Praise for Sarah Morgan

'A gorgeously sparkly romance'
— Julia Williams

'The perfect book to curl up with'
— *Heat*

'Full of romance and sparkle.'
— *Lovereading*

'I've found an author I adore — must hunt
down everything she's published.'
— *Smart Bitches, Trashy Books*

'Morgan is a magician with words.'
— *RT Book Reviews*

'Dear Ms Morgan, I'm always on
the lookout for a new book by you...'
— *Dear Author blog*

Sarah Morgan is the bestselling author of *Sleigh Bells in the Snow*. As a child Sarah dreamed of being a writer, and although she took a few interesting detours on the way she is now living that dream. With her writing career she has successfully combined business with pleasure, and she firmly believes that reading romance is one of the most satisfying and fat-free escapist pleasures available. Her stories are unashamedly optimistic, and she is always pleased when she receives letters from readers saying that her books have helped them through hard times.

Sarah lives near London with her husband and two children, who innocently provide an endless supply of authentic dialogue. When she isn't writing or reading Sarah enjoys music, movies, and any activity that takes her outdoors.

Readers can find out more about Sarah and her books from her website: www.sarahmorgan.com She can also be found on Facebook and Twitter.

Sunset in Central Park

SARAH MORGAN

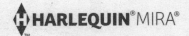

Harlequin MIRA is a registered trademark of Harlequin Enterprises Limited, used under licence.

First Published in Great Britain 2016
By Harlequin Mira, an imprint of HarperCollins*Publishers*
1 London Bridge Street, London, SE1 9GF

Sunset in Central Park © 2016 Sarah Morgan

ISBN 978-1-848-45472-9

0716

Our policy is to use papers that are natural, renewable and recyclable products and made from wood grown in sustainable forests. The logging and manufacturing processes conform to the legal environmental regulations of the country of origin.

Printed and bound by
CPI Group (UK) Ltd, Croydon, CR0 4YY

Dear Reader

As a child I was always in awe of my mother who could name every plant we ever passed, often by its Latin name. I used to test her, trying to catch her out. I'd tug her arm and point to some obscure leaf or flower, often hidden behind another, and ask 'what's that?' She always knew. I badly wanted to be such an expert, able to impress people with my depth of knowledge. Sadly, that has yet to happen (although I'm confident with 'rose') but one of the great things about writing is that you can create characters who are everything you're not.

The heroine of this story, Frankie, is most definitely an expert. Like my mother, she can take a few stems of greenery and arrange them in such a way as to make a person stop and admire. Frankie is a strong, independent woman who is very good at her job and she is in control of every part of her life except one – her love life. Taking that leap requires her to put aside her tarnished beliefs about love. The one person who might be able to do that is Matt, the older brother of her best friend.

Friends-to-lovers is a theme I love exploring. I enjoyed watching Frankie and Matt's long friendship turn into something deeper, and seeing Frankie learn to trust after years of keeping barriers between herself and the world.

Thank you for picking up this book! I hope you enjoy *Sunset in Central Park*, and that reading it brings some reading sunshine to your day. Don't forget to look out for Eva's story, *Miracle on 5th Avenue*, coming later in the year and if you're on Facebook, I hope you'll join me there. https://www.facebook.com/AuthorSarahMorgan

Love Sarah
Xx

This one is for my dear
friend Dawn, with much love.

The course of true love never did run smooth.

—William Shakespeare

Chapter One

Sleeping Beauty didn't need a prince. She needed strong coffee.

—Frankie

She'd expected hearts, flowers and smiles. Not tears.

"Crisis unfolding, two o'clock." Frankie tapped her earpiece and heard Eva respond.

"It can't unfold at two o'clock. It's already five past three."

"Not the time, the position. Crisis is unfolding ahead of me and to the right."

There was a pause. "You mean by the apple tree?"

"That's what I mean."

"Then why not just say 'by the apple tree'?"

"Because if you're going to make me wear an earpiece and look professional, I'm going to sound professional."

"Frankie, you sound more like the FBI than a floral designer. And how can there be a crisis? Everything is running smoothly. The weather is perfect, the tables are pretty and the cakes are looking stunning if I say so myself. Our bride-to-be looks radiant and the guests will be arriving any minute."

Frankie stared at the woman crumpled against the tree trunk. "I hate to tell you this but right now the bride-to-be isn't looking radiant. We have tears. I am the last person to make an observation on the psychology of weddings and all the fluff that surrounds them, but I'm guessing that's not the usual response. If they reach this stage, it's because they think marriage is a good thing, am I right?"

"Are you sure they're not happy tears? And how many tears exactly? One tissue or a whole box?"

"Enough to cause a world shortage. She's crying like a waterfall after heavy rain. I'm starting to understand why they call it a bridal shower."

"Oh no! Her makeup will be ruined. Do you know what happened?"

"Maybe she decided she should have gone with the chocolate ganache instead of the orange sugar icing."

"Frankie—"

"Or maybe she saw sense and decided to get out now while there's still time. If I were about to get married, I'd be crying, too, and I'd be crying a hell of a lot harder and louder than she is."

A sigh vibrated in her ear. "You promised to leave your relationship phobias at the door."

"I closed the door, but they must have sneaked in through the keyhole."

"The mood for this event is sunny optimism, remember?"

Frankie stared at the bride-to-be, sobbing under the apple tree. "Not from where I'm standing. It's been a dry summer, though. The apple tree will be pleased to be watered."

"Go and give her a hug, Frankie! Tell her everything will be okay."

"She's getting married. How can everything be okay?" Sweat pricked the back of her neck. There was only one thing she hated more than bridal showers, and that was weddings. "I will not lie."

"It's not a lie! Plenty of people live happily ever after."

"In fairy stories. In real life they sleep around and get divorced, invariably in that order." Frankie made a huge effort to smother her prejudices. "Get out here now. This is your area of expertise. You know I'm no good at the touchy-feely thing."

"I'll handle it." This time it was Paige who spoke and who, moments later, strode across the neatly tended lawn, cool and composed despite the New York heat and humidity. "What was she doing immediately before she started crying?"

"She took a phone call."

"Could you hear any of the conversation?"

"I don't listen to people's conversations. Maybe the markets crashed or something, although judging from the size of this house it would need to be a big crash to make a difference." Frankie pushed her hair away from her sweaty forehead. "Can we do these events indoors from now on? I'm dying." It was the sort of day that made your clothes stick to your skin and made you dream of iced drinks and air-conditioning.

She thought longingly of her small apartment in Brooklyn.

If she were home now she'd be fiddling with cuttings, tending the herbs on her windowsill and watching the bees flirt with the plants in her tiny garden. Or maybe she'd be on the roof terrace with her friends, sharing a bottle of wine as they watched the sun set over the Manhattan skyline.

Weddings would be the last thing on her mind.

She felt a touch on her arm and glanced toward her friend. "What?"

"You're stressed. You hate weddings and all things bridal. I wish I didn't have to ask you to do them, but right now—"

"Our business is in its infancy and we can't afford to turn them down. I know. And I'm fine with it." Well, not *fine* exactly, Frankie thought moodily, but she was here, wasn't she?

And she understood that they couldn't be choosy about their clients.

She, Paige and Eva had started their event-and-concierge business, Urban Genie, only a few months earlier after they'd lost their jobs at a large Manhattan-based events company.

Frankie gave a little smile, remembering the giddy excitement and sweaty fear that had come from starting their own company. It had been terrifying but there had also been a powerful feeling of liberation. They had the control.

It had been Paige's brainchild, and Frankie knew that without her she would very likely be out of a job right now. Which would mean no way to pay her rent. Without the money to pay her rent, she'd have to leave her apartment.

Unease rippled through her, as if someone had thrown a pebble into the quiet, smooth pond that was her life.

Her independence was everything.

And that was why she was here. That and the loyalty she felt toward her friends.

She pushed her glasses back up her nose with the tip of her finger. "I can cope with weddings if that's what comes our way. Don't worry about me. She—" Frankie nodded her head toward the woman under the apple tree "—is your priority."

"I'm going to talk to her. If the guests arrive, stall them. Eva?" Paige adjusted her earpiece. "Don't bring the cakes out yet. I'll let you know what's happening." She walked over to the bride-to-be.

Frankie knew that whatever the problem was, her friend would deal with it. Paige was a born organizer with a gift for saying exactly the right thing at the right time.

And she possessed another gift, crucial to the success of events like these—she believed in happy endings.

As far as Frankie was concerned, people who believed in happy endings were delusional.

Her parents had separated when she was fourteen, when her father, a sales director, had announced that he was leaving her mother for one of his colleagues.

And as for everything that had happened since—

She stared blindly at the ribbons fluttering in the breeze.

How did people do it? How did they manage to ignore all the statistics and facts and convince themselves they could find one person to be with forever?

Forever didn't exist.

She shifted restlessly. Paige was right. There was nothing on earth she hated as much as weddings and all things bridal. They filled her with a sense of foreboding. It was like watching a car driving along the freeway, heading toward a pileup. There was a hideous inevitability to it all. She wanted to cover her eyes or shout out a warning. What she didn't want to be was a witness.

She saw Paige put her arm around the sobbing woman and turned away. She told herself that she was giving them privacy, but truthfully, she didn't want to look. It was too raw. Too real. Looking stirred up memories she preferred to forget. Fortunately, her job wasn't to manage the emotions of the clients; it was to provide a floral display that reflected the tone and mood of the event.

The mood was supposed to be happy, so she'd chosen creams and pastels to complement the beautiful linens. Celosia and sweet pea nestled alongside hydrangea and roses in glass pitchers chosen to satisfy the bride-to-be's request for simplicity.

Of course, *simplicity* was a relative term, Frankie thought as she surveyed the two long tables. Simplicity could have meant feasting from picnic baskets, but in this case the tables gleamed with silverware and the shimmer of crystal. Charles William Templeton was a lawyer with a famous clientele and sufficient funds at his disposal to ensure that his only daughter, Robyn Rose, could have any wedding she wanted. The Plaza was booked for the following summer. Frankie was relieved Urban Genie wasn't involved with that event.

The brief for the bridal shower had been garden elegance with a touch of romance. Frankie had managed not to wince as Robyn Rose had mentioned Flower Fairies and *A Midsummer Night's Dream*. Thanks to Eva, who had no trouble turning their clients' romantic visions into reality, they'd more than met the brief.

They'd rented chairs and customized them with ribbon that coordinated with the table setting. Handmade silk butterflies were artfully positioned around the garden, and acres of lace created the feel of a fairy grotto. You could almost believe you were in a fairy tale.

Frankie gave a half smile.

Only Eva could have thought it up.

The only nod to simplicity was the mature apple tree currently sheltering the sobbing bride-to-be.

Frankie was bracing herself to start holding off guests when Eva appeared by her side, her cheeks pink from the sun.

"Do we know what's happening?"

"No, but I can tell you it's not all celebration. Paige needs to work magic."

Eva glanced around wistfully. "It all looks so pretty and

we've worked so hard to make it perfect. Normally I *love* bridal showers. I always think of it as a final celebration before the bride and groom ride off into the sunset."

"Sunset is what happens before darkness, Ev."

"Can you at least *pretend* you believe in what we do?"

"I do believe in what we do. We're a business. We manage events and we're damn good at it. This is just another event."

"You make it sound so clinical, but there's a magical side to it." Eva straightened the wing of a silk butterfly. "Sometimes we make wishes come true."

"My wish was to run a successful business with my two best friends, so I guess you're right about that. There's nothing magical about it, unless managing to function after an eighteen-hour day is magical. And coffee is definitely magical. Fortunately, I don't have to believe in happy endings to do a great job. My responsibility is the flowers, that's all."

And she loved it. Her love affair with plants had begun when she was young. She'd taken refuge in the garden to escape the emotions inside the house. Flowers could be art, or they could be science, and she'd studied each plant carefully, understanding that each had individual needs. There were the shade-loving plants like ferns, ginger and jack-in-the-pulpit, and then there were the sun worshippers, like lilacs and sunflowers. Each needed an optimum environment. Planted in the wrong place, they would wither and die. Each needed the perfect home in order to flourish.

Not so different from humans, she mused.

She loved selecting the right flower for the right event; she enjoyed designing displays of plants but most of all she loved growing them and watching the changing seasons. From the extravagant froth of blossom in the spring to the elegant russets and burnt orange of the fall, each season brought its own gifts.

"The flowers are beautiful." Eva studied the bunch of flowers artfully arranged in the pitcher. "That's pretty. What is it?"

"It's a rose."

"No, the silvery one."

"Centaurea cineraria."

Eva gave her a look. "What do normal people call it?"

"Dusty miller."

"It's pretty. And you used sweet peas." Her friend drew her finger wistfully over the flower. "They were my grandmother's favorite. I used to leave bunches of them by her bed. They reminded her of her wedding. I love the way you've put this together. You're so talented."

Frankie heard the wobble in her friend's voice. Eva had adored her grandmother, and her death the previous year had been devastating. Frankie knew she missed her horribly.

She also knew that Eva wouldn't want to have a wobbly moment at work.

"Did you know the sweet pea was discovered by a Sicilian monk three hundred years ago?"

Eva swallowed hard. "No. You know so much about flowers."

"It's my job. What do you think of this? It's Queen Anne's lace," Frankie spoke quickly. "You'll like it. It's very bridal. Perfect for you."

"Yes." Eva pulled herself together. "When I get married I'm going to have that in my bouquet. Would you make it for me?"

"Sure. I'll make you the best bouquet any bride has ever seen. Just don't cry. You're a mess when you cry."

Eva scrubbed her hand over her face. "So you'd be happy for me? Even though you don't believe in love?"

"If anyone can prove me wrong it's going to be you. And

you deserve it. I'm hoping Mr. Right rides up on his white horse and sweeps you away."

"That would attract some attention on Fifth Avenue." Eva blew her nose. "And I'm allergic to horses."

Frankie tried not to smile. "With you, there's always something."

"Thank you."

"For what?"

"For making me laugh instead of cry. You're the best."

"Yeah, well, you can return the favor by handling this situation." Frankie saw Paige hand Robyn another tissue. "He's dumped her, hasn't he?"

"You don't know that. It could be anything. Or nothing. Maybe she has dust in her eye."

Frankie glanced at her friend in disbelief. "Next you'll be telling me you still believe in Santa and the tooth fairy."

"And the Easter bunny." Composed again, Eva whipped a tiny mirror from her purse and checked her makeup. "Don't ever forget the Easter bunny."

"What's it like living on Planet Eva?"

"It's lovely. And don't you dare contaminate my little world with your cynical views. A moment ago you were talking about Mr. Right."

"That was to stop you from crying. I don't understand why people put themselves through this when they could just stab themselves through the heart with a kitchen knife and be done with it."

Eva shuddered. "You've been reading too much horror. Why don't you read romance instead?"

"I'd rather stab myself through the heart with a kitchen knife." And it felt as if she'd done just that. She was looking at Robyn Rose, but she was remembering her mother, incoherent with grief on the kitchen floor while her father, white-faced, had stepped over her heaving body and walked out the door, leaving Frankie to clean up his mess.

She stared straight ahead and then felt Eva slide her arm through hers.

"One day, probably when you least expect it, you're going to fall in love."

It was a remark typical of Eva.

"That's never going to happen." Knowing that her friend was emotionally vulnerable, Frankie tried to be gentle. "Romance has the same effect on me as garlic does on vampires. And besides, I love being single. Don't give me that pitying look. It's my choice, not a sentence. It's not a state that I'm in until something better comes along. Don't feel sorry for me. I love my life."

"Don't you want someone to snuggle up to at night?"

"No. This way I never have to fight for the duvet, I can sleep diagonally across the bed and I can read until four in the morning."

"A book can't take the place of a man!"

"I disagree. A book can give you most things a relationship can. It can make you laugh, it can make you cry, it can transport you to different worlds and teach you things. You can even take it out to dinner. And if it bores you, you can move on. Which is pretty much what happens in real life." Unlike her father, her mother had never married again. Instead, she burned through men as if they were disposable.

"You're going to make me cry again. What about intimacy? A book can't know you."

"I can live without that part." She didn't want people to know her. She'd moved away from the small island where she'd grown up for precisely that reason—people had known too much. Every intimate, deeply embarrassing detail of her private life had been public knowledge.

Paige walked back to them. "The phone call was the groom." Her voice was crisp and businesslike. "He called it off."

Eva made a distressed sound. "Oh no! That's dreadful for her."

"Maybe it isn't." Despite the fact she'd already guessed what had happened, Frankie's stomach churned. "Maybe she had a lucky escape."

"How can you say that?"

"Because sooner or later he'd cheat on her and break her heart. Might as well be now before they have kids and a hundred and one Dalmatian puppies and innocent bystanders are injured in the fallout." Not wanting to admit how gutted she was to have been proved right yet again, Frankie leaned forward and removed the Queen Anne's lace from the pitcher.

"A hundred and one puppies of any breed would put pressure on a marriage, Frankie," Eva said.

"And not all men cheat." Paige checked the time on her phone, and the diamond on her finger caught the sunlight and glinted.

Seeing it, Frankie felt a flash of guilt.

She should keep her mouth shut. Eva loved dreaming and Paige was newly engaged. She needed to keep her thoughts on marriage to herself.

"It will be different for you and Jake," she mumbled. "You're one of those rare couples that are perfect together. Ignore me. I'm sorry."

"Don't be." Paige waved her hand and the diamond glinted again. "You and I don't want the same thing, and that's fine."

"I'm a killjoy."

"You're the child of divorced parents. And it wasn't a

happy divorce. We all have a different perspective on life, depending on our own experience."

"I know I overreact, though. It wasn't even my divorce."

Paige shrugged. "But you lived through the fallout. It would be crazy to think that wouldn't affect you. It's like washing a red sock with a white shirt. Everything ends up tainted."

Frankie gave a half smile. "Am I the white shirt in that analogy? Because I'm not sure I'm white-shirt material."

Eva studied her. "I agree. I'd say you were more of a combat jacket."

"Robyn has gone upstairs to fix her makeup." Paige steered the conversation back to work. "The guests will be arriving any minute. I'm going to talk to them."

"We're canceling?"

"No. We're going ahead, but now it's not a bridal shower—it's a party. A celebration of friendship."

Frankie relaxed slightly. Friendship she could cope with. "Nice. How did you pull that one off?"

"I pointed out that friends are there for the bad times as well as the good. They were invited to share the good, but if they're true friends they'll be right there by her side for the bad."

"And bad times are always improved by champagne, sunshine and strawberries," Eva said. "Here she comes."

Frankie reached for the next pitcher of flowers and Paige put her hand out to stop her.

"Those are beautiful. What are you doing?"

"The flowers are supposed to match the mood of the occasion, and these are too bridal."

Without waiting for Paige's approval, Frankie tossed the bridal Queen Anne's lace into the border and watched as the flowers hit the dirt.

She tried not to think of it as symbolic.

* * *

The three friends arrived home an hour or so before the sun was due to set.

Sweaty, irritable and miserably unsettled by the events of the day, Frankie searched in her purse for her keys.

"If I don't get inside in the next five seconds I'm going to melt right here."

Paige paused by the front door. "Despite everything, it went well."

"He dumped her," Eva murmured, and Paige frowned.

"I know. I was talking about the event. That went well. We should celebrate. Jake's coming over. Why don't we all meet up on the roof terrace for a drink?"

Frankie didn't feel like celebrating. "Not tonight. I have a date with a good book." She wasn't going to think about how Robyn Rose was feeling. She wasn't going to worry about whether she was all right or whether she'd ever have the courage to love again. That wasn't her problem.

Fumbling, she dropped the key and saw Eva exchange a glance with Paige.

"Are you all right?"

"Of course. Just tired. Long day in the heat." And part of that heat had come from being exposed to a boiling cauldron of emotions. Frankie retrieved the key and wiped her forehead with her palm.

"You should wear a skirt," Eva said. "You would have been cooler."

"You know I never wear skirts."

"You should. You have great legs."

Frankie made a blind stab at the door but it wouldn't open. "I'll see you tomorrow."

"All right, but we thought you might need distraction after the bridal shower so we bought you something." Paige dug her hand into her bag, the bag that held everything from cleanser to duct tape. "Here." She handed over a parcel and Frankie took it, touched by the gesture.

"You bought me a book?" She opened it and felt a thrill of excitement. Her bad mood evaporated. "It's the new Lucas Blade! It's not out for another month. How did you get this?" Almost salivating, she held it against her chest. She wanted to sit down and start reading right away.

"Eva is well connected."

Eva's cheeks dimpled into a smile. "I mentioned to dear Mitzy that you love his work, and she used her power as a grandmother to force him to sign you a copy, although why you want to read a book called *Death Returns* I do not know. I'd be up all night screaming. The only good thing about that book is his photo on the jacket. The guy is insanely hot. Mitzy wants to introduce me to him, but I'm not sure I want to meet a man who writes about murder for a living. I don't think we'd have much in common."

"It's signed?" Frankie opened the book and saw her name in bold black scrawl. "This is *so* cool. I was thinking of pre-ordering it but the price is shocking because he's so successful. I can't believe you did this."

"Your idea of horror is a bridal shower or a wedding, but you did it anyway," Eva said, "so we wanted to treat you tonight. This is our thank-you. If it scares you and you want company, bang on the door."

Frankie felt her throat thicken. This was friendship. Understanding someone. "I hope it does scare me. That's what it's supposed to do."

Eva shook her head, bemused. "I love you, but I will never understand you."

Frankie smiled. Maybe not understanding. Maybe friendship was loving someone even when you didn't always understand them. "Thanks," she muttered. "You guys are the best."

The key finally slid into the lock and she stepped into the sanctuary of her apartment. She closed the door and the first thing she did was pull off her glasses. The frames were heavy and she rubbed her nose gently with her fingers and walked through to her pretty living room. The space was small, but she'd furnished it well, with a few good pieces she'd found on the internet. There was an overstuffed sofa that she'd rescued and covered herself, but what she loved most about her apartment were the plants. They crowded every available surface, a rainbow of greens with splashes of color, leading the eye toward the small garden.

She'd turned the small enclosed space into a leafy refuge.

Gold flame honeysuckle, *Clematis Montana*, and other climbers scrambled over trellises while pots overflowed with a profusion of trailing plants. Vinca and bacopa tangled and tumbled over the small area of cedar decking that caught the sun at certain times of the day, and a Moroccan lamp sat in the center of the small table for those evenings she chose to sit alone rather than join her friends on the roof terrace.

Peace and calm enveloped her. The prospect of an evening reading a book she'd been looking forward to for months lifted her mood.

This was her life and she loved it.

Not for her the stomach-churning roller-coaster ride that was *love*. She didn't need that and she certainly didn't want it. She never wasted an evening staring longingly at her phone, hoping it would ring, and she'd never cried her way through a single tissue, let alone a whole box.

She flipped open the book, but she knew if she read the first page she'd be hooked, and first she needed to shower.

Tomorrow was Sunday and her schedule was clear, so she could read all night if she wanted to, sleep late and no one would care.

One of the many benefits of being single.

She put the book down, wondering why everyone else seemed so eager to give up that precious status.

Much as she loved her friends, she was glad she lived on her own. Paige and Eva had shared the apartment above hers for years and even though Paige was now spending more time at Jake's apartment, she still spent at least half the week in her old room. Frankie suspected that decision was driven as much by her friend's desire not to leave Eva alone as a need to maintain her own space.

Eva's romantic longing for a family was something Frankie understood but didn't share. Her experience was that family was complicated, infuriating, embarrassing, selfish and, on too many occasions, hurtful. And when it was family that hurt you, the wounds were somehow deeper and slower to heal, perhaps because the expectations were different.

Her experiences growing up had influenced so much of who she was and how she chose to live her life.

Her past was the reason she couldn't attend a wedding without wanting to ask the couple if they were sure they wanted to go ahead.

Her past was the reason she never wore red, hated skirts and was incapable of sustaining a relationship with a man.

Her past was the reason she felt unable to go back to the island where she'd grown up.

Puffin Island was a nature-lover's paradise, but for Frankie there were too many memories and too many islanders who bore a grudge against the name of Cole.

And she didn't blame them.

She'd grown up cloaked by the sins of her mother, and

her family's reputation was one of the reasons she'd made the move to New York. At least here when she walked into a store, the other people weren't all talking about her. Here, no one knew or cared that her father had run off with a woman half his age, or that her mother had decided to heal her insecurities with affairs of her own.

She'd left it all behind, until six months earlier when her mother had stopped moving around the country from job to job and man to man and settled in the city.

After years of very little contact with her only child, she'd been keen to bond. Frankie found every interaction excruciating. And woven in between the embarrassment, anger and discomfort was guilt. Guilt that she couldn't find it inside her to be more sympathetic toward her mother. Her mother had been the prime victim of her father's infidelities, not her. She should be more understanding. But they were so *different*.

Had they always been that way? Or was it Frankie's fault for going out of her way to make sure they were different? Because the clearest memory that lingered from her teenage years was her absolute determination to be nothing like her mother.

Stripping off her shirt, she walked into her little kitchen and poured herself a glass of wine. Paige and Eva would no doubt spend the evening chatting, dissecting every moment of the event.

Frankie had no wish to do that. It had been bad enough at the time without going through every detail again, and it wasn't as if they didn't know what had gone wrong. The groom had dumped the bride. The way she saw it, a dead body didn't need a post-mortem if you could see the bullet hole through the skull, and right now she needed to take her mind off everything to do with weddings.

Stepping into the shower, she washed away the stresses of the day.

It could have been a disaster, but with her usual smooth efficiency, Paige had rescued the situation.

Robyn's friends had been wonderful, supporting her and saying the right things. There had even been laughter as they'd shared champagne and Eva's cakes. Instead of an impending wedding, they'd celebrated their friendship.

Frankie wrapped herself in a towel and stepped out of the tiny bathroom.

Friendship was the one thing that could be relied on.

Where would she be without her friends?

And although she wasn't in the mood for drinking and talking on the roof terrace, there was comfort in knowing they were only a few steps away.

She'd snuggle up with her book and lose herself.

She pulled on black yoga pants and a T-shirt, put some cheese on a plate and sat down to read. Immersed in another world, she almost leaped out of her skin as an enormous crash came from the kitchen.

"Holy crap."

Yanked from a fictional world of horror, it took a moment for logic to kick in and tell her that one of the herb pots carefully balanced on her windowsill had fallen.

She didn't need to investigate the source of the accident; she already knew.

Not a serial killer, but a cat.

"Claws? Is that you?" Still holding her book, she walked through to the kitchen, saw the soil and shards of terracotta scattered across the floor and a terrified cat with fur the color of marmalade. "Hey—you need to look where you're walking."

The cat shot under the kitchen table, eyeing Frankie from a safe distance, her fur almost vertical.

"Did you scare yourself? Because you scared the hell out of me." Calm, Frankie put her book on the table and stooped to clear up the mess. The cat shrank farther under the table. "What are you doing down here? Where's Matt? Is he working late?"

Matt, Paige's brother, owned the house and lived on the top two floors. It was Matt, a landscape architect, who had found the old, neglected brownstone years before and lovingly converted it into three apartments. The four of them lived there in almost perfect harmony. Along with the cat Matt had rescued.

Frankie disposed of the shattered pot and the soil and reached for a tin of cat food. She carried on talking, careful not to make any sudden movements. "Are you hungry?"

The cat didn't move, so Frankie opened the tin and tipped it into the bowl she'd bought after the cat's first visit.

"I'll just leave it here." She put the bowl down.

Claws approached with the watchful caution she always showed toward humans.

As someone who approached people in much the same way, Frankie empathized.

"I don't know how you're getting down from Matt's apartment, but I hope you're being careful where you tread. Wouldn't want you to be hurt." Although it was a bit late for that. She knew Claws had been abused and neglected before Matt had rescued her. As a result, the cat trusted no one except Matt, and even he was scratched if he made any sudden movements.

Claws sniffed cautiously at the bowl and Frankie stood back, giving the animal space.

Pretending to ignore her, she topped off her wineglass,

cut a few more slices of cheese and sat down at the kitchen table that had been a housewarming gift from her friends. It was her favorite place to sit, especially first thing in the morning. She liked to open the windows and watch the sunlight stream over her garden. It was a suntrap, catching the light and warmth from early in the morning.

"We should probably celebrate." She raised the glass. "To being single. I can go where I like, do what I like, I'm dependent on no one. I sail my own ship through whichever waters I choose to navigate. Life is good."

Claws took another sniff at the food, keeping one eye on Frankie.

Finally, she started to eat and Frankie was surprised by the sense of satisfaction that came from knowing the animal was beginning to trust her. Maybe she should get a cat of her own.

Unlike some humans, cats understood the notion of personal space.

She opened the book and started to read where she'd left off.

She was halfway through the third chapter when she heard a knock on the door.

Claws froze.

Frankie pushed a piece of paper in the book to mark her place, trying not to be irritated at the disturbance. "It will be Eva or Paige, so there's no need to freak out. They've probably run out of wine. Don't break any of my plant pots while I answer the door."

She tugged open the front door. "Have you drunk so much that you can't—oh."

Matt stood in the doorway, although *stood* wasn't really the right word, she decided. He virtually filled the space. He topped six feet, his shoulders broad and powerful from all the heavy lifting he did at his job. He could have been intimidating, but a faint smile tilted the corners of his mouth and softened the rough edges of masculinity. There were a dozen reasons why a woman might take a second look at Matt Walker, but it was that bone-melting sexy smile that guaranteed he was never short of female company.

"So far this evening, I haven't drunk a drop. Hoping to remedy that soon." He glanced from her to the door. "You should use that security chain I fitted for you."

"Normally I do. I thought you were Paige."

He smelled good, she thought. Like summer rain and sea breeze. It made her want to bury her face in his neck and breathe him in.

She wondered which of them would be more embarrassed.

Definitely her. Matt wasn't the kind of guy who was easily embarrassed.

"Am I disturbing you?" He scanned her damp hair and she pushed at it self-consciously.

When it was wet it turned an unflattering shade. "Rust" one boy had called it at school after she'd been caught in a heavy rainstorm. When she blushed, which she was now doing thanks to her wayward imagination, her face clashed horribly with her hair.

"You're not disturbing me, but if you're looking for Paige and Eva they're up on the roof terrace."

"I wasn't looking for them. I've lost my cat. Have you seen her?"

"She's here. Come in. I opened a bottle of wine." She issued the invitation without a second thought because this was Matt. Matt, whom she'd known forever and trusted.

"You're inviting me in?" His eyes gleamed. "I'm honored. It's Saturday night and I know how much you love your own space."

The fact that he knew her so well was one of the things that made their relationship so easy and comfortable.

"You have owner's privilege."

"There's such a thing? I never knew that. What other benefits am I entitled to that I haven't been claiming?"

"The occasional glass of wine is definitely on that list." She opened the door wider for him and he strolled past her into her apartment.

Her gaze lingered on his shoulders. She was human, wasn't she? And Matt had an impressive set of shoulders. The kind you could lean on, if you were the leaning type. She wasn't. Even so, there was no denying that the man was sexy from every angle, even from the back. Of course, the fact that she found him sexy was her secret and it was going to stay that way.

She could enjoy her own private fantasy, safe in the knowledge that no one was ever going to find out.

Frankie closed the door behind him. "How did you lose your cat?"

"I left the window open but she's never had the courage to climb through it before. I don't know whether to be pleased that she was finally brave enough to explore or worried that she felt the need to escape from me."

"Mmm, I guess that depends on whether this is a onetime thing. Do women often try and escape from you?" *No,* she thought. *Of course they didn't.*

"All the time. It's hell on the ego." He was cool and relaxed and her heart gave a little kick, as it always did around him.

She ignored it, as she always did.

Unlike her mother, she didn't think sexual attraction was an impulse that had to be acted on. She'd rather have a long-term friendship than short-term sex any day. In fact, there were a million activities more appealing than sex, which she'd always found to be fraught with complications, unrealistic expectations and pressure.

If they gave out grades for sex, you'd be a D minus, Cole, with nothing for effort.

She frowned, wondering why that memory had come into her head now.

The guy had been a total jerk. She wasn't going to give a second thought to a man whose ego was so big it had needed its own zip code.

Matt, on the other hand, was a good friend. She saw him most days, sometimes on the roof terrace where they met for drinks or movie night and sometimes at Romano's, the local Italian restaurant owned by Jake's mother.

Their friendship was one of the most important relationships in her life.

Which was one of the reasons she tolerated his cat.

"I think you should be pleased she wandered down to my apartment. Shows she's slowly gaining confidence. With luck she'll eventually stop trying to scratch us all to the bone. She's in the kitchen." She walked through and he followed her, scanning the profusion of pots on the windowsill.

"You're growing herbs now?"

"A few. Sweet basil and Italian parsley. I grow them for Eva."

"There's an Italian parsley? All those trips to Italy I took in college and I never knew that." He strolled across to the window and stared out across the small garden. "You've done a good job with this place. I'm lucky having you living here."

They talked all the time about a range of subjects but he rarely made personal comments. She hated the fact that it flustered her.

"I'm the lucky one. If it weren't for you I'd be living in an apartment the size of a shoe box and storing my clothes in the oven. You know how it is in New York." Embarrassed, she stooped to stroke the cat and Claws shot under the table for protection. "Oops. Moved too fast. She's nervous."

He turned. "She's getting better. A few months ago she wouldn't have paid you a visit." He sat down on one of the kitchen chairs and Claws immediately crept out and jumped onto his lap. "Thanks for feeding her."

"You're welcome." Frankie watched as Claws gave a slow stretch. The cat lost her balance and shot out her claws, but Matt curved his hand over her back, holding her securely against the hard muscle on his thigh.

Frankie stared at that hand and the slow, reassuring stroke of his fingers and felt herself grow hot.

"Something wrong?"

"Excuse me?" Frankie dragged her eyes from the mesmerizing movement of his fingers and met his amused gaze.

"You're staring at my cat."

Cat? Cat. "I—" she'd stopped staring at the cat a long time ago. "She's still skinny."

"The vet said it will take a while for her to regain all the weight she lost when she was shut in that room." There was a grim set to his mouth that reminded her that there were limits even to Matt's patience. And then he smiled. "Have I seen that T-shirt before? The color suits you."

"What?" Unbalanced by both the smile and the comment, she stared at him.

She didn't think Matt would ever mock her, which could only mean—

"Do you want something?" She looked him in the eye. "Because you can just ask straight out. You don't have to do the whole 'you look nice in that T-shirt' thing to soften me up. Thanks to you I live in the best apartment in Brooklyn, and on top of that I've known you forever so you can pretty much ask anything and I'll say yes."

"Another owner's privilege?" He gently lifted the cat and set her down on the floor. "You probably shouldn't have told me that. I might choose to invoke that clause in our agreement."

Was he flirting with her?

Confusion jammed her thought processes.

She always knew where she was with Matt but suddenly she was in unfamiliar territory.

Of course he wasn't flirting. They never flirted. She didn't know how to flirt. Her expertise, honed over a decade, was in putting men off, not in encouraging them.

And anyway, Matt would never be interested in her. She wasn't sophisticated enough or experienced enough.

She needed to say something light and funny to restore the atmosphere, but her mind was blank.

Matt watched her steadily. "I paid you a compliment, Frankie. You don't have to strip it down and check it for bugs or incendiary devices. You just say thank you and move on."

A compliment?

But why? He never paid her compliments. "This T-shirt is five years old. It's not that special."

"I didn't say I liked your T-shirt. I said I liked the way you look in it. I was complimenting *you*, not what you were wearing specifically. Did you mention wine?" Smoothly he changed the subject and she turned to pick up the bottle, frustrated with herself.

Why did she have to turn it into such a big deal? Was it really so hard to flirt?

Eva would have had the perfect response ready. So would Paige.

She was the only one who had no idea what to say or do.

She needed to get a "how to" book. How to flirt. How not to make a fool of yourself around a man.

"Montepulciano. Unless you'd rather a beer?"

"Beer sounds good."

She stooped and pulled one out of the fridge, forcing herself to relax. She was going to type "how to flirt" into a search engine later. She was going to practice a few responses so this never happened again. If a guy paid her a compliment, she should at least know how to respond instead of treating every comment as if it were an incoming computer virus. "How was your day?"

"I've had better." He snapped the top off the beer. "Too much work, not enough time. Remember that piece of business I won a few months ago?"

"You've won loads of business, Matt."

"Roof terrace on the Upper East Side."

"Oh yes, I remember." This conversation was better. Safe. "It was a real coup. Is there a problem with planning?"

"Not planning. That's all good. What isn't good is the fact that Victoria left yesterday."

Frankie had trained with Victoria at the Botanic Gardens and she'd been the one to recommend her to Matt. "Doesn't she have to give you notice?"

"Technically yes, but her mother's sick so I told her to forget it and just get herself home."

That was typical of Matt. He was a man who appreciated the importance of family. His was a tight-knit unit, not a fractured mess like hers. "She's not likely to be back soon?"

"No. She's moving back to Connecticut so she can be closer."

"Which leaves you without a horticulturist when you're in the middle of a big project." Roof terraces were Matt's specialty, and his projects ranged from residential homes to large commercial properties. "What about the rest of your team?"

"James's expertise is hard landscaping, and Roxy is keen and hardworking but has no formal training. Victoria had started to teach her the basics but she doesn't have the skills to put together a design." He set the bottle down on the table. "I'm going to have to recruit, and hope I get lucky. Fast." He drank and Frankie eyed the strong column of his throat and the dark, grainy shadow of his jaw. He was strikingly handsome, his body hard and strong. He spent half his working day with his sleeves rolled up covered in dirt, but even dressed casually his innate sense of style shone through. It was that restrained eye for design that had built his business.

If she *had* been interested in men, he would have been a prime candidate.

But she wasn't interested. Definitely not.

People told you to play to your strengths, didn't they? And she was very, very bad at relationships.

Matt put the beer down and for a brief moment his gaze met hers. He gave her a look laden with intimacy and it made her heart pump a little faster and her breathing quicken.

Crap, her mind was playing tricks.

She had an overactive imagination courtesy of an underactive sex life.

She looked away. "I know a lot of people. I'll make some calls. Roof terraces need special skills. It's not just about planting pretty flowers. You need trees and shrubs that will provide year-round color."

"Exactly. I need someone who understands the complexities of the project. Someone skilled and easy to work with. We're a small team. There's no room for egos or prima donnas."

"Yeah, I get that." It was stupid to be flustered when she'd known Matt pretty much forever. The fact that he'd matured from lanky boy into insanely hot man shouldn't affect her as much as it did.

He was her best friend's older brother and he'd grown up on the same island as her, off the coast of Maine. He'd experienced the same frustrations associated with small-town living, although of course his experience had been nothing like hers. No one's had been like hers.

After her father's affair had been exposed and he'd left them for a woman half his age, her mother's response had been to have affairs of her own. She'd told anyone who would listen that she'd married too young and planned to make up for lost time. In an attempt to rediscover her youth and confidence, she'd cut her hair short, lost twenty pounds and started borrowing Frankie's clothes. There had been no man too young, too old or too married to escape her mother's attentions.

Frankie had discovered that a reputation wasn't something that had to be earned. You could inherit it.

No matter what she did, on Puffin Island she'd always be the daughter of "that woman."

It was as if her identity had merged with that of her mother.

Some of the boys at school had assumed she was the shortcut to a life of sexual adventure. One in particular.

Frankie pushed the memory away, refusing to allow it space in her head. "Do you want something to eat? I don't have Eva's skills, but I have eggs and fresh herbs. Omelet?"

"That would be great. And while you do that, tell me about your bad day. Paige said it was a bridal shower." Matt picked up his beer. "I'm guessing that's not your favorite thing."

"You're right about that." She didn't bother denying it. What was the point when Matt already knew her better than most?

"What happened?"

"Oh, you know—usual thing. Groom backed out, bride cried, yada yada—" She smacked the eggs on the edge of the bowl, keeping her tone light, pretending it was of no consequence, whereas, in fact, she felt as if she'd spent the afternoon in a cocktail shaker. Her emotions were both shaken and stirred. Despite her best efforts to suppress them, memories engulfed her. Her mother setting fire to her wedding album and cutting through her dress with kitchen scissors. The agonizing family gathering for her grandmother's eightieth birthday where her father had brought his new girlfriend and spent the entire afternoon with his hand up her skirt. "Paige rescued the whole thing, of course. She could smooth a storm in the ocean. The food was good, the flowers were spectacular and the bride-to-be's parents still paid the bill so it had a happy ending. Or as close to a happy ending as life ever gets." She pulled a fork out of the drawer and beat the eggs the way Eva had taught her, until they were light and fluffy.

"You must have hated every minute."

"Every second. And the whole of August seems to be nothing but bridal showers. If it weren't for the fact we've only just started the company, I'd take an extended vacation." She snipped a selection of herbs from the pots on the windowsill. As well as the parsley and basil, there were chives and tarragon all growing in a tangled, scented profusion of green that made her small kitchen feel like a garden. She chopped them and added them to the eggs. "It started me thinking about stuff I haven't thought about in ages. Why the hell does that happen? Drives me insane."

His gaze was warm and sympathetic.

"Memories do that to you. They pop up when you least expect them. Inconvenient."

"Annoying." She added a knob of butter to the skillet, waited for it to sizzle and then poured in the eggs. "I'm not good at weddings. I shouldn't be doing them. I'm a killjoy."

"I didn't realize weddings were something you could be good or bad at. Surely all you do is buy a gift, show up and smile."

"The first two parts of that I can handle. It's the last one that gives me a problem." She tilted the pan, spreading the mixture evenly.

"The smiling?"

"Yeah, you're expected to be a cross between a cheer-leader and a groupie. The mood should be happy and excited and I just want to warn them to run while they still can. I'm hoping that one day Urban Genie will be successful enough to turn them down and focus on corporate events. I think I'm allergic to weddings in the same way some people are allergic to bee stings." While the eggs were cooking, she prepared a simple green salad, threw together a dressing of olive oil and balsamic vinegar and put the bowl on the table.

"So the only way to get you to say 'I do' would be to give you a shot of adrenaline?" There was humor in his voice and she smiled too as she eased around the edges of the omelet and folded it in half. The surface was golden brown and perfect.

"I'd need more than adrenaline. I'm as likely to say those words as I am to walk naked through Times Square." She picked up her glass and took a sip of wine. "Look at us. It's Saturday night and you're spending it in my kitchen with a deranged cat. And me. You need to get a life, Matt."

He put his beer down. "I like my life."

"You're a man in your prime. You should be on a hot date with four Swedish blondes."

"That sounds like hard work. It also sounds like something Eva would say, not you."

"Yeah, well, sometimes I try and sound normal." She took another sip of wine. "When you're on an alien planet it's important to try and blend in."

"You're not on an alien planet, Frankie. And you don't have to be anyone you're not. Certainly not with me."

"That's because you already know all my secrets, including the fact that the T-shirt I'm wearing is five years old." She slid a perfect omelet onto a plate, added a chunk of crusty bread and handed it to him. "Ignore me. I'm in a weird mood tonight. This is what the word *bridal* does to me. All that talk of fairy-tale romance unsettles me." And being with Matt unsettled her, too. Being this close to him made excitement shimmer across her skin and desire burn low in her body. She recognized sexual attraction. She just didn't know what to do with the feeling.

Her phone rang and she checked the caller ID and ignored it.

Perfect timing. If ever she needed to be snapped out of a sexual fantasy it was now.

Matt glanced at her. "Don't you want to get that?"

"No."

Curiosity gave way to understanding. "Your mother?"

"Yes. She's trying to bond with me, but that involves telling me about her latest twentysomething boyfriend, and tonight I'm not in the mood. It's Saturday night. No one invades my space."

"I'm invading your space."

Her heart gave a little kick. "You own the space."

"So we're back to owner's privileges." Matt gave her a long look and then picked up his fork and started to eat. "Does your mother know you lost your job and set up Urban Genie?"

"No."

"You're worried she'd fuss over you? Paige will tell you our mom always says you never stop worrying about your kids."

Frankie felt a pang. "My mother wouldn't fuss. She's not really interested in what I do. As you know, we're not close."

"Do you wish you were?"

"No." She disposed of the eggshells. "I don't know. Maybe. It's been years since we had a proper conversation about anything. I'm not sure we ever did. Most of our verbal exchanges were on the lines of 'clean your teeth' and 'don't be late for school.' I don't remember ever really talking." Maybe that was why she wasn't good at it. Or maybe it was just her nature to be private. "Let's talk about something else."

He glanced across the room. "Most people keep pots and pans in their kitchens. You have shelves of books."

"I can't fit them all in the living room. And anyway, I love books. Some people like looking at paintings. I like looking at books. What are you reading at the moment?" She relaxed. Books were something they often talked about. It was a comfortable, safe subject.

"Haven't read anything for a month. Business has exploded. The moment my body hits the bed I'm unconscious." He took another mouthful of food and glanced at the bookshelf again. "What's the brown one on the end? I can't see the title." His tone was casual and she followed the direction of his gaze.

"It's Stephen King. *The Stand.* Why? Do you want to borrow it?"

"No, I have that one, but thanks." He gave her a thoughtful look and then returned his attention to his food.

Frankie had the feeling she was missing something.

"Is everything okay?"

"Everything is great. This omelet is fantastic. I didn't realize you were such a great cook."

"Food always tastes better when you're not the one who cooked it."

"You're not eating?"

"I ate some cheese earlier while I started a new book. Reading food."

He stuck his fork into the salad. "Reading food?"

"Food you can eat while you're reading. Food that doesn't require any attention. Can be eaten one-handed while I turn the pages with the other. You don't know about reading food?"

"It's a gap in my education." There was a tiny smile on his lips. "So what else qualifies as reading food?"

She sat down and puffed her hair out of her eyes. "Popcorn, obviously. Chocolate, providing you break it into chunks before you settle down. Chips. Grilled cheese sandwiches if you cut them into bite-size pieces."

He reached across the table and picked up the book she'd been reading. "The latest Lucas Blade? I thought this wasn't out for another month."

"Early copy. Turns out Eva's favorite client is his grandmother, and I get to be the one who benefits from that friendship."

"Well, now I understand why you need to eat while you read. I'll borrow it when you're done with it. I love his work. So that's what you were doing when I knocked? You were sitting here reading?"

Frankie nodded. "I'm halfway through chapter three. Gripping."

He put the book back on the table carefully. "Can I ask you something?"

"Sure, although I haven't guessed the twist yet if that's what you want to know."

"It isn't." He'd finished his food and put his fork down. There was a pause. Her heart started to thud a little harder.

He looked serious, but surely if something was wrong he would have said so right away.

"What do you want to ask me?"

He pushed his plate away and lifted his gaze to hers. "How long have you worn glasses you don't need?"

Oh, God.

Had he really just said what she'd thought he'd said?

What was she going to say? She looked at him stupidly. "Excuse me?"

"When I knocked on the door you were reading, but I saw your glasses on the stand in the entryway so you can't be long-sighted. Of course you could be short-sighted, but you read the title of that book perfectly just now. Which leads me to believe you're neither." His tone was neutral. "You don't need them, do you?"

Flustered, she lifted her hand to her face.

Her glasses. She'd forgotten to wear her glasses.

She remembered taking them off when she'd walked through the door. She hadn't put them back on because she hadn't been expecting company.

"I need them." What should she do? She could squint and trip over a chair, but it was a bit late for that. "It's complicated." Lame, Frankie. *Lame.*

"I'm sure it is." Matt's tone was gentle. "But the reason you need them has nothing to do with your vision, does it?"

He knew.

Horror washed through her. It was like arriving at work and discovering you'd forgotten to dress. "If you've finished, you should probably go." She snatched the plate from him, her face burning. "Claws is scratching my sofa. And I need to get back to my book."

The book she could read perfectly well without glasses.

Matt didn't budge. "We're not going to talk about this?"

"Nothing to talk about. Good night, Matt." She was so desperate for him to leave she stumbled over the kitchen chair on her way to the door. The irony almost made her laugh. If she'd done that sooner, he might never have guessed. "Have a great evening."

He stood up slowly and followed her.

"Frankie—" The gentleness of his tone somehow intensified the humiliation.

"Good night." She pushed him through the door and Claws shot out with him, clearly unimpressed by the level of hospitality.

Frankie slammed the door, narrowly missing his hand.

Then she leaned against it and closed her eyes.

Crap, crap and *crap*.

Her cover was totally and utterly blown.

Matt let himself into his apartment and dropped his keys on the table.

He'd known Frankie since she was six years old and for the past ten years, since she'd moved to New York, she'd been a constant feature in his life. He didn't just know her, he *knew* her. He knew she burned easily and always wore sunscreen. He knew she hated tomato, romance movies, the subway. He knew she had a black belt in karate. And it wasn't just those basic facts that he knew. He knew deeper things. Important things. Like the fact that her relationship with her mother was difficult and that her parents' divorce had affected her deeply.

He knew all those things, but until tonight he hadn't known she didn't need the glasses she always wore.

He ran a hand over his face. *How could he have missed that?*

She'd worn glasses for as long as he could remember, and he'd never once questioned her need for them. He'd noticed that she fiddled with them when a situation made her nervous or uncomfortable, as if they offered her some reassurance, but he'd never understood why her glasses would be reassuring. They were possibly the ugliest thing he'd ever seen. The frames were thick and heavy and an unappealing shade of brown, as if they'd been trodden into a patch of damp earth. They were unattractive, and knowing her the way he did, Matt was sure that was the reason she'd chosen them. They were armor. Razor wire, to repel unwanted intruders.

Relationships, he thought. Was anything in life as complicated?

Claws rubbed against his legs and he bent to stroke her.

Who was going to break the bad news to her that she was cute as hell with or without ugly glasses? The fact that she seemed unaware of it just increased the sexiness level. There was so much she didn't know about herself.

The cat sprang onto the sofa, digging in her claws, and he gave a humorless laugh.

"Yeah, she'd probably do the same thing if I told her that. Dig her claws in me. Then she'd hide under the kitchen table. You and she have a lot in common."

Grabbing a beer from the fridge, he took the steps up to the roof terrace.

The setting sun sent shards of red and orange over the Manhattan skyline.

New York was a city of neighborhoods, of buildings that rose tall and proud into the sky, of blaring cab horns, hissing steam and the never-ending noise of construction. It was a city of iconic landmarks: the Empire State Building, the Chrysler Building, the Flatiron Building. The ultimate dream destination for many, and he understood that. Tourists arrived and immediately felt as if they were extras on a movie set. You saw them pointing it out. *That's where they filmed* Spiderman, or *that's where Harry met Sally.*

And it was a city of individuals. The wealthy, the poor, the lonely, the ambitious. Singles, families, locals and tourists—they all crowded together on this patch of land that nudged the water.

"You going to stand there admiring your kingdom all night or are you going to share a beer with me?"

Matt turned sharply and saw Jake sprawled on one of the loungers, a beer in his hand. He swore under his breath. "You scared the shit out of me."

Jake grinned. "Big tough guy like you? Never."

"What are you doing here?" Normally he would have been happy to see his friend, but right now he wanted space to process this new information on Frankie. What else didn't he know about her? *What else was she hiding?*

Jake raised the bottle toward Matt. "I'm drinking your beer and enjoying your view. Best view in Brooklyn."

"You have your own roof terrace. And the reason I know that is because I built it for you. You also have your own beer."

"I know, but my roof terrace and my beer don't come with your scintillating company."

"Last time I looked it was my sister's scintillating company that was taking most of your time and attention." He saw Jake open his mouth to speak and cut him off quickly. "Do not even think about telling me what it is about my sister that takes most of your time and attention. I don't want details. I'm still getting used to the idea that the two of you are together."

"You're going to be my brother-in-law. It's official. There's going to be a ceremony. In a way you're marrying me."

Matt almost cracked a smile. "I'm going to file for divorce."

"On what grounds?"

"Unreasonable behavior. Breaking and entering and—" he eyed the beer "—theft and misappropriation of property."

"I always said you would have made a fine lawyer." Jake leaned back and closed his eyes. "Bad day?"

There had been nothing wrong with his day. It was his evening that hadn't gone according to plan.

Matt sprawled on the lounger next to his friend. "Have you ever thought you knew someone and discovered you didn't?"

"Every damn day. What's her name?"

"What makes you think it's a woman?"

"If you thought you knew someone and then discovered you didn't, that person could only be female. Mystery, thy name is woman. And you're in luck, because Uncle Jake is here to give you advice on that."

"Or Uncle Jake could just drink his beer and shut up."

"I could do that, but because I'm your friend I'm going to give you the benefit of my infinite wisdom on the fair sex. Do not expect to understand a woman. You don't need to. It's like traveling to a foreign country where you don't speak the language. You can get by with a few phrases and hand gestures. But don't tell your sister I said that or she'd throw the ring I gave her into the East River."

"Talking of Paige, why are you up here with me instead of downstairs with her?"

"She's taking a call. Building her empire."

"You couldn't just hang out until she'd finished? What about Eva?"

"Eva is watching some movie where everyone is kissing and crying so I thought I'd enjoy the sunset and catch up with an old friend." He eyed the beer and grinned. "And then you showed up. So what happened with Frankie? What did you find out that you didn't know before?"

"What makes you think this has anything to do with Frankie?"

"Because I've known you a lot of years." Jake took a mouthful of beer. "And you've had feelings for Frankie for every single one of those years."

"How the hell do you know that?" He shifted uncomfortably. "Am I that easy to read?"

"No, but you're protective of the people you care about, and you're extra protective when it comes to Frankie. You don't need to be an expert in human relationships to see that she matters to you. As far as I can see, it's always been Frankie."

"Not always. I was engaged to Caroline."

"A temporary lapse from which you recovered, fortunately for our friendship."

"You didn't like Caroline?"

"She was the female equivalent of a hand grenade, a small curved object designed to cause maximum destruction." Jake paused. "She had me fooled for a while, though. Frankie is nothing like her."

Matt didn't disagree. He and Caroline had met in college and their relationship had been more like a kick in the balls than a blow to the heart. It had lasted twelve intense months and it had woken him up to what he wanted. Not just wanted, *needed*. Trust. Honesty.

"Frankie hides a lot."

"Maybe, but the difference is that Frankie doesn't hide it because she's manipulative or conniving. She hides it because she's scared. I joke about women being difficult to read but Paige is pretty much an open book and as for Eva—she's not just an open book, she's an audiobook. Everything she feels comes out of her mouth with no filter. Which makes it simple for guys like me. But Frankie—" Jake pulled a face "—she's different. She's guarded."

"I know." Matt didn't mind the fact that she was guarded. What he minded was the fact that she was guarded around him. Why would she feel the need to wear glasses around him? Didn't she trust him?

"What? You expect her to open up and spill all her secrets to you?" Jake shook his head. "You expect too much."

"I expect trust. Is that too much to ask?"

Jake shrugged. "It's everything. Trust is serious. More serious than sex. Think about it. When you trust someone, you're giving them the power to hurt you." He drained his beer. "That's scary stuff. Like saying, 'Hey, here's a really sharp knife. Stab me in the chest with it anytime you like.'"

"I would never hurt Frankie."

"That isn't the point."

"So what is the point?"

"She had a rough time growing up, you know that. Her mom is scary. Remember the last time she visited? She pinned me against the wall. I almost lost my virginity right there in Frankie's kitchen. It's no wonder Frankie is guarded."

Matt remembered Paige telling him that boys had hit on Frankie at school, assuming she was like her mother and that sex was guaranteed.

Like mother, like daughter.

"I don't know how to handle it."

"You'll figure it out. Getting wounded creatures to trust you is your special gift. If you don't believe me you only have to look at that damn cat."

"Are you comparing Frankie to a cat?" Matt shook his head. "How did you ever get any woman, let alone my sister?"

"I used my abundance of natural charm." Jake yawned. "How's work? You never return my calls. Are we breaking up?"

Matt was too preoccupied to smile. "I'm snowed under. I'm in the middle of a big project and I've lost a key player." His skill lay in design and hard landscaping and much of that was already completed. They still had to deal with lighting and furniture. He'd planned three log seats, and had completed one of them. His problem was the planting and it would remain a problem until he could find someone to take Victoria's place. "I need to try and recruit someone with Frankie's skills."

Jake shrugged. "So ask Frankie."

"What?"

"Why bother trying to find someone like Frankie, when you can have Frankie. If she has the right skills, give her the job."

"She already has a job."

"So you'll need to be creative. Find a way." Jake paused. "The best way to get someone to trust you is to spend time with them. You have the perfect excuse right there under your nose."

Matt stared at Jake, wondering why that solution hadn't occurred to him. "Sometimes," he said, "you're not a bad friend."

"I'm the best friend on the planet. You love me. That's why we're getting married. And we're going to live happily ever after."

"Until I divorce you."

"You couldn't afford to divorce me. We haven't signed a prenup."

Chapter Two

If you want unconditional love, get a dog.

—Frankie

"We had a call from Mega Print. Remember them? We ran their office party last month." Paige checked all the requests that had come through overnight. "The vice president of sales wants regular dog walking. Can we cover that?"

"I'm on it. I manage everything canine." Eva slid into her chair and toed off her running shoes. "Matt recommended a fantastic dog-walking business called The Bark Rangers on the Upper East Side and so far our clients are impressed. The owners are twins. My new favorite game is trying to tell them apart. They're called Fliss and Harry."

"You can't tell a man and a woman apart?"

"Harry is short for Harriet. I'll give them a call."

Paige frowned. "Matt recommended them? He has a cat. When did he need dog walking?"

"The twins' brother is a client of his. I think they play poker occasionally. Daniel Knight?"

"The lawyer? I've met him. Brilliant by all accounts, not to mention smooth and charming."

"Single?"

Paige laughed. "Very. He's also as dangerous as they come. Definitely doesn't mate for life."

Eva sighed. "Not my type, then. I'll have to keep looking." She perked up as she checked her schedule. "I used to loathe Mondays when we worked for Star Events, but now I love them." Through the floor-to-ceiling glass behind her, Manhattan basked in a pool of blazing sunshine. Urban Genie operated out of Jake's company building—he ran a digital marketing firm and had generously let them use one of his boardrooms as they got their own company off the ground. "I love running my own business. And my blog followers tripled overnight so the work side of my life is perfect. Which, of course, means that my love life is totally crap because everyone knows both parts can't go right at the same time."

"You need to teach me how to flirt." The words came out before Frankie could stop them and Eva stared at her.

"Excuse me?"

"Flirt. You know. That thing you do with men without even thinking about it."

"Er—it's true that I flirt if I have someone to flirt with, but it's been so long since I met anyone I've probably forgotten how to do it." Eva slumped in her seat. "There are so many men in Manhattan. They're everywhere. And I don't meet a single one of them. My life is a manless, sexless desert. And the con—"

"The condom in your purse has expired. We know. You keep telling us." Paige gave her an exasperated look. "It's boring, Ev!"

"It's a tragedy, that's what it is. Here I am, a warm, willing woman, and no one wants me. And you're not allowed to comment, Paige, because you're getting regular sex."

"I'm going to buy you a brand-new condom."

"Don't bother," Eva said gloomily. "It will only expire again and I'll feel guilty that it had a wasted life. Anyway, back to flirting. I can rack my brains and try to remember how to do it if that would be any help. Who are you planning on flirting with?"

Frankie felt her face heat. "No one specific. It's precautionary training. Like self-defense or basic cookery."

"Basic flirting. Flirting 101. No problem. I'll book you in for a one-on-one session." Eva reached for her phone. "When do you want to start?"

"Not now. I need to be in the right mood."

"We'll do it over a bottle of wine. It will loosen you up."

"You think I need loosening up?"

"Let's put it this way—your starting point is glaring at every guy as if you're thinking of stabbing him between the shoulder blades with a sharp implement, so we have a way to go."

"Am I that bad?"

Eva exchanged glances with Paige, who shook her head.

"You're lovely as you are. Why do you want to flirt?"

"I hate being tongue-tied when guys say things. I want to memorize a few swift, witty comebacks, that's all." She watched as Eva slid her phone into her bag. "Why have your followers tripled?"

"Not sure. It might have been the photo I posted to Instagram." Eva opened the drawer of her desk and selected a pair of shoes with heels that could have doubled as a lethal weapon. "I took a photo of a cupcake and it looked delicious."

"Were you in the photo, too?"

"It was a selfie." Eva slid her feet into the shoes with all the delight of Cinderella discovering the glass slipper fitted.

"Were you dressed at the time? Because there's your answer."

"I was dressed!"

Paige was sending a response to the vice president. "Be grateful she wasn't eating a banana or that might have qualified as Most Embarrassing Moment."

Frankie didn't respond.

Right now when it came to Most Embarrassing Moment, she had the edge.

She'd spent the whole of Sunday reliving the moments that had followed Matt's discovery that her vision was perfect. Feeling as naked and exposed as a snail that had been extracted from the protection of its shell, she'd virtually pushed him out the door.

Had she even said goodbye?

She couldn't remember. All she remembered was planting her hand on his chest—a strong chest, very muscular—and giving it a good, hard shove. Of course, Matt being built like a linebacker, he could have resisted if he'd wanted to. He hadn't. Which either meant he'd been as keen to exit the apartment as she was to see him leave, or that he'd been weakened by the shock of discovering that she was wearing glasses when she didn't need to, and embarrassing didn't begin to describe *that* moment.

Frankie squirmed in her seat.

What must he think of her?

She wanted to slink under the table and never come out again, but that would be about as mature as her reaction when he'd raised the subject on Saturday.

She wished she could put the clock back.

There were so many more dignified ways she could have reacted. A light, flirtatious response would have been perfect.

"Did you see Matt yesterday?" She kept her tone casual and Paige glanced up from the screen.

"Briefly. Why?"

"No reason. I wondered if he mentioned anything." Like the fact that he had a deranged woman living in his apartment. A deranged woman with perfect vision.

"He mentioned he's overloaded with work. I promised to feed Claws tonight because he's going to be late. He's going to owe me big-time for that favor. I might need a bodyguard."

"I am generally considered to be a people-pleaser and the fact that I'm not volunteering to do it in your place tells you what I think of that cat." Eva stood up. "I'm willing to call the Bronx Zoo if you like and ask if they have any tips for feeding predators. Maybe we could open the window and poke a piece of meat through with a long pole."

"I'll feed her." Frankie shrugged as they both looked at her. "Why not? She's just a cat." And it would give her an opportunity to leave a note in Matt's apartment. She'd apologize for being rude. Then she wouldn't have to do it face-to-face.

Which meant that she could add cowardice to her other flaws, but never mind.

Turning back to her work, she answered an email from a client who wanted flowers delivered to his wife on a monthly basis.

"Claws isn't *just a cat*. She is a psychotic cat," Eva said. "She scratched me so hard last week I thought my bone was going to fall out through the hole."

Paige shuddered. "That's vile."

"It was vile. Lucas Blade could use that animal in one of his books as a murder weapon."

"What did you do to her?"

"Nothing! I was trying to hug her! She was abandoned and mistreated. I was trying to show her that not all humans are evil."

"You have to let her work that out for herself, Ev. You can't love someone who doesn't want to be loved."

"Everyone wants to be loved. If they don't, it's because they're afraid."

Frankie pressed Send on her email. "Or because they think that love is just too much trouble."

"That's another way of saying they're afraid. Don't worry, I learned my lesson. I'm not going near her again. From now on I'll be projecting my positive feelings from a safe distance." Eva's phone rang and she picked it up and wandered out of the room, the fabric of her tiny scarlet skirt skimming her long, tanned legs.

Frankie stared after her, wondering how it felt to be that sexually confident. "Did she forget to dress? If she goes outside wearing that skirt there will be a riot."

Paige jabbed the charging cable into her phone. "She looks amazing, doesn't she? We went shopping yesterday when you were lost in your book. Your response to stress is to read, ours is to shop. How was it, by the way?"

"I didn't make it past the third chapter."

"That's not like you. What's wrong?"

"Nothing is wrong."

"Frankie—"

"It's Matt." She closed her laptop. "He found out I don't need to wear glasses."

"He— Oh." Paige let out a long breath. "How? When?"

"Saturday night. He came down looking for Claws. I was on my own and I wasn't expecting anyone. I was reading and cooking and—I wasn't paying attention. Long day." She closed her eyes briefly. "I can't believe I was so careless."

"Is it really such a big deal?"

"It's a huge deal."

"Why?" Paige sat back in her chair. "Frankie, it's not as if he's a stranger. Matt has known you since you were a kid. He knows pretty much everything there is to know about you."

"He didn't know I wear glasses even though my vision is perfect."

"How did he react?"

"I don't know. I pushed him out the door without asking." Remembering made her want to crawl under the table. "There were a million things I could have said or done. I could have smiled and said I manage fine without my glasses in the apartment but no, I gave him a shove that would probably have injured someone less powerfully built than your brother."

"If he upset you, I'll kill him." Paige sounded annoyed. "Did he say something tactless?"

"I didn't give him the chance. It wasn't his fault. It was me. All me." She dropped her head in her hands. "What is *wrong* with me? I'm a sane, independent woman. I'm good at my job—"

"You're excellent at your job."

"Yeah, I really am. And I know I'm a disappointing daughter, but I'm a great friend even though I don't hug enough for Eva." She lifted her head. "All I'm saying is that in every other aspect of my life I'm pretty normal and function well. Why am I such a basket case around men?"

"Do you seriously need me to answer that?"

"No, but I should have the emotional intelligence not to let the antics of my mother affect my life like this. Matt said he liked me in my T-shirt—he paid me a compliment and I responded as if he'd covered me in anthrax."

"This is why you want to learn to flirt?"

"I want to learn to be *normal*." She looked at her friend in despair. "What am I going to do?"

"Do you mean about the glasses, Matt or men in general?"

"All of it! How can I wear glasses around him knowing that he knows? I'll feel stupid. And what do I say next time I see him?"

"Whether you wear glasses or not is your choice, Frankie. If you feel more comfortable wearing them, then wear them. And as for what happened on Saturday—" Paige thought for a moment "—you should probably talk to him about it."

"I was leaning more toward pretending it never happened." If she could ignore it, she would. "I could leave him a note saying sorry I was weird."

"You don't have to do that, Frankie. He knows you."

"You mean he knows I'm weird."

Paige smiled. "No. I mean he knows what you grew up with. I don't understand why this bothers you. This is Matt we're talking about. Not some stranger."

It was precisely because it was Matt that it bothered her. Exposing the depth of her hang-ups to a guy she'd known forever and found attractive was mortifying.

Generally she didn't care what men thought about her, but she cared what Matt thought.

"You're right. I should have an adult conversation. But I can't turn 'hey, I wear glasses but I don't need them' into anything that sounds remotely mature."

Eva walked back into the room. "That was Mitzy. She wants to officially be one of our clients, and before either of you say anything, I know she's never going to be our biggest earner, but I love her. What's the matter with you two?" She peered at Frankie. "You're wearing your doomed face and Paige is wearing her problem-solving face. What's happened?"

"I have a doomed face?" Just for a moment Frankie wished she had Eva's confidence. Never in a million years would she go out in public wearing a skirt that short.

"You have the face you wear when things are going wrong."

Paige stood up and picked up some pages from the printer. "Matt worked out that she doesn't need glasses."

"Oh." Eva's brow cleared. "Is that all? I thought something awful had happened."

"That is awful."

"Why? Wearing glasses is part of who you are. It's part of your individuality."

"You mean my hang-ups."

Eva shrugged. "Hang-ups are individual. The important thing is that you mustn't be afraid to let people know the real you. That's what intimacy is."

"I don't want intimacy! That's why I wear the glasses—to repel intimacy."

"Yes, but—" Eva caught Paige's eye. "But I strongly defend the right of the individual to wear whatever they like, so I'm making no comment. Is that why you want to know how to flirt? So that next time he talks about your glasses you can turn it into seduction?"

"I wear the glasses so I can be sure I never reach the point of seduction."

Eva looked baffled. "I love you, but I will never understand you."

"That goes both ways. And if you don't comment on my glasses, I won't comment on that thing you call a skirt."

"Hey, I am rocking this skirt." Eva's cheeks dimpled into a smile as she rotated her hips in a sensuous movement that would have caused multiple collisions had they been in public. "Don't you love it?"

"I've seen wider hair ribbons, but yes, it's cute. Now tell us about Mitzy." She needed to stop thinking about Matt and focus on work. "What does she need from us? If she can get me early copies of all Lucas Blade's releases, I'll do pretty much anything for her."

"She wants me to bake him a birthday cake."

Paige clipped pages together. "Does she really want a cake or is it just an excuse to spend another afternoon talking to you?"

"Does it matter? She's so kind. And wise." Eva's voice thickened. "She reminds me of Grams. And she treats me as if I'm family."

Eva had such a rosy view of family it made Frankie feel guilty that she couldn't feel better disposed toward her own.

"Go and see her, Ev. I'll make up a bunch of flowers for her, and don't charge her for the cake."

"I don't think she minds paying. Money isn't the problem. But she's lonely."

And so are you, Frankie thought, making a mental note to spend more time with her friend. As an introvert, she didn't seek human contact the way Eva did. She loved her friends, but she was equally comfortable in her own space with her books and her plants. But she knew that with Paige spending more time with Jake, Eva would be spending more time alone.

"Her grandsons don't visit?"

"One of them rarely leaves Wall Street and Lucas, the one who writes those scary books you love, rarely leaves his apartment unless he's on a book tour. Apparently, his deadline is looming and he's Mr. Moody. She wants me to fill his freezer with healthy food, too, so he doesn't fade away or turn into a vessel for junk food."

Frankie thought about what had happened to the main character in the opening scene of Lucas Blade's new book. Then she looked at Eva, who was so gentle you could have knocked her over with one flick of a soft sweater. "I don't think you should be visiting some reclusive dangerous guy in his apartment by yourself."

"Who said he was dangerous? I never said he was dangerous."

"You said he was moody."

"Well, he lost his wife," Eva said reasonably. "He's allowed to be moody."

"His books are dark, Eva. I mean read-with-the-lights-on dark. That man's mind works in ways that even freak me out."

"I'll have to take your word for it because I'd rather give away my shoe collection than read a horror story. But you can relax. I'm taking the food to Mitzy and she is going over there with Peanut."

"Who is Peanut?"

"The dog. Very cute. I walked him last time I was there. Much more appreciative than Claws. He's one of those tiny dogs that fits in a handbag. Lucas bought him for Mitzy, which was actually very thoughtful so he can't be that dangerous, can he? But thank you for caring."

"Well, be careful." Frankie checked her schedule. "I need to go to the flower district tomorrow morning. Final preparations for the Myers-Topper birthday bash on Friday."

Paige glanced up. "How is the planning for that going?"

"All good. We're doing a hedge wall, tree rental and fresh flowers. Anyone want to join me?"

"At the flower district at five in the morning?" Eva recoiled. "No, thanks. I'd rather pull out my own eyelashes, which is probably what I'd have to do to stay awake if you got me up at that time."

"I'll come. I love it and they sell great coffee in that little bistro." Paige sent another document to the printer, stood up and stretched. "Time to go. I have a meeting over on Fifth. Are you sure you're happy to feed Claws? Because if you are then I won't hurry home."

"I'll feed her."

She'd leave a note for Matt and that would be the end of it.

Matt would sense she didn't want to talk about it, and being a guy it was a fair assumption that he wouldn't want to talk about it, either. Neither of them would ever mention it again.

"You'll need the keys to Matt's apartment." Paige rummaged in her bag and pulled them out. "Here. Good luck."

"I'm feeding the cat. I need cat food, not luck." Frankie dropped the keys into her purse. "How hard can it be?"

Eva opened her mouth and then caught Paige's eye and closed it again. "I'm not saying a word. But if I were you I'd take a weapon along with the cat food. And wear armor."

"I always wear armor."

But now she'd lost a layer.

Her glasses.

Tired and hot after a day when too much of it had been spent outside in sweltering heat, Matt let himself into his apartment and paused as he heard voices.

He lived alone.

There weren't supposed to be voices.

He walked into his kitchen and stopped. His intruder was on all fours under the table. All he could see was a perfectly curved bottom in faded denim, but he would have known that bottom anywhere.

He admired it for a moment, but decided that this time he'd hold the compliment.

Instead, he cleared his throat.

Frankie banged her head on the table and swore. She emerged gingerly, glasses awry, rubbing her head with her fingers. "What are you doing here?" She pushed her glasses up her nose, as if challenging him to comment.

He said nothing, but felt a flash of disappointment that she still felt the need to wear them in front of him.

"This is my apartment. I live here."

"How long have you been standing there?"

"A while." Or maybe he wouldn't hold the compliment. It was bad to hold things in, wasn't it? "Long enough to admire your butt."

Confusion clouded her eyes. "Instead of staring at my butt, you should be dealing with your pet. Your cat has issues."

Not only my cat, he thought. "I wouldn't argue with that."

"She was happy enough to eat my food on Saturday, but apparently she needs to be the one who decides where she eats. She wasn't impressed that I was the one that put food in her bowl."

"She's giving you problems?"

"Nothing a therapist couldn't sort out given a couple of years." She pushed her hair back from her face and he reached forward and gently removed her glasses.

"You don't need to wear those when you're with me."

"Matt—" She made a wild grab for them but he folded them up and slid them into his pocket.

"What do you think they do, Frankie? Cover up the fact you have pretty eyes?" They were a washed shade of green and they reminded him of a Scottish hillside or an English garden after a shower of rain. She looked so disconcerted he wanted to hug her. "You need to stop hiding."

"I'm not hiding."

"You're hiding. But you don't ever need to hide from me." Knowing that he'd pushed her enough for the time being, he turned and put his laptop on the table. "Thanks for feeding Claws. That's twice in one week. I owe you for the favor, plus extra for danger money."

"You don't owe me anything." She was balanced on her toes, poised to run, and he decided that the best way to get her to relax was to talk about work.

"I spent the morning trying to find a horticultural specialist who can step in and replace Victoria. Do you have time to take a look at the plans? I'd love to hear your thoughts." He was banking on the fact that Frankie was too passionate about her job not to be intrigued by the project that was currently occupying his every waking moment, and he was right.

"Sure." The wary expression on her face faded. "Tell me about the project. What was the brief?"

"Architectural style with sustainability. It's a multifunctional space. General living, family time, some corporate entertainment. They have a social conscience. Green roofs reduce heating and cooling costs. They're reducing their carbon footprint. Everybody wins, including me."

"It's not winning if it gives you a nervous breakdown.

Couldn't Victoria have stayed another few weeks to give you a chance to find someone?"

"Her mother is sick. That has to be her priority. I understand that. Maybe I'm more sympathetic to that than most because of Paige." He didn't elaborate. He didn't need to. Frankie knew all about the health issues his sister had suffered growing up. "It will work out." He'd learned early on what mattered in life, taught himself to fix what he could fix and find a way to live with what he couldn't.

"I made a few calls today." Her tone was casual. "People I know whose skills are perfect for you. Most of them are busy. One of them will be free in October."

Knowing how busy they were at Urban Genie, he was touched. "You did that for me?"

"You need help." She dismissed it as nothing but he knew it wasn't nothing. She'd taken time out of a horrendously busy schedule to try and help him.

"Thanks. I appreciate that."

"You'd do the same for us."

He noticed she chose the word *us* rather than making it more personal.

Frankie, he was realizing, had a big problem with personal. Far bigger than he'd first thought.

"The problem is that October is too late for this project. I need someone who can hit the ground running, who knows how I think and who has the same creative vision."

"And where are you going to find someone like that?"

"I'm looking at her."

Those green eyes widened. "You mean me?"

"I saw your expression when I described the project— admit it, you're interested."

"It's true that roof gardens have their own charms and

challenges but I have a job. Urban Genie is in its infancy and—"

"And you already told me you have a few too many wedding events this summer. You hate them. Delegate those to someone else and come and work with me." He handed her the plans and saw the panic and indecision in her eyes.

"I can't."

"Take a look at the plans and think about it. Talk to Paige and Eva. It's not as if I'm asking you to relocate to Alaska. You can still help with Urban Genie. Just reduce your hands-on work for now. What's the name of that supplier you've been working with?"

"Buds and Blooms."

"You'd be giving them an opportunity to grow their business, you'd be helping me and you'd be doing work you love. Let someone else deal with the froth of weddings. Design me a roof garden. At least think about it. It's only for the summer. One project." His gaze caught on a piece of paper on the table. "What's that? You wrote me a note?"

She made a strangled sound and scrabbled for the paper. "You can't read it!"

"You wrote me a note I'm not supposed to read?"

"I assumed I'd be gone by the time you read it." She snatched it from the table, cheeks scarlet.

"Aren't you going to at least tell me what it says?"

"I was apologizing for Saturday, that's all." She was adorably flustered and Matt resisted the urge to take the note from her fingers.

"Why would you feel the need to apologize?"

"Hey, I don't know. Maybe because I almost trapped your hand in the door two seconds before I shut you out of your own apartment." She shoved the paper into the pocket of her jeans and shot toward the door.

"It's your apartment." This time he was determined not to let her leave without finishing the conversation. "You live there."

"But you own it."

"I made you feel uncomfortable."

"It's not you, it's me. It's all me."

They reached the door at the same time.

"Wait." He planted his hand in the center of the door panel to prevent her leaving and saw her freeze.

"What are you doing?"

"I want to say something and I want to do it without worrying about you severing one of my limbs in the door." He could have stepped back but he didn't. If what it took to get her to open up to him was to invade her comfort zone, then he'd invade it. But he'd try and invade it as sensitively as possible.

"Look, I know you think it's strange that I'd wear glasses when I don't need them but—"

"You don't have to explain."

"I do. You're wondering why on earth anyone would do something that weird." She'd dipped her head and all he could see was the sweep of her dark lashes and the delicate freckles that dusted her nose like pollen.

"I'm not wondering that because I already know the answer."

"You do?"

"You think it puts a barrier between yourself and the world. Or rather, men." The temptation to touch her was almost overwhelming. "What I don't understand is why you're so upset that I know."

"Because it's a deeply personal thing."

"That's what a relationship is, Frankie. It's about knowing the deeply personal things that other people don't see. We've known each other a long time."

"And there's such a thing as 'too much information.'" If she pressed any closer to the door she would leave an imprint.

"It's called intimacy, Frankie. It's what happens when two people know each other well. And for the record, I don't think it's weird."

Finally, she looked at him. "You don't?"

"No. But as we're being honest with each other, it's only fair to tell you that you're wasting your time."

"Excuse me?"

"You have beautiful eyes, and they're beautiful with or without the glasses. And to save you examining that comment in minute detail I can tell you that yes, it was a compliment." He removed his arm and opened the door, gently nudging her through it. "Have a think about working with me and thanks again for feeding my cat."

Reining in his protective instincts, he closed the door before he could do something inappropriate like haul her into his arms.

There was plenty of time for that.

This was only step one.

It wasn't as if they weren't going to see each other again. And at some point she was going to realize that he still had her glasses.

Chapter Three

A compliment is a gift. Accept it gratefully.

—Eva

Beautiful eyes?

He thought she had beautiful eyes?

Frankie wandered through Manhattan's flower market in a daze that had nothing to do with the early start or the fact she hadn't slept.

"I love this place." Paige slipped her arm through Frankie's. "It's calming, isn't it?"

"What is?" Frankie wasn't concentrating. She couldn't stop thinking about the moment she'd been trapped between Matt and the door. He hadn't actually touched her, but he might as well have because she'd been so agonizingly aware of him it had been almost impossible to breathe. The avalanche of unfamiliar feelings had come as a shock. It wasn't as if she was the kind of person who thought about sex all the time. Hardly ever, in fact. She'd accepted that it didn't play an important role in her life, and even though she was intelligent enough to know that at least part of the reason for that lay with her parents, she hadn't ever considered that it might change.

But it was changing. Or maybe it would be more accurate to say that Matt was changing it. He hadn't touched her, but she'd found herself wanting to touch him. She'd wanted to grab him and kiss him, an impulse that had left her more than a little freaked out. Fortunately, she'd managed to stop herself, but what she hadn't been able to stop was the strange feeling inside her, the almost breathless excitement that she associated with Christmas Eve and the last day of school. Being close to him seemed to flick a switch in a part of her she'd never accessed before. And she had to remind herself to breathe, something she'd managed to do without prompting up until this point in her life.

Paige elbowed her. "You're not listening to me. You need strong coffee." She dragged her into the small coffee shop and ordered two espressos. "This will wake you up."

Frankie didn't tell her that her problem wasn't going to be solved by coffee.

She wasn't sure how to solve it. Two cold showers hadn't worked.

They drank the coffee and Paige talked about new clients while Frankie tried to forget the hard strength of Matt's body against hers and focus on business.

Boosted by caffeine, they tackled the flower market. Nestled between Seventh Avenue and Broadway, the market was a hidden jungle of plants surrounded by soaring tower blocks of glass and steel. It was five o'clock in the morning but despite the early hour, the place was bustling with people.

They went into one of the many stores and Frankie leaned forward and stuck her nose in a bunch of blooms. "These are perfect." She picked a large bunch and stashed it on a metal shelf to buy later, before carefully selecting another bunch.

"They're pretty. So did you speak to Matt?"

Frankie almost dropped the flowers. How could just hearing his name make her clumsy? She was like a teenager in the throes of her first major crush. Except that she'd never felt this way when she was a teenager. "I wrote him a note, but then he showed up while I was feeding Claws and I scrunched it up because I'm a coward."

"He didn't say anything?"

"He said a couple of things." Unsettling things. Things that had danced around her brain and kept her awake when she should have been sleeping.

You have beautiful eyes.

She'd been so taken aback by the compliment, she'd said nothing. Eva would have made a lighthearted remark in response. Paige probably would have done the same.

She'd been mute.

And this morning she'd found her glasses in her mailbox.

She wondered if it was a test to see if she'd put them back on.

Frustrated with herself, she turned her head and stole a surreptitious glance in the mirror that ran along one side of the store. The glasses dominated her face, which had been her plan when she'd chosen them.

Paige leaned over to examine a box of cream roses. "Did he mention work?"

"Work?" Unable to see how anyone could think her eyes were beautiful, Frankie turned back to her friend. "You mean did he tell me about Victoria leaving? Yes. He's been trying to recruit someone. After he mentioned it on Saturday night, I called a few people I met on my course at the Botanic Gardens, and people I've worked with since then, but so far no luck. I'm still working on it."

"He wants you to do it."

Her pulse skipped. "That's not going to happen."

"Why not? You love roof gardens! They're your favorite thing. Why wouldn't you do it?"

Because forgetting how to breathe for the short time she was currently with him was one thing, but having to remind herself right through an entire working day was something else. What if she forgot and suffocated? And then there was the whole electric-current feeling that she didn't seem able to switch off. She wasn't sure she'd survive feeling that way for an entire day. She couldn't possibly work with him.

And maybe that made her a coward, but better to be a coward than be asphyxiated by longing. Because that was what it was. She might be embarrassingly inexperienced, but she recognized desire.

She imagined the autopsy report: death by sexual frustration.

"We've only just started Urban Genie. I can't go and work for another company."

"I'm not suggesting you go into partnership with Matt, just help him with this project over the summer."

"We have two events the week after next."

"Both of which you've already planned. Buds and Blooms has a great team. They did a good job on the Harrison Real Estate event last week. If they have any problems, they can call you."

It was the same argument Matt had used. "I don't think it's a good idea."

"Why not?"

"Because mixing business with personal is never a good thing."

Paige burst out laughing. "It's not as if you're having sex with him!" Laughter was replaced by curiosity. "Are you?"

"No!" But now Paige had mentioned it, Frankie's brain was crowded with new images. Images of Matt naked, that strong, muscular body intimately entwined with hers. "Of course not. Why would you even ask that?"

"Possibly because your face is scarlet."

"That's because I hate talking about sex in public. I don't think working with Matt is a good idea, that's all. I should be focusing my attention on Urban Genie."

"This isn't like you. I thought you'd want to help."

"I did help! I made some calls. I plan on making more later."

"But why not do it yourself? You're the sort of person who would do anything for your friends." Paige hesitated. "If it weren't for Matt, we'd all be living in a shoe box."

"You're playing the guilt card?" And it worked, because she knew that if it wasn't for all these new, unfamiliar feelings she would have helped Matt in an instant. Not only because it was a way of avoiding all the bridal showers they had booked that summer, but because he was a friend and Paige was right. She would always, always help a friend.

"Is this about the whole glasses thing? Has my brother upset you? Is that why you don't want to help?"

"No." Heat spread around the back of her neck. "He's a great guy. Strong, principled, decent—" *and insanely hot.*

And it was the insanely hot part that was stopping her volunteering to help.

Normally she didn't have any problems around men. It

was simple. She wasn't interested. But with Matt it was different. With Matt it was—confusing.

Paige touched her arm. "Matt has always looked out for me. He's always been there for me."

"I know." The Walker family loyalty was something she envied. Instead of trying to cause each other maximum stress and embarrassment, they pulled together. It was a family dynamic so far removed from her own experience she barely recognized it.

"It would be good to be able to return the favor for once."

"Except I'd be the one returning the favor."

"You'd do the work, but it would have an impact on all of us. We're a team." Paige paused. "You and Matt think alike and you have similar taste and style when it comes to all things outdoors. He thinks you're so talented. After you did the planting for his roof terrace he wouldn't shut up about how smart you are. And I know you admire his work, too. I would have thought you would jump at the chance to do something together."

Do something together?

Images danced across her brain and heat spread across her neck. "I'll think about it."

Paige studied her. "Are you sure this isn't about the whole glasses thing? Because—"

"It's not about the glasses thing."

It was about the door thing. And the compliment thing. And the chemistry thing.

Mostly, the chemistry thing.

"Has he told you that the client has built financial penalties into the contract so if the job falls behind it costs Matt directly?"

"No. He didn't mention that."

Guilt intensified.

Paige was right; she had her apartment and her independence because of Matt.

True, she paid him rent, but it was a friendly rent. And it was stupid to worry about the chemistry and her reaction to him. She needed to learn to handle it.

Brooding, she made her purchases and they walked on through the market.

Towering plants, specialty cut flowers, tropical flowers and dried botanicals crowded the sidewalk on both sides, creating a lush avenue with a sultry feel. Usually it calmed her, but not today.

Paige reached out to touch the leaves of a tropical palm tree. The thicket of greenery blocked out the sound of traffic and for a moment it was possible to forget they were in the middle of the city. "Talking of Urban Genie, we need to discuss the Smyth-Bennett engagement party in a couple of weeks."

Frankie's heart sank.

Another engagement party.

"What is there to discuss?"

"They want to change the brief."

"Isn't it a bit late for that?"

"They're the clients." Paige shrugged. "They want something more romantic. Or rather, the bride-to-be does and the groom-to-be is going along with it."

"How have we ended up doing so many romantic events?" She stuck her face in a bunch of flowers. "Whatever happened to product launches and corporate functions?"

"We have those booked in, too, but it's summer and love is in the air."

"Francesca! Francesca! Is that really you?"

Recognizing her mother's voice, Frankie shrank back into the nearest store. "Oh crap, *no*."

Paige turned. "Stay calm."

"Why? Can we hide? Is it too late? Why is she here? How did she find me?"

"I don't think she was looking for you. I'm guessing it's a chance encounter."

Frankie moaned. "Party dress?"

Paige peeped around the flowers. "Purple. Sparkly. Short. It's either a party dress or she's cheerfully dressed for breakfast. She's channeling the showgirl look."

"Kill me now. This place is heaving with people. I know some of them. If she talks to me for more than five seconds I'll have to move to Seattle."

"Then we'll make this quick because I can't see myself in Seattle. I'd love the coffee, but the climate would kill me." Paige stepped into the street and Frankie followed her, grabbing her arm.

"Is she on her own?"

"No."

"Is he younger than us?"

"Hard to tell, but he's certainly a long way from retirement." Paige braced her shoulders, the way she did when she handled a difficult client. "Good morning, Mrs. Cole."

"Paige!" Gina Cole teetered up to them, clutching the arm of a man Frankie guessed to be in his midtwenties. "How many times have I told you to call me Gina? Mrs. Cole makes me sound so *old*. You're looking very pale, Paige. I hope you're not sick again, honey."

"I'm not sick." Paige kept her tone civil. "It's five thirty in the morning and—"

"You need a good foundation. I can recommend one, although personally I like to layer different products and I'm a total fan of strobing. Look at my skin. You wouldn't guess I haven't been to sleep yet, would you?" She tugged at the arm of the man next to her. "Have you met Dev? Dev, meet Paige and Frankie. Frankie is—" there was a brief moment of hesitation "—my daughter."

"No *way*." Dev responded with the appropriate amount of disbelief, and Frankie caught Paige's eye.

Seeing her friend's amusement made her feel better, until she saw her mother slide her hand over Dev's butt and squeeze.

"Mom—"

"Have you girls been up all night partying, too?"

"No. We're working."

"Well, I guess that explains your appearance. These things matter, Frankie! You don't want to let yourself go, honey. You are *never* going to attract a man looking as if you raided a charity store. I could transform you if you'd let me. Underneath that shaggy hair and those baggy clothes—" Gina waved a manicured hand and the bangles on her wrist jangled "—you have the same body shape as me. You could look like me if you tried harder."

Horrified, Frankie backed away. She'd spent her life trying hard not to look, or be, anything like her mother. "I like the way I am."

"You could be pretty. Don't you think she could be pretty, Dev?"

To his credit, Dev had more sense than to answer that.

"It's good to see you, Mrs. Cole," Paige intervened, "but I hope you'll excuse us now. We're choosing flowers for an event and we're on a deadline."

"What event? I found out this week that Star Events laid

off a bunch of staff. You lost your job over two months ago and you didn't even *tell* me? I'm your mother. I was worried about you."

Frankie was thrown. Her mother never worried about her. If anything, it was the other way around. "That's why you've been calling so often?"

"Of course. I wanted to tell you you're better off without them. The *hours* they made you work. Inhuman. Not getting enough rest is bad for your skin and no one is going to fall in love with you if you're looking old and ugly. Don't worry about the money. Dev could give you a loan. He's in banking." She snuggled closer to Dev and patted his arm. "Only twenty-nine and already on his way to the top, can you believe that? Right now I'm his favorite way of spending money. Fortunately, he's nothing like your father. Lord, that man was miserly. I expected him to charge me rent just for sitting on my own sofa. That's one of the advantages of dating much younger men. They know how to live in the moment. He lives very close to here, by the way."

Frankie felt the color drain from her cheeks. "My father?"

"No! That man is so lily-livered he hasn't been in touch since the day he walked out, you know that!" Her laugh was high-pitched. "I'm talking about Dev!"

"You should go, Mom. If you haven't been to bed yet, you must be tired."

"I didn't say we hadn't been to bed. I said we hadn't been to sleep." Gina gave Dev a playful nudge. "This man is an *animal* I tell you. He exhausts even me, and I have more stamina than most. That's another reason I love younger men. You have no idea how many times he can—"

"Mom!" Frankie barked out the word, mortified. Heads around her turned in curiosity and she was transported back to her teenage years when it had felt as if everyone was staring at her. "We don't need details."

She'd grown up with details. They were scarred into her brain.

Would she have had fewer issues if her mother hadn't been so free with the details?

"How I ever raised such a prude I will never know. You need to loosen up. People say it's impossible to meet a man in Manhattan, but I say they're looking in the wrong place."

"Mom—"

"*Use it or lose it.* Who was it who said that? I can't remember." Gina Cole frowned, until she remembered that frowning was bad for her and quickly smoothed her forehead with her fingers. "If you need money or a place to stay—"

"I don't. I make my own money and I have my own place."

And she had her own issues, personal to her.

Thanks, Mom.

"Of course you do! Owned by Paige's handsome brother." Gina winked and stepped closer to Frankie. "Now *that's* a man with brains, looks and money. Matt is that irresistible combination of smart and sexy. I read a feature on him the other day. He was wearing a tool belt and making a seat out of a log. Those *abs*. I swear I—"

"Please, Mom!"

"Please what? Oh, don't worry about Dev. He's not the jealous type."

Shame spread over her like a rash, not least because she'd had the same thoughts herself and the idea of having anything in common with her mother was horrifying. And mingled in with the shame was anger that her mother could contaminate a relationship that was precious to her. What if she said something similar to Matt? Frankie would die. It had been the same growing up. The embarrassment and shame had clung to her like a cloak, visible to everyone who looked. *Like mother, like daughter.*

"We have to go. We're working."

"So you got another job?"

"That's right. And I need to do it right now. Have a good day, Mom." Frankie started to walk away, nausea churning in her stomach.

"Wait! When are you going to invite us around? We're family, Frankie."

Frankie paused, wishing the burning in her gut would ease and trying not to imagine the horror of her mother bumping into Matt. What if she said something embarrassing? Or worse. What if she flirted?

This was the reality of family and it wasn't the cozy, comforting thing Eva fantasized about. It was like opening a bag expecting to find sugar, only to discover that someone had substituted salt.

"I have a lot going on right now."

"It's been ages. And how is dear, sweet Eva? Still missing her grandmother? We should go out together one night. All the girls together. It would be fun. Call me to arrange it and for goodness' sake throw away those hideous glasses and get yourself contacts. No man is going to want to sleep with you in those. See you soon!" She walked away and Frankie sagged against the wall.

"What is *wrong* with her? She invented inappropriate. I'm sorry. I don't know what to say."

"What are you sorry for?"

"All of it. For her tactless remarks about your health, for

spouting the lurid details of her sex life around the flower market and for saying those things about Matt. I want to die, but then she'd take charge of my body and do something unspeakable with it."

"You don't have to apologize." Paige slid her arm through her friend's. "You're not responsible for your mother."

"I feel responsible."

"Why? None of it is your fault."

Wasn't it? Frankie felt the familiar gnawing of guilt in the pit of her stomach. The truth was she felt responsible and always had.

When it had first happened she'd discovered that guilt could be so big it could swallow a person whole. She'd been paralyzed by indecision, not knowing what to do for the best. The only thing she'd been sure of was that she didn't want to inflict her problems on anyone else.

Gradually, the guilt had faded, like a terrible wound that eventually heals but never quite goes away.

She went weeks, months even, when she never thought about it. And when she did think about it, usually in the dark hours of the night, she kept it to herself.

It wasn't something she ever intended to share. Not even with her closest friends. The time for that was long past.

"Can you imagine if Matt had overheard that? I'd definitely have to move to Seattle. And I hate the way she calls us *girls* as if we're all eight years old. I don't think a woman of fifty-three should call herself a *girl*. There's something undignified about it. Or delusional. I'm not sure which." Struggling with emotion, she dived back into the store and rubbed her hand over her cheek. Her eyes and throat burned. "I can't bear it. Another rich guy the same age as me. And why don't these men ever say no?"

"I don't know, but it's not your problem." Paige rubbed her arm gently, her voice warm with sympathy. "I'm sorry we bumped into her."

"So am I. All she ever talks about is sex. She loves embarrassing me."

"I don't think she's thinking about you at all. She's thinking about herself."

"Let's change the subject. Talk about something. Anything." Frankie focused on the bright blooms. Flowers always calmed her. Nature was never embarrassing. "Talk about you. Please. Or work. Work is good. As long as it's not weddings."

"Did I tell you we won that piece of business for New York fashion week? They emailed me late last night."

"That's a real coup. The event is in September?" Frankie made a huge effort to push her mother out of her head. *Use it or lose it*, she'd said.

Frankie had lost it. She'd definitely lost it.

"Yes. It will be our biggest event yet, so that's a piece of good news."

"That is good news." Her heart was beginning to slow. The awful burning humiliation receded, but still the words remained. *Use it or lose it.* The phrase was buried in her head like a tick burrowed into an animal's fur. What was the rule when you'd never really had it? How could you use something you didn't know what to do with? Other women her age were generally sexually experienced. Frankie's experience boiled down to a few awkward embarrassing encounters from which she'd been relieved to walk away. And the detail of those was something else she'd never shared with anyone. "How are things with Jake?"

"Good. He's pressing me to move in with him."

"Oh." The four of them had lived together in the brownstone for a long time. Frankie realized she hadn't given any thought to that changing. "How do you feel about that?"

"Mixed feelings. I love being with Jake and his apartment is spectacular, but I love Brooklyn, too." Paige hesitated. "And I'm worried about Eva."

"Me, too. She was pretty emotional at that bridal shower the other day. But she's doing better than she was at Christmas."

"She puts on a brave face, but she misses her grandmother horribly. She pushes through the day, but she still cries at night sometimes. I hear her." Paige stood back to allow someone carrying a large plant to pass them. "I can't imagine how it must feel to have no family at all. Eva told me the other night that she feels like a boat that slipped its moorings. She's bobbing in the sea alone."

Frankie felt a flash of guilt. "Now I feel terrible for complaining about my mother."

"Don't. Your mother makes everything worse, not better."

"But at least I'm connected to someone. What do we do about Eva?"

"I wish she'd meet someone. And before you frown, I know relationships aren't everything, but I think that's what she needs. She needs to find someone who appreciates how special she is. She needs a family of her own."

"I wouldn't want her to meet anyone right now. She's vulnerable. What happens when it all goes wrong? She couldn't take the heartache." The thought of Eva hurt made her own chest ache. "She's so trusting."

"Not all relationships end in heartache, Frankie."

"Plenty do, and it would break Eva. What if she falls in

love and the guy turns out to be a lying cheating piece of—"
Anger rushed through her. "I'd kill him."

"He could turn out to be decent, honest and the best thing
that happened to her."

"In which case I might not kill him. But I've never in
my life met a guy that would be good enough for Eva." She
hesitated. "Except maybe Matt."

"Matt? My brother Matt?"

"Why not? They're great friends. They're always laughing and teasing each other." Maybe that was the answer. If
Matt were with Eva, she'd stop thinking things she shouldn't
be thinking.

"They're friends but there's no chemistry between them."

"He's smoking hot and she's beyond gorgeous. What more
do you want?"

"You think my brother is smoking hot?" Paige looked at
her curiously and Frankie wished she'd kept her mouth shut.

"I have eyes, don't I? All I'm saying is that I think those
two would be good together and if it was Matt with Eva then
I wouldn't have to kill him. I know he'd be good to her."

Paige's expression turned from curious to thoughtful.
"They'd kill each other. She'd make him watch romantic
movies and he'd turn to drink. No, I'd pick someone different for him. And anyway, Eva would never tolerate Claws,
and Matt wouldn't part with the cat so that's their first major
argument right there. She'll find someone and, in the meantime, she has us. Thank goodness for friendship."

Frankie didn't disagree. Without her friends she never
would have survived the difficult parts of her life. "I'll stay
with Eva the nights you're at Jake's."

"You'd do that?"

"I don't want her to be on her own and miserable."

"That's good of you, but there's a flaw in that plan."

"Which is?"

"She'd know you were only doing it for her."

"Isn't that what friendship is? Doing something for someone you care about?"

"Yes, but she'd be mortified if she knew I'd heard her crying and even more mortified if she knew I'd told you. She thinks she should be over losing her grandmother by now."

"That's crap. You don't ever get over something like that. The best you can hope for is to learn to live alongside it."

"I know. Let's see how we go. In the meantime, I'll carry on doing what I'm doing, dividing the week up. Maybe you can find reasons to look in on her the nights I'm not there. You don't need to stay. So what else do you need to buy here?" Paige paused by another display. "Those pale pink roses are gorgeous."

"No pastels. I want strong colors. Vibrant. Energetic. Electric. Futuristic. A fusion of color and scents." She dug the list she'd made out of her bag and scanned it, anxious to do something that might stop her thinking about her mother.

They were surrounded by color. Pinks, purples, blues and yellows. Hydrangeas in more colors than she'd thought possible.

It should have been relaxing, but meeting her mother had fired up her tension levels.

She picked up some long-stemmed roses. "I didn't ask where she was living."

"Your mother? Do you want to know?"

"No. There's no point. She won't be there long." Unable to concentrate, she stared down at the roses. "I can't remember the last time we had a proper conversation. You speak to yours all the time, and about normal things. Mine just keeps encouraging me to have sex. Is there something wrong with me?"

"There's nothing wrong with you. Your mother isn't an easy woman to deal with. Are we buying those roses? Because if not I think we're about to be charged rent for holding them for so long."

Frankie drove a hard bargain for the roses, talked colors and stems and then they strolled out of the store together and back into the street.

The sweet, sugary smell of the flowers filled the air, masking traffic fumes and city smells.

Thanks to Paige, she felt calmer.

She tried to imagine what life would look like without her friends.

It didn't look good.

She stopped walking. "I'll help Matt."

"You will?" Paige sounded surprised. "What made you change your mind?"

"You did, reminding me about friendship. Matt helped me out when I needed somewhere to live. I can't ever repay him for that. But I can do this."

It was work, that was all. She was helping a friend.

There was nothing more to it than that.

Chapter Four

Friends are like bubble wrap. They protect you against hard knocks.

—Eva

Frankie stood on the roof terrace and shaded her eyes with her hand. The sun was baking and there wasn't a breath of wind. New York in the peak of the summer months was stifling.

She'd seen the "before" photos and spent hours studying Matt's construction concept, but plans and reality were two different things. He'd transformed a bland outdoor roof space into what promised to be a luxurious rooftop garden, perfect for both relaxing and entertaining. Clever use of brick, textured stones and different woods had created an architectural element that would be a significant part of the design.

It was stunning.

She felt a kick of excitement. For her, this was so much

more rewarding than choosing flowers for a wedding. Those lifted the moment but this—she stared around her, imagining how the place would look when it was finished—this could lift a life.

She, more than anyone, understood the importance of green space and nature for health and happiness.

For her a garden wasn't a luxury, it was a necessity.

Through the turmoil of her childhood, their beautiful garden had offered peace and sanctuary.

No matter what she told her friends, there were times when she missed Puffin Island. Not the people or the past, but the place. She missed the sea air and the call of the gulls. Most of all she missed the feeling of being surrounded by nature. But she'd learned that with clever planting she could create the same feeling in her own backyard. And she could create the same thing for other people.

She turned her head and looked at Matt, who was deep in conversation with James and Roxy, two members of his team who were finishing off the hard landscaping.

His arms were folded, a stance that emphasized the well-developed muscles of his upper body. He rested one scuffed boot on a stack of concrete slabs.

Sunlight shimmered across his dark hair and a pair of sunglasses concealed the expression in his eyes but she could see by the way he angled his head and occasionally nodded that he was listening carefully to the discussion.

Some men did all the talking, as if their voice was the only one worth hearing, but Matt wasn't like that. Matt was a listener.

She'd worried that working closely with him might feel awkward, but it was turning out to be easier than she'd anticipated. Apart from the fact that every time she wore her glasses he removed them, they were getting along just fine. She'd had very few moments where she'd forgotten to breathe and there had been no suggestion of intimacy, no repeat of that unsettling moment in her apartment. Of course that might have been because there was nothing intimate about working in the blaze of summer heat with a team of people.

Every two minutes someone asked him a question. He was the one everyone turned to for ideas and solutions, and not just because he was the boss. He was the one with the creative vision and the skills to do what it took to make that vision a reality. He was the brain behind the designs, but he was also the muscle. Literally. He spent his days hauling heavy weights up and down New York rooftops and it showed. His T-shirt hugged shoulders that were thick with muscle, and his legs were solid and strong.

Heat flared low in her stomach and she swiped her forehead with her arm. It was the ultimate injustice to feel sexual excitement when she knew if he ever laid a finger on her it would fizzle to nothing.

She was a D minus.

Matt ended his conversation and strolled over to her. "Everything okay?"

No, it wasn't okay.

"I'm hot." She spoke without thinking and saw the corner of his mouth twitch. "I mean, *it's* hot. The weather. Not me. The weather is making me hot. In an increased body temperature way, not—" Her voice trailed off and he lifted an eyebrow.

"Not what?"

She glared at him. "You're not funny."

"Do I look as if I'm laughing?"

His mouth was firm and serious and his eyes—well, she couldn't see his eyes because they were hidden behind a pair of dark glasses. But he didn't look as if he was laughing. He looked…he looked…

She swallowed. He looked tough and sexy, rumpled and just rough enough around the edges to turn that low hum of desire up a few notches.

This was where a flirting lesson would have been helpful. She could have said something that would have defused the situation and made them both laugh. Then they could have moved on. Instead, she felt as if she was being boiled in oil. The atmosphere rippled with sexual undercurrents she had no idea how to handle and it didn't help that he was standing so close to her. Far too close. In fact, all he had to do was lower his head and—

"This roof terrace is roasting," she said lamely. "I could fry an egg on the deck."

"Maybe you should take a layer off." His husky voice stroked across her skin and her gaze skidded to his.

What the hell was he playing at? This was Matt. *Matt.* And he was telling her to take her clothes off? She was so far out of her comfort zone it was like hanging off a sheer cliff by her fingernails.

"No, thanks. Talk me through the project. I took a look at Victoria's plans. They're good. I'll stick with her suggestions and maybe add a few more ideas. What are your thoughts on furniture? Seating?" Other women flirted. She talked about furniture. Not only that but she was babbling, too, her torrent of words a direct contrast to Matt's watchful silence.

She had a feeling he was waiting for her to talk herself out.

And there it was again, that strange electric feeling be-

hind her ribs. Her skin felt sensitive, as if all her nerve endings had suddenly woken from a deep sleep.

"The main seating will be three log benches." His calm,
steady voice was a direct contrast to her fluttering nerves.
"They'll blend with the rustic environment, and the weight
will mean they won't be blown around by the wind."

"Sounds good. Are you building those yourself? You're
so good with your hands. I mean in the sense of making
things, not anything else." Oh, what was *wrong* with her?
His soft laughter was the final straw and she covered her
eyes with her hands.

"Enough! I can't do this."

"Do what?" Still laughing, he eased her hands away from
her face. "What can't you do, honey?"

His fingers were warm and strong and she wondered if
he could feel her pulse racing. "Have these conversations!"

"What's wrong with the conversation?"

"I'm saying all the wrong things."

"There is no *wrong thing* with me." He paused. "And
you're right. I am pretty good with my hands."

She had no idea whether the log bench was still part of
this conversation or whether they were talking about something else. And if they *were* talking about something else,
then—

Her head was spinning.

She stood, face burning in the heat, both her tongue and
her tummy in knots.

Finally, he stepped away from her, giving her space.

"You should come and see the bench I've already made.
It's down at the workshop. We have other stuff there you
might be able to use."

Okay, so now he was talking about work. Work she could handle.

Back in her comfort zone, she felt herself relax. "Given any thought to shade?"

"I've recommended a pergola. They were checking their budget but it looks as if they'll go with that."

"How are you going to get the construction equipment and supplies onto the roof?"

"I'm using materials that can be carried up in the elevator, otherwise we would have had to hire a crane and then you can kiss goodbye to $25,000. Is this the point where you tell me you're going to need a crane to haul all the soil you're planning on using?"

She tucked her thumbs into her pockets. "No. It's a roof terrace, so a lightweight, fast draining soil mix will keep the weight to a minimum." She'd forgotten how much she enjoyed the challenge of designing a roof terrace. There were so many aspects to consider, from privacy and outlook to the extremes of weather.

"Planters?"

"There are a couple of options." She glanced around, picturing it in her mind. "You could use lightweight fiberglass planters, or fiberstone. The mixture of stone and fiberglass would be a good choice."

"When they're weathered, they look like stone." He nodded. "That would work well. You should definitely take a look at what we have in the workshop. There might be something there you can use."

"Does the client have the budget for drip irrigation?"

"They thought they didn't but I helped them see the light by pointing out how much it would cost them to replace the plants that are going to die when they don't remember to water them twice a day." He pulled her to one side as James walked past, carrying a large paving slab. "Any thoughts on planting?"

His fingers were firm on her arm and Frankie felt ripples of excitement spread through her body and pool low in her pelvis.

Seriously? He was trying to stop her being flattened by concrete and she found that exciting? Her body had to be the strangest, weirdest, most incomprehensible thing on the planet. When she wanted to respond to a man it didn't happen, and when she didn't want to, it did.

Concentration wasn't something she usually struggled with, so it annoyed her to find unwanted thoughts creeping into her head. It was like walking in a forest and finding yourself attacked by midges or mosquitoes. She wanted to bat them away or spray them with something toxic.

"Frankie?" Matt's gentle prompt reminded her that they'd been in the middle of a conversation.

She hoped he hadn't noticed the lapse.

"I'd stick to a simple color palette and keep it looking natural. You want to screen the terrace to give privacy, but not obscure the view of the city."

"The building restricts plant height to six feet."

"I like evergreens, and their small leaves make them perfect for roof terraces. Large leaves shred more easily in the wind." She looked around, scanning the skyline, relieved to have an excuse to look somewhere other than at him. "We're overlooked by that apartment block, so we need to consider how to keep it feeling private."

"We thought some low-cost reed screening."

"That would work." Years of experience allowed her to

picture how it would look. "Have you considered planting an evergreen magnolia in that corner?"

He followed her gaze. "I hadn't, but it's a good idea. Anything else?"

She strolled the length of the roof terrace. As she moved away from him, her breathing normalized. "English boxwood. Maybe some ivy. We don't want to block the view in this direction."

"The view is about as perfect as it gets."

"It's iconic New York." She stepped back. "We need to think of air flow." She went through a mental list of options. "Tell me more about this pergola. And your plans for a water feature."

He talked her through it, while Frankie concentrated on the view and tried to remember to breathe in and out.

"I'm going to work on this tonight." She scribbled a few notes on her pad. She still preferred to work with a paper and pencil most of the time, and her pad was full of sketches and ideas.

"Don't sacrifice your evening for me." He rolled up the design plan. "I appreciate the help and it's true that there's time pressure, but I don't expect you to kill yourself over it."

"It's not a sacrifice. It will be fun."

"An evening doing a planting design is fun?"

"There might be wine involved. Since we started Urban Genie there is no such thing as an evening off." She paused as one of his team presented him with a form to sign.

He scrawled his signature in bold, black ink. "Did you check it, Roxy?"

"Yes, boss." The girl grinned and gave a little salute. "Learned that lesson the last time."

Matt watched Roxy walk away. "It's Friday night. When did you last go on a date?"

Frankie stared after the girl, wondering how she could bend down in jeans that tight. "I don't think she heard you."

"I wasn't talking to her, I was talking to you."

"*Me?* Oh——" She hesitated, knowing that her answer wasn't going to paint a picture of her as the epitome of urban sophistication. "Well—I don't know—I've been busy—I don't date that much." What was the point in lying when he already knew she wasn't a party animal? "When I date, I almost always regret it so I'm just as happy spending the evening thinking about plants."

He removed his sunglasses slowly. "Why do you regret it?"

His eyes were the most incredible blue, warm, interested and focused on her.

She felt as if her insides were slowly melting. "I'm not good at it."

"It's dating. The only requirement is to spend time with someone. How can you not be *good* at it?"

The fact that he'd even ask her that question revealed the massive gulf in their life experience and expectations, as well as how little he knew about her dating history. And how little he seemed to understand her hang-ups, despite the whole glasses incident. And why would he? Matt was confident and self-assured. Dating was unlikely to be something that made him consider therapy.

"It's the pressure." She tried to explain. "Will you like them and will they like you. Do you have to be more this or less that. Dating a stranger is pretty fake, isn't it? People project an image. You see what they want you to see and they often hide who they really are. It's like going out with a mask on. I don't have the energy for it." It was an understatement. She found it monumentally stressful, which was why she'd cut it out of her life.

"How about going out and being yourself? Does that ever happen?"

"That doesn't usually work."

"How can being yourself not work?"

She was acutely conscious of the people working around them and wondered how the conversation had blended so seamlessly from talk of buds and blooms to her own phobias.

And it wasn't just the conversation that unsettled her. It was the way he focused on her, with that lazy, sexy gaze, as if she was the only person on the roof. In New York City. *In the world.*

She'd always felt safe with Matt, but right now she didn't feel safe. She was trying to stay in her comfort zone and he seemed determined to nudge her out of it. Which wasn't like him.

She was filled with a whole bunch of feelings she didn't recognize and had no idea what to do with.

"I don't expect you to understand. When you're with a woman it's probably very simple."

He lifted his hand and pushed her hair back from her face. She felt the rough pads of his fingertips brush gently against her skin and started to tremble.

"When I'm with a woman," he said softly, "I want her to be herself. If someone isn't interested in who you really are, or in showing you who they really are, you're probably wasting your time dating them."

He let his hand drop but the trembling didn't stop. It was as if he'd hit a trigger point. She saw his face through a blur of sunlight and the feverish patterns created by her own brain.

When I'm with a woman...

All she could think was *lucky woman*.

The atmosphere was electric and she felt that strange rush of awareness brush across her skin. Her heart was pounding so hard she expected the entire crew to pick up the rhythm.

"Are you seeing someone at the moment?" Why, oh why had she asked him that question? She didn't want to know. She truly didn't want to know. She rubbed her hands over her arms, wondering how she could have goose bumps when it was so hot.

"I'm not seeing anyone."

"There's no one who interests you?"

"There is someone who interests me a great deal."

"Oh." Frankie felt as if she'd been kicked in the stomach. "Well, that's—exciting."

Not in a million years would she have expected his announcement to bother her as much as it did. Misery descended like a thick winter mist, smothering her good mood.

She wished she hadn't asked but at the same time she was glad she had because at least it would stop her thinking dreamy thoughts and having anxious moments worrying that their relationship might be changing.

That comment about her having beautiful eyes had been just that—a comment.

For some men dating was virtually a hobby, but Matt was different.

Matt, she knew, wasn't the sort of man to sleep his way through the female population just because he could. Nor was he the sort of man who needed a woman on his arm to inflate his ego. If he was interested in someone then she must be special.

Her ribs ached with the acid burn of jealousy.

She saw a brief vision of the future, of evenings spent on the roof terrace, with Matt and his girlfriend entwined together on one of the low cushions.

"I'm happy for you." She said the words, even though she didn't feel them. "That's great."

What sort of woman had caught his attention? She'd be beautiful, obviously. Smart. That went without saying. And sexually confident. Definitely someone who would know how to flirt when the situation called for it.

Not the sort of woman who wore glasses when she didn't need them.

"It's not great." He tucked the plans under his arm. "It's complicated."

Frankie had no idea what to say to that. She felt horribly inadequate. She was the *last* person to give anyone advice on relationships. "Relationships are always complicated. That's why I don't bother. I have no idea what a normal, healthy relationship looks like. And there I go again—being the rain cloud on someone's patch of sunshine. Ignore me. If you want advice, talk to Eva. When it comes to love, she has all the answers. And she believes in it, which helps."

"I don't want to talk to Eva."

Was he saying that he wanted to talk to *her*?

She was trapped between wanting to escape and wanting to be a good friend.

She had absolutely nothing of use to say on the subject of love, but that didn't mean she couldn't listen. This was Matt. Matt, who had given her a lovely home for years. "I can't give advice, but I can listen if you want to talk."

And if she turned green with envy, at least she'd match the plants.

"You'd do that?" There was a hint of humor in his voice. "Even though dating is your least favorite subject?"

"I don't want some woman messing you around. I like you." Oh, crap. She shouldn't have said that. "We're friends. Of course I like you. If you want to talk, talk. Tell me about this woman you're interested in. She must be pretty special if you like her."

"She is."

His words added another bruise to the many that were accumulating.

"Why is it complicated? I assume she's not married or still at school?" Seeing his brows lift she blushed and shook her head in apology. "Sorry. This is why you shouldn't be talking to me. When it comes to love, my every thought is warped. So what's the problem? Just tell her straight out. Or are you afraid she isn't interested?"

"She's interested."

"Well, of course she is!" Envy made her irritable. "She'd have to be crazy not to be interested. You're the whole package, Matt—the three Ss, as Eva calls it."

"The three Ss?"

"Single, sane and s—" She was going to say *sexy*, but she suddenly realized how easily that could be misinterpreted. If he knew she found him sexy, she'd never be able to look him in the eye again, and that was already hard enough after the whole glasses incident. "Solvent," she muttered. "You're solvent."

"Single, sane and *solvent*?" He sounded amused. "That's all it takes? That doesn't sound like a very high bar."

"In Manhattan, you'd be surprised," Frankie said darkly. "All I'm saying is, if you're interested in someone, there shouldn't be a problem. A million women would jump at the thought of having you in their lives."

There was a pause as Matt scanned the skyline. "I don't want a million women. I want one woman, and she's scared of relationships. She's not good at trusting, so I'm taking it slowly."

Something in his tone made her glance at him sharply, but he'd slid the sunglasses back onto his nose and she could no longer see his eyes.

Frankie was confused.

Surely he wasn't saying—?

He didn't mean—?

A delicious, terrifying excitement ripped through her. She went from envy to euphoria. She was filled with an equal amount of joy and heat. Matt was interested in her. *Her. She* was the woman. The thought made her dizzy with elation. Her palms felt sticky and her heart pounded like drums in a rock band. And then it dawned on her that if he knew she was interested and he was also interested, the next logical step would be to take things to the next level. That would be what he was expecting. That was what normal people did, wasn't it? That was the reason he was telling her how he felt. And if they took things to the next level—

Reality poked its way through the joy, puncturing her elation like a needle pressed against a child's balloon.

Euphoria gave way to pure panic.

"On second thought, forget it. You want to stay away from relationships that are complicated." She was stammering, tripping over her words. *Stay away from me.* "It's too much trouble. Seriously, Matt, don't go there."

Admiring someone from a safe distance was one thing. When you thought they weren't interested and that it could never go anywhere, it was a safe hobby. But this—this was different. It was like admiring a tiger in a zoo and suddenly realizing that someone had removed the glass between you. There was nothing stopping his coming close.

Up until this moment she'd had no real idea that Matt was interested in her, but now she knew that he was, it changed everything.

It made the impossible possible and she found the possible terrifying.

"I've never been afraid of complicated, Frankie. I've never been the kind of guy who thinks something worth having has to be easy to get."

"Well, you should be afraid." *Breathe, Frankie. In and out. In and out.* "Complicated is bad. If it's complicated, maybe you should rethink. You deserve to find someone special. A nice, dependable, uncomplicated, sweet girl who isn't going to mess you around." She articulated each word carefully, her tone transmitting the message *and that's not me*.

"Frankie—"

"And talking of working on a plan, that's what I'm doing. I'll talk to you tomorrow."

She stepped back from him, tripped over a bag of cement and virtually sprinted toward the stairs that led from the roof to the top floor of the house.

No way was she going to let this go any further, not just because she believed all relationships were doomed but because it would be impossible to get closer to Matt without his discovering all the things about herself she made a point of keeping secret.

Because he knew about the glasses, he thought he knew her. What he didn't know was that the glasses were just the tip of the iceberg.

* * *

Roxy stood with her hands on her hips, watching Frankie bolt. "Do you have that effect on many women, boss?"

Matt swiped his hand across the back of his neck and thought about his cat. "I'm starting to think I do."

"What did you say to her?"

"Nothing. Not a damn thing." Well, he'd said a few things, but he'd barely gotten started.

Roxy pushed her baseball cap away from her eyes and scratched her head. "You must have said *something*. She ran as if she was being chased by a pack of zombies."

"I have a way with women."

"In fact, you do—" she grinned at him "—but today your natural charm obviously failed you. Maybe you should go after her, in case she falls and breaks her ankle or something. She looked seriously freaked out. She probably saw you checking out her butt."

"I wasn't checking out her butt."

"You were definitely checking out her butt."

Matt gave her a stern look. "Whatever happened to respect?"

"I have so much respect for you, boss, I don't know where to put it."

It was a struggle not to smile. "You could put it right here, Roxy. Right here where I can see it."

"Hey, do you even doubt it? You gave me a job when no one else in the world would, and you helped me find childcare. You've got to allow a girl a bit of hero worship."

This time he did smile. "How is the baby?"

"Stop calling her a baby. She's two years old, Matt!"

"Are you getting any more sleep?"

"Some, but she's awake early and ready to play. I don't

mind. I love her so much it fills my whole chest. Even when she wakes at four in the morning and my eyelids are sealed closed and I'd sell my soul for another five minutes of sleep, I still love her. I'm reading to her lots at the moment. I found a stack of books in the thrift shop. She loves them." She took a gulp from her water bottle. "She'd be perfect for you, boss."

"Generally I like them a little older."

Roxy choked. "Not Mia—Frankie. She'd be perfect."

"Since when did you become an expert on relationships?"

"Having a really bad one gives you an advanced qualification. Almost like a college degree. You become an expert. I bet I could have letters after my name."

"Do you have any particular letters in mind?"

Roxy grinned. "DMWM."

"I'm not even going to ask."

"Don't Mess With Me. I kept it clean, because I'm a mom now and I don't want Mia growing up hearing shit. I mean stuff. Things. I don't want her to grow up hearing things. And I want her to know that if a relationship makes her feel bad, she should get out. She shouldn't hang around, like I did."

Something about the angle of Roxy's chin prompted the question. "Has Eddy been bothering you again?"

"Since the last time you showed him the door? No." She gave a half smile. "Man, he was terrified. His *face*. And you didn't even touch him. You just told him to get out, and gave him a scary look. How do you do that?"

"Scary facial expressions are my party trick." He paused. "You're not going to get back with him?"

"Never. He doesn't want to know Mia. What sort of man doesn't want his own child? And he made me feel bad about myself." She put the top back on her water bottle. "I won't be with a man who makes me feel bad. Life can be crap all by itself. I don't want to invite crap into my home. And I don't want Mia growing up seeing that kind of relationship. I want her to know she can choose something good. That she deserves it."

Matt looked at the fierce stamp of her features and felt the same deep respect he had on the day she'd appeared at the door of his office. "You're an impressive person, Roxanne."

"Hey, don't go falling in love with me, because that whole boss-employee thing never works. It's the power thing—" She shook her head and there was a twinkle in her eye. "No. Just no."

"I'll try and remember that."

"Frankie would be perfect for you. She's supersmart. Knows all the Latin names for flowers and everything. I heard her saying them under her breath. And she's got a great body. When did you last have a serious relationship?"

Matt stirred. "It's been a while."

He thought of Caroline, sobbing and wailing, begging him to forgive her, telling him it hadn't meant anything, a moment of madness because she'd been drinking. Telling him what they shared was still there. That it wasn't gone.

For Matt, it was gone. Maybe he could have forgiven a drunken fling. What he couldn't forgive were the lies. She'd taken a knife and slashed through the trust they'd had. Without trust, everything was gone.

He decided it was time to end the conversation. "I have things to do. I'm leaving you in charge, Rox."

"Me?" Her chest puffed out. "So now I'm the boss?"

"You're the boss."

"Do I get a raise?"

"In your dreams." He already paid her way above the going rate for unskilled labor and they both knew it.

"But I can hire and fire?" She eyed James. "You'd better watch your step."

James was in the process of hauling large concrete slabs. Sweat darkened his T-shirt, and his hair was plastered to his head in spikes. "I wish you would fire me. Then I could get out of this damn heat and go home."

"Put a dollar in the swear jar." Roxy put down the water bottle. "I'll help you, wimp."

James rolled powerful shoulders and shot a glance at Matt. "Why did you take her on?"

"Right now I can't remember but I'm sure I had a good reason."

"I'm thinking of going back to law. She can't follow me there." James stomped back across the roof and Roxy grinned after his retreating back.

"He loves me, really. Can't imagine him as a lawyer, can you? These things you have to do right now—do they involve Frankie?"

"No. Not that it's any of your business, but I need to put in some hours at the workshop."

"You mean you want to play with your chain saw. I get it. Nothing like power tools for working off tension. Boys with toys. I know all about it."

"I'm not a boy."

"Yeah, I know that, too." She blew her hair out of her eyes and eyed his biceps. "I'm trying not to focus on that side of things. I've never worked for a sexy boss before. This is all new to me."

He sighed. "Roxy—"

"Hey, the boss I had before I got pregnant was sixty-five

and weighed two hundred and thirty-eight pounds. I'm still getting used to the novelty of having something to look at during my working day, so give a girl a break. Go. I'll be fine. I'm going to finish the decking and clear up. And I'll make sure James works until the heat fries him to a crisp. Don't worry about us. We're the A team."

He wasn't worried about them. He was worried about Frankie.

He'd never seen anyone so freaked out.

She'd run away so fast his ego probably should have sustained permanent damage, except he knew that the reason she'd sprinted away was not because she wasn't interested but because she was.

That cheered him up and he paused to help James move one last slab. "Can you manage here?"

"No worries." James's muscles bunched. "A man's love life has to take priority."

Matt decided that one of the downsides of working in a small team was that everyone had an opinion on his love life. "I'm going to the workshop. We still have two rustic seats to carve."

"I get it. Nothing like hammering and sawing to take your mind off problems of the heart. Women, huh?" James gave him a sympathetic slap on the shoulder. "There's no understanding them."

"That's because you're a dumbass," Roxy said cheerfully. "We're easy to understand if you take the time. Oh, and boss? I wouldn't be too worried."

"Why is that?"

"Because she was checking out your butt, too."

That, Matt decided, was the best news he'd had all day.

Chapter Five

Before you run from something, make sure whatever is chasing you can't run faster.

—Paige

Romano's was crowded, even for a Friday night. Owned by Maria, Jake's adoptive mother, the Sicilian restaurant was a thriving Brooklyn eatery. Tonight all the tables were full and a line stretched around the block. The restaurant was noisy and busy, the spacious room echoing with the sound of conversation, the clink of cutlery and the occasional shouts from the kitchen. Delicious smells wafted through the space, the aroma of roasting peppers mingling with the Mediterranean scent of oregano and garlic.

Frankie slid into the booth by the window where Paige and Eva were already seated. "I'm in trouble. Serious trouble."

Eva choked on her water. "You're pregnant?"

"*What?* No!" Appalled, Frankie glanced around to check

Matt slid into the seat next to Frankie.

She held herself rigid, hardly daring to breathe.

Being near him shouldn't make her this nervous, should it?

She felt the hard length of his thigh against hers and tried to shift away, but she was already pressed up against the wall and had nowhere to go.

"We interrupted your conversation." Matt reached for the menu. "Eva, what were you saying about sex with dinosaurs?"

"*Since* dinosaurs, not with dinosaurs. My preference is for sex with humans, but that hasn't happened in a long time. I don't want to talk about it. It's depressing. And anyway, Frankie was just telling us she's in trouble."

Frankie shot her friend a quelling glare. "Forget it!"

"Why are you giving me that look? We're all friends here. If we can talk about me having sex with dinosaurs, we can talk about you being in trouble. It's only Matt, and sometimes it's helpful to have a male perspective on things."

Not this time.

"You're in trouble, Frankie?" Matt closed the menu without looking at it. "What sort of trouble?"

Damn the man. He knew exactly what her trouble was. "I'm not in trouble."

Eva frowned. "But you said—"

"It was nothing! Forget it."

"So here's my male perspective—" Matt pressed his thigh against hers. "It's a mistake to turn your back on a problem, or run from it."

Her mouth dried. "Why?"

"Because it's going to follow you. That problem is just

going to keep right on treading on your heels, so you might as well turn and face it."

She faced him and saw the wicked gleam in his eyes.

Her insides melted. He was the sexiest man she'd ever seen. "I tend to black the eye of problems that follow me."

"That's good. Confront it." His gaze was locked on hers and she felt her heart rate increase.

"What if the problem refuses to go away?"

"Maybe it's not a problem. Maybe the problem is that you're scared."

"What?" Eva looked baffled. "I have no idea what the two of you are talking about. Can we order before I die of starvation?"

Matt transferred his gaze from Frankie to Eva. "For a woman who never has sex, you have a healthy appetite."

"Sex isn't the only form of exercise on the planet, you know."

Frankie wished everyone would stop talking about sex. Between that and the searing heat in Matt's gaze, she was ready to combust.

Fortunately, Maria arrived at their table to take their order and the conversation moved on to more general things.

On the surface it was a normal Friday night, but under the surface there was a new tension. And there was Matt's thigh, pressed against hers. Solid muscle.

He reached across and helped himself to bread. The sleeves of his shirt were rolled back, revealing strong forearms. His skin was bronzed from the sun and dusted by dark hairs.

She imagined those hands on her skin, slow and skilled. Patient.

She imagined those hands holding her face steady as he kissed her.

Oh *God*, she wanted him to kiss her so badly, which made no sense at all because she'd never even enjoyed kissing much. Her mind always wandered and she ended up thinking about plants or books.

"How's Roxy getting on?" Paige reached for her drink. "Is the childcare working out?"

"Thanks to you. She's coping well. They gave her a friendly rate, didn't they?"

"We're putting a lot of work their way," Paige said. "They were happy to help. By the way, that dog-walking business you recommended, The Bark Rangers, is brilliant. I met the twins and they're great, although I will never be able to tell them apart in a million years."

"Glad it's working out." Matt was calm and relaxed. "I'll let Dan know next time I see him."

Frankie was relieved by the change of subject.

Somehow she stumbled through the rest of the meal but then Matt suggested gathering on the roof terrace for drinks and a movie.

She needed space, and he wasn't giving her any. Every time she tried to inch away from him he was right there.

They finished their meal and the general agreement was that they'd go back to the roof terrace and watch a movie, but Frankie bowed out.

"I have work to do." As Matt was the one who had given her the work, he couldn't exactly argue with that. And he couldn't exactly abandon Jake and the others. "You guys go ahead without me."

That was her plan, but when they arrived back at the brownstone they shared, Paige and Eva didn't follow Matt and Jake up to the roof terrace. Instead, they stood on either side of Frankie like bookends.

"It's time we talked." Eva took the keys out of Frankie's hand and let herself into the apartment.

"I think I'm best left alone tonight."

"I'm not leaving you alone. I'm not good with tension. It unsettles me and keeps me awake and I'm horrid when I'm tired." Eva pushed open the door and toed off her shoes. She had an enviable ability to instantly make herself at home anywhere.

"Why are you tense?"

"Not me, you. You're the one who is tense. And we want to know what's happening between you and Matt."

Frankie froze in the doorway. "Nothing is happening."

Paige pushed her inside. "Have the two of you had a fight?"

"No! Why would you even think that?"

"You were scratchy with him."

"Scratchy?"

"Yes. You made Claws look warm and friendly in comparison." Eva pushed the door closed, trapping her inside. "Do you have any wine in your fridge?"

"Why? I was going to work and then read my book—"

"Tough. Your book can wait. I'm not leaving until we've sorted this out." Eva made straight for the kitchen and Frankie looked pleadingly at Paige, who shrugged.

"I agree with her. You were scratchy. What's going on? Is it hard working together?"

"No! And I've never had a fight with Matt."

Eva popped her head around the kitchen door. "You've never worked with him before. Everything changes once you work with someone. And Matt can be as controlling as Paige. Everything has to be done his way. Is he driving you insane?"

"I'm not controlling," Paige protested, and then pulled a face when they both looked at her. "Well, maybe I am. A little. But in a good way. Because I like things the way I like them."

Frankie cut them off. "There's nothing going on and there's nothing weird. We work well together. He's smart and creative and—" she shrugged "—we're a pretty good team." They were a far better team than she could possibly have envisaged. Not only because Matt was easy to work with, but because they were naturally in tune with each other's ideas. When it came to garden design, they had similar taste.

"So what's the problem?"

Should she tell them? Yes, because she had no idea how to handle this. "I think he likes me." Saying it sent adrenaline shooting around her body. Her heart flew, like a leaf caught up in the wind.

"Of course he likes you. You've been friends for years, and—" Paige's eyes widened. "Oh. You mean he *likes* you."

"I knew it. Let's drink to that." Eva poured the wine, her expression triumphant. "He's taking things to the next level. He's had enough of being friends. He wants more. Holy crap. This is exciting. I may not ever have sex again, but it's good to know that my two best friends are."

"Wait! Stop!" Frankie lifted her hand. "We're not taking anything to the next level. There won't be any sex!"

Paige handed her a glass of wine. "You told me you find him attractive."

"Matt is a friend. We've been friends for years. He respects my work." It sounded lame, even to her. "He respects *me*."

"You're worried he wouldn't respect you if your relationship changed?"

"I know he wouldn't. I don't want his opinion of me to change."

"Why would it?"

"Isn't it obvious? Look at me!"

Eva curled up on the sofa. "I'm looking. I see an attractive, confident professional woman whose major flaw is her inability to comprehend that diet Coke is not a healthy breakfast."

"If you think that's my major flaw then you haven't been paying attention. There is no way, *no way*, I would ever get involved with Matt!"

"Why not? The guy is smoking hot." Eva shot an apologetic look at Paige. "Sorry. Is that weird?"

"No." Calm, Paige reached for her wine. "It would only be weird if *I* found him smoking hot."

"It's not him, it's me!" Couldn't they see that? "Can you imagine what would happen if Matt unzipped my sweatshirt? All my baggage would tumble out. He'd be flattened under the avalanche of issues I keep hidden inside these clothes. Buried alive." All her hang-ups, her inadequacies, her tension—it would be right there in his hands and she'd never be able to look him in the eye again.

"He knows about the glasses already," Paige pointed out.

"Yes, but there are other things. Bigger things. And he doesn't know about those."

And neither did they, because she'd never told them. And she never would. That was one deeply embarrassing episode of her life she intended to bury deep.

Eva stood up. "Forget wine. This situation needs chocolate cake. I'll be back soon." She vanished from the apartment and Paige put her glass down carefully.

"Matt has a few issues of his own after Caroline."

"I know. But there are issues and there are issues, and mine are—" Frankie gestured with her hand "—big issues."

"And you think this will come as a surprise to him? It's not as if he doesn't know you."

"Believe me, there's plenty he doesn't know."

Eva came back into the apartment in time to catch the end of the conversation. She was carrying a large chocolate cake.

"This was today's experiment. It has a secret ingredient. And Matt is more than capable of handling your issues. That man can handle anything. I've never seen him stressed." Eva cut the cake into generous slices. "Actually, that isn't true. I saw him stressed when Paige and Jake got together, but that's different. Paige is his sister and all bets are off when it's a sibling."

"How would you know? You're an only child."

"But I'm an expert on relationships. It's my superpower. Believe me when I say Matt would handle your issues with both hands tied behind his back." Eva picked up a fork. "That's one of the qualities that makes him hot."

"I don't want him to handle me. As you say, the guy was messed around plenty by Caroline. I'm not adding to the trauma."

"I'm confused. Are you protecting him or yourself?"

"Both of us!"

"Caroline lied." Paige dug her fork into the cake. "She wasn't honest. You're nothing like Caroline. Matt trusts you. But if you're not interested, just tell him straight. Matt will respect your feelings and leave you alone." She took a mouthful and closed her eyes. "Sublime, Eva. What's the secret ingredient?"

"If I tell you, I'll have to kill you and eat you and I'm already way over my daily calorie allowance with this slice of cake."

Frankie stared at her cake without touching it. "I *am* interested. That's the problem."

Eva paused with her fork halfway to her mouth. "You're interested? In Matt? That's the problem you were talking about earlier?"

"Yes! I'm interested, and I don't want to be." Frankie felt as if her heart was going to burst. "My head is a mess. I shake when he stands near me and I've got this weird feeling here—" she rubbed her fist against her chest "—and when he's talking I can't concentrate because I'm always thinking about—"

"About?"

"Stuff."

"Stuff?" Eva put her fork down. "You mean sex?"

"Why is that a problem?" Paige looked baffled. "If you both feel the same way then what's stopping you getting together?"

"The fact that I'm bad at relationships. *Really* bad. If I was going to have a relationship the *last* person I'd have it with would be someone like Matt."

Paige finished her cake. "Someone you care about and do, in fact, like."

"That's right."

"And find seriously hot."

"Right again."

Paige put her plate down. "Frankie—" her tone was patient "—most people would think that meeting someone you like and find hot is a good place to start a relationship from. But you're saying that makes them wrong for you?"

"Yes. If—*when*—I mess it up, it would really matter. None of the guys I've had bad relationships with before have mattered. I haven't cared enough for it to matter. That's what made them perfect."

"No, Frankie," Paige sounded exasperated, "that is what made them less than perfect. Are you seriously saying you'd rather have a relationship with a guy you don't care about and don't find attractive than with a guy you really like?"

"That's what I'm saying."

Eva opened her mouth and closed it again. "Do you even realize how crazy that sounds?"

"Why is it crazy? When I mess up a relationship with a guy I don't particularly like and have no feelings for, no one gets hurt. It doesn't matter. Everyone walks away intact. It would be different with Matt. I *like* him. I care about him. With Matt it would matter. One of us, or both of us, would get hurt."

"So your brilliant master plan is to carry on having relationships with guys you don't like so that when it all goes wrong it doesn't matter."

"Exactly. And now that you understand the problem, I need you to tell me how to fix it. Do I ignore it and hope he ignores it, too? Do I talk about it face-to-face? Tell him I'm not interested?"

"You *are* interested." Eva finished her cake. "And he already knows that."

"He can't possibly know that."

"Matt is an experienced guy and you are a terrible liar."

That possibility hadn't occurred to Frankie. "You seriously think he knows?" She put the cake down untouched.

"Yes, but that's a good thing."

"It is not. If he knows, I'm going to have to move to the Arctic."

"No one is moving anywhere. I have a better idea," Paige said. "Take the next step and see what happens. You want to kiss him, so kiss him."

"There is no way I would kiss him. It would kill any feelings dead." Frankie thought about it. "Which I suppose might be a pretty effective way of handling this situation."

"Why would it kill feelings?"

"Because kissing is one of those things that looks amazing in the movies and is deeply disappointing in real life. But it could be the perfect answer. If we kissed, maybe we'd both realize it was a *big* mistake and get on with our lives."

There was a brief silence.

"Brilliant idea," Eva said casually. "Go for it. I'm sure you'll both be cured in an instant and we can all go back to normal. Now eat your chocolate cake and let's watch something on Netflix."

Chapter Six

Just because a man doesn't ask for directions, doesn't mean you shouldn't show him the way.

—Paige

Matt was on the phone when he heard the door. Still talking, he opened it, hoping it was Frankie. Preferably dressed in her underwear.

His sister stood there. She was wearing a tailored dress and her perfectly smoothed hair told him she was on her way to a meeting. It was Monday morning, and he knew her day would be planned, hour to hour, because that was how Paige lived her life.

He scanned her face, instinctively checking her color.

It was a habit he'd developed years before when her color had often been an indicator of her state of health. Pale skin and lips with an ominous blue tint had set off alarm bells. She'd been born with a heart condition and even now, after successful surgery and years of good health, he found it hard to break the habit.

It made him overprotective, a trait he knew drove Paige crazy.

That didn't bother him. The way he saw it, part of an older brother's role was to drive his sister crazy.

He stood to one side to let her in and finished his phone call. "I'll increase the order if you'll halve the cost." He waved a hand to the coffee machine and Paige strolled across the kitchen and poured herself a mug while Matt negotiated a price he could live with.

When he finally ended the call she was sipping coffee, her hands wrapped around the mug.

"I'd forgotten how good you are at driving a hard bargain. I still remember the residents of Puffin Island muttering dark threats when you raised your prices for cutting their grass in the summer. You were fourteen years old."

"There was a lot of grass and it was a hot summer." He scrolled through the ten emails that had dropped into his inbox during his call. "Much as I love reminiscing, I have a meeting in an hour and it's probably going to take me an hour and a half to get there. Is everything okay? What can I do for you?"

"It's more about what I can do for you." She lowered her mug slowly. "I can help you."

His sister was a born organizer—a skill, in his opinion. That was one of the reasons her business was guaranteed to be a success. The downside was her tendency to try and organize him along with everything else.

"I appreciate the thought, Paige, but I already have more business than I can handle."

"I'm not talking about your business. I can't help you with that. I can help with your love life."

He already had his staff interfering with his love life. The last thing he needed was his sister's input. "I don't need help with my love life."

"You're wrong about that."

"You think you know more about how to run my love life than I do?" *Stupid question*, he thought and saw her smile.

"I know I do."

"Let me put this another way," he said carefully. "What makes you think you have the *right* to interfere with my love life?"

"Maybe because you interfered with mine?"

He couldn't argue with that.

"I thought that was water under the bridge. I seem to recall that I groveled for a humiliating length of time."

"I didn't find it humiliating. I found it satisfying. It's not often that you admit you're wrong."

"It's a family trait. And you have a cruel streak."

"I'm your sister. It's in the job description."

"I'm starting to miss the time when you were too ill to argue with me. Look, I'm willing to take whatever is coming to me but you've chosen a bad moment to take revenge. I told you I have a meeting."

"This isn't about revenge. I really can help you. And you owe me. I fixed the babysitting problem for your Roxy."

"She isn't *my* Roxy, and I put you in touch with a great dog-walking business, so I figure that makes us even. And I can handle my own love life, Paige." This time he wasn't joking. "There's nothing wrong with my judgment."

"Are you sure? Because you proposed to Caroline."

"Ouch." Only a sibling would have thrown that in his face.

"It's the truth, but don't be too hard on yourself. You were blinded by blond hair and an impressive rack. The blood drained out of your brain and landed—well, we both know where it landed. That doesn't matter now. She was completely wrong for you, everyone knew that, and you had the sense to end it. But when you find a woman who is perfect for you, it's important not to mess it up."

He knew what was driving this conversation. He'd seen it before, when Paige had been sick, when Eva had been bullied—the three women stuck together like Velcro.

"We're talking about Frankie."

"I'm glad to know there's still some blood left in your brain."

"I can handle it, Paige."

"Mmm." Sounding unconvinced, she took another sip of her coffee. "So how's it going?"

Familiar with every nuance in her tone, he put his phone down on the table. "Has she said something?"

"I'm a woman. I'm your sister. And I'm not stupid." Her eyes lit up. "I'm so excited. My brother and my best friend."

"Paige, it's not—"

"No, and it never will be if you don't let me help! And if you're about to tell me that this is none of my business, don't waste your breath. You owe me this one."

Matt forced himself to clamp his mouth shut.

"Fine. Interfere. But this is a onetime thing."

"I prefer to call it helping."

"I don't care what you call it—I'd rather deal with this my own way."

"Even if your way sucks and will probably ruin your chances *and* your friendship with Frankie? Relationships have always been straightforward to you. All you have to do is look at a woman and she goes weak at the knees. Don't ask me why. I don't get it, personally. Not that I'm saying you're hideous or anything—"

"Thank you."

"One of your exes did once tell me that your unique appeal is that you look like a bad boy but inside you're a good guy. Which gives a girl the best of everything."

Matt was intrigued. "Which ex-girlfriend?"

"I always protect my sources. But what I'm saying is that you've never had to think about it. You've never had to work at it. You pretty much picked who you wanted."

He was starting to find the conversation more than a little uncomfortable. "Paige—"

"Frankie isn't like that. She finds relationships scary, and you're freaking her out, Matt! Don't think about our experiences, or our parents', think about Frankie and what her life has been. Her father had an affair with a woman barely out of college, and Frankie was the one who virtually nursed her mother through her meltdown. Since then she has seen her mother hop from one lover to the next like a rabbit on steroids. It's hardly surprising she thinks relationships are doomed. And she doesn't want to doom a relationship with someone she cares about. You need to take it slowly. Stand back and let her come to you."

He'd tried taking it slowly and he'd realized that if he waited for her to come to him he'd be waiting forever. He had no intention of doing that.

"I know what I'm doing, Paige."

Paige topped up her coffee. "Dating has pretty much always been an embarrassing and humiliating experience for Frankie. You've put her on her guard, Matt. Why do you think she didn't want to join you on the roof terrace last night? You pushed her out of her comfort zone and she was all hot and bothered."

Good.

He wanted her hot and bothered. He wanted her out of her comfort zone.

"I've got this, Paige."

"Matt—"

"I said I've got this."

"Men! Fine, be stubborn. But don't blame me when it all goes wrong." Paige finished her coffee and put the empty cup on the counter. Her gaze fixed on an invitation propped on a shelf. "What's that?"

"Wedding invitation. Sounds as if you're seeing plenty of those right now."

"Only as part of work." She picked it up. "Ryan, Emily and Lizzy? The guy is marrying two women?"

"Lizzy is Emily's daughter. Adopted daughter, although I think they might be related. Niece or something." He picked up his laptop and slid it into his bag. "It's Ryan Cooper. Do you remember him? We were at school together. The family lives in—"

"Harbor House. I love that place. It has incredible views over Puffin Point. I babysat Rachel Cooper a couple of times."

"That was a while ago. She's teaching at Puffin Elementary now."

Paige scanned the invitation. "So Ryan is getting married and it's a beach wedding. Lobster bake. Dancing at the Ocean Club. Sounds like the perfect way to spend a summer weekend. Puffin Island at its best. It'll be fun. You're going?"

"Yes. Ryan is a friend. It should be a great weekend."

She put the invitation back. "The invitation says 'and guest.' Who are you taking?"

He hadn't planned on taking anyone, but an idea took root in his mind.

"I'm taking Frankie." It would do them both good to get away from the city. New York in the summer was heaving with tourists and the heat was suffocating. Sea air would be welcome.

Judging from his sister's expression, she didn't agree. "Frankie wouldn't go to Puffin Island if she was drugged and unconscious."

"Why not?"

"First, there's the fact that this is a romantic beach wedding and we both know how much Frankie loves romantic weddings. And then there's the biggest obstacle of all—"

"Which is?"

"Frankie hasn't been back to the island since she left for college."

"You're exaggerating." Conscious that he was going to be late, Matt picked up his phone and slipped it into his pocket.

"And you're annoying! She's my best friend, Matt. I'd know if she had been back."

He stilled, shock trickling through his veins like ice water. "You're serious? She's never been back to the island? Not once?"

"No. Why would she? It doesn't have happy memories for her."

"But—" He dragged his hand over the back of his neck, trying to process this new information. "Shit."

"Well, that's eloquent."

"I thought—"

"What did you think?"

He'd thought that he knew her, but he was starting to understand just how little he knew.

And how much he wanted to know.

"I think it's time she went back."

His sister gave him an exasperated look. "You'll never persuade her, but what if you did and then someone was mean to her? Have you thought about that?"

"No one is going to be mean to her." He kept the sudden rush of anger firmly leashed.

"How do you know that?"

"Because I'll be there. The whole time."

Paige rolled her eyes. "Mr. Protective. Are you taking a white horse and a suit of armor?"

"No. Just my natural charm."

"You're annoying sometimes."

"You're annoying a lot of the time." But he saw the anxiety in her eyes and relented. "I know she's your friend, but you're going to have to trust me on this."

"But—"

"I said you're going to have to trust me." He scooped up his jacket. "Now, go and meddle in someone else's love life because you've spent long enough on mine."

Frankie had only visited his workshop a few times before. A large space beneath his offices, he used it for storage and also for any construction work that couldn't be done on-site.

The doors opened onto an outdoor area stacked high with planters and paving slabs. A few large trees stood tall in their tubs, ready to be delivered to his various ongoing projects.

Today he was working on the second of three log benches

that were destined for the roof terrace. James and Roxy were working on-site so Frankie and Matt were on their own.

Frankie tried not to think about that.

Instead, she stared at the thick tree trunk. "Cedar?"

"Red cedar." He pulled a tape measure out of his pocket. "It's pretty easy to shape and will withstand the extremes of temperature."

She didn't have to ask what he meant. She'd lived through plenty of New York summers and winters.

"It's going to look great."

"I think so." He measured the log and made some calculations. "While I do this, why don't you take a look at the planters? See if there is anything there you think will work. If not, we can design something specifically to fit the space."

"Okay." She'd spent the last three nights planning the talk they were going to have. The one where she told him he had to stop looking at her and standing so close to her and all the other things he was doing that disturbed her equilibrium. But today he seemed to be more preoccupied by his work than by her.

She dropped to her haunches to take a closer look at a terracotta planter. Deciding it wasn't right for her needs, she moved on and paused by the log bench he'd already completed.

Like his sister, he had a high attention to detail, and it showed. The piece was a testament to his skills as a craftsman and designer.

She glanced across to where he was turning the thick tree trunk into a stylish rustic seat.

Watching him work was like watching an artist. He used a level to measure where to make the cuts, his movements careful and precise. Only when he was satisfied that he had the line he wanted did he pick up the chain saw. He flipped down the visor on his helmet and moments later the sound of the saw cut through the air. He'd been using a chain saw since his late teens, when his father had realized this was more than just a hobby and had made sure he was properly trained.

She remembered him being called out to help on numerous occasions when heavy snow had felled trees on the island where they'd lived. Like other members of the community, Matt had waded in and helped without question.

It seemed he hadn't lost any of his skill. He didn't just carve the bench, he understood the wood. He knew its strengths and weaknesses. He understood how to make the best product and his eye for style and design was faultless.

He cut the basic outline and then shaped it. Every cut had to be just right. Every angle perfect. It was fascinating to watch him work.

For a brief unsettling moment Frankie had a vision of him in bed with a woman. He'd be good, she thought, and immediately looked away.

What did she know about being good in bed?

Nothing.

She was a D minus with nothing for effort.

She was so busy wondering why that thought kept plaguing her that it was a few moments before she realized the whine of the chain saw had ceased.

Glancing across she saw that he'd stripped off his shirt, along with all the protective clothing. Wiping a hand over his brow, he reached for a bottle of water from the cooler and emptied it over his head and shoulders.

His chest gleamed with droplets of water and Frankie felt her mouth dry. Was he doing it on purpose to gain her attention? No. He wasn't even looking at her. And why shouldn't he take his shirt off? This was his space. He could do what he liked here.

She'd known him forever but this was the first time she'd seen him without his shirt.

His jeans rode low on his hips and hard, pumped-up muscles rippled and gleamed in the fierce beam of sunlight that shone in through the window. He had a couple of scratches on his arms and another on his shoulder, although whether they were courtesy of an aggressive cat or an aggressive rosebush, she didn't know.

She felt weird, slightly light-headed, as if she'd drunk a bottle of beer too fast or gone a day without eating. *It was the sun*, she thought, and pulled her hat out of her back pocket.

She was a redhead and had to cover up in the sun.

Working on the roof terrace had been easier because the other members of his team had been there. But now they were alone.

Matt swiped the water from his eyes with his fingers, glanced across and his gaze collided with hers.

She felt as if she'd suffered a direct hit from a meteorite.

His eyes darkened and then he gave a slow smile. "Too damn hot for this sort of work."

"Yes." She jammed her hat down over her eyes. It was the heat that was making her crazy. The heat. Nothing else. Turning away, she focused on the planters but there was only so much staring you could do at a pot, and the more she tried not to look at him, the more she wanted to.

She was burning alive.

Hot and frustrated, she dropped into a crouch to take a closer look at the nearest planter.

A pair of scuffed, reinforced work boots appeared in her line of vision. "Stand up, Frankie."

"What?" Was she even capable of standing up? She wasn't sure, and she didn't want to try it and find that her knees gave way. Landing on her nose would be another embarrassing moment to add to the long list of embarrassing moments. "Why?"

"Because we're adults. It's time we talked." He reached down and hauled her upright as if she weighed nothing.

She stood awkwardly, conscious of the soil on her fingers and the sweat on her brow. The heat and humidity meant that her hair was having a wilder party than usual. She didn't need a mirror to know she probably looked like a sheep that had collided with an electric fence. "I don't have anything to say. And you have to stop crowding me."

He was too close to her and she could see the smooth, bronzed skin and the dip and curve of powerful muscle.

She backed away until her retreat was blocked by one of the trees. Branches poked through her T-shirt like accusing fingers, pushing her back toward him.

Matt closed in on her. "Am I making you uncomfortable?"

"Yes! You're making me uncomfortable."

"Good." He gave a sexy smile that melted her bones.

"Back off. You're invading my personal space and if I move back any farther I'll be hanging off this tree like a Christmas decoration." She risked a glance and was instantly trapped by his gaze, hypnotized by the look in his eyes. It was a look she hadn't seen before in all the years she'd known him.

"Matt—"

"What?" His voice was husky and it stroked over her senses like a velvet glove.

"You know what." She stood still, frozen by the delicious inevitability of what was to come.

He was going to kiss her.

Yes, do it. Let's get this over with and then he'd discover the truth and they could both get on with their lives.

She closed her eyes tightly, trying to breathe, waiting for the touch of his mouth, but instead of kissing her he brushed the tips of his fingers along her jaw, raising the anticipation to almost unbearable levels.

She was helpless, drugged by the deceptive gentleness.

"If two people who are single and unattached have feelings for each other, I don't see why they shouldn't act on those feelings, do you?"

It was a struggle to speak. "Are you talking in principle or specifically?"

"I'm talking about us, Frankie." The way he emphasized the *us* made her breath catch.

"In that case, yes, I can see why we shouldn't act on any feelings. I think that would be a big mistake. You're a friend. You're important to me."

"You don't think friendship is a good basis for a relationship?"

"In this case the friendship is too valuable to lose. It's not worth it." She was finding it difficult to breathe. "You're too close, Matt."

He didn't move. "Do I make you nervous?"

"I'm not nervous. I have a black belt in karate. I could fell you like a tree." It was a lie. They both knew it was a lie.

"You don't need to be scared, Frankie."

"I'm not—" She felt his thumb brush her lower lip and

stopped breathing altogether. "Okay, now you're definitely too close. You have to let me breathe. What the hell are you doing?" And then it came to her. The answer. "You're doing this because I'm a challenge."

His thumb stilled. "What?"

"I'm a challenge. That's why you're interested."

"Frankie—"

"Men love a challenge, don't they? Particularly when it comes to dating. You're thinking, hey, I know she's not great at this but I can be the one to transform her."

"That is so messed up I don't know where to start."

"You don't start. You give up and we pretend this never happened. I forget it, you forget it, we all forget it. I *am* messed up, like Claws. You need to stay away from me." Why couldn't she stop *talking*? It was as if every thought she'd ever had was determined to find its way out of her mouth.

"You're nothing like Claws. I don't want to transform you, Frankie. I'm interested in *you*, not some fake version of you." His mouth was still dangerously close to hers. "I like who you are. I've always liked who you are."

"You don't know who I am. Not really."

"I know you're a smart, creative, incredibly sexy woman. And I also know you have a few relationship issues."

A few?

"I have more than a few relationship issues. If you piled them up, North America would have a new mountain range. I would dwarf the Rockies. You have no idea."

"I do." He paused. "You're not your mother, Frankie."

Even the mention of her mother made her want to crawl under a stone. "I know. I've worked hard to make sure I'm not."

"Maybe you've worked a little *too* hard."

"What's that supposed to mean?"

"That you've focused so hard on not being her, you don't know how to be yourself."

"That's crap. Matt, I don't want to dent your ego but I just don't find you attractive."

"I know you find me attractive."

"That's arrogant." She met the amused shimmer of his gaze.

"You've been looking at me." He slid his hand into the heavy mass of her hair, drawing it away from her neck. "And the reason I know that is because I've been looking at you, too. And I think it's time we did more than look."

Excitement and nerves mingled together in a suffocating cloud.

Oh crappity crap, crap, crap.

She had no idea what to do. No idea how she was supposed to respond.

She was an expert at keeping men at a distance.

She had no experience in letting men close.

She didn't know how to do that.

Matt was an important part of her life. Letting him close would ruin everything they'd built over the years. Part of her badly wanted to do it, anyway. Part of her wanted to find out where this dizzying excitement ended. One kiss should do it. One kiss would be enough to kill it all.

Beads of sweat clung to her forehead. She felt as if she was caught in a riptide, pulling her far out to sea, away from the safety of the shore.

What had she learned in the swimming lessons she'd had when she'd been growing up on Puffin Island? She'd learned that the best way to deal with a riptide was not to try and swim against it. You swam with the tide then gradually peeled off and swam back to the safety of the shore.

"You're a really sexy guy, Matt. A million women would be interested in you. You don't need me."

"Have dinner with me tonight."

Was he even listening to her? "Thanks, but no. Having dinner would complicate everything."

"We have dinner together almost every Friday."

"Today is Monday." If she grabbed him now and kissed him, it would all be over.

She lifted her hand and then let it drop again. She couldn't do it.

His brows rose. "The night of the week makes a difference?"

"No. The fact that we'd be on our own makes a difference. It would make it more like a date."

"It wouldn't be *like* a date," he said slowly, "it would *be* a date. That's what this is. A date. I'm asking you to have dinner with me. Just the two of us."

"And I'm saying no."

"So let me get this straight. You don't mind having dinner with me when it's not a date, but when it's a date, you're not interested."

"That's right."

"Do you know how crazy that sounds?"

"About as crazy as thinking we could have an intimate relationship and stay friends."

"Frankie, we've known each other for more than twenty years." He was patient. "Nothing is going to stop us being friends."

"I will not go on a date with you, Matt."

"Why not?"

"We could start with the fact that when it ends I could lose my home."

"When the date ends?"

"When the relationship ends. Because we both know that's what we're talking about here. When men talk about dinner, what they really mean is sex. We'll have dinner and then you'll want to end up in bed and that's where it will all fall apart."

He looked dazed, as if he'd been hit around the head with a heavy object. "Frankie—"

"Let's just forget we ever had this conversation."

"So you won't have dinner with me because you think dinner might lead to sex, which would lead to a relationship, which would end." He said it slowly, as if he was trying to make sense of it.

"That's right." Her stress levels were in the red so she was relieved that finally he seemed to understand. "Now can we—"

"Not every relationship ends, Frankie, and even if it did I can one hundred percent guarantee that your home and your security would never be affected by anything that happened between the two of us." He jammed his fingers into his hair. "I sound like a mortgage broker."

"You'd have sex with me, you'd give me a D minus with nothing for effort, then it would be awkward and I'd have to move." The words fell out of her mouth without her permission and she froze in mortified horror.

Had she really just said that? Normally her problem was opening up to guys, not closing herself down. The last person she'd dated had said that getting personal information from her was like trying to break into a vault, and yet here she was gushing like a waterfall after heavy rain, spilling secrets she'd never shared with anyone.

Maybe he hadn't heard her.

Please don't let him have heard me.

His stunned silence told her that her prayers were going unanswered.

She stared at the floor, appalled. Her face was hot, and the heat had nothing to do with the weather.

How did she dig her way out of this one?

She'd ignore it and hope he would ignore it, too.

"I love my home and I don't want to move," she said quickly. "So there's no way I would have sex with you, which means dinner is also out of the question."

"Who told you that you were a D minus?"

Oh God.

She wanted to die. Really fast. Right now.

"Forget it. It's not—"

"Tell me."

"I don't want to talk about it! Let's just say I wasn't top of the class. I bet you'd score straight As, so let's just forget it and move on." Could it get any worse? Her relationship with Matt was turning into the dance of the seven veils. Piece by piece, he was exposing her. First the glasses and now this. Soon she'd have nothing left to hide. She felt emotionally naked. "I don't want to talk about it, but believe me when I say you don't want to have sex with me. I'm flattered that you find me attractive, but the truth is that sex really isn't my thing."

"What do you mean, it's not your thing?"

Did the guy never stop asking questions? "People are good at different things, aren't they?" Her voice rose. "I'm brilliant with plants. Recognizing them, growing them, ar-

ranging them—all of it. I can cook well enough not to poi-
son myself, I know enough about technology to fix my own
laptop when it crashes and I'm a pretty good friend. Sex,
I'm not good at."

"Is that what he told you? The D minus guy?" His tone
was grim. "If you feel as if you're being graded then it's no
wonder you're stressed about sex. It's supposed to be about
pleasure, not pressure."

"Yeah, well, there you go." She puffed her hair out of her
eyes. "For me, it's all pressure and no pleasure. And if the
whole performance scoring isn't enough, there's the issue
of the apartment."

"Will you forget the damn apartment for five minutes?"

"No, I won't! It's my home. Do you have any idea how
much I love living there?"

"I know how much you love it, Frankie." He pressed his
fingers to the bridge of his nose and breathed deeply. "No
one is ever going to make you leave the apartment. It's yours
for as long as you want it, so can we separate that from this
conversation?"

It seemed as if the only way to make him understand
was to be blunt, which also required humiliating herself.
"I won't have sex with you, Matt. I'm not that into it. I'm
not surprised he gave me that grade. And I'm not good with
all the feeling, emotional stuff that goes with relationships.
Unlike Eva, I'm not a feeling person. Now, can we move
on? I really don't want to talk about this any longer, and if
you're any sort of friend you'll move to one side and pretend this conversation never happened."

"The conversation where I asked you to have dinner with
me and you somehow turned that into having really bad
sex and losing your apartment?" There was a gleam in his

eyes. "That sounds like a hell of an evening. I'm not surprised you said no."

"Good. So in that case—"

"I'll pick you up at seven."

"What? I thought you agreed—"

"I agreed that the date you described sounds less than
appealing, but that's not the evening we'll be having. Do I
find you attractive? Yes. Would I like to have sex with you?
Yes to that, too. Am I inviting you to dinner but secretly
intending that dinner turns into sex? No, because I'm not
fifteen, Frankie. Believe it or not, I'm capable of thought
and actions that aren't driven by my hormones and I can go
on a date with a woman without having to sleep with her."

"I don't want to go on a date. Don't use that word."

"Fine. It's not a date, it's dinner with a friend." He stepped
back from her. "I'll see you at seven."

Dinner with a friend? She gaped at him. "Well, I—"

But she was talking to herself because he'd gone.

Chapter Seven

One person's danger is another person's good time.

—Eva

"So you're having dinner," Eva said carefully, "but it's not a date."

"That's right. I tried to put him off but it didn't work and now I'm stuck. I should have just kissed him! That would have sent him running." Frankie threw all her clothes on the bed. She was shivery with nerves. She hadn't eaten a thing since breakfast. Which was ridiculous, because this was Matt. Matt, whom she'd known forever. Except the version of Matt she'd known forever wasn't the one who had been looking down at her with those lazy blue eyes and that sexy smile. "What do I wear? You know about this stuff. It's your superpower."

"I need more information. If it's not a date, what is it?"

"I don't know! We both need to eat, that's all." Except that she wasn't sure she'd be able to eat anything at all. Her stomach was so full of butterflies there was no room for anything else. "Can't two people have dinner without dissecting meaning and motivation?"

"Of course they can," Eva soothed. "We'll call it a— nondate."

A nondate.

Frankie stared at the clothes on her bed in despair. "I want to look good. I don't want to embarrass him. But it's important that I send out the right message."

"What message is that? I'm confused."

She was confused, too. "That we're just friends. This isn't a relationship or anything."

"You and Matt already have a relationship. A lovely relationship."

"We do." Frankie's knees were shaking and she gave up and sat down on the bed. She was terrified, but underneath the panic was a ripple of something else. Something more dangerous. Excitement. Anticipation. *Matt.* "We do have a good relationship, so why are we messing with that? What are we doing?" She gave a moan and sank back into the pile of clothes. "You have to tell him I'm sick."

"I'm not telling him that. Get up. I can't see your clothes if you're lying on them." Eva dragged her up again.

"I don't own anything suitable. I spend my days wrestling with rosebushes. When I see clients I wear my white shirt and my black pants. I spend my evenings in sweats and a T-shirt."

"We already know he likes you in those. He likes you whatever you're wearing."

She knew that was true. She'd seen the way he looked at her. And the way he looked at her made her feel...feel...

"I can't wear sweats and a T-shirt to dinner."

"Where is he taking you?"

"I don't know. He didn't tell me." Or maybe he had and she'd blocked it out. She'd heard nothing after the words *I'll see you at seven*. She'd tried to tell him that no, that wasn't going to happen, but by the time she'd found her voice he'd already walked away, and then James had arrived to pick up another load of materials and after that there was no opportunity.

"It's not helpful that he didn't tell you," Eva said. "If you've been asked on a date then it's only fair to know what to expect." She caught Frankie's eye and gave a weak smile. "Except that this isn't a date, so those rules don't apply. Wear anything."

"What does *anything* look like? This is why I hate dating. If it was just a couple of hours I could stand it, but the stress starts hours before the actual date."

"Calm down. This is Matt. You don't need to be scared—"

"I am scared! Everyone is scared of something, right? Heights? No problem. Dangle me off the edge of the Empire State Building and I wouldn't break off the conversation. Rats? Cute, especially their tails. Spiders? Hand me a large hairy one and I'd be totally cool."

Eva paled. "Do you honestly think I'd hand you a spider of any sort?"

"Figure of speech. I was talking about me. My phobias. It's dating, by the way. That's my phobia."

"That's because you've only dated losers, but Matt is different. You need to calm down or you'll be in a state by the time you leave."

It was because Matt was different that she was in a state. "I don't know what to wear."

"Wear a dress."

"I don't own a dress of any sort. I haven't worn one since that arrogant ball-brain put his hand up my skirt at prom. He said, 'It's time you lost your virginity,' and I said, 'I feel the same way about your hand.' They had to ice his wrist."

"I know. I was there. And that whole incident was hideous, but it was a long time ago, Frankie."

"He was the beginning of a long line of dating disasters." She stood up, knowing she was being unfair. She was expecting her friend to understand, but she hadn't given her all the information, had she? She'd never told her about the D minus. She'd never told anyone. Except Matt.

Matt knew.

She gave a moan and covered her face with her hands. "Why don't you go instead of me?"

"Because Matt didn't ask me, and also I'm busy tonight."

"What are you doing?"

"I'm having a cozy night in on my own." Eva's tone was bright and Frankie looked at her, her own problems receding.

"Paige is out with Jake?"

"He got tickets to some premiere uptown. Lucky them. And don't look at me like that. I'll be fine. I'm looking forward to being on my own."

"Liar."

"Okay, maybe I'm not exactly looking forward to it but it's good for me to get used to being on my own."

Frankie felt something squeeze inside her. "Are you feeling sad?"

Eva gave a wobbly smile. "Every now and then, but I'm doing fine so you don't need to worry."

"You should go out with Matt. That way I don't get the stress and you don't have to sit on your own brooding. It's the perfect solution."

"It's not the perfect solution. He asked you, not me."

"You two would be perfect together. Him with all his strong family values and you with the whole Cinderella thing."

"What Cinderella thing? You want me to wear rags and clean his apartment?"

"No, but you both believe in love. You'd be a perfect couple."

"Except for one major drawback—I'm not interested in Matt that way, and Matt isn't interested in me. He's interested in you." Eva turned back to the clothes, rejecting two pairs of black yoga pants. "I agree these are slim pickings. Are you sure I can't persuade you to borrow one of my dresses?"

"No, thanks. No offense, but your dresses all have 'take me' written all over them."

"In that case I wish someone would pay attention. Okay. No dress. Move over so I can take a better look at what we're working with." She rifled through the clothes on Frankie's bed and fished out a pair of emerald-green leggings. "These might work. They're pretty. When did you buy them?"

"I didn't. You and Paige bought them for me when you had that day in Bloomingdale's."

"I remember. That was a great day. I never see you in them. Don't you like them?"

"I like them," Frankie conceded, "but I don't want to ruin them by wearing them."

"They're supposed to be worn."

"I never know what to wear them with."

"I have a beautiful silk tunic that would look perfect. And a matching purse. I'll fetch them in a moment, but first show me your shoes. I don't want to make two journeys."

Frankie pulled out two pairs of running shoes, several pairs of Converse, three pairs of sturdy boots and two pairs of flats.

Eva rejected them all. "Don't you have anything with a heel?"

"My last pair of heels snapped when I got them caught in that grill on Fifth Avenue."

"We're the same size. I'll lend you something."

"I don't want to wear heels. I love my flats. I like being able to walk."

"Heels give you an excuse to hold his arm—" Eva caught her eye again "—which obviously you don't want to do," she said hastily, "so you might as well wear flats. Great idea."

"None of this is a great idea. What are we going to talk about?"

"The same things you talk about when we're all there." Eva carried on sorting through Frankie's clothes. "Plants, roof terraces, Claws, crazy cab drivers, the volume of construction in Manhattan—the choice of subject matter is endless. What *is* this?" She held up an old gray T-shirt with a hole in the shoulder and Frankie shrugged.

"I know it's old but it doesn't matter because I wear it to bed."

"Not anymore you don't." Eva started a pile on the floor for disposal.

"I live on my own. Who cares what I wear to bed?"

"I care. I won't be able to sleep upstairs, thinking of you down here wearing that."

"I love you, but there are times when I think you're very strange."

"The feeling is mutual." Eva added another T-shirt to the pile on the floor. "What if there's a fire in the night? A hot fireman might come and rescue you and you'll be wearing this ugly gray thing."

"If there was a fire in the night I hope the fireman would

be thinking about the two of us not burning to death, rather than judging my fashion choices."

"This was a choice?" Eva tossed another T-shirt on the growing pile. "Your wardrobe is an abomination. It's no wonder you don't know what to wear to dinner with Matt. There's nothing here."

The reminder of dinner brought the gnawing feeling back to Frankie's stomach. "I don't know why he wants to do this."

"Because he likes you," Eva said patiently, "and he wants to spend time with you."

"I should have kissed him. That would have ended it there and then."

"If he asks you on a second date you can still try that." Eva reached out and wound one of Frankie's curls around her finger. "You have truly beautiful hair. I don't suppose you'd let me—"

"No."

"But you don't know what I—"

"Still no."

Eva sighed and let her hand drop. "How about just a tiny glimmer of lip gloss? Just to emphasize your mouth."

"I don't want to emphasize my mouth or any other part of myself. I'm having dinner and it ends there." Because if it didn't end there that would mean—

She swallowed and met Eva's gaze.

"Stop it!" Eva stood up. "You need to stop dissecting everything and get ready. Go and have a shower and I'll fetch the tunic." She walked to the door and then paused, a wistful look on her face. "I'm so happy for you. I can't believe the two of you are finally going on a date."

"It's not a date!"

"Of course it isn't," Eva soothed. "All I meant was, I hope you have an amazing time on your—er— dinner that's not a date. Nondate. It's a nondate."

"So what's happening?" Paige was eating a slice of toast with one hand and scrolling through her emails with the other. "Where are you going with your favorite tunic?"

"I'm lending it to Frankie. She has a date with Matt." Eva danced around the room, humming to herself. "But don't call it that or you'll freak her out. They're on a *nondate*, which is a whole new way of dating for people who are freaked out by dating. Which is basically Frankie."

Paige finished her toast. "A nondate. Sounds interesting. So what happens if they have a good time?"

"I don't know." Eva shrugged. "I guess they go on a second nondate and before they know it they're nondating on a regular basis. Maybe there will even be a nonengagement and a nonwedding. As long as the cake is real, that's all I care about."

Paige raised her eyebrows. "You don't think you're jumping ahead slightly?"

"Someone has to. Frankie has been stuck in the same place emotionally for far too long. And she's been stuck in the same place with her wardrobe, too. This has to end. I'm going to quietly slip a few things into her apartment and hope she doesn't notice." Eva frowned. "I hope Matt just grabs her and kisses her."

"Stopping you right there." Paige raised a hand. "I don't want to think about my brother kissing."

"I bet he's an amazing kisser."

"No! Don't want to think about it. Go. Give Frankie the

tunic." Paige picked up her phone. "Are you sure you don't mind if I stay with Jake tonight?"

"Mind? Why would I mind? I'm not your mother." Eva adopted a serious face. "I hope you're using protection, Paige, and making good choices."

"You know what I meant."

"I know what you meant. You're worried I'm going to sit in a sodden heap all night, but I promise I'm not."

"I don't like leaving you."

"Please! Am I twelve years old? I'm looking forward to having some 'me' time. I'm going to give myself a beauty pampering and have a Netflix marathon. Bliss."

Paige gave her a long look. "You're sure?"

"I'm sure. You don't have to watch over me. It's true that sometimes I'm sad, but that's to be expected. I lost the only family I have and I miss her horribly. Sometimes life sucks. We all know that. I know you and Frankie both think I'm marshmallow, but I'm pretty resilient."

"I know you are." Paige gave her a hug. "And you're not alone. We're your family, too."

"I know, but tonight I don't need a babysitter. Go and fan the flames with Jake. But not so many flames you need the fire department. I'm still getting over the shock of see-ing what Frankie wears to bed." Patting her on the shoul-der, Eva pulled away. "I have serious work to do. I need to make sure our Frankie doesn't bolt the door and refuse to go on this date."

"That isn't going to happen."

"You didn't see her. She was close to having a panic attack."

"Matt will handle her. And by the way, I'm making ex-cellent choices, even though I may not choose to disclose all of them to my mother."

Chapter Eight

Relationships are like Halloween. Scary.

—Frankie

Matt's approach was to keep it low-key and casual, and as little like a *date* as possible, and the moment he saw how nervous Frankie was he knew he'd made the right decision.

"Frankie—"

"What? *What?* Do I look okay? You didn't tell me where we'd be going so it was hard to know what to wear. I'm probably not wearing the right clothes—"

"You look incredible. Can you walk in those shoes? Because we're going to be walking."

"Of course I can walk. You're mixing me up with Eva, whose shoes are like high-rise apartments. You think I look incredible? You like the tunic?" She tugged at the silver tunic and he smiled.

"I hadn't noticed the tunic, but now you mention it—" He saw her snatch in a tiny breath.

"Oh, that's smooth."

"It's not smooth." He slid his fingers under her chin and tilted her face to his. "It's the truth. It's called a compliment."

She skewered him with a glare. "Compliments make me uncomfortable. Back off."

"I'm not backing off. And you'll get used to the compliments in time. Are you ready? I have a cab waiting."

A few days before he might have been amused and a little exasperated that she could feel nervous around him when he'd known her for most of his life, but that was before he'd understood how much there was about her that he didn't know. It wasn't about the length of a relationship, he realized, it was about the depth. Now he knew she had secrets.

And he wanted her to share them with him.

He wanted to know who had told her she was a D minus.

But right now he wanted to stop her thinking about the evening ahead. He changed the subject as they walked to the cab, recounting a funny story about a client he had met a few days ago who had wanted to plant an instant apple orchard.

"Instant? How can it be instant? Does she think you have magical powers?" The wary look in Frankie's eyes was replaced by laughter as they stepped inside the cab.

"She saw a picture in a magazine and wanted her garden to look just like that. She'd read that you could buy mature trees, and thought that was all that was needed. We had a frank conversation." He relaxed back in his seat, glancing out the window as the cab drove over the Brooklyn Bridge toward Lower Manhattan.

"So you told a client no?"

"I listened and then proposed a different approach. I don't ever take a job that I know is a bad idea. In the short term

she would have been a client but when her apple orchard
withered and died she would have been an ex-client, and my
reputation would have been mulched along with the apples."

"And now she's probably in love with you."

Matt laughed. "I wouldn't go that far, but we definitely
reached a level of understanding."

"Where does she live?"

"Maine." Eventually he was going to bring up the subject
of Puffin Island, but not yet.

"So you need to be careful which species you recommend."

"Because of the cold climate?"

"Cold climate, short growing season and diseases."

"That's what I told her." But it was good to hear it con-
firmed. Her depth of knowledge always impressed him.
"She wants to grow Pink Lady."

"Forget it. She can also forget Braeburn, GoldRush and
Granny Smith. They don't ripen before the first freeze so
they don't have the flavor. I'd go with Beacon or Snow.
Honeygold and Honeycrisp would work, too, but whatever
you're planting you need to prepare the soil and do some
significant ground work, otherwise your poor apple trees
will be foundering."

"Noted."

They discussed it in more detail as the cab wound its way
through Manhattan going north and he noticed that when
she stopped thinking about being on a *date* she was relaxed.
He also noticed that the tunic she was wearing brought out
the incredible green of her eyes. Her hair fell in a tangle of
fire and flame past her shoulders, and her nose was slightly
pink from the sun. "I'm going to talk to some local apple

growers and in the meantime, I promised to come back to her with a drawn-up plan."

"Victoria has gone. Who is doing that for you?"

"I was hoping you would."

"I'm already helping with your roof terrace! What do you think I am, a robot?"

"No. I think you're capable and talented." He thought a great number of other things, too, things that kept him awake at night and messed with his focus, but he restricted his compliments to her work. "And it's because you're capable and talented that I intend to pick your brains about this garden. I thought you could involve Roxy. Pass on some of your expertise."

Her gaze softened. "I like Roxy. And you're generous, taking her on."

"She's a hard worker and she deserves a break." He leaned forward and spoke to the cab driver and Frankie glanced out the window.

"This is Central Park."

"That's right."

"This is our date?"

"What date? We're not on a date."

The cab pulled up and Matt paid and nudged a protesting Frankie out of the car.

"I want to pay."

He shook his head and then remembered how strongly she felt about paying her own way. "You can pay on the way home. Alternatively, you could pay me back by giving me help I can't get from anyone else."

She waited while he closed the door of the cab. "So you're asking me to help you with this job as well as the other one? Even if I have the time I can't advise you properly without seeing the garden. I'd need to walk around it and get a feel for the place. I'd need to know more about the soil—"

"So that's a yes? Thank you."

"I didn't say—" She made an exasperated sound. "You're manipulative."

"I'm a man who knows how to pick the best person for the job." It was so much more like one of their normal exchanges that he smiled, and after a second she smiled back.

"Paige does that same thing."

"What thing?"

"That thing where you charm people into giving them the answer you want to hear."

"You think I'm charming?"

"No. I think you're superannoying."

"Are you hungry?"

"Honestly? Not really. Dating makes me nervous and being nervous kills my appetite." She stopped dead and there was a hint of desperation in her eyes. "I warned you I was no good at this. I'm supposed to be making sparkly conversation and seducing you with my wit and my body, but so far all I've done is talked about apples."

"First, we're not on a date. Second, we're in a public place so it's probably best if you don't seduce me, and third, I happen to find apples interesting."

"Matt—"

"Frankie," he kept his tone patient, "you're trying too hard. Just be yourself."

"I'm nervous. Look—" she held out her hands "—I'm shaking. If you gave me a drink now, I'd spill it."

"I asked you out because I like you. You, not some version you think you're supposed to be. You just have to be you, that's all. It's not hard, Frankie."

"Me." She looked unconvinced. "Okay, I'll try that."

He took her hand and tugged her against him, keeping her away from skateboarders and horse-drawn carriages. Central Park on a summer's evening in August was crowded and colorful and they headed into the park, leaving behind the insanity of the city, the bright lights and the blare of cab horns. They passed joggers and tourists, lovers strolling hand in hand, musicians and a bride and groom posing for wedding photographs.

"Wedding alert," he drawled. "Keep your eyes straight ahead."

"There's no escaping it." She gave a wry smile and glanced up at the canopy of trees. "It's beautiful. After a week of staring at towers of steel and glass, I needed a nature fix. This was a great idea."

"I love Central Park. It's one of my favorite places in New York. When I first arrived here I missed Puffin Island and I used to come here for my dose of green. It's a place where you can escape from the crazy energy of this city. There's a bench I adopted as my own where I did most of my studying. That's the best thing about the park. Finding your own place."

They strolled along a narrow, winding path, through sunlight and shadow, past borders tumbling with flowers.

"What would you have done if I'd worn high heels?"

"I knew you wouldn't."

"How did you know?"

"Because I know you." Except that it turned out he didn't know her anywhere near as well as he'd thought he did, or wanted to. And he was planning on doing something about that.

He looked at her and found her looking at him.

He stopped walking and so did she.

The air stood still. There wasn't a breath of wind, and all sound vanished.

A single strand of her hair curved around her cheek toward her mouth, as if saying *this way*. He wanted to follow those shining strands with the tips of his fingers and explore the line of her jaw with his lips. He wanted to get close enough to count the freckles that dusted her nose. He wanted to pull her in and kiss her, right there among the trees and flowers, laughing children and barking dogs.

It was the last two that stopped him hauling her into his arms. When he finally kissed her, he wanted it to be in private.

He stepped away from her and glanced up toward the sky, trying to act normally. Trying to act as if his blood wasn't racing and his heart wasn't pounding. "Did you know you can do bat walks here in the summer?"

There was a brief pause. "Bat walks?" Her husky tone suggested she was suffering in the same way he was.

"I only found out recently. If I'd known, I would have taken my sister years ago."

A laugh escaped her. "Paige would hate it."

"It's a brother's duty to scare his sister senseless."

He chose a route that took them along meandering woodland paths, and they strolled through dappled sunlight, enjoying the outdoor space.

For his own sake he steered the conversation onto safe topics.

He asked her about Urban Genie and she told him about some of their more recent business wins.

"We're working long hours, but somehow those hours don't seem so long when you're working with your friends.

Sometimes we're laughing so much it feels more like one of our nights off." She related a couple of stories that made him smile, and then she asked him about his business and he found himself telling her about his current dilemma.

His business was growing so fast he'd reached a point where he had to make a decision on whether to expand or turn down work. What he really wanted to do was find a way to sponsor Roxy for training but then they'd be another person short.

"She shows a real aptitude and she's keen, but that's not enough. She needs to learn the scientific fundamentals of plant care so she can take on maintenance programs for the clients."

"She could do classes evenings and on weekends ?"

"But she needs to be there for Mia."

"When I was training there was a woman who took six years to get her certificate. They're very flexible about allowing you to do whatever fits with your schedule."

He was surprised to discover how helpful it was to talk it through with her, because usually he made all his decisions alone. It was the way he operated.

They reached Bow Bridge as the sun set and stood gazing at the views of Central Park West and Fifth Avenue, watching as the tops of the trees glowed red in the fading light.

"Sunset in Central Park," she murmured. "It doesn't get any more perfect."

They were standing side by side, close but not quite touching.

He wondered if she was as aware of him as he was of her.

And then she turned her head to look at him and he saw the heat of his own desire reflected in her eyes.

Her mouth was a soft, inviting curve. All he had to do

was lower his head, but he didn't. He'd made up his mind that by the time he kissed her she was going to want it so badly she wasn't going to be thinking about her performance.

Instead, he stepped back and held out his hand. "Our table is booked for eight fifteen."

She hesitated and then took his hand and they walked along the path to the famous Bethesda terrace.

"I feel as if I'm on a movie set whenever I come here."

He smiled. "Which movie? *One Fine Day*, *Home Alone 2* or *Ransom*?"

Their voices and footsteps echoed and he paused under the elegant arches, looking toward the famous fountain.

"I'm more likely to think of *The Avengers*. Or that episode of *Dr. Who*. I'm not a lover of romantic movies."

"Me neither."

"You're a guy. You're not supposed to enjoy them." She strolled toward the fountain. "Aren't you going to ask me my favorite movies?"

"I already know your favorite movies. *Psycho*. *Rear Window*. You're a Hitchock addict."

"Why wouldn't I be? The guy was a genius. You're forgetting *Vertigo*. I love that movie."

"You also love *The Shining* and *Alien*."

"The first one. Ridley Scott."

"I love his work."

"He should have won best director for *Gladiator*. He was robbed." She glanced at a couple who were locked in an embrace by the fountain and then looked away quickly. "So there's nothing else for you to find out about me. You already know everything."

Not everything, but he intended to work on that.

They walked along the path that skirted the lake, watching the last glimmers of light play across the still surface of the water.

"We're eating at the restaurant on the lake?"

"Yes." He opened the door of the restaurant and she walked past him. He breathed in the subtle floral scent of her and felt her bare arm brush against his.

All evening she'd been the one who was tense, but now it was his turn.

"This is perfect." She settled into her chair and gazed at the water. "I've lived in New York almost all my adult life and I've never eaten here."

"Jake took Paige here a few weeks ago."

They ordered, and Frankie sat back as the waiter poured their wine.

"Does it feel strange knowing the two of them are together?"

"Yes. I'm still getting used to it, even though Jake is my closest friend. I have an overprotective streak when it comes to my sister."

"It's a good trait."

"It drives her crazy."

"But if you asked her, I bet she wouldn't want it to be any different. You two are lucky. When I was growing up I would have done anything to have someone to share the crap with."

"You had Eva and Paige."

"But that's not the same as having someone on the inside. Friends can listen, sympathize and support, but there's a difference between supporting from the outside and living through it." She paused. "There are some things you can't even share with your friends."

And that was something else he hadn't known. He'd always assumed she shared everything with Paige and Eva.

There was music playing in the background but he didn't hear it.

"What things?"

There was a long, protracted silence.

He saw the rise and fall of her chest and he sensed she was on the verge of telling him something, but then she gave a little smile and a shake of her head.

"All I'm saying is that you can't really understand the workings of a family unless you've lived inside it."

"Your parents' divorce must have been tough."

"Not just the divorce. The years leading up to it, too." She took a sip of her drink. "It would have been pretty cool to have a sibling. She could have taken some of the heat off me, particularly if she enjoyed partying and dressing up. I'm not good at that. It's a constant disappointment to my mother that she has a more exciting social life than I do. Still, on the positive side, the one thing I can be sure of is that she is never going to want to borrow my clothes." The lightness of her tone was intended to mask the hurt but it didn't.

"You might have had a brother, and that wouldn't have helped with the whole dressing-up thing, either. Not only that, we boys are notoriously bad at remembering to call our mothers so a brother might not have been much help relieving the load."

"You don't call your mother?"

"I *intend* to call, but somehow the week gets away from me and then she calls me, and then it's too late for me to impress her by calling her. Sometimes she doesn't call me, either. She calls Paige, and they talk about me behind my back, probably agreeing I'm useless. Having a sibling isn't all roses."

"You and Paige are pretty close."

"That's true, but it's also true that there were plenty of times growing up when I was tempted to throw my sister into the deepest part of Penobscot Bay, so don't paint it too rosy."

"I know life isn't all rosy, but I still think you're lucky." She sat back. "Your family is as close to picture-perfect as it gets."

"No family is perfect, Frankie. We have our irritations and scratchy moments. If you don't believe me, join us for Thanksgiving. Paige gets her planning and organization gene from our mother so you can imagine the two of them together in the kitchen. It's like two generals with different strategies trying to agree on a battle plan. Everyone takes cover."

Frankie laughed. "I love your mom."

"She drives Paige insane because she's so protective."

"I guess that runs in the family." Her gaze lifted to his and he thought how much he wanted to take whatever it was that was hurting her and fix it.

"I guess it does."

Their food arrived and for a while the conversation revolved around the perfectly cooked dishes. They ate sea scallops, followed by a creamy risotto and a perfect salad.

They were surrounded by the hum of conversation, the clink of glasses, the occasional bubble of laughter, but he ignored it all. His only interest was in her.

"You're not wearing your glasses."

"There didn't seem any point, now you know I don't need them." Frankie focused on her plate and he noticed the contrast between the dark sweep of her thick lashes and the rich cream of her cheek.

"I'm glad. I don't want you to hide from me."

"The food is delicious." She put her fork down. "So where in Maine is this garden you want me to help you plan? Is it coastal? Because that will make a difference to the variety of apple we recommend. Also how far south they are."

"It's on Puffin Island." If he hadn't been watching her face, he might have missed her reaction. "They're a couple from Boston who bought a house on the northwest side of the island for summers. They're redesigning the house and the garden. My parents bumped into them in Harbor Stores and that's how they heard about me. You know how it is."

"Yes." Frankie picked up her spoon and stirred the coffee that had been placed in front of her. "I know exactly how it is. So you're going back to Puffin Island for a job? That's quite a commute."

The tension was back and he wondered how she could think she wasn't capable of feeling.

She had so many feelings they were almost bursting out of her.

"I'm not anticipating having to make more than a couple of visits. The guy is a partner in the same law firm as my father. It's a favor."

"You're not charging?"

"I'm charging. The favor is that I'm willing to travel to Puffin Island. It's not exactly down the street. We've agreed I'll do a detailed design, both landscaping and planting, and then hand it over to a local company."

"Sounds good. Take photos and I'm happy to put together some ideas for you. When are you planning on going?"

"Weekend after next. I'm already there for a wedding so

it makes sense to combine the two. An old friend of mine is getting married. You might know him. Ryan Cooper?"

"Not personally, but I know who he is. His family owned that amazing house overlooking Puffin Point. White clapboard and stunning views."

"That's the one. My invitation includes a guest." He paused, feeling like a man poised to dive off the high board into deep water. "Come with me, Frankie."

Her cup hit the saucer with a clatter. "You're not serious."

"Why wouldn't I be?"

"For a start because it's a wedding, and you know how much I hate weddings, and second, because it's Puffin Island. You've put together my two least favorite things and expect me to say yes?" Her coffee sat untouched in front of her. "I can't believe you'd even ask me. My face is on every Wanted poster in town." Her words made his chest ache, as did the thought of how bad it must have been for her. A small community could be supportive or suffocating, but either way there was no escaping. No hiding. No anonymity.

There was no doubt that the local population had an obsession with what their neighbors were doing, and he knew some people hated that element of island living. Matt didn't feel that way. People were people wherever you lived. He enjoyed living as part of a community. The way he saw it, give-and-take made the world a better place. He tried to make her see it that way, too.

"We'd have fun, Frankie. A weekend away from crazy, insane New York. We could breathe sea air, walk in the forest, eat ice cream, browse in Ryan's wife-to-be's new gift store."

The candle between them flickered and for a moment he saw a wistful look in her eyes.

Then she shook her head.

"And we could play that really fun game called 'Avoid Frankie.' That's the one where the locals cross the street so they don't have to come face-to-face with me. If you haven't already played it, then you should. It was an island-wide activity at one point."

Knowing the islanders as he did, he found that hard to believe. It was true that everyone knew what was happening to everyone and that strangers were often treated with suspicion, but on the whole he'd found the people to be kind and supportive. She was painting an image he didn't recognize. "That wouldn't happen."

"Not to you, maybe. I'm not going back to the island. That part of my life is over. Finished. In the past."

"If you won't go back, then it's not over or finished."

"You and I both know islanders have long memories."

"I do know. David Warren still reminds me of the time I stole hay from his field for Paige's rabbit because I couldn't be bothered to walk to the pet shop. Doesn't mean he doesn't give me a warm welcome when I'm home."

"That's you!" Her exasperated tone was layered with notes of panic. "I haven't been back to Puffin Island since I left for college. Why would I?"

Even though his sister had told him the same thing, it still shocked him to hear it. "Because you were raised there. It was your home until you were eighteen."

"I don't think of it as home."

"But you do think of it." He knew she did and he suspected she thought of it more than she would admit.

"The place has nothing but bad memories for me."

"So how about we try and put some better ones in their place?"

"Maybe we'd just pick up a whole new set of bad ones to add to the bucket load I already have."

"That wouldn't happen. I'd be with you the whole time."

Her brows rose. "Will you be riding your white charger and carrying a sword? Just clarifying, so that I recognize you. I don't believe in fairy tales. I happen to know Prince Charming doesn't exist. And just so that we're clear, I don't believe in true love, happy-ever-after, or any of that crap, either."

"As long as you still believe in Santa, we're good." His reward for lightening the tone was a begrudging smile.

"Him, I believe in."

"That's a relief. I was beginning to think we had nothing in common. Come with me, Frankie." He spoke softly. "Put that ghost behind you. Move on."

"It wouldn't be moving on. It would be going back."

"Everything moves on. Even Puffin Island. And sometimes you have to go back to move forward. There is no reason for you to stay away."

"My mother was responsible for breaking up at least one marriage on that island. Alicia and Sam Becket. It was a hideous time."

Matt had heard plenty of rumors about the Beckets' unconventional marriage but he decided this wasn't the time to mention it.

"Even if that's true—and plenty would argue that you can't break something sturdy—you are not your mother. You are not responsible for how she chooses to live her life. You're not responsible now, and you weren't responsible then." He wished he could make her see that.

"Maybe you're right and it would do me good to go back because I've built the place up into this horror island that

Lucas Blade could very well put in one of his books, but part of me is—"

"Scared?"

"No! I'm not *scared*. I'm not that pathetic." She gave him a furious look and then her shoulders drooped. "All right, I'm scared. Turns out I *am* that pathetic."

"You're not pathetic. You had a bad time and it's left bad memories. We all tend to avoid things that bring us down."

"What do you avoid?"

He finished his coffee. "I'm not good with hospitals. After all those visits with Paige—" He paused, fielding the images that rushed at him. "I walk through the door, smell that hospital smell, see medical staff with serious faces and white-faced relatives sipping disgusting coffee out of flimsy cups and I'm right back there, feeling the tension and seeing my parents' attempt to cover up their anxiety. I can't bear people talking about health and hospitals. I shut down. Close off."

Sympathy darkened her eyes. "Those were bad times."

"My point is that we all have things we'd rather avoid, Frankie. It doesn't make us pathetic, it makes us human."

"Well, I'm superhuman, and I'm not going. You'd have to drug me and tie me to the plane. I'll look at your photos, I'll talk about your apple orchard, but I'm not setting foot on Puffin Island." She picked up her coffee and took a sip.

He watched her. "If you change your mind, let me know."

"I'm not going to change my mind."

He didn't try and persuade her.

He'd planted a seed. Now he was going to let it grow.

She was a coward. Not only because she was afraid to set foot on the island again, although that was definitely part of it, but also because she knew that going to the island with

Matt would mean taking their relationship to the next level. And then it would end.

She didn't want it to end.

Tonight was the most fun she could remember having, but underneath the laughter and the conversation had been a seam of shivery tension and excitement that made her breathless.

She could almost have believed in happy endings, except she knew better.

Frankie sat in the cab, watching glittering, nighttime New York slide past outside the windows like a glamorous movie set.

It was late, but the streets were as crowded as they were in the middle of the day.

She could have been people-watching, or thinking about Puffin Island and all the things Matt had said, but all she could think about was him. The powerful length of his thigh close to hers but not quite touching, the width of his shoulders against the back of the seat.

The physical awareness was intense and unfamiliar. She didn't understand how she could feel this way. He'd taken her hand a couple of times in the park while they were walking, that was all. But she was fast discovering that sexual awareness was rooted in more than just touch. It could be triggered by a smile, a word or a look, like the one he'd given her over dinner that had made her feel as if she was the only woman in the restaurant.

And she realized that the most deliciously arousing thing of all was how well he knew her.

It was as if he could see inside to all the parts of her she kept hidden. It should have felt scary, but instead it gave her a warm, excited buzz as if all the energy she usually directed into hiding who she was had suddenly been redirected.

She stole a glance at him and he turned his head and gave her a half smile. It was as if he understood everything she was thinking.

There had been a moment in the park where she'd been convinced he was going to kiss her, and then another moment on the bridge while the sun was setting. She'd almost gone up in flames with want and need, and when he hadn't kissed her she'd been torn between relief that they'd postponed the moment when he was going to discover she was terribly bad at sex and frustration because she'd wanted him to kiss her so badly.

And now the nerves were back because she had no idea what happened next.

Her rulebook for relationships didn't look like other people's.

Did she invite him in for coffee?

Did she say good-night at the door?

She worried all the way back and the worry intensified as they crossed the Brooklyn Bridge, the lights shimmering across the gunmetal surface of the East River.

She paid the cab driver and walked to the door to her apartment, wishing she could calm the feelings in the pit of her stomach.

Hand shaking, she reached into her pocket and pulled out her keys. "Tonight was fun."

She was as jumpy as a kangaroo on a trampoline.

Matt reached out his hand and her heart danced in an excited rhythm. This time he was definitely going to kiss her. The chemistry was so powerful, even she could feel it and she waited, hardly daring to breathe, wanting it desperately and yet at the same time terrified because she knew that once he kissed her that would be it. *He'd know.* Anticipation danced across her nerve endings, sending a thousand volts of electricity through her body.

Her eyes started to close. She swayed and then felt his fingers brush against hers as he took the keys from her and opened the door to her apartment.

"Good night, Frankie." His voice came from close to her ear, rough, male and thickened with intimacy. He was close enough that she could see the rough texture of the stubble that shadowed his jaw.

"Matt—"

"Sleep well."

She opened her eyes and stared into his.

Sleep well? That was all he was going to say?

He'd been racking up the tension all night, and he wasn't going to kiss her?

Damn it, if he wasn't going to kiss her then she'd kiss him. They needed to get it out of the way once and for all. She reached out to haul him toward her, but her hand closed over thin air. And he didn't notice because he was already walking away from her.

This, she thought dizzily as she stared after his retreating back, was why she avoided relationships.

She would never in a million years understand men.

Chapter Nine

If your glass is half-full, open another bottle of wine.

—Paige

Frustrated and unsettled, Frankie closed the door of her apartment. She was too wound up to sleep. Her mind was full of thoughts that were too uncomfortable to examine closely. Thoughts about getting naked with Matt. Hot, sweaty thoughts. *Exciting thoughts.*

Crap.

The date had been nothing like she'd expected it to be. She'd thought it would go the way all her dates went—a few awkward hours together where the conversation didn't quite gel—the verbal equivalent of bumping noses when you kissed. Instead, it had been relaxed and fun. Matt had made it fun.

Central Park. Why had no one thought to take her on a date there before?

The answer was obvious. Because no one knew her as

well as Matt did. It was always restaurants or a movie. And all her relationships collapsed long before the moment when her date might have realized that being outdoors was her favorite thing.

As far as she was concerned, there had been only one real thing wrong with the evening.

He hadn't kissed her.

On the other hand if he *had* kissed her, it would have ruined the evening. Knowing that she wasn't going to sleep, she decided that she might as well return Eva's purse.

It took a while for her friend to answer and when she finally opened the door, Frankie backed away in shock.

"What happened to your *face*? If you're auditioning for a horror movie the part is yours."

"It's a face mask, Frankie. It's supposed to make me beautiful."

"I hate to break this to you, but they lied. You should have read the small print."

Eva smiled and the mask started to crack. "How was your date? I mean dinner," she corrected herself quickly. "Dinner. I know it wasn't a date."

"It was—" how could she describe it? It had been magical, exciting, *terrifying* "—it was different."

"Different 'good', or different 'get me out of here'?"

"Good."

"Where did he take you?"

"Central Park. We walked, we talked and then we had dinner."

"Was it stressful?"

"It was pretty much perfect." Apart from the point when he'd invited her to Puffin Island, but she was trying not to think about that.

And he hadn't kissed her.

Dammit, why hadn't he kissed her?

"Thanks for the loan of the purse. I'll have the tunic cleaned." Distracted, Frankie handed over the purse and took a closer look at Eva's face. "Did you get some of that stuff in your eyes? They look bloodshot."

"Oh!" Eva lifted her fingers to her cheek, flustered. "Maybe. Clumsy me. Do you want to come in? We could hang out for a while and open a bottle of wine." She opened the door wider but Frankie shook her head.

She was about to ask where Paige was and then remembered that she was with Jake. Which meant Eva was on her own with plenty of time to brood. *How could she have forgotten that?* "Paige is staying with Jake tonight. Are you going to be all right?"

"Of course I'm enjoying a quiet night in on my own. I'd forgotten how good it feels to do that once in a while. I'm going to rinse this thing off my face and settle down with popcorn and Netflix."

"What are you going to watch?"

"I don't know. Something you would never watch in a million years. There will be kissing. And happy endings. We both know romantic movies are your idea of hell. See you tomorrow!"

The door closed between them and Frankie returned to her apartment, wondering why she felt uneasy.

Eva was an adult. If she'd wanted company she would have said so.

She took a shower and settled down with her book but for once the words, even those written by Lucas Blade, didn't hold her attention. She kept thinking about Matt and mingled in there was concern for her friend.

Eva had said she was fine, but what if she wasn't?

If Paige had been home, she wouldn't have worried. Paige was so much better than Frankie was at delivering emotional support when it was needed. Not that Frankie considered herself a bad friend because she didn't. She was rock-solid, loyal and deeply caring in her own way, but she was the first to admit that in an emotional crisis, she wasn't good. An excess of emotions unnerved her. It always had. Whether she'd been born that way or whether it had been created on the blustery seas of her parents' divorce she didn't know, but whenever emotions were intense she wanted to slide into a dark hole and hide until the storm passed. She felt inept and useless.

But tonight there was no Paige, which meant that Eva was on her own.

The thought nagged at her, preventing her from relaxing.

She reached for her phone, wondering if she should text her friend, but then put it down again.

What good would that do? She'd say "Are you okay?" and Eva would reply "Yes. You?"

She was probably deep into a romantic movie.

Impatient with herself, Frankie tried to read her book but she couldn't focus. Ten minutes later she glanced at the clock.

What if Eva wasn't watching anything?

What if she'd poked herself in the eye again trying to remove the face mask? Her eyes had been red and—

"Crap." Frankie sprang off the sofa so fast the book thudded to the floor. Eva's eyes hadn't been red because of the mask. They were red because she'd been crying.

Moments later she was hammering on Eva's door.

This time it took longer for Eva to answer. The face mask was gone but her eyes were still red. "What's wrong?"

Frankie wanted to say that nothing was wrong with her, but stopped herself. Eva was selfless and giving and was unlikely to put her own needs first. "You invited me in."

"You hate romantic movies."

"We can talk. I feel like talking."

"What about?"

"Stuff—" Frankie floundered. "Problems," she said vaguely and Eva looked confused.

"You hate talking about your problems. You bottle them up, boil, simmer, kick things around the room. Then you attack them like Boudicca repelling an invading army."

"Yeah, well, tonight I'm trying a new approach." Frankie shoved her way through the door and saw Eva's clothes strewn over every available surface in a rainbow of pastel colors and sparkle. "Oh my—were you burgled?"

"No."

"Someone emptied out your drawers."

"That was me. I was looking for my peach silk scarf."

"Did you find it?" Frankie eyed the piles of clothes, knowing she'd never find anything in that mess. How did one person ever get to wear all of that?

"I think Paige might have borrowed it."

"And you criticize my clothes."

"The clothes themselves, not the way you store them."

"You appear to be using the floor as storage. Do you want help sorting through this stuff? We could hold a yard sale and give the proceeds to damaged cats or something."

"I'm doing enough for damaged cats by tolerating Claws despite her temper issues, and anyway, everything you see here has importance and meaning. I don't want to get rid of any of it. There isn't a single piece here I don't love."

"Seriously? What about this—" Frankie snatched up a green knitted sweater. "I've never seen you wear it."

"Gran knitted that." Eva's eyes filled and she plopped down onto the sofa, ignoring the pile of clothes. "Sorry. Ignore me."

"I'm the one who should be saying sorry." Horrified, Frankie folded the sweater carefully and sat down next to Eva. "Don't cry. Please don't cry. I'm clumsy and stupid and Paige will kill me for upsetting you."

"It's not you, it's me. This happens. And it's fine."

"It's not fine. What can I do? Do you need a glass of water? A hug?" Frankie patted Eva's shoulder awkwardly and felt a rush of frustration. Why was she so hopeless in these situations? "Talk to me, Ev."

"It's just a bad moment, that's all. It will pass. I'll get through it. I'm using you as my role model."

"Me?"

"Yes. You and Paige are the strongest people I know. You've both handled serious crap in your lives and carried on. I'm trying to be more like you and less marshmallow."

"You don't want to be like me. I'm a mess." Frankie pulled at a peach scarf that was half-hidden under one of the cushions. "Is this what you were looking for?"

"Yes! And I think you're amazing." Eva blew her nose. "You're so independent. So strong and together. You're inspiring and brave."

Frankie thought of the way she'd responded to Matt's suggestion that she go with him to Puffin Island.

You'd have to drug me and tie me to the plane.

"I'm not brave, Ev. And I love the marshmallow side of you. Don't ever change."

Her friend's words made her feel like a fraud.

She knew she wasn't an inspiration for anyone. If she was strong and together would she really be so afraid to go back to Puffin Island? Would she really be so terrified of taking the leap with Matt?

"I want to change the way I am. I'm tired of feeling bad. Any tips greatly received." Eva reached for another tissue. "If you want to help, you can distract me. Tell me about your evening with Matt. You said it was perfect."

"We walked in Central Park. We talked. We had dinner. It involved food and conversation."

"But it wasn't a date."

"No. It definitely wasn't a date."

"So there were no romantic moments?" Eva seemed so disappointed Frankie was tempted to make one up just to see her friend smile.

"He did grab my hand a couple of times."

Eva brightened. "Truly?"

"Probably to stop me running off."

"Why would you run off?"

"He mentioned Puffin Island. He wants me to go back for a weekend with him." She toed off her shoes and curled up on the sofa next to Eva. "He's combining a job with a friend's wedding." Knowing that Eva would ask, she added the name. "Ryan Cooper."

"I know him. He's hot."

"He's also off the market because he's marrying his very pregnant girlfriend, Emily, in a romantic beach wedding."

Eva looked dreamily across the room. "I would *love* to style a beach wedding. And you're invited? Lucky you. This is what I mean about you being an inspiration. Most people who'd been through what you've been through would be too scared to go back, and you're scared, too, but you're doing it, anyway."

Frankie opened her mouth. There was no *way* she was going back. "In fact, I'm not—"

"Don't waste your breath telling me you're not brave, because you are. I know you're scared, but doing something even though it scares you is the definition of brave."

"Yes, but I'm not—"

"You *are*! You are brave. And I'm going to remember that every time I hit a rough patch thinking about Gran. It's hard, but I'm going to get through it. I feel better already." She scrunched up the tissue she'd been using. "I'm glad you're going back. I've never said anything before but I was worried about you staying away. And there are so many wonderful things about the island."

Oh hell, how was she going to extract herself from this?

Frankie's throat was so dry she felt as if she'd swallowed sand. "Name one."

"The smell of salt and sea. That feeling you get when you walk on the cliffs and you stare into infinity and realize how big the world is and how small you are. The wind in your hair, the seagulls, small children with big smiles and melting ice creams."

Frankie felt a tug deep inside her, a yearning for something long forgotten. "I miss those things, too."

"And then there are the wonderfully quirky people."

"Those, I don't miss."

"The other day I read about a man who had died in his apartment in Harlem. No one discovered his body for five weeks. *Five weeks.* That would never happen on Puffin Island."

"True, and they wouldn't need a post mortem because they'd already know why he died."

"I know." Eva slid the scarf through her fingers. "That's one of the brilliant things about the place. I love New York. I wouldn't want to live anywhere else, but I do wonder what it would be like living here if I didn't have you, Paige, Matt and Jake. I'd be horribly lonely."

"You do have us. We're a community right here. You don't need to be on an island to be part of a community, Eva. You just need to reach out to people, and you do that naturally. I don't know what's going to happen in our lives— none of us do—but I do know you'll never be lonely. You're like a lightbulb. People are always drawn to you because you brighten their day."

Eva's eyes filled. "That's possibly the nicest thing anyone has ever said to me."

Frankie grabbed the box of tissues. "I've made you cry again."

"But in a good way."

"Is there a good way to cry?"

"Of course there is. Don't you ever cry?"

"No. I have a heart of stone."

Eva blew her nose. "Frankie, you have so much heart it's bursting out of you."

"That sounds messy. Not that anyone is going to notice in this apartment of yours. You'd better clean up before Paige comes back or she'll freak." Frankie flopped back against the sofa, wondering how to extract herself from this misunderstanding. "A wedding on Puffin Island is the perfect combination of all the things I hate in life."

"I know. But you're going, anyway. You're incredible. And I'm sure no one is going to mention the past. It's been ten years. Paige told me you bumped into your mother last week. Was that difficult?"

"Horrible. I can't believe I'm saying this because we both know I'm not the biggest supporter of team Happy-Ever-After but I actually wish she'd meet someone she cares about. None of her relationships ever stick."

Eva wrapped the scarf around her neck. "If she were a saucepan, she'd be Teflon coated."

Frankie laughed. "That's my mother. Nonstick."

"Love is complicated."

"You can say that again. And that's why some people prefer to avoid it altogether. I'm one of them."

"That's not true. Take tonight—you're up here with me when you'd rather be on your own. That's love. Not romantic love maybe, but still love."

"Who said I wanted to be on my own?"

"I know you. You were stressed about your evening, and when you're stressed your response is to lock yourself away and read or fiddle with your plants. But you're here. With me. Because you know I'm upset. You're the best friend on the planet."

Frankie's throat thickened. "Friend love is different."

"Not really. Romantic love should be supported by a backbone of strong friendship. A man can be the best kisser in the world, but I wouldn't want to be with him if he wasn't my best friend. Listen to me, getting all emotional. Your least favorite thing. You see what I mean? You're brave. You face what needs to be faced even when you don't like the way it looks. Like my face when I cry."

"Don't cry." Frankie's discomfort had nothing to do with

the fact that she was sitting on a pile of Eva's clothes. Her friend had placed her on a pedestal and she was going to fall hard.

"It's late. You should probably go to bed."

Frankie looked at her friend, remembering the times Eva had been there for her. "Have you got the ingredients for that amazing hot chocolate you make?"

"Yes. Do you want to take a mug downstairs?"

"I was thinking I might stay the night. In Paige's room." Frankie said it casually. "It would be fun. You have whipped cream?"

"I always have whipped cream. You never know when you might need it."

"Tonight is one of those times."

"We could curl up and watch a movie together." Eva brightened and then subsided. "Are you sure you're not doing this for me? Because truly I'm fine. and—"

"I'm not doing it for you. I'm doing it for me. I don't want to be on my own."

It was true

She didn't want to be on her own or she'd start panicking about her upcoming trip to Puffin Island.

Of course she could have told Eva that she'd misunderstood and that she had no intention of ever visiting the place again, but Eva was only just holding it together.

Frankie had no idea why Eva had chosen her as a role model. All she knew was that if she was a source of inspiration, then she'd better do something inspiring and brave.

Chapter Ten

If your glass is half-empty, you're less likely to spill it.

—Frankie

Matt was hauling the first log seat into place on the roof terrace when Frankie planted herself in front of him the following day.

"So this trip to Puffin Island—" The words tumbled out like a river in full flow. "Not that I'm telling you I'm coming because I still think it's a crazy idea, but if I *did* come, where would I stay? It's all right for you, you can stay with your parents, but the moment people recognize me they will be closing doors in my face and locking up their husbands and sons. I'll probably have to camp in a field so I need to know what to take."

Matt eased himself upright.

She'd clearly been stewing on it all night, but he sensed the shift from a definite no to a maybe. He wondered what had made her change her mind.

"You won't be camping in a field and I have no intention of staying with my parents." He didn't say that was because what he planned to do to Frankie definitely couldn't be done in front of his parents. "Why don't you leave the accommodation issue to me? There are rooms at the Ocean Club. Ryan and Emily have a few places reserved for people who don't live on the island."

"What does that mean? That we'd be staying together?"

"That's what I'd like." He saw something that looked like panic flicker in her eyes. "What's the problem, Frankie? You don't like my company?"

"You know I like your company."

"That's all that matters. The rest can take care of itself."

The tension between them was off the scale. Moonlight or sunlight, sunrise or sunset, it was always there, the blood-pumping chemistry.

"You make it sound simple, but it isn't." She wrapped her arms around her waist. "I don't know what this is, Matt. Is it friendship? Is it dating? Is it a weekend of—what?"

"Do we have to define it that specifically?"

"Yes. If I know what's expected, I'll know if I have the skills to be what you want me to be. Generally it's a good idea in life not to take on things that play to your weaknesses."

She made it sound like a job interview.

"You don't need skills to spend a weekend with me, Frankie. And I don't want you to be anyone but yourself."

"That doesn't usually work out so well."

"It works for me."

She bit her lip. "What's the plan?"

"We'll arrive Friday morning and visit the site so that we can take some measurements and soil samples. Then

Saturday is the wedding. I thought we could have a day to ourselves Sunday and come back that evening." He tried to make it sound low-key and relaxed but she still looked anxious.

"A day to ourselves? What would we be doing?"

"If I said we'd be laughing, enjoying plenty of interesting conversation and an indecent amount of mind-blowing sex, what would you say?"

Color streaked across her cheeks. "I'd say the first two sound fine."

"You have something against mind-blowing sex that I need to know about?"

"Yes! Starting with the fact that I don't even know what that is! I told you—sex isn't really my thing. If that's why you're inviting me, you should take someone else." She spoke in a breathy, nervous voice that connected with something deep inside him.

"Frankie—"

"You don't believe me, so I'm going to prove it to you." Without warning she snatched her hands out of her pockets and grabbed him by the front of his shirt.

Then she tugged him toward her, rose on tiptoe and kissed him.

Shock froze his system. His mind went blank. The world around him faded to nothing more than white noise.

For a split second he stood there, absorbing the fact that he was finally kissing Frankie. Or rather, she was kissing him.

He felt her start to pull away and cupped her face in his hands, keeping her mouth locked against his. No way was he letting her go. *No way was this ending.* Desire exploded through him, raw and real, and he slid one hand down her back and pulled her against him. His other hand he pushed into the soft mass of her hair, holding her head steady for his kiss. She might have started it, but now he was taking over.

Her mouth was soft and warm and he felt her melt into him. He sensed her uncertainty, but he also felt the hunger in her. A hunger that matched his. Raw sexual desire rocked his balance and he slammed his hand against the nearest solid surface, a fence panel waiting for one of his clients in Brooklyn. He clamped his hand low on her hips and pressed her close to the hard throb of his erection. He wanted her with an intensity he'd never felt before. They were both fully clothed and yet somehow this kiss was the single most erotic experience of his life.

He had no idea how it would have ended had the blare of a car horn from the street below not brought them back to the real world.

She dragged her mouth from his and stared at him, her breathing shallow.

He hoped she wasn't expecting him to speak because right at that moment there was only one part of his body that appeared to be functioning.

She touched her fingers to her lips and took a step back, a move that pushed her back against the fence. "What did you do that for?"

It was a struggle to focus. "What?"

"Kiss me. You kissed me!"

"Honey, you kissed me."

"But you kissed me back." She dragged her hand through her hair and then lifted it from the back of her neck, as if she was too hot.

He sympathized. If he was any hotter he'd combust.

"I've always considered kissing to be a pastime at its best when it's a shared experience."

"I wanted to get it out of the way."

As far as he was concerned all they'd achieved was throwing lighter fuel on a burning fire, but he was willing to play along.

"I guess we did that."

"Yes. So now we know."

"Yes." His eyes dropped to the soft curve of her mouth. "Now we know."

She eyed him. "Just to be clear, if our relationship is a Monopoly board, we haven't passed Go."

"But at least we're not in jail. That's always a good thing." Although if you could earn yourself jail time for bad thoughts, he would be heading for a long stint inside.

"We bought you something." Paige placed four bags on her desk and Frankie roused herself from daydreams about Matt.

That kiss had been nothing like she'd expected. Nothing like anything she'd experienced before. She'd started it, but somehow the balance of power had shifted instantly. There was no doubt that Matt had been the one in charge. She was trying to work out how that could have happened but the whole thing was a dizzying blur. Never in a million years would she have thought kissing could have felt so— so— intense. She could still feel it. The firm pressure of his hands on her face, the skill of his mouth, the sheer heat of it. It had been a discovery, a lightning bolt—

Crap, she was starting to sound like Eva.

Giving herself a mental slap, she reached for the bags. "Those look expensive."

"It's a thank-you for all your hard work getting this company off the ground."

"You worked hard, too."

"I might have treated myself to the odd thing." Paige grinned and Eva balanced on the edge of Frankie's desk, her blue skater skirt riding up her thighs.

"Open them. We tried to compromise between what you feel comfortable in and what we think you'd look great in."

"Is this a makeover?"

"It's a thank-you." Eva pushed the bags toward her. "I was feeling really crappy the other night and you helped me. I know you hate deciding what to wear, so I hope I've made it easy for you. There's an outfit for traveling, which can be easily smartened up when you go to see your client. Then there's something to wear to the wedding and something to wear on the beach."

"I hadn't decided what to wear to the wedding." Frankie wrestled through tissue paper and extracted a feather-light length of slippery emerald green silk. "It's a dress? I don't—"

"It's not a dress. It's a jumpsuit and it's going to look stunning on you. It might be windy and you don't want to spend your whole time trying to stop the other guests seeing your underwear. And on that note I took the liberty of buying you a few more personal things."

"You bought me lingerie?"

"If you have an accident and you're taken into the emergency department I don't want your mismatching underwear to distract them from saving you. And as I was the one who threw away that gray abomination you called a nightdress, I figured I owed you."

Lingerie.

She wasn't stupid. She knew why Eva had bought her lingerie, and it wasn't because she wanted her to look good in the event of an encounter with the emergency services.

She wanted her to look good in the event of an encounter with Matt.

Although that might be a total car crash, too.

If anything, the kiss had made things more terrifying, not less, because now she had further to fall. The ultimate disappointment when they finally made it to bed would be crushing.

She tucked the silk jumpsuit back into the bag and peered into the others. "You two have spent a fortune."

"Doing something scary is always easier if you're looking good. I also bought you a new sweater."

"Are we bankrupt?"

"No, we're doing well." Paige handed her a small bag. "I know you hate lipstick, but this is so neutral it barely counts. It will look good with the jumpsuit for the wedding. Summery and light." She paused. "We're proud of you."

Frankie felt like a fraud. "You didn't have to do this."

"You're the one who is doing it, and we think you're incredible. You're strong and fearless." Paige gave her a hug and then pulled away as Frankie's phone rang. "You'd better get that."

Fearless?

They had no idea.

She'd never been more scared of anything in her life, but whether it was the thought of being with Matt or the thought of returning to Puffin Island, she didn't know. The whole thing was now a tangled mess of stress in her head.

Needing to escape, Frankie snatched up her phone and walked out of the office.

Paige flopped into her chair. "Do you think she's going to wear it?"

"I don't know. I hope so because Matt is going to need therapy if she wears something like that gray T-shirt to bed."

"He's so crazy about her, I have a feeling he wouldn't care."

Eva gave her a dark look. "You didn't see the T-shirt. Even Marilyn Monroe couldn't have carried that off."

Chapter Eleven

If you live your life looking backward, you'll never
see what lies ahead.

—Eva

There were two ways to reach Puffin Island. One was to
take the ferry that ran regularly between the island and the
mainland, and the other was to catch the short flight across
the bay.

Because they only had a long weekend, Matt opted for the
flight. "Ryan arranged it. He pointed out that the traffic will
be bumper to bumper on the coast road in the summer, and
he's right. And we need to arrive in time to see the garden."

Frankie didn't care if they traveled by donkey. It was the
destination that bothered her.

She walked toward the small aircraft, feeling sicker and
sicker, wondering if it was too late to change her mind.

She no longer cared about being Eva's inspiration. All she
cared about at that moment was not inflicting this on herself.

Only a narrow stretch of water stood between her and her past.

She was so anxious she'd even stopped thinking about the kiss.

The pilot's name was Zachary Flynn. Eva would have observed that he was "hot," if in a slightly dangerous way. The only thing Frankie cared about was that she'd never met him before.

For her, that was the key factor.

At least he was unlikely to open the door of the plane and drop her into the choppy waters of Penobscot Bay. If she didn't know him, then he couldn't bear a grudge.

The Cessna seaplane was perfect for short flights between the islands, and Frankie stared down at the glittering expanse of the bay, the yachts, the islands with fishing boats bobbing in sheltered harbors.

She was conscious of Matt sitting beside her, powerful and real. At one point he reached across and gave her hand a squeeze in a gesture that was designed to be reassuring, but instead made nerves spring to life in her stomach.

She knew he was intending to take their relationship to another level. Unfortunately, she knew that the moment he laid a finger on her the level they'd hit would be the basement not the penthouse. True, the kiss hadn't quite turned out the way she'd anticipated but she was under no illusions about the rest of it.

But there was no time to worry about that now because she could see the island and the runway in the distance.

She glanced around anxiously as they landed, half expecting to see a posse of locals holding a banner saying Leave Our Island, but there was no one except the staff who manned the small airstrip during the peak summer months.

"Car rental is all fixed." Zach tossed Matt a set of keys. "It's the silver one at the far end of the parking lot. Be careful as you drive the last half mile to my place. Camp Puffin is heaving with people, but you'll be fine once you reach Seagull's Nest. The place is fully stocked, but if there's any particular brand of beer you like you might want to pick it up on your way through."

Frankie hauled her bag over her shoulder and she and Matt walked toward the car. "We're staying in the camp?"

"Zach owns a cabin that he rents out. It's right on the water. I thought you might prefer to be away from town."

She did prefer it. Somewhere away from town and away from all the people she was dreading meeting sounded good. She was touched that he'd been so thoughtful. "Where does Zach live if he doesn't stay in the cabin?"

"In Castaway Cottage."

Everyone born on the island knew Castaway Cottage. It nestled in the perfect curve that was Shell Bay, looking out toward Puffin Rock and the wild Atlantic Ocean beyond.

Frankie had lost count of the number of hours she'd spent on that beach on her own, dreaming of climbing onto a raft and escaping. "I knew the woman who used to live there. Kathleen Forrest. She died a few years ago."

Matt slid into the driver's seat and Frankie into the passenger's. "How did you meet her?"

Memories tumbled down on her, as if she'd opened a cupboard that was too full. "The day my Dad walked out, I walked out, too." And she still felt guilty about that. Her mother had told her afterward that half the island had been out looking for her. "I ran all the way along the coast path and ended up at Shell Bay. I was the only one there, or at least I thought I was. I cried myself dry and then Kathleen appeared with a flask of hot chocolate. She wrapped me in a blanket and took me back to the cottage." Frankie frowned. "I remember hesitating in the doorway and muttering something about her being a stranger. I've never forgotten her answer."

"Which was?"

"'On Puffin Island there is no such thing as a stranger, only a friend.'"

Matt nodded. "That sounds like something she would say."

"She called someone on the town council to let them know I was safe. They'd all been out looking for me."

"Why did you run in the first place?"

Frankie stared out the window. She'd never told anyone the reason. "I guess it was shock." That part wasn't a lie. She *had* been in shock. Panicked and confused. Not only had her father walked out, she'd been put in a hideous position and had no idea how to handle it.

"Your mom must have been worried sick." Matt glanced at her and something in his searching gaze made her wonder whether he'd guessed there was more to the story.

"She was too shocked about my dad to be thinking much about me." Frankie tried to shake off the past. "So where are we going first?"

"If you're in the mood for talking about apple trees, I thought we'd go and do the site visit. Then we can call in at the harbor and pick up some supplies on our way to the cabin."

Harbor Stores was the center of island gossip. She wondered if he'd think she was a coward if she stayed in the car for that part and let him pick up what they needed.

He drove like a local, taking back roads that avoided the

center of town and finally ended up on a road that skirted the forest.

The couple who wanted the apple orchard gave them a warm welcome. They had a pitcher of iced tea waiting and Frankie sipped her drink while she and Matt studied the garden and discussed the options.

Although Matt wasn't a trained horticulturist, he had plenty of ideas and experience, and one big advantage. He'd grown up on Puffin Island. He understood the climate and the challenges of planting in this environment.

Two hours later they climbed back into the car and Matt drove toward the harbor.

"That was useful. It's a comparatively sheltered garden. It will be easier than I thought."

"We are going to need to spend some time preparing the soil first."

"Agreed." They were approaching the road that led past the harbor, and Frankie shrank down slightly in her seat. She wasn't ready to see people. She hadn't worked out how to handle it.

Matt pulled into a parking space and turned to look at her. "I can go on my own if that's what you'd prefer."

Then she'd have to confess to Paige and Eva that she'd stayed in the car.

"No. Let's do this." She reached down to release her seat belt and his hand covered hers.

"You're not going to war, Frankie." His voice was soft. "Most of the people in there won't remember anything about that time. Half of them probably don't know your mother."

"Let's hope not, otherwise I'll be hiding behind you." She tried to make a joke of it. "Good thing you have broad shoulders."

She walked into Harbor Stores feeling as if she was walking the plank. The bell on the door sounded, announcing her arrival, and heads turned.

Here we go.

Her face burned and then she felt Matt's arm curve around her waist protectively.

"Relax." He murmured the word in her ear. "Almost everyone in here is a tourist. What do you want to eat tonight? Before you answer I need to warn you that if I'm cooking, you have a choice of three things."

"Three? That's all?" She was relieved to have an excuse to focus on him. "Spell it out."

"Pizza, pasta and duck legs in orange sauce."

"That's fancy."

He gave her a wicked smile. "It's the dish I cook when I want to get laid."

"Does it work?"

"I guess we'll find out later."

Her heart skipped a beat and for a moment she forgot about the locals. "I don't want to ruin your record, so let's go with pizza."

They made their choices and took the basket to the checkout. Frankie was beginning to think that Matt might be right and that this wasn't going to be as bad as she'd feared, when she turned and bumped into an elderly lady carrying a bag of apples. Her hair was as white as the snow that blanketed the island during the long winter months; her skin was wrinkled and paper thin, but her blue eyes were sharp and alert.

Hilda Dodge.

Recognizing her immediately, Frankie turned to make for the door but the woman shot out a hand and caught her arm.

"It's Francesca, isn't it?"

Crap. Coming back here had been a mistake. *A big fat mistake.*

Hilda had lived next to the Beckets. She'd probably seen Frankie's mother climbing in and out of the bedroom window. And now they were going to talk about it in glorious detail. They were going to reminisce, right next to the vegetable aisle, where no doubt the color of her cheeks would make the heap of glossy vine tomatoes look washed out.

"It's Frankie."

"We haven't seen your face here for—" Hilda's head bobbed as she did the calculation "—it must be almost ten years."

Ten years, one month, six days and five hours.

"I went to college." *I ran away and never came back.* That's how strong and brave she was.

"I remember you well. You, Paige and that other girl— pretty blonde who lived with her grandmother—"

"Eva."

"That's her. Eva. My memory isn't what it was. The three of you were thick as thieves. And you were so shy."

"Excuse me?"

"So many times I tried to talk to you after that business with your parents, but you always crossed the road so that you wouldn't have to speak to me." Hilda leaned in and lowered her voice. "I was the same age as you when my parents divorced. Such a shock. Like coming home and finding someone has knocked your house down. In an instant, everything you're used to has gone. Vanished."

It had felt exactly like that. As if her world had collapsed.

Frankie stared at her. "You— I assumed—"

"I wanted you to know that you had our support. Everyone on the island felt the same way. When you went missing that day—" Hilda's eyes filled and she patted Frankie's arm "—we all went out looking for you. Everyone. We searched the fields and the forest. We were all praying you hadn't gone into the water. When Kathleen called to say she had you safe in the cottage—well, a few prayers of thanks were said that night."

They'd said prayers of thanks?

"I—"

"We've missed seeing you around, although I understand why you needed to leave this place and have a fresh start. Too many memories here." Hilda gave her a quick hug. "Still, it's all behind you now. And you're home, that's the main thing."

Home? "I live in New York now, Hilda. That's my home."

"Once an islander, always an islander. You can't get away from it, pumpkin. Enjoy your stay. The whole island is excited about the wedding."

In a daze, Frankie let Matt guide her to the door and back to the car.

He pulled out of the space, avoiding the line of traffic queuing for the ferry.

Frankie's head was still spinning. She sat in silence, processing what had just happened. "Aren't you going to say it?"

"Say what?"

"I told you so. You told me it was in my head. People crossing the road."

"First, I grew out of saying 'I told you so' when I was around nine years old, and second, I don't think it was all in your head. I love this place, but I'm the first to admit that it has downsides, and one of those downsides is the interest people take in other people's business."

"Maybe." But looking back, she could see that Hilda might have been right. *She* was the one who had crossed the road because she'd been too ashamed to face anyone. "I assumed I knew what they were thinking. What they were going to say to me."

"You're not the only person who goes around imagining that they know what people are thinking."

"You don't do that."

He shrugged. "I'm human. I do it sometimes, but generally I find it more reliable to wait until a person tells me what they think, rather than making a guess. Not only does that make sense to me, but also I'm a guy. I don't have female intuition."

"Neither do I, it seems." Frankie leaned her head back against the seat and let the memories flow over her. "I was *so* scared of her."

"Hilda? She's virtually an island elder. Growing up, we were all a little scared of her. But she has a wicked sense of humor and she'll do anything for the people of this island. Look on the positive side. You went into Harbor Stores and came out alive. In fact, you did better than that. You were hugged by Hilda. That's a ticket to island approval right there."

That much was true.

Frankie felt some of the tension leave her. She had built it up in her head. Her own embarrassment had led her to avoid people and she'd confused who was avoiding whom.

Once an islander, always an islander.

Maybe she didn't feel as if this place was *home* exactly, but she had to admit that it had charm. A charm she'd forgotten. Or maybe it wasn't that she'd forgotten, more that the beauty of the place had been blackened by the events surrounding her parents' divorce.

Matt paused to allow traffic to pass and then took the road that led toward Camp Puffin on the eastern side of the island.

Frankie gazed out the window across the rolling fields to the sea. It glistened and sparkled in the sunshine, a perfect day for sailing. The bay bobbed with boats, and in the far distance she could see the mainland. "It's pretty here. I never spent much time on this side of the island."

"You never spent a summer at Camp Puffin?"

"No. Paige didn't do it because she wasn't well enough. But you know that, of course." And she'd been relieved to have an excuse not to spend the summer alongside the other kids. Some of them had been fine, but there had been a group of older boys who had made her life a misery. It had been hard enough to cope with the teasing at school, without extending the torture through the long days of summer. It was a relief to escape from it for a few months. "Eva and I used to make our own camp in the cave on the bay just beyond South Beach. Do you know it?"

"I know it well." The smile on his mouth made her wonder how well.

At night the cave had been a favorite hangout for teenagers seeking privacy.

"We buried a box in the cave. Each of us put something personal in it."

"I hope you buried it deep or that box is probably floating somewhere close to Greenland now. The wedding is on South Beach, so we can look for it." Matt slowed as the road turned to a dirt track. It skirted the forest and headed directly to the camp. "There's a path from here that leads over the cliffs to Castaway Cottage."

"I walked it a couple of times." She'd been fourteen years old and isolated, with a secret she couldn't even tell her closest friends. "I often walked as far as the cottage, but I never went inside apart from that one time. I used to sit on the rocks and stare at it for hours." Until the welcoming glow of the lights and the curl of smoke from the chimney had increased her feeling of isolation and she'd returned over the cliffs to the shards of her own shattered family. "I remember it being cozy. Kathleen had framed photos of seabirds on the walls and in the kitchen there were huge jars filled with sea glass she'd picked up herself from the beach. Everything about the place made you think of the ocean. I remember wishing I could stay there forever, wrapped in that blanket, listening to the waves crashing onto the rocks. And Kathleen was so kind." So kind that she'd almost told her everything.

Almost.

And that was the reason she'd never knocked on the door again. She hadn't trusted herself not to blurt it all out. And the secret wasn't hers to tell. It was a burden she'd unwillingly carried through her life.

"So you do have some good memories of the islanders."

They drove past the main camp buildings and took the narrow track that led up the coast. Frankie saw groups of kids in kayaks bobbing in the water close to the shore, and another group building a camp on the beach. They were laughing, gathering pieces of driftwood and arguing with each other. *Making memories.*

Did she have good memories?

"Maybe I do, but they were eclipsed by everything that

happened. After my dad left, my mom was so upset I didn't know what to do." She watched as two of the girls tried to wedge the driftwood into the sand, laughing and falling over each other. "There were days when she didn't get out of bed at all. I was scared to leave her. That went on for months. People called around every day to check on us. Whenever I went into Harbor Stores people patted me and told me they were sorry for my troubles. We had a casserole on our doorstep every single day. And then Mom decided she'd had enough of being the victim so she got herself a makeover, went out partying, got drunk with Sam Becket and the rest is history. The casseroles stopped. After that I kept waiting to have one tipped over my head."

"From what I heard the Beckets' marriage was in trouble long before your mother decided to rediscover her youth."

"I never heard that."

"You were probably too young to pick up on it. If the rumors were correct, he had numerous affairs."

Frankie absorbed that information. "He had other affairs? Why didn't I know that?"

"You've never been one for gossip. It's one of the things I like about you."

Her heart gave a little jolt. "There's more than one thing about me that you like?"

"Are you flirting with me?" He gave her a teasing smile that made her heart pump hard against her chest.

"I don't know how to flirt. I was going to research it, but I've been too busy."

"You can research flirting?"

"You can research anything. There's probably even some online training you can do."

"Flirting 101?" He kept his eyes on the track as he negotiated the uneven surface, but the smile on his face widened. "So if you weren't flirting, that means it was a serious question. I'll answer, but I should probably warn you I'm into high numbers so it could take a while."

"You're full of crap, Matt Walker."

"I think you mean charm."

"And does that charm usually work for you?"

"I guess we're going to find out." He shot her a glance and she saw the burn of heat in his eyes but she didn't have time to analyze his words because moments later he was pulling up outside a cabin. "We're here. This is Seagull's Nest."

The simple log cabin nestled on the cliff where the forest met the sea. It had its own private deck suspended above the beach and on a day like today when the sea was rough, the waves spattered spray across the broad planks.

Charmed, Frankie slid out of the passenger seat.

The cabin was idyllic but secluded. Until today, she'd assumed they'd be spending the night surrounded by other wedding guests. She'd pictured group celebrations, drinking and hilarity.

She hadn't imagined anything like the intimacy of Seagull's Nest.

"Do you have a key?"

"In the door." Matt lowered the bags. "No one bothers much with keys around here, which comes as a bit of an adjustment to us New Yorkers."

He pushed open the door and Frankie walked past him, his body brushing against hers.

Her insides were a tumble of sexual awareness and nerves, which was crazy because this was Matt. Why should she feel so nervous when she'd known him forever?

Except that this wasn't the Matt she'd known. This Matt was new to her.

The cabin was simple but stylish, the perfect hideaway for a romantic weekend. The large bed had been made up with fresh linen, and a bunch of scented flowers had been placed in a vase by the bed. The window was open and the cabin was filled with the smells of summer and the faintly salty air.

It was charming. And romantic.

Which was lovely, except she didn't do romantic. She was clueless, and pretty soon Matt was going to discover just how clueless. What was he expecting? She was pretty sure that the list of reasons he liked her was going to dwindle to low single figures once he discovered more about her. She'd tried warning him but either he hadn't been listening or he'd assumed that she was exaggerating the problem.

Or maybe he was one of those men who thought he was such a sex god he'd be able to get past the problem.

Which simply increased the pressure.

She was going to be the first woman he didn't manage to turn on. Like an old, rusty engine that no amount of love and care could restore to working order.

She longed to have a normal, healthy attitude toward relationships. She should be flirting and laughing with anticipation. Instead, she wanted to run into the forest and hide as she'd done as a child.

Losing her nerve, she backed toward the door. "This place is for lovers."

"Yeah, that's right." He slid his arm around her and hauled her back against him. "Is there something wrong with that?"

Everything was wrong with that.

Now she was here, all her insecurities came rushing back.

The fact that sex had never played a big part in her life had never bothered her much, and she realized now it was because it had never mattered enough. She'd never cared enough to be disappointed. To her, sex had been an activity fraught with complication and weighed down by uncomfortable memories of the past. But she'd never experienced the same electrifying urgency she felt with Matt.

She wanted him desperately. So desperately that the hum of physical awareness was something that seemed to be permanently switched on whenever she was near him. It had been that way since the kiss. And she wanted to kiss him again. She wanted to rip at his clothes and explore, a feeling she'd never had before. She wanted all of him, and the only thing stopping her was the fear that she was going to disappoint him. And herself. What if reality didn't live up to the promise and expectation? Never before had she felt this delicious, intoxicating excitement. It was like being injected with a drug, and she didn't want the feeling to vanish.

"Talk to me." His voice was soft. "Tell me what's wrong."

"This is never going to work." Given everything he knew about her, she saw no reason not to be honest. She hated keeping secrets. She already had more than enough of those locked inside her. "Every time I go to bed with a man it's a disappointment. I'm bored. He's bored. You'd probably have more excitement trawling the internet. I can't—I mean I've never—" And that was something else she'd never told anyone. "Never mind."

"You could never bore me, Frankie." He slid his thumb across her burning cheek. "And you don't need to be stressed."

"I'll decide what I want to be stressed about." If a situation had ever been more stressful she couldn't remember it. "I'm an adult. I own my stress levels."

He smiled. "Sometimes the way to handle something you're afraid of is just to do it."

"Like going to the dentist, you mean?"

He raised an eyebrow. "I'm pretty confident the experience will be a few steps up from that. Do you trust me?"

"Of course, but that has nothing to do with this." She made another desperate attempt to make him understand. "I don't think I'm very sexual. I'm not built that way. Or maybe the whole thing with my mom has just made me so tense I can't relax enough to do it. I don't know, but I do know that you being insanely hot isn't going to change anything. You think this is going to work because you're a rampant sex god who is going to be the one to show me what I'm missing?"

"No, I know this is going to work because I care about you and you care about me. And also because I want to rip your clothes off the whole time. That's another clue right there." He lowered his head and brushed his lips across her neck. "Stop thinking about how it was before, and focus on how it is now." He was so self-assured, every movement was smooth and confident whereas she was a shivering wreck.

She closed her eyes, trying to control the waves of sensation. Her heart was thumping so hard she thought he must be able to feel it. "Matt—"

"Have I ever hurt you before?"

"No, but we've never—"

"No is all you need to say. You don't need the *but*. If I do anything you don't like, or that makes you feel uncomfortable, all you have to do is say and I'll stop." His hand curved around the back of her neck and his lips trailed from her neck to her jaw, hovering tantalizingly close to her mouth. She wondered if he was doing it on purpose, teasing her, making her wait. Waiting increased the tension, and underneath the tension was excitement.

Her nerves and uncertainty didn't change the fact that she wanted him with every fiber of her being.

She didn't have the chance to speak because he lowered his mouth to hers, kissing her in a slow, seductive exploration that made her pulse pound. It was every bit as exciting as it had been the first time, and she gave a little moan and grabbed for the front of his shirt. This part she could handle. If only he'd stop at this, they'd probably ace it.

He pushed her back until her shoulders were pressed up against the door. She could feel the hardness of his thighs caging hers, and feel the thickened pressure of him against her. Trapped, she gave a little moan and wrapped her arms around the solid power of his shoulders.

Kissing Matt was a whole-body experience. She felt it right through her, little shivers of excitement chasing across her skin and sliding into her limbs. Her hands tightened on his shoulders, her fingers digging into hard male muscle. She was grateful for his strength because she wasn't confident she could rely on her own body to keep her upright. Fortunately, she didn't need to worry about that because he kept her clamped against the solid power of his body, holding her trapped while he kissed her. His mouth was hot and hungry, his kiss both demanding and explicit. His free hand slid upward, cupping the heavy weight of her breast through the thin layers of her clothing. It was the first time he'd touched her so intimately and she tensed. He paused and then dragged his thumb slowly over the tip. Sensation shot through her like a lightning bolt and she moaned against his mouth. The craving was so acute it was hard to stay still. She felt his hand tighten on her hip, holding her still while the other continued to tease every nerve ending in her body with slow, delicious strokes that left her shaking. She could feel the hard, heavy ridge of him pressing against her and still he kissed her, holding her trapped.

Suddenly, it wasn't enough. She wanted more. She didn't want him touching her through her clothing; she wanted to feel all of it and she urged his hand down to the hem of her shirt. Without lifting his mouth from hers, he flicked open the buttons and pulled off her shirt, so that all that was between her and him was the confection of silk and lace that Eva had insisted she wear. She didn't feel him unfasten it but he must have because she felt the soft slide of fabric whisper over her skin as it slid to the floor. And then he drew her deeper into the warmth of his mouth and she closed her eyes. His tongue slid in slow, delicious circles that sent her excitement levels soaring. Until that moment she'd had no idea that pleasure could be agonizing.

Without warning, he scooped her up and carried her to the bed.

He deposited her onto a downy nest of cushions and throws and she sank into a swirling world of sensation as he finished undressing her. Matt ripped off his shirt and she had a brief glimpse of taut muscle before he came down on top of her. The hair on his chest grazed supersensitive skin and then he was kissing her again.

The window was open, and the only sounds were the hiss of the sea as it lapped at the sand and the uneven tone of Matt's breathing as he kissed his way down her body and eased her thighs apart.

For Frankie, sex had always been a deeply unsatisfying

fumble in the dark, but the cabin caught the full force of the late-afternoon sun, the warmth of the rays spilling over her skin and spotlighting every inch of her naked body.

She felt the maddeningly gentle flick of Matt's tongue at the top of her thighs and tried to wriggle away.

"Stop!" Mortified, she tried to push him away. "You can't do that!"

"Why not?"

"It's too embarrassing—"

"It's embarrassing because you're not used to being naked in front of me? You'll get used to it."

"Matt, I won't, I—oh—" She closed her eyes as he touched her and a thousand bolts of sensation shot through her body. "You can't—it's daylight."

"That's not a reason to stop, that's an observation." The soft humor in his voice made her squirm but he held her still, keeping her hips pinned to the bed with his hands.

"Can we at least wait until dark?"

"If we wait until dark, I'll put the lights on. No difference."

"Matt—"

"Trust me. I want you to trust me." His roughened tone made her face burn. He eased his way back up her body and smoothed his hand through her hair. "Relax. You're safe, Frankie. I promise I'll always keep you safe." He trailed the tips of his fingers over silky, sensitive skin, his touch feathery light. He knew exactly where to touch her, how to touch her. And then he followed the same path with his mouth, until he strayed close to that secret part of her. She felt the warmth of his breath, the touch of his fingers and then the slow, expert slide of his tongue.

A moan left her lips and she clamped her mouth shut, shocked by herself.

Previously she'd always been held back by the past, but right now the past was nowhere. There was only the present.

Her hips shifted against the sheets, but he held her fast, his tongue exploring her aching flesh. He did things to her no one had ever done before, his wickedly clever mouth and fingers driving her excitement levels into the stratosphere. She forgot she was lying naked in a beam of sunlight, forgot that this was Matt, forgot everything except the squirming, delicious pleasure he created with the slow stroke of his tongue and the intimate invasion of his fingers.

She lay in that impossibly intimate pose, naked in front of him, and utterly vulnerable. She felt her body ripple and tighten as he urged her toward an elusive, mysterious peak. Pleasure escalated, reaching an agonizing pitch, and she felt her body spasm and clench around the pressure of his fingers. She came, dimly aware that she was crying out Matt's name and telling him not to stop, her body racked by shudders.

Finally, she lay limp and closed her eyes tightly.

She felt him move, easing up the bed so that he was lying next to her.

"Frankie—" His voice was rough. "Look at me."

Look at him? Was he kidding? She was never going to be able to look at him again. She covered her face with her hand but then felt his fingers close over her wrist, drawing her hand away. "Leave me, Matt. Seriously. Just—leave me. I'll make my own way home. We never have to look at each other or have a conversation again. Tell everyone at the wedding that I died."

There was a pause and when he spoke there was a trace

of amusement in his voice. "Just so I get the story right, what was the cause of death?"

"Embarrassment." She felt his fingers on her arm, stroking gently.

"Why are you embarrassed?"

"Do you seriously need to ask?"

Because she'd completely come apart in front of him. She'd yelled his name. She was pretty sure she'd begged him at one point—

Her face was so hot she could have charred a burger, and Matt curved his palm over her cheek, forcing her to look at him.

"There's nothing wrong with enjoying sex, Frankie. And there's definitely nothing wrong with you."

To her utter mortification she felt the hot scald of tears in her eyes.

Crap, *crap*, she never cried. Never.

"Look at me, Frankie—" He pulled her hands away from her eyes and cursed when he saw the glistening dampness on her skin. All traces of amusement faded. "Don't cry, honey. Shit, don't cry. I'm sorry if I embarrassed you. Next time I'll take it more slowly. We'll do it in the dark if that's really what you want."

"It's not you, it's me. I don't know why I'm crying. I never cry—" she scrubbed the heel of her hand over her face "—except I never knew I could feel like that. I thought I couldn't—I thought I was—I don't know who I am anymore."

He pulled her against him, wrapping her in his arms, enclosing her in warmth and strength. "You're the same person you've always been, except you've learned something new about yourself. We all find out new things about ourselves all the time, Frankie. That's not a bad thing."

It didn't feel bad, it felt good. All of it felt good and she wanted more.

How could she possibly want more?

She kept her face pressed against his chest, absorbing his strength and the male scent of him.

Tentatively, she slid her hand down his thigh, feeling hard muscle and rough body hair, savoring the differences. Then she covered him with her hand.

His breathing changed but he said nothing. Just lay there as she explored the thickened length of him, touching him in ways she'd never touched anyone before.

Her tummy clenched, her whole body consumed by an agonizingly sweet ripple of desire.

"Matt?"

There was a pause and then the breath hissed through his teeth. "What?"

"I want you." It was a simple statement but it expressed her feelings perfectly. She'd never meant anything more in her life.

He rolled her under him and his eyes burned like blue fire. He shifted his position and she felt heaviness and the intimate brush of his body against hers. The buzz of awareness was back, only this time it was a thousand times more powerful because she knew there was more to discover.

And she wanted him to be the one to show her.

His mouth brushed across her jaw, lingering, suggestive. "If you think that was good, I can't wait to show you how good it's going to feel when I'm inside you."

His words made her breath catch. The anticipation was so acute it was painful.

Feelings and emotions engulfed her, spilling over, drowning her.

"Matt—" She dug her fingers into the hard muscle of his shoulders. "Please. I want—"

He silenced her words with his mouth, kissing her with slow, deliberate skill until she was writhing under him. Just when she thought she was going to die of wanting, he eased his mouth from hers long enough to lean across and reach for something.

Her heart rate rocketed.

She didn't know which surprised her most, the fact that this was really going to happen or the fact that she really wanted it to. She'd been so scared to let this happen, but now the moment was here she couldn't remember why.

She wrapped her legs around him and pressed close but Matt took his time, sliding his hand down her body, teasing her with skilled, knowing fingers until she was so desperate she could barely stay still. Through the sound of her own breathless gasps she heard his voice close to her ear, urging her to relax and trust him.

She felt him shift position, and the anticipation was so shocking in its intensity that she held her breath. His hand slid under her bottom and she felt the intimate brush of his body against hers, and then he was inside her, entering her with slow, heavy thrusts, taking his time, allowing her body to adjust to the thickened pressure of his.

She hadn't realized she was digging her fingers into his shoulders until he paused.

"Breathe, honey." His voice was rough and raw. "I'll take this slowly."

She discovered that she didn't want to take it slowly and

slid her fingers into the silk of his hair, drawing his head down to hers.

From there it was nothing but sensation. She felt the skilled stroke of his tongue and the roughness of his jaw brush against sensitive flesh. She felt his hands, strong and purposeful, moving over her, positioning her as he wanted her.

Every thrust took him deeper, sending awareness and emotion rushing through her. She slid her arms around him thinking that this was Matt; Matt, whom she'd known forever.

The shock and wonder of it fused her brain.

She arched into him, wondering how anything could feel this mind-blowingly good. For the first time in her life she wasn't tense, she wasn't worrying that she wasn't feeling anything because now she was feeling everything.

He slid his fingers into hers and dragged her arms above her head.

She moaned his name against his mouth and he moved with a skilled, steady rhythm that drove her wild. She didn't have to think about what to do because her body did it by itself, or maybe it was just that Matt knew what to do.

With a blinding flash of revelation she realized that everything she'd ever believed about sex, and everything she'd believed about herself, had been wrong. She wasn't bad at it and she didn't hate it.

She loved it, and with the right person it felt perfect.

And Matt was the right person.

And as that thought settled in her brain, he thrust deep and brought pleasure crashing down on both of them.

Chapter Twelve

Surprise is the spice of life. Use liberally.

—Eva

Frankie lay with her head on Matt's chest, her legs entwined with his. She felt the graze of body hair and the solid weight of muscle trapping her against him. Her body felt heavy and unfamiliar, as if he'd taken it apart and put it together again differently. It had been less a slow seduction than a wild unraveling. There were aches and tingles she didn't recognize. Feelings she didn't recognize.

She'd never craved intimacy, but now she'd experienced it she wondered how she'd lived without it.

"I have a confession."

"Hmm?" His eyes were closed. He hadn't spoken a word since he'd devoted himself to disproving every belief she had about herself.

"I do like sex."

"No kidding. I may never be able to move from this bed

again. I'll probably live but it's too soon to be sure." His arm was locked around her, and she felt the delicious pressure of his leg on hers.

There was nothing in Matt's words to cause her anxiety, but still she sensed a subtle change in him that she couldn't identify. She decided it was probably down to her own inexperience. What did she know about the way men usually behaved after sex? Nothing.

"Are you wishing we hadn't crossed the line?" she asked.

He opened his eyes and turned his head to look at her, a ghost of a smile on his mouth. "Which line is that? I think we crossed a few."

She felt heat seep into her cheeks. "The line between friends and lovers."

"Ah—that one. No. Are you?"

She decided she could happily drown in those ocean-blue eyes.

"No." Looking at him made her feel dizzy with longing. "What happens now?"

"Right now? I lie here and hope my heart rate eventually returns to normal. I'll let you know when that happens."

"I'm being serious."

"Honey, so am I." He shifted onto his elbow so that he could see her properly. "What would you like to happen now?"

"I only have limited experience to draw on, but normally at this point the man says, 'Thanks, I'll call you,' and then walks out and never calls."

"I don't have the energy to haul myself across the room to get a glass of water, let alone walk out the door. And I'm naked." There was a wicked gleam in his eyes. "Which is a complication."

"Once you've recovered your strength it's still an option."

"It's not an option for me." He lowered his head and gave her a lingering kiss. "I've known you a long time, Frankie. I know you think relationships always end badly, but ours isn't going to. Stop thinking about it."

"Okay." She desperately wanted to ask him if he meant their relationship wasn't going to end badly, or wasn't going to end at all, but she knew that question was wildly inappropriate so she bit her tongue and said nothing. She was craving reassurance and hated the feeling.

He stroked his fingers gently across her cheek. "There are a million things I could say to you now, but it's not the right time."

So there *was* something wrong.

"Tell me."

He shook his head. "No." He eased away from her and her heart bumped.

She'd *known* he was hiding something. "I want to know what you're feeling."

"You're not ready to hear how I'm feeling, but let's just say I'm not going anywhere. Will you do me a favor?"

"I already did. Several times."

"Are you flirting with me?"

"I might be. But obviously I'm a flirting virgin so I'll need you to be gentle with me."

He gave a slow smile and lowered his mouth to hers. "I can be gentle if I need to be." And his kiss was just that. A slow, gentle stirring of her senses that soon had the blood throbbing through her veins. Just when she thought she was going to explode, he lifted his head. "Stop worrying, Frankie. Stop analyzing everything and enjoy the moment."

She wondered if the reason he wanted her to focus on the

moment was because he knew it wasn't going to last. Was that what he thought she wasn't ready to hear?

Crap, what was *wrong* with her?

She was in bed with the sexiest man on the planet, who showed no signs of walking out, but still she was lying here waiting for that to happen.

He was right. She needed to stop analyzing, and she needed to stop using her mother's butterfly approach to relationships as an example of normal.

"If all the moments are going to be as good as the ones we just had, I guess I could do that."

He hauled her under him in a possessive gesture and she gasped as he settled himself between her thighs.

He was the most gorgeous guy she'd ever met.

And he was in her bed.

Her bed.

She, Frankie Cole, wasn't a D minus.

With Matt she felt sexy and womanly and—

Happy.

It was the last coherent thought she had for a long time.

Matt stepped out of the shower, knotted a towel around his hips and strolled back into the bedroom. Frankie was still lying in the bed, the sheets wrapped around her legs, her hair a blaze of fire across the pillows.

Her eyes were closed, her thick lashes forming a dark crescent against cheeks the color of whipped cream. He watched her for a moment, feeling like a man who had misjudged a distance and accidentally stepped off a cliff.

He'd had good sex before, but what he'd shared with Frankie had been so much more than good sex.

He'd been focused on helping her discover something

about herself that she didn't already know. It hadn't occurred to him that in the process he'd discover something
about himself, too.

He was used to being in control of his life. He'd thought
he had *this* under control.

Turned out he'd never been more wrong about anything.

The knowledge shook him to the core.

Her eyes opened. She looked at him for a sleepy moment
and then her mouth curved into a sweet smile. "Are you
watching me sleep? That's boring."

Nothing she ever did could be boring.

He wanted to join her in bed, but he didn't trust himself
not to say something that would freak her out.

Knowing Frankie as he did, he knew it wouldn't take
much, and he didn't want those barriers to go up again. He
wanted her to stay like this. Unguarded. Trusting.

"Get dressed. I'm taking you to dinner."

"We bought pizza."

"I'm not in the mood for pizza." And he needed to get
away from the cozy interior of the cabin, where the intimate
cloak of darkness would make it all too easy to say something he knew she wasn't ready to hear.

"You mean like a date?"

He dressed quickly, before he could change his mind.
"It's dinner. Label it any way that makes you feel more
comfortable."

There was a pause and then she slid out of bed, her hair
falling over her shoulders in fiery spirals. "It's definitely a
date." She said it in a husky, slightly amused tone that played
havoc with his willpower.

He wanted to throw her straight back onto the bed, keep
her there and never let her go.

Shit. He was in trouble.

"Great." He backed toward the door, crashing into a small table. He caught the lamp before it fell to the floor. "I'll be on the deck when you're ready."

She gave a puzzled frown. "But—"

"Don't rush." Matt walked into the door frame and Frankie winced.

"Are you—?"

"I'm fine." His shoulder throbbed, but it was nothing compared to the rest of him.

He strode out onto the deck and leaned over the railing, staring down at the ocean.

Tonight it was calm, lapping at the beach in deceptively gentle waves. He contemplated diving into the chilly water, but Frankie emerged moments later.

She was wearing a pair of close-fitting black jeans and a green silk top that made him wish he'd taken that swim.

Instead, he drove her to the Ocean Club. The restaurant was crowded and lively and they were welcomed at the door by a pretty girl with a big smile.

"Matt and Frankie? I'm Kirsti. Ryan told me you might be coming. He said I'd recognize Frankie because she has amazing hair. And he was right—you remind me of a pre-Raphaelite painting. I studied art at college," she said by way of explanation. "We held a table for you, just in case. It's busy everywhere at the moment, partly because it's peak tourist season and partly because of the wedding, of course. You haven't been back in ten years, is that right?" She beamed at Frankie. "I bet you're glad to be home. If you can squeeze your way through the crowd, I'll show you to your table." She turned, ponytail swinging, and walked through to the far side of the restaurant where glass doors opened straight onto a spectacular terrace overlooking the beach.

Matt felt Frankie's hand slide into his and he turned to look at her. "Is this place all right for you?"

"I love it."

"The comment about your hair didn't upset you?"

"She paid me a compliment. You taught me how to accept a compliment."

He'd taught her other things, too, like how to match the rhythm he set, how to trust her body, how to trust *him*.

Her gaze lifted to his and he saw the same raw desire he was feeling reflected in her eyes.

The noise around them faded. He could feel his pulse pounding.

And he realized that coming here had been a mistake. They should have stayed in the privacy of their cabin, where he would have been free to do what he wanted to do without fear of being arrested. If they were living in the Stone Age he would have dragged her back to his cave and never let her leave.

Frankie squeezed his hand, her eyes questioning. "We should go."

For a moment he thought she was suggesting they leave and he was about to agree when she gestured to Kirsti.

"Yeah." His voice sounded rough and unsteady and he saw Frankie frown slightly before she tugged at his hand and they walked to where Kirsti was waiting.

"We have three big parties inside tonight so it's a bit rowdy. This is better for a romantic evening. More intimate."

Great. Just when he was trying to dial down the intimacy, he was given moonlight and candles.

He managed a nod. "It's great. Thanks."

The table was set at the far end with stunning views over the bay. A candle flickered in the center of the table, and the scent of flowers filled the terrace.

"The lobster is good." Kirsti handed them menus. "So is the salmon. I'll be back in a moment to take your order. You can start with a glass of champagne on the house, courtesy of the boss."

"Ryan's giving away free drinks?"

"Savor the moment. That's what love does to you. Turns your brain to mush, so it seems. And it's Friday night, too. It's going to cost him a fortune."

Frankie picked up the menu. "Will you be at the wedding?"

"I wouldn't miss it. I've been waiting for this to happen to Ryan for a long time. And I'm at least partly responsible for the fact he and Emily got together. Matching people up is my special gift and I always knew they'd be a perfect couple." Kirsti left Matt and Frankie together, pausing by a neighboring table to scoop up a couple of empty glasses and exchange a few words with a young couple and then disappearing toward the crush at the bar.

"She's a romantic, like Eva. The two of them would be best friends in under two seconds." Frankie scanned the menu. "I can't believe Ryan remembered me. I only met him a couple of times."

"You're more memorable than you think you are, Frankie."

She put the menu down. "Because my mom blazed a trail of destruction through the island."

"That's not what I meant. The place has changed. Moved on, just as we have. Look around you." He gestured with his head. "Do any of these people know what this place was like ten years ago?"

"I guess not. This building was a wrecked boatyard when I was growing up. Ryan has transformed the place."

"He's a smart businessman. This isn't an easy place to make money but he's tripled the number of visitors to the island since the Ocean Club opened. It's good for the local economy."

Kirsti arrived back at their table. "Olives on the house." She placed a small bowl in the center of the table along with their drinks.

They'd finished ordering when Ryan appeared on the terrace.

Matt rose to his feet and his friend clapped a hand on his shoulder.

"Well, if it isn't the city boy." His greeting was warm. "We're honored to have some New York style at our wedding."

He and Ryan had been at school together, met up infrequently when they were at college and had drinks whenever they were both back on the island.

Ryan's gaze settled on Frankie. "Still the same amazing hair." He stepped forward and gave her a hug and then turned to Kirsti. "Just checking you're not wrecking the place in my absence."

"You shouldn't be here! How's Emily? You'd better hope that baby doesn't come before the wedding."

Judging from his relaxed expression, Ryan wasn't too worried. "I hope it doesn't, too. We can't cope with extra guests. We already have half the island coming."

"More than half. Tomorrow is going to be a beautiful day and the beach is the perfect place to get married." Kirsti patted his shoulder. "Go home. Get some sleep. That's going to be in short supply soon."

"Thanks for the reminder." The two of them vanished toward the kitchen and Matt watched as Frankie picked up her drink and stared out to sea. The soft expression on her face was gone.

All it took was the word *wedding*, he thought.

"Can I ask you something?"

"Sure." There was a pause as Kirsti brought over their food and set the plates down on the table.

Matt waited for her to move away before he carried on talking.

"When I asked you to come here that night in Central Park you said no. You were adamant that you didn't want to do it. And then you changed your mind. Why?" It was something that had been puzzling him.

She lowered her drink. "It was because of Eva."

"Eva persuaded you it was a good idea?"

"No. It was a misunderstanding." She gave a wry smile. "We were talking, and somehow she got the idea that I'd said yes to you and she saw it as an example of facing your fears. For some reason she sees me as an inspiration for doing tough stuff. Can you believe that?"

"Why didn't you tell her she'd misunderstood?"

"How could I? Ev is struggling right now. She misses her grandma terribly. She's grieving." She was silent. "Look, I know I'm a fake. I'm not brave at all. I'm a coward. I'm not here because I want to face my fears. If it were up to me I'd happily carry on hiding from them. I'm here because knowing I'm doing something hard apparently helps my best friend get out of bed in the morning. That's all it is. It's not a big deal."

How could she think that? "I'd say doing the thing you find hardest because you think it will help your friend is a big deal."

"I'm still not convinced I should show up to the actual event. I don't want to ruin the wedding."

"Why would you ruin the wedding?"

"I'm not good at weddings, Matt. I know most people think they're happy events, but I don't see it that way. You probably think I'm crazy."

"I think you're someone who has seen the fallout of a bad relationship more than you've seen the good. And you saw it at an age where it made a big impression. If you'd been older, you might have had more examples to balance it out."

"I've stopped counting how many relationships my mother has had. Every time I see her break up with another man it reinforces my belief that relationships don't stick." She sighed. "Which brings us back to the wedding. What do I say to the bride and groom?"

"You just say that you hope they'll be happy. I assume you do hope that?"

"Of course I hope they'll be happy. It's just that—"

"You don't believe they will?"

She shrugged. "I've seen it go from dizzy delight to dreadful too many times to be able to have faith in it." She glanced at him. "This is the part where you tell me your parents have been together for almost three decades, just to prove I'm wrong."

"I'm not going to tell you something you already know. You're a smart woman, Frankie. There are plenty of examples of love out there, but when you've seen something different I guess that's what's in your head. It's hard to shake that off."

And that, he knew, was the biggest obstacle in their relationship.

"That's it exactly. That bride-to-be at the event a few weeks ago—she looked as if her life had crumbled around her. It reminded me of my mom after my dad walked out. Let's change the subject." She finished her champagne. "There's something I want to ask you. It's personal."

"I think I've already proved I don't have a problem with personal."

"Yeah, well, this is uncomfortable personal, not intimate personal." She hesitated. "You probably don't want to talk about it."

Tension rippled across his shoulders. "You want to ask me about Caroline."

"You were engaged."

"Yes. Until she had an affair with her college professor." It wasn't his favorite topic of conversation, but he didn't want her to feel there was anything she couldn't ask him. "It's not a secret, Frankie."

"Did you think about taking her back?"

It didn't mean anything, Matt. I was stupid. I want you to forgive me.

"For about five seconds, which was how long it took for my brain to kick in."

"Because of the affair?"

"Because she lied about it." He thought about the lies, the evasion, the complicated games. "If a person is willing to lie to you once, how can you ever be sure they won't lie to you again? The trust was gone. If there's no trust between two people, what is there? No relationship is perfect. No matter how much love there is, there's a strong chance you're going to hit rocky times at some point. Life is unpredictable. It can throw out the unexpected and the challenging. Coping with that requires trust and honesty."

"So she broke your heart, crushed it under her shoe, but still that hasn't put you off relationships."

He understood what she was asking. "That one relationship didn't work out, but that doesn't mean relationships never work out. One single experience isn't representative of all of them."

"I wish I could feel that way."

"I was lucky enough to see plenty of examples of good, solid relationships growing up. My parents, my aunts and uncles—I didn't have your experience."

"Aren't you worried you might get hurt again?"

"If I'm hurt, I'll handle it." His gaze held hers. "Whatever the reason, I'm glad you decided to come this weekend."

"So am I." Frankie rested her chin on her palm and stared out across the ocean. "Would you ever move back here?"

"No. I don't want to live in a place where someone holding hands with someone else is a major news story. And anyway, I love the city. But that doesn't mean I don't love visiting this place." He glanced out at the bay, at the boats and buoys bobbing. "It has a lot of good memories for me. A lot of firsts happened here. First time sailing, first time surfing, first time kissing a girl." That brought a smile to her face.

"Who was she?"

"*That* question I'm not answering."

"You're such a gentleman."

"We'll pretend that's the reason, because then I won't have to confess that it's because I was embarrassingly clumsy and bad at it."

"Can't imagine that."

"It was a while ago. I've learned a thing or two since then." They'd spent time together before but now everything was infused with a new layer of awareness and meaning.

Frankie put her fork down. "Can we go?"

"Now? You don't want dessert or coffee?"

"Yes, but I want other things more and it's all about priorities." Her gaze dropped to his mouth and Matt felt the intense heat of arousal rush through his body.

He stood up, reached for his wallet and dropped some bills on the table. "Let's go." He reached for her hand, clamped her by his side and walked through the restaurant as quickly as he could without knocking over tables.

At the bottom of the steps, he turned right instead of left.

"Where are we going?" Frankie kept pace with him. "The car is the other way."

"We're not going to the car. We're going to the beach."

"The beach?"

"You've never had sex in the cave. We're going to fix that."

"What? We can't!" She gave a disbelieving laugh and dug her heels hard into the ground. "Matt, we're not seventeen."

"Be grateful for that. It took me five fumbly minutes to get a girl out of her bra when I was seventeen. My moves are much smoother now." He pulled her in and lowered his mouth to hers. This time there was no resistance, no hesitation. She kissed him back until the blood was pumping in his brain. He felt her press against him and reluctantly he lifted his head "Can you run in those shoes?"

"If I need to."

"You need to. I don't mind everyone in the Ocean Club guessing why we're leaving our meal half-eaten, but I'd rather they didn't actually witness it." Locking her hand in his, he led her down the path to the beach.

"I can't believe we're doing this. When did you last have sex on this beach?"

"Honestly? I've never had sex on this beach but I'll try anything once."

They reached the sand and she stopped. "Eva will kill me if I ruin these shoes."

"Take them off."

"No way! I'll hit my foot on a rock and have to be flown back to the mainland for surgery. The whole island will know it was because I was on the beach having sex. I do not want to be anyone's cheeky headline."

"I'll carry you."

"If you do that you won't be able to see where you're going. Agh!" She squeaked in surprise as he lifted her and threw her over his shoulder.

"Put me down!" Laughing, she thumped his back with her fists. "Matt! You're behaving like a caveman."

"A man who is about to have sex in a cave is entitled to behave like a caveman." He strode across the beach, the wash of light from the Ocean Club above them illuminating the sand. He crossed South Beach, scene of numerous lobster bakes and drunken teenage parties and headed to the adjacent cove.

The sounds of the Ocean Club were drowned out by the sound of sea on sand, and he paused by the entrance to the cave and pulled off Frankie's shoes.

Only then did he lower her feet onto the sand.

Unbalanced, she grabbed the front of his shirt. "I can't believe you did that."

"No talking. Me Tarzan, you Jane. Get inside the cave."

"Tarzan lived in a jungle. What if someone else is in here?" She peered into the darkness.

"There isn't. They banned sex in here a few years ago after the lifeboat crew had to rescue a couple of naked teenagers who lost track of time and almost drowned. There was a town meeting where they tried to decide what to put on the sign. 'No sex, high risk of drowning' was voted out in favor of 'No nighttime bathing.'"

"So we're not supposed to be here?"

"We're breaking every rule in the book. How does that feel?"

"Surprisingly good." She wrapped her arms around his neck. "I've spent my life trying to live down my family's reputation but tonight I intend to live up to it."

He smiled, loving this new side of her. "Who are you and what have you done with Frankie?"

"Are you complaining?"

"Hell, no." He scooped her into his arms again and carried her deep into the cave, holding his phone out for light. "Which do you prefer? Grainy sand or sharp rocks?" His voice echoed and rocks glimmered and gleamed in the dim light.

"You make it sound so erotic." But there was a tremor in her voice, and her breath was warm on his neck. "Matt—" she sounded breathless "—what if we lose track and drown?"

"I'm a great swimmer." He lowered her until her feet touched the sand. Then he drew her top over her head and pushed it into his pocket.

"What are you doing?"

"I don't want to risk the tide washing it away and having to explain to the locals why Frankie Cole is walking along Main Street topless."

"If I'm taking my shirt off, so are you." She tugged roughly and buttons flew. "Oops."

"You're an animal." Laughing, he cupped her face in his hands and kissed her. He felt her fingers fumbling with his zip and moaned as she dropped to her knees in front of him. "Frankie—"

"I've never done this before so if I do it wrong, you'll have to tell me."

He braced his hand on the rock in front of him, his breath leaving his body in a hiss as she drew him into the soft warmth of her mouth. "Holy shit—"

"Am I hurting you?"

"No."

"Are you sure? Because I heard you moan."

He dropped his head onto his arm. "It was a good moan."

"Oh—" She sounded smug. "In that case there are a few other things I'd like to try—"

He was about to ask what other things but then she did something with her tongue that wiped coherent thought from his brain.

He tightened his fingers on the rock, the sharp edges digging into his palm. Sensation rushed toward him like a wave and he swore under his breath and eased away from her.

"What's wrong?" She sounded breathless and he had to force the words from his mouth.

"Nothing's wrong." It was a struggle to speak. "Just give me a minute."

She rose to her feet and he wrapped his arm around her waist and hauled her close, burying his other hand in her hair. He'd never wanted anyone the way he wanted her.

Sealing his mouth over hers, he dragged her jeans down over her legs and helped her wriggle out of them. Then he closed his hands over her bottom, feeling warm bare skin under his palms. All that was left between him and her was skimpy, silky underwear that proved no barrier at all.

She gasped against his lips. "Eva bought me that underwear you just ripped."

"Great choice. I approve."

She laughed, breathless. "You didn't even see it."

"No, but it came off easily and that's the main thing."

Her laugh turned to a whimper as he slid his hand between her legs.

"Matt—"

He trailed the tips of his fingers over the silken seam of her flesh and then slid deep. Her fingers dug hard into his hair and her breathing fractured.

"Oh, God—now—please—I don't want to wait—"

Still kissing her, he fumbled in his pocket for his wallet and she gave a murmur of protest that he smothered with his mouth.

"I'm trying to protect you."

"Oh—"

He could tell from her tone that she'd forgotten about that. He could easily have forgotten, too, if it hadn't been for the fact that protecting Frankie was big on his agenda. He never, ever wanted to hurt her.

He paused long enough to deal with the condom and then lifted her so that she straddled him.

She licked at his lips and trailed her tongue over his jaw. "If you drop me, I'll kill you."

"I lift concrete slabs on a daily basis. I think I can manage to hold one fragile female without having an accident."

"Fragile? You think I'm fragile?"

"I think parts of you are fragile." He smothered her words

with his mouth, shifted the angle of her body and entered her in a long, smooth thrust. Engulfed by the silky smooth heat of her, he closed his eyes. "Am I hurting you?"

"No! God, no—" She tried to move but he was the one in control, and he kept his mouth on hers and his hands locked on her hips as he drove into her.

This time there was no slow, drawn-out seduction, just a fast, frantic slaking of need.

He felt the first ripples of her orgasm tighten on his shaft and thrust deeper, hearing her cry out as they both reached that peak at the same time.

Slightly dazed, he lowered her carefully to the sand.

She rested her head against her chest. "We just had cave sex."

"I know."

"Standing up."

"I know." He stroked his hand through her hair. "And if you don't stop talking about it, it's going to happen again."

She lifted her head. "I want it to happen again, but not here."

"Where? In the back of the car? Up a tree? Name it. Happy to help."

"You've had sex up a tree?"

"No, but for you I'd manage it. Tarzan, remember?"

She was laughing. Breathless. "Let's go back to the cabin."

He didn't argue.

Chapter Thirteen

A wedding is an excuse to have your cake and eat it.
—Paige

Frankie slept deeply and woke late. If she'd been in her apartment back home in New York, she would have woken to the honking of horns and the wail of police sirens, but here on the island all she could hear was the sound of the waves breaking onto the rocks. She lay there in the delicious fog between wake and sleep, savoring the peace.

Matt's arms were locked around her and her legs were trapped between his.

Moving would have meant waking him, so she stayed still and that suited her just fine.

It should have felt strange, waking up next to a man, but it didn't.

She examined that thought for a few minutes and came to the conclusion that the reason it didn't feel strange was because it was Matt.

Yesterday when she'd arrived she'd felt nothing but stress and tension. Somehow it had all seeped away.

She'd had sex. Amazing, mind-blowing sex. And she'd done it again and again, not just in the bed but on a beach.

In a moment he'd wake, and she had every intention of repeating the experience. She studied his face in minute detail, pondering on what the dark stubble on his jaw would do to her sensitive skin.

She couldn't wait to find out.

Her phone lit up on the nightstand and she gingerly reached for it, trying not to wake him.

There was a text from Eva. A single word.

Well?

Knowing exactly what she was asking, Frankie grinned and texted back.

Well what?

Are you on your own in bed?

Frankie hesitated. This part she could share, couldn't she?

No.

A few seconds later her screen lit up again.

OMG!!! Random stranger or Matt?

"I hope you're not spilling our secrets to my sister." Matt's voice was sleepy and sexy and she turned her head, guilty.

"It's Eva. She wanted to know if we shared a room. I hate lying. Do you mind?"

"The fact that you hate lying is one of the things I like about you, remember? And they'll drag the information from you at some point so it might as well be now."

She put the phone back on the nightstand and snuggled closer. "What else do you like about me?"

"You want a list?

"Maybe. A short one."

He shifted so that he was on top of her. "I love your hair."

"Oh, please—you start with my hair?"

"I love it." He slid his fingers through her curls. "I love your freckles—"

"You're picking all the things I'm supersensitive about!"

"We're not talking about the things you like, we're talking about the things I like." He lowered his head and kissed her. "I love that you're so honest."

"Blunt."

"Honest. I like it." His expression grew serious. "I love that you'd come here, to a place that scares you, just because you wanted to support your friend. I love that you offer to stay in the apartment with her, even though you like your own space—"

"She told you about that?"

"Paige did. I love how smart you are, I love your sense of humor—"

"Do you love the fact that I'm a sex addict?"

"That's the best part." He kissed her and she laughed and wrapped her arms around his neck.

"You're entirely responsible for that flaw."

"If it's a flaw, I'm happy to take the blame for that one." He kissed her and she felt her body melt.

"How do you do it?"

With a groan he lifted his mouth from hers. "How do I do what?"

"Make me want you like this? I'm desperate. Again."

"I think you have a lot of sexual energy to use up. I'm happy to help you out."

"Your generosity is one of your best qualities." She gasped as he slid his hand under her bottom. "Do we have to go to this wedding?"

He stilled. "You don't want to?"

"I'm scared. I admit it. So far we've bumped into a few people and they've all been welcoming, but half the island is going to show up to this wedding. What if someone says something to me?"

"I hope plenty of people will say things to you. Things like 'great to see you back on the island, Frankie' and 'good to meet you.'" He lowered his forehead to hers. "Nothing bad is going to happen, sweetheart."

The endearment made her heart turn over. "You don't know that."

"I do. I'm going to be there with you the whole time. If anyone so much as looks at you the wrong way, I'll drop them headfirst in the ocean." His blue eyes gleamed. "You know I can be a bit overprotective. It's one of my flaws. I'm working on it."

"A *bit* overprotecive? Matt, I've watched you with Paige. You could get a part-time job as a bodyguard." She teased him, but deep down she loved that side of him. As someone whose parents had never given much thought to protecting her from anything, it felt surprisingly good to be with someone who cared how she was feeling.

"It's different with Paige. She's my sister. It was my job to

keep her out of trouble, whereas with you—" he shifted position so that he was cradled between her thighs "—with you
my purpose is to get you into as much trouble as possible."

"I had no idea you had such a bad side, Matt Walker."

"I keep it hidden." He eased into her and she moaned as
she felt the thickened thrust against sensitive flesh.

"How long am I going to feel this way? When am I going
to get bored?"

He lowered his mouth to hers and she felt him smile
against her lips. "Never," he murmured, "as long as I have
anything to do with it."

Somewhere in the deep recesses of her mind a tiny part
of her knew this was too good to be true; but what he was
doing to her, what he was making her feel, drowned out the
voice of anxiety. Swamped by sensation, she closed her eyes
and went with the fairy tale.

Matt stood under the hard jet of the shower and closed his
eyes. He would have dragged Frankie into the shower with
him had it not been for the fact that he needed a few moments to pull himself together. He'd wanted her to open up
to him, and she had. And the fact that she'd trusted him
enough to do so had somehow deepened the intimacy. He'd
been stunned by her response, but what had shocked him
more was the strength of his own. He didn't think his feelings for her could go any deeper, but it seemed he'd been
wrong about that.

What would happen when they were back in New York?
Back to their regular lives?

He wanted to freeze time and keep her here, insulated
from the outside world. He was almost tempted to skip the
wedding. He would happily have spent the rest of his life

holed up in this cabin with Frankie. The rest of the world could go to hell as far as he was concerned.

"Matt—" Frankie stood in front of him, his phone in her hand "—it's Ryan."

Feeling guilty at being caught in the middle of contemplating ways of getting out of attending his friend's wedding, Matt reached for a towel and took the phone from her.

Distracted by the tiny dip at the base of Frankie's throat, he listened as his friend outlined the problem. "I'm sorry. That's bad news." Struggling to focus, he averted his eyes. "So you're going to fly to the mainland? How long will that take? No, that's no problem, we'll wait here until you text us." He ended the call and Frankie looked at him expectantly.

"What's happened?"

He reached out and pulled her against him, kissing the smooth, pearl-like skin at the base of her throat. "We have another couple of hours in bed."

"That sounds good." She slid her arms around his neck. "Any particular reason?"

"Ryan and Emily have a mini wedding crisis." He moved her hair to one side and kissed her neck, breathing in the scent of her. "The florist has appendicitis and was flown to the mainland in the night. Unfortunately, she took the key to the store with her so there is no way of getting the flowers. They're delaying the wedding a couple of hours to give Zach time to fly across to the mainland and get the key."

"It's going to take hours to fly there, and what if she's in surgery and they have to hang around?"

"I guess that's a chance they're going to have to take. They don't have a lot of options."

There was a protracted silence and then she eased away

from him reluctantly and took a deep breath. "I'll do the flowers."

Knowing how much she hated weddings, it hadn't even occurred to him to ask her. "You?"

"It's their wedding day! They want it to be perfect. I'll do it. Call Ryan back." She stepped away, as if she didn't trust herself not to change her mind. "If I can't get access to the store, then I'm going to need to raid someone's garden."

"Frankie—" He knew that this was a big deal for her. Part of him wanted to explore the change in greater depth but they didn't have the luxury of time. "Are you serious?"

"I never joke about weddings, Matt." Her wry humor made him smile.

"In that case I'll call Ryan back." He cupped her face in his hands and kissed her hungrily. "I hope he appreciates the sacrifice I'm making."

"Stop distracting me!" She pushed at his chest. "Call him. And some clues as to what the bride is wearing would be good."

Matt made the call, half his attention on his friend and half on Frankie. She ignored the green silk jumpsuit she'd already laid out on the bed and instead pulled on a pair of yoga pants that fitted her like a second skin.

Her hair was still damp from the shower she'd had before him, and she pulled it into a ponytail and grabbed her purse. "Well?"

"Ryan doesn't know what she's wearing. Apparently, it's a closely guarded secret, but he thinks Brittany will know. And in the meantime Kirsti is sending out a text to all the islanders asking for access to their gardens. They have a system that they use in an emergency where they can text everyone. Islanders with flowers in their gardens are all responding to Ryan, and he's emailing me a list so that you can take your pick."

"You're telling me the islanders are giving me permission to trespass on their property and pick their flowers?"

"That's right."

"Has he told them it's me? Frankie Cole?"

"They know and I'm sure they're just hoping you can fix this problem for Emily and Ryan. What do you need apart from flowers?"

"I don't know—I—something to tie the flowers together. And I need to pack this wedding outfit because if I'm wearing yoga pants in the photos Eva and Paige will kill me."

"I'll put it in the car and we can change once we've done the flowers." He checked his email. "Take a look—some of them have already replied and listed the flowers they have."

She scanned the contents of the emails while she slid her feet into her shoes. "Brittany and Zach—is that the same Zach who flew us in?—they seem to have a well-stocked garden. Wait a minute—is that Brittany Forrest? Kathleen's granddaughter?"

"Yes. We can be at Castaway Cottage in ten minutes."

Matt hung their clothes in the back of the car, drove along the track that led out of the camp and took the road that led to the north of the island.

"I haven't had time to tame my hair. I'm going to look as if I've been in an explosion. Eva and Paige are definitely going to kill me. I was supposed to look groomed and elegant."

"You look sexy and gorgeous. The sort of woman a man might be tempted to drag into a cave for hot sex."

"Yeah?" She shot him a lingering look. "That's a look I'm not familiar with."

And he wasn't familiar with the slow, sexy smile she gave him. "That smile suits you. Want to pull over and try forest sex?"

"Focus! We only have a couple of hours and if you start talking about sex I won't be able to concentrate. You know weddings don't bring out the best in me. How many bridesmaids? Flower girls?"

"How would I know? I'm a guy."

"If I'm making hand-tied bouquets, I need to know the number." She pulled a notepad out of her bag and made a few sketches.

He realized that she was focusing on the flowers instead of feeling nervous about the wedding and being back on the island.

Castaway Cottage was a pretty clapboard beach house, and the front door was already open as Matt pulled up.

The ugliest dog he'd ever seen ran out to greet him.

"Jaws! Get back in here now!" A female voice bellowed through the doorway and Matt walked forward with a grin.

"Hi, Brittany."

"Matt!" She gave him a warm hug, followed by an anxious look. "Can you fix this? This is Em's big day and we wanted everything perfect. We need a miracle."

"I've brought you a miracle, and her name is Frankie." He turned to find Frankie on her knees making a fuss of the dog, who rolled at her feet in ecstasy.

Brittany raised her eyebrows. "Well, that's an unusual reaction. Most people take a while to warm up to our dog. Of course that's partly our fault for calling him Jaws, which isn't exactly a name guaranteed to endear him to people. I love him, but I'm the first to admit he's not the most visually appealing animal on the planet."

"I think he's gorgeous." Giving Jaws a final pat, Frankie rose to her feet. "Do you know any of the details about this wedding?"

"What details do you need?" Brittany filled her in. "Take anything you want from the garden. I want Emily's day to be perfect and we're all grateful to you for stepping in. Is there anything else you need?"

"Wire to tie the bouquets. And ribbon? Hair ribbon would do."

Brittany pulled a face. "Wire is easy. Ribbon, not so much. I'm not a hair ribbon person, but I know someone who is. I'll text Ryan and ask him to bring over everything Lizzy owns. In the meantime I'll fetch wire."

"That's fine. We can add ribbons later. What color is the bride wearing?"

"The bride is very pregnant." Brittany's eyes glittered with humor. "So she's wearing a cute cream dress. Our friend Skylar designed it."

"So we need to try and detract from the bump?"

Brittany laughed. "I'm sure you're great at what you do, but I can tell you that nothing on the planet is going to disguise that bump."

"Not disguise, but I don't want to make the bump seem bigger by making the bouquet too puffy."

Brittany led them around the side of the cottage and they followed her through a gate and into the coastal garden that hugged the back of the house.

Frankie's expression turned from surprise to wonder and she glanced at Brittany. "You're a gardener?"

"Hell, no. I'm an archaeologist. I'm more likely to kill the plants while I'm digging than do anything healing to them. This garden was my grandmother's baby. She spent every spare moment here. She passed away a few years ago, but one of her friends—our neighbor—still comes and tends it."

"It's beautiful. Calming. Unbelievable for a coastal garden—how does it survive the harsh winters?"

"No idea. You'd think all the plants would freeze like the rest of us."

"It's not the freezing that's a problem, it's the thawing. You want them to remain dormant." Frankie bent down and examined the soil in the bed nearest to her. "Seaweed mulch."

"Yeah?" Brittany glanced at Matt and grinned. "If you say so."

"It's great for the soil and the slugs hate it."

"Grams fought a constant war against slugs." Brittany pushed her hands into her pockets. "You think there's something here that can make a decent bouquet for Em?"

"Plenty. Is there anything you don't want me to touch?"

"Strip it bare if you need to."

"*Phlox Carolina*—the white one." Frankie walked toward the border closest to her. "We call it wedding flox. And there's *Leucanthemum vulgare*—" She was talking to herself, distracted, excited as she stepped eagerly into the garden, and Brittany raised a questioning eyebrow toward Matt, who shrugged.

"I don't know what that is, either, but no one knows flowers like Frankie so we can leave her to it."

"Great. In that case, I'm going to finish getting ready. Feel free to use the kitchen table to assemble your masterpiece. Yell if you need anything. And don't let Zach feed Jaws any of the bacon."

She left them to it and Frankie dug her sketches out of her bag.

Matt watched her. "What can I do?"

"Stand still and hold whatever I hand you." She moved around the garden like a butterfly, pausing, admiring, snipping and gathering.

In under ten minutes she had a large armful of flowers and foliage. "I can work with this. Let's take this through to the kitchen and I can start making up bouquets."

The kitchen of Castaway Cottage was the heart of the house. A large table dominated the center of the room, and shelves were adorned with driftwood, jars of sea glass and shells.

Matt could imagine Frankie sitting there, lost and confused by what was happening at home.

The front door was open and Jaws ambled in and out freely, trailing sand from the beach beyond. Sunlight played over the polished floorboards and the rug in striped blue tones added to the beachy feel.

It was at times like this when he missed the island.

In the height of the summer it was idyllic, but Matt knew that when winter came the place would take on a different feel. Snow would blanket the roads and the garden, turning it into a mysterious frozen wonderland. The community would be stripped down to locals and a few die-hard winter sports enthusiasts.

Zach put mugs of strong coffee on the table. "I cooked bacon and there are fresh rolls in the basket. Help yourselves. It will be a long time until you eat. I'm going to change." He walked out of the room and Matt filled a roll with bacon while Frankie worked.

"You should eat something. You must be starving after all that exercise."

"I'll eat in a minute. I have three of these to make."

"Give me a job."

"Could you cut me some lengths of string?" Frankie pushed it toward him and went back to work with the flowers.

He cut string and watched as she transformed a heap of flowers into a stunning bridal bouquet. Her fingers worked swiftly as she snipped stems and twisted leaves.

"For someone who hates weddings you're certainly good at this."

"This isn't about weddings, this is about flowers. And it's not going to be perfect. It would have helped to see the dress, but it's the best I can do."

Her best was impressive. She held up the bouquet, a froth of creamy white blooms with delicate floral tendrils tumbling like a train.

He knew nothing about bridal bouquets but even he could see the artistry in her creation.

"Wow." Brittany paused in the doorway, "You have real talent."

Frankie gave her a quick smile. "Thank you. One down, two more to go."

Interesting, Matt thought, that she accepted the compliment from a woman without question but whenever he did the same thing she floundered and flapped.

Or maybe it had something to do with the fact that the compliment had been work-related rather than personal.

Brittany poured herself a coffee and watched as Frankie tied the other two bouquets. "Awesome. Are you done? If so, we should probably get going. Half the island is waiting for us."

Matt saw Frankie's expression change. So did Brittany. "Is something wrong?"

"No. I—" She paused. "I haven't been back to the island in a long time, that's all."

"Is that a problem? Are you worried about not knowing many people? Because Zach and I can introduce you and—"

"That's not it. If people don't know me, that's probably better." Frankie put the scissors down carefully. "My family isn't very popular around here and the locals have long memories."

"Now I'm intrigued." Brittany finished her coffee as Zach walked back into the room. "What did you say your last name was?"

"Cole."

Brittany opened her mouth to speak again but it was Zach who stepped forward. He put his hand on Frankie's shoulder and gave it a squeeze.

"Whatever your reputation, it will be eclipsed by mine. I'm the big bad wolf of the island. They'll be too busy frowning at me to notice you."

"They're not that bad." Brittany tidied up the table, gathering up pieces of stem and leaves. "They've accepted you. Mostly."

"Exactly. I often feel as if I'm still on trial. They're waiting for me to step out of line." But Zach looked more amused than annoyed and Brittany hooked her finger into the front of his shirt and tugged him toward her.

"Just so we're clear, I love it when you step out of line." She stood on tiptoe, kissed him briefly on the mouth, then turned back to Frankie. "Don't worry about the locals. You will have a hero's welcome. And now we should go or Emily will start freaking out."

Zach raised an eyebrow. "I've never seen her freak out."

"She freaks out in a quiet, tense way, and I don't want her

freaking out. I don't want this baby arriving in the middle of the wedding." Brittany strode around the kitchen stuffing various items into her purse. "So there's a party tonight at the Ocean Club. I hope you're both coming? Dance until your feet ache and all that."

Matt wondered how Frankie would react to that but she nodded.

"If the locals haven't chased me off the island by then, that would be fun."

"No one is chasing you anywhere." Brittany placed the bouquets carefully in a box. "I texted Ryan and he's bringing every ribbon Lizzy owns. She's insisting on wearing a tiara and fairy wings. We'll meet him at the beach and make a decision about which is best." She glanced at them. "Are you guys going to change? Because you might as well do that here. Saves you flashing the locals in the beach parking lot."

Matt fetched their clothes from the car.

Frankie changed into the jumpsuit made of emerald-green silk, which made her eyes look luminous and brought out the bright copper shades in her hair.

Distracted, Matt fumbled with the buttons on his shirt. "You look incredible."

"Thanks." But her smile was anxious and he knew that despite Brittany's reassurances, she was worried.

As they pulled into the beach parking lot he turned to look at her.

"You're going to have fun, I promise. You look great, although random amazing sex would be easier if you wore a dress or a skirt."

"Callum Becket thought the same thing in tenth grade, which is why I never wear dresses."

It was the first time she'd told him anything specific about that time when she'd lived at home.

People were pouring past them on their way to the beach but Matt didn't move.

"What happened?"

"My mom had just broken up his parents' marriage. He was mad and full of raging teenage hormones. He seemed to think that as our parents were at it like rabbits, we might as well do the same. We were at the prom and he got two of his friends to hold me down while he stuck his hand up my dress. My new red dress. I'd been so excited about wearing it—" Her breathing quickened, but she must have seen the expression on his face because she gave a quick smile. "Don't worry—Paige and Eva appeared just in time. Without his friends, Callum was pretty weak. I almost broke his wrist. He couldn't write for a few days. But I decided I didn't want it to happen again so I gave up wearing skirts except when school demanded it. And I took up karate so if it ever happened again I'd be able to floor the guy with a scissor kick. And now I've probably scared you."

"Are you kidding?" What he felt was anger, but he didn't tell her that. "It's incredibly sexy having a girlfriend who can floor me with a scissor kick. Anytime you want to try that, go ahead."

"How is it you manage to make me smile about things I never smile about?"

He slid his hand into her hair and brought her mouth to his. "Callum isn't going to be here, in case you were worried about that. The Beckets left the island years ago, so there is zero chance of you bumping into him." He felt her relax.

"Good. Because I wouldn't have wanted to have to break his other hand."

"I would have done that for you."

"Really? You seem like a man who uses intellect and reason to solve most problems."

"That's always my first approach. But I've been known to revert to Plan B when the situation calls for it." He hid his anger behind a smile. "We should go. They're waiting for these flowers."

They walked down the path to the beach but as they rounded the corner, Frankie stopped.

"That's quite a crowd. I hadn't expected so many people."

"They're a friendly crowd, Frankie."

She stirred. "Let's hope so."

He hoped so, too, otherwise he'd be tempted to put Plan B into action.

Chapter Fourteen

Marriage is the triumph of hope over reality.

—Frankie

It felt as if most of the island had turned up at South Beach to see Ryan marry Emily.

The beach was a splash of color, with outfits ranging from swimwear to floaty silk. Chairs had been placed in rows on the sand, and the cries of the seagulls and the crashing of the waves were interspersed with laughing children and barking dogs.

Everyone seemed to know each other and Frankie stood still, poised on the edge, feeling like the outsider. If she lingered here, perhaps no one would notice her and once the ceremony started she could melt away unseen.

She was about to run that plan past Matt when Ryan spotted them. He strode across the beach and pulled Frankie into a hug. "You're the hero of the hour. You shouldn't be hovering at the edge of the beach—you should be right in the front row. You're our guest of honor."

Front row?

Frankie's stomach lurched. Sitting right in the front would mean there would be nowhere to hide. She'd be right there, watching while they exchanged vows. She'd be expected to wear a soppy, dreamy look on her face. It wasn't a look she'd perfected. "No! I couldn't possibly—you must have lots of people who—"

"Oh, Ryan is right, you must—" This time it was Hilda who spoke, and a pretty blonde woman with two children close by added her voice to the general atmosphere of persuasion.

"There's definitely room up there. I'm Lisa, by the way. I own Summer Scoop, the ice cream shop on Main Street. If you have time, you must pay us a visit. Ice cream cones on the house."

"Or we could buy a tub and take it home," Matt murmured in Frankie's ear, "and I could lick it off your naked body."

It made Frankie want to laugh, and in trying not to laugh she forgot to feel tense about the prospect of sitting in the front row at someone's wedding.

"Are you planning on doing that on Main Street?"

"It's possible. I'll try and let you know before it happens." Matt took her hand and led her to the front. Some faces she knew, and some she didn't. Some said how pleased they were to see her back on the island, some said how pleased they were she'd found flowers she could use for Emily. All were welcoming and friendly.

Finally, she slid into a spare seat in the front row. "I shouldn't be sitting here."

Matt sat down next to her. "Smile. You're going to have fun."

She wanted to ask how he thought she'd have fun when Hilda sat down on her other side.

"Remember, once an islander, always an islander." She patted Frankie on the knee before turning to talk to the woman on the other side of her.

Frankie glanced around, saw soft smiles and misty eyes and wondered what was wrong with her. She felt nothing except faint panic and mild nausea.

To distract herself she focused on the small group of children who were fidgeting and holding recorders ready to play and then on Ryan, who was standing with another tall, dark-haired man who looked familiar.

She was trying to work out where she'd seen him before when Matt leaned toward her.

"He's the Shipwreck Hunter."

"Excuse me?"

"That guy you're staring at, wondering where you've seen him before? His name is Alec Hunter. He's a historian. He presented that series on shipwrecks that kept most of the nation's women glued to their TV sets."

"Of course." She'd loved every moment of that series, and she'd bought his book. She was about to ask Matt another question when the crowd fell silent and the group of children started playing their recorders.

Because she was still looking at Alec, Frankie witnessed the exact moment Ryan turned his head and saw Emily. It was a rare moment of unguarded emotion. Everything he felt showed in his eyes. She wondered how anyone had the courage to give that much of themselves.

Emily finally reached the front and Frankie automatically checked the bouquet. Considering how little time she'd had, and the restricted materials, she was satisfied. The shape ensured that it drew the eye away from Emily's bump, not that either she or Ryan seemed to be disguising the fact that she was pregnant. Ignoring protocol, Ryan lowered his head to Emily's and kissed her until the little girl standing next to them gave his jacket an impatient tug.

Brittany grinned at her in sympathy. "Ryan, you're supposed to kiss the bride *after* the ceremony," she said, and the little girl giggled.

She was holding the posy Frankie had made; her blond hair was caught up in a glittery tiara, but what really made Frankie smile was the pair of fairy wings she'd clearly insisted on wearing.

Hadn't Eva had a pair at that age? Whenever they'd played make-believe games, Eva had been a fairy. Frankie had chosen elf or wizard.

Her mind wandered and she barely heard the words that Emily and Ryan exchanged.

Halfway through Lizzy started fidgeting and Ryan scooped her into his arms, holding her while he and Emily finished exchanging vows.

Frankie watched as the little girl's hand closed over his shoulder. Something about the way Ryan held the child made her throat thicken. Lizzy was at that age where she believed adults had all the answers, and that daddies were heroes.

Once, she'd thought the same.

Coming to terms with the realities of her father's human frailties had been part of her transition from child to adult.

She saw the way Ryan was looking at Emily and wondered if her father had looked at her mother the same way on their wedding day.

At what point had it all gone wrong? Had it been good at the beginning and gradually fractured or had there been flaws, weaknesses, from the start?

As she watched, Ryan took Emily's hand and Frankie

stared, mesmerized by their entwined fingers, slender and delicate threaded through firm and strong.

In the background she heard their voices as they spoke, but all she saw were those clasped hands. They were holding each other as if they had no intention of ever letting go.

And then the ceremony was over and Frankie saw Ryan slide his hand behind Emily's head and lower his mouth gently to hers.

He didn't kiss her. Instead, he said something quietly that was for Emily alone.

It was only because Frankie was seated so close that she could read his lips.

I love you. Always.

Always?

Frankie felt an ache in her chest. How could you promise something you couldn't possibly be sure of? What happened? Did love change or did people change?

She thought of her father, of promises and lies, and wondered when one had turned to the other. Had he meant the vows he'd said on his wedding day? Had he believed them and broken them or had he never really believed them in the first place?

She saw Ryan's hand slide from Emily's head to her bump and linger there protectively while they shared a look that excluded everyone else. It was the most intimate, private moment Frankie had ever witnessed, and for that single fleeting second she actually believed that this was real. It surprised her, but what surprised her most was the deep-seated hope that it *was* real. That these two people had something that could last.

She wanted to believe that, she really did.

And then it was over and there was laughter and clapping and people crowded forward to offer their congratulations in person.

Frankie stayed still, all the words jammed inside her.

Matt's hand covered hers. "Are you all right?"

Was she? She wasn't sure. Her head was filled with questions that she couldn't answer. She wanted to talk to him, because Matt had a wise and measured view of the world whereas she saw everything through a distorted lens. But this wasn't the place for that conversation. She couldn't sit in the front row at someone's wedding and discuss whether love was something that could really last.

Watching Ryan and Emily, she almost believed that it could. It was like glimpsing a patch of blue sky in the middle of a storm. And the blue sky spread, as the wedding turned into a beach party and the guests ate lobster steamed in seaweed and cooked in wash kettles over open fires using water from the ocean.

As darkness fell, Ryan slipped his jacket around Emily's shoulders and pulled her in for a dance on the sand. And when Lizzy tried to join them he lifted her, too, and they danced in the firelight, the three of them together.

A family.

Frankie felt something she'd never felt before. A yearning, a deep, aching, empty place inside herself she hadn't realized existed.

Ryan had provided a stack of picnic blankets and Matt grabbed two plates of food and guided Frankie to a patch of sand slightly away from the main celebration.

She curled up on the blanket, listening to the strains of laughter and music. Matt sprawled next to her. "Tell me what you were thinking back there."

"That this is the nicest wedding I've ever been to."

"That's it? That's all you were thinking."

She sat cross-legged and stared out to sea. "I've never really believed the whole happy-ever-after fairy tale, but Ryan and Emily seem so in love with each other."

"You don't believe they are?"

"I want to believe it." She picked at her lobster, wondering how much to say. "When relationships go wrong, do you think it's because they were always wrong or because the people changed?"

"You're asking me if people can be in love and then not be in love? Yes, I think that can happen. Life can put pressure on any relationship, but a strong relationship can survive it. My parents were under a lot of pressure when Paige was ill. They had some tough times, but they supported each other. I guess what I learned from watching them is that if you're honest in a relationship, if you're not afraid to say how you're feeling and listen to how the person you love is feeling, then you can work it through. You can find a way." He paused. "You're thinking about your parents?"

"I remember picking up their wedding photo once and thinking that they looked happy. I had so many questions about that photo. They were smiling at each other, as people do in wedding photos, and I wanted to know if it was real. Did my dad love her when they got married and then fall out of love? Or did he never love her?"

"Your mom never talked about it?"

Frankie shook her head. "At the beginning she was so upset and angry she couldn't say a good word about him, and afterward she didn't want to talk about him at all."

And Frankie had had questions. So many questions.

"You're not in touch with him, are you?"

"He sent me a birthday card when I was fifteen and I've heard nothing since."

There was more, of course, so much more, but at that moment Ryan rounded everyone up and the party moved up to the sleek surroundings of the Ocean Club, where cocktails and champagne were served along with delicious seafood.

Frankie noticed Alec Hunter again, but this time he was dancing with a beautiful woman with blond hair that poured over her shoulders like liquid gold. They were laughing together, and Frankie saw the flash of diamond on one of her fingers.

Everyone seemed to be in love, she thought.

People took that risk, time and time again. They jumped, even knowing that they could fall. She felt like a child shivering on the edge of a swimming pool, watching everyone else in the water, afraid to jump in herself in case she drowned.

Everyone was so much braver than she was.

"You're doing too much thinking and not enough dancing." Matt pulled her onto the dance floor, ignoring her protests.

"I'm not great at dancing—"

"That's what you said about sex and look how wrong you were."

She laughed. "Do you want to say that a bit louder? I'm not sure Hilda heard you."

"Oh, she heard me, and if she didn't she'll hear it from someone else. That's how things work on Puffin Island." Grinning, unrepentant, he twirled her skillfully and she landed breathless against his chest.

"I suppose you think that was smooth." She gasped as

he dipped her and then pulled her close. "Okay, that *was* smooth. Show-off."

"There are other things I could show you. Bigger things."

"That really would shock Hilda. You're a good dancer."

"So are you." He buried his face in her neck and she felt the warmth of his breath against her skin and closed her eyes. She'd never felt this way before, ever.

"I didn't think I could dance."

"I'm making it my mission in life to show you all the things you have wrong about yourself." His mouth moved to her ear. "Shall we get out of here?"

"I don't want to offend the bride and groom."

"The bride and groom left half an hour ago but no one noticed. The secret is to leave without a fuss." He took her hand and they weaved their way through the high-spirited crowd, through the door of the Ocean Club, but this time instead of taking the path to the beach as they'd done the night before, he headed back to the car.

He drove back to Seagull's Nest and opened the door to the cabin. "It's still warm out. Do you want to sit on the deck for a while?"

The deck was bathed by moonlight and the only sound was the soft crash of the sea hitting the rocks beneath them.

"I'd like that."

Despite the fact that she was tired, Frankie was in no hurry to go to sleep.

She'd been dreading this weekend, but now she wished it could last forever.

She settled herself into the nearest chair and moments later Matt joined her. He had a bottle of champagne and two glasses in one hand and a sweater in the other.

"Are you cold?"

"A little." She took the sweater gratefully and wrapped it around her shoulders, watching while he poured champagne.

"To you."

"Why are we drinking to me?"

"Because you saved the day and you survived sitting in the front row of a wedding. That deserves a toast."

She took a sip of champagne. "I never thought I'd say this but it was a nice wedding."

"But…?"

"No." She shook her head. "There are no buts. Not this time."

"You're saying you believe they might be happy?"

She smiled. "You think I'm crazy, don't you?"

"No." He tilted his chair back and rested his feet on the railings. "I think that stuff with your parents affected you badly. Your dad's affair—when something like that happens it's bound to shake your belief system."

It wasn't something she talked about, but for some reason it was easy to talk to Matt. He wasn't one of those people who thought listening was waiting for a gap in the conversation just so that they could talk about themselves. He didn't just listen, he *heard*.

"I knew about it, Matt." The words spilled out, as they so often seemed to do around him. "I knew he was having an affair. For six months before he finally walked out, I knew and knowing was horrible. I didn't know what to do. I was fourteen years old and I was in charge of a secret that could blow my family apart."

Matt didn't move. For a moment she wondered if he'd heard her and then he stirred.

"You never told anyone?"

"No. My dad made me promise not to say anything."

"He *knew* that you'd found out?" The legs of the chair landed on the deck with a thud. He turned to face her, shock etched on his features. "Frankie?"

"I found them together. I walked in on them having sex."

"Shit." Matt dragged his hand over his face. "In your house?"

"In my parents' bedroom. My mom was away and I was supposed to be staying out late for drama club but it was canceled so I came home early. Mom had given me a key. Dad didn't know that. I don't think they talked much by that point. So I let myself in and then I heard my dad moaning and I thought he was hurt or something so I ran upstairs. The bedroom door was open and I—" She shook her head. "It doesn't matter. Let's just say that they saw me so there was no pretending for anyone. I locked myself in my bedroom and my dad was hammering on the door. I don't know what he did with her. She must have left, I guess."

"Did you recognize her?"

"Vaguely. She worked with him. He made me promise not to say anything right then. He kept saying 'You don't want to break up our little family, do you?' and 'It's grownup stuff, Frankie, and you would never understand.' And he was right about that—I didn't understand. When my mom came home I stayed in my room and said I was sick. Which was true."

He took her hand, warming it between both of his. "You never told her?"

She shook her head. "I had this secret and it was so huge it was as if another person had moved in with us. It sat at the dining table, and lay in my bed. I could never get away from it." She stared out across the ocean, at the gunmetal sea and the dark shadows of the rocks. "I couldn't concen-

trate. My grades dropped. A couple of my teachers asked
if things were all right at home and I always said they were
fine, but in reality my whole world was crumbling and I
had no idea how to glue it back together."

"You didn't tell Eva and Paige?"

"No. They knew things weren't great at home, but I didn't
give them the details. I didn't want them to have the burden
of knowing, and also I think part of me still hoped that if I
didn't talk about it, it might all go away. I think deep down
I was still kidding myself that it might have worked out."

"It didn't."

"No. I often wonder what would have happened if I hadn't
come home early that day. If drama club hadn't been canceled, I would have stayed at school and I never would have
known. She would have left the house before I came home
and I wouldn't have caught them. I wouldn't have been in
this situation where I couldn't look at my dad across the dining table. My mom thought I was going through a moody
teenage phase and she used to send me to my room."

There was a pause and Matt's fingers tightened on hers,
firm and strong. "Are you telling me that you blamed yourself?"

"Not at first. At first I was confused because I'd thought
my parents were happy. That was the scariest thing. If they'd
had fights or seemed unhappy then I would have seen it
coming, but I didn't see anything at all. And it made me
wonder what I'd missed. I still do that. I look at couples and
I wonder what's going on beneath the surface. What they're
thinking *really*. Are they happy *really* or is it all a lie?" She
stared down at their hands. "After he left and my mother
fell apart, I blamed myself. I was scared. She was in such
a bad way I didn't know what to do. I just wanted her to be

herself again. I kept thinking that if I hadn't found him with that woman, maybe he would have stuck around. Instead, my mom decided to prove she had everything a younger woman had, and my life went from scary to embarrassing. And the worst thing was I missed my dad. I was mad at him, but I still missed him so much. I had this great empty hole in my chest. I thought we were close. I couldn't understand how he could just walk away from me."

Matt stood up and pulled her to her feet, wrapping her in a tight hug. "I'm glad you told me."

"I'm glad I told you, too." She breathed in the scent of him, soaked up the strength. "At least now you know why I'm a mess. I don't want to think about how many men my mother has been with since. She's like a butterfly, flitting from plant to plant, sucking the best from all of them. Do you understand now why I don't trust relationships?"

"I understand, but Frankie—" he eased her away from him and smoothed her hair back from her face "—have you ever wondered whether the reason you're afraid of relationships comes from what happened with your father, rather than your mother? He lied and cheated and then expected you to lie, too. He was the person you looked up to, and loved, and he let you down. It seems to me that's the relationship that damaged you, honey, not your mother."

She sat in silence, letting his words soak in. "But—"

"When the person you love and trust most in the world lets you down, where do you go from there?"

She stared at him.

Was he right?

For years she'd thought her problems stemmed from her mother's lifestyle choices. From the evidence that relationships were mostly fleeting and didn't last.

She thought about her father. He'd walked away without looking back, unimpeded by responsibilities or memories. He'd thrown them off like a snake shedding its skin, teaching her that there was no bond that couldn't be broken, no declaration of love that couldn't be withdrawn.

"You're right." Her voice was croaky. "Why didn't I see that? I was always closer to my dad growing up. He called me his 'baby,' his 'little girl.' If something happened at school, he was the one I told first. He taught me to swim, he took me sailing. He was like a god to me. When it all happened, at first I didn't believe it. I didn't know what to do. Every little secret he asked me to keep destroyed another part of our relationship. He made me part of his deception and I found that hard to forgive. I didn't know whether to tell my mother or not."

"You were fourteen. No fourteen-year-old should have to make that decision."

"I lost all respect for him and—" she paused "—I lost my ability to trust."

"Of course. The one person every little girl should be able to trust is her daddy." His tone was rough. "Did you tell her? Did your mom know that you knew?"

"No. She was wrecked after my dad left. Some days I stayed home from school because I was afraid to leave her on her own. She kept sobbing over photo albums, staring at every image, wondering if he'd actually loved her then or if it had all been a lie. It almost destroyed her that he had an affair with someone half her age. I was scared to leave in the morning and scared to go home after school. I didn't know what I was going to find. Paige and Eva took turns coming home with me. That went on for ages, and then suddenly she woke up one morning and decided enough was enough. She got her hair cut, lost some weight, starting taking things from my wardrobe—" She shook her head. "It was almost easier to deal with her being upset because that only involved me. This new version of her involved the whole community. She drank too much and twice the police chief drove her home. I wanted to die. And I started to hate the island. Somehow, over time, I managed to equate this place with all the bad things that happened. I couldn't wait to go to college."

"And how do you feel about the place now?"

Matt's arms were locked around her like a safety barrier, and she stared at the flicker of moonlight on the surface of the ocean.

The world around her looked different.

"I'd forgotten how much I love it. It's so peaceful. You could live here and not know a single thing that was going on in the rest of the world. Also, it feels different. Back then it was all about my parents, but this weekend has felt as if it's about me. About us. And it's given me a different perspective on the past."

"You mean talking about your father?"

"Not just that. I used to think the locals crossed the street to avoid me, but now I realize *I* was the one crossing the street because I was embarrassed to look them in the eye."

She leaned her head on his shoulder. "I think about it a lot. Whether I should have told my mother. Whether I should tell her now. Most of the time I think there's no point, but there's this big secret sitting between us like a wall and I can't get past it. Before Dad left I was so scared and confused, and after there seemed no point because by then she knew anyway, and I was afraid of making it worse. She hated my dad, and I was afraid she'd hate me, too, if she knew."

"They were both adults, Frankie. You were the child. You shouldn't have had to carry that burden and make those decisions."

She felt the stroke of his fingers through her hair. "You think I should tell her?"

"No. But I wonder if it might help you feel better."

She looked at him. "Your relationship with Caroline didn't stop you trusting?"

"No." His fingers brushed her cheek. "It shook my trust for a little while and maybe I'm more careful because of it, but my foundations weren't rocked in the way yours were."

She wrapped her arms around his neck. "You're not that careful. You're here with me. A Cole. We have a reputation for being unreliable heartbreakers."

His eyes glittered in the darkness. "Did I mention that I like to live dangerously?"

"Did I mention that I'd like you to rock my foundations?"

He raised an eyebrow and a smile touched his mouth. "Are you flirting with me again, Ms. Cole?"

"I think I might be but I still don't have much experience. I'm working on it."

"Happy to help you with that." He swung her up in his arms and carried her into the cabin.

Chapter Fifteen

She who dreams is not always asleep.

—Eva

Matt and Frankie spent the next day rediscovering the island, eating ice cream from Summer Scoop and buying gifts from Something Seashore, Emily's new gift store. Lisa was doing a brisk trade behind the counter but she gift-wrapped each of Frankie's purchases with meticulous care.

"Normally I run Summer Scoop, but Emily wasn't expecting to get pregnant when she set up her business, so we're all helping out." She measured a length of ribbon and snipped. "You've made some good choices here. Your friends are lucky."

"You have beautiful things." Frankie glanced around the store, her gaze lingering on handmade striped cushions and glass jars full of sea glass. There were so many items that tempted her, but she'd restricted herself to a basket of seashells that she was planning to use in floral displays, and gifts for her friends.

She wanted to buy something for Matt, but he didn't leave her side so there was no chance of doing anything secretive. The fact that he was so protective of her didn't irritate her the same way it did his sister. It made her feel safe, and loved.

Loved?

She frowned. Not loved. Cared for would be a better expression.

"Emily has a good eye, and she stocks the work of local artists whenever she can. Much of the stuff you see here was made on the island." Lisa carefully packed Frankie's purchases into a stylish linen bag. "Everyone wants to take a piece of the seashore home with them."

In the glass cabinet in front of her was a necklace of interwoven silver starfish. It was unusual and intricate.

Lisa smiled. "Pretty, isn't it? It's one of Skylar's. Do you want to take a look?" She reached for the key to the cabinet but Frankie backed away.

"I'm not a jewelry person. I'm a gardener. I spend most of my life up to my elbows in dirt. That's the reality of my life."

There was no place in her life for a starfish necklace, no matter how pretty. When would she wear it? It wasn't really *her*, although lately her definition of what was her had changed radically.

"Unless you're up to your neck in dirt, you could still wear a necklace under your shirt. It would be like wearing sexy underwear. Just because no one can see it, doesn't mean it doesn't feel good wearing it. It's original. A one-off. You won't find another like it." Lisa turned as a door opened behind her and two small blond heads appeared.

"Excuse me one second—these two belong to me. They're the reality of *my* life."

Frankie blinked. "Twins?"

"Double the trouble." Lisa gave a wry smile. "Meet Summer and Harry." She walked away to deal with the children, and Frankie reached for the bag, taking one last look into the glass cabinet.

The starfish necklace caught the light, twinkling against the bed of midnight-blue velvet, winking at her.

Ridiculous, she thought. She couldn't begin to afford it and she certainly didn't *need* it. She'd be better off buying a new pair of gardening gloves to replace the ones that were full of holes. Or a few new T-shirts.

What was it about being on vacation that made you part company with common sense?

She turned her back on it and left the store.

Matt followed a few moments later.

"That place is dangerous," she muttered. "It should be called Mega Temptation, not Something Seashore."

"Sometimes it's good to give in to temptation." He took her hand and led her away from the busy main street to one of the quieter roads. "Close your eyes."

"Why?"

"I have a surprise for you."

"I've already seen it. I was impressed." She nudged him with her elbow. "Hey, that was more flirting. How am I doing?"

"You're doing great. And now will you close your eyes? Humor me."

She closed her eyes and felt his fingers brush the back of her neck and an unfamiliar weight settle on her skin. "You didn't—" She lifted her fingers to her throat and opened her eyes. "You bought me the necklace?"

"It's intended to be a positive reminder of the island, and our weekend."

The weekend wasn't something she was ever likely to forget.

"You shouldn't have done that."

"You don't like it?"

"I love it." She was stammering. Overwhelmed. "That's not the point."

"The fact that you love it is exactly the point. And if you're worried that you don't have any occasion to wear it, then don't. I'll take you somewhere you can wear it."

He made her feel special. Or maybe it was the way he was looking at her that made her feel special. But underneath the euphoria that came from being with him, something else lurked. Questions. What did it mean? What happened next? "I don't know what to say."

"You say thank you. That's it."

"But—"

"You're worried it comes with strings attached? You think I'm giving you this so that I can have my evil way with you?"

"You can do that for free."

"Damn. If I'd known that, I wouldn't have bothered."

The humor in his eyes made her feel better and she stood on tiptoe and kissed him.

"Thank you."

She wished she could switch off her brain. She wished she could stop asking herself what it all meant.

They wandered back to the harbor and when they'd had enough of dodging tourists, they visited the house where she used to live. Frankie was surprised to find it looked different from how she remembered it. The freshly painted outer walls gleamed in the hot August sunshine, and a bright red swing took pride of place in the garden. She thought of all the times she'd returned home with a sense of dread, never knowing what mood her mother would be in, and realized that the dark times had colored the house in the mind.

"It feels strange being here. It's not how I remembered it."

"Things rarely are."

She stepped away from the house and breathed in the sea air. "I'm almost sorry to be going home."

"Me, too." Matt turned her to face him. "We can come back again anytime you like."

We.

The word made her catch her breath.

She'd never been a *we* before. Or an *us*.

It felt as strange and unfamiliar as the light press of the necklace against her skin.

Seeing her mother's life crumble had made her determined to forge an independent life, and she'd done that to the detriment of her relationships.

Before they left the island they made one more visit, this time to Matt's parents.

"Aren't they going to think it's strange you being here and not staying with them?"

"My parents understand that I don't want to have scorching sex under their roof, and anyway, they had a houseful of friends this weekend."

"That's what I remember most about your house growing up. It was always full of people and your mom was always cooking." But she wondered what Lillian Walker would think of the fact that her son was involved with a Cole.

As it turned out his mother was as warm and welcoming as ever, and if she guessed at the change in their relationship, she didn't comment.

They ate lunch in the pretty garden, home-cooked food that Lillian threw together with the effortless ease of someone who entertained regularly.

"How was the wedding?"

They talked about the day, explained what had happened with the flowers and the conversation moved from Frankie's skill with flowers to Urban Genie.

"I worry your sister is working too hard." Lillian glanced at Matt. "Not that she'd tell me, of course. She hides everything from us."

"The business is growing fast and she's working hard." Matt didn't lie. "But she's happy. And she's well. Jake keeps a close eye on her, but don't tell her that. He tries to do it without her noticing."

"Jake's a good man." Lillian served the food. "The number of times he showed up at the hospital when she was ill—I was thinking of booking him a bed." She paused, her attention caught by Frankie's necklace. "That's pretty. I remember seeing it in Something Seashore."

Frankie tensed. How did she respond to that?

How did she prevent awkward questions?

"I bought it for her," Matt said easily, and Frankie saw his mother's gaze linger on the necklace and then shift to her son, registering the significance.

"It's a pretty piece," she said. "Skylar is a talented artist. I've bought one of her photographs for your dad for his birthday." And just like that the subject changed and Frankie was once again reminded that Matt's mother was nothing like hers.

Lillian Walker respected her son's privacy and accepted his choices.

Gradually, Frankie relaxed, soothed by the warm family atmosphere.

"We're spending three weeks in Europe in late October." This time it was Matt's father who spoke. "I have to be in Italy on business, so we're adding in a little vacation time."

"But we'll be back for Thanksgiving," Lillian said quickly. "You know you're welcome. We'd love to see you."

Matt didn't hesitate. "I'll be here."

"Frankie, I hope you'll come, too." Lillian's tone was casual. "And bring Eva. How is she? I worry about her."

They'd always made her feel like one of the family, Frankie thought. In some ways she'd felt more at home in Paige's house than she had in her own. It was no wonder Matt had no trouble believing in love. He'd grown up with it right under his nose.

"Eva has her ups and downs but she's doing okay."

"She's lucky to have you and Paige." Lillian stood up and cleared the plates. "What time is your flight?"

"Four o'clock."

Michael Walker raised his eyebrows. "You'll be caught in traffic driving back into the city."

He and Matt argued for a few minutes about the best route, and Frankie helped Lillian clear the table.

"It's good to see you back on the island." Lillian opened the dishwasher and started loading plates. "It must have been daunting to come back after all this time."

Frankie wondered how she knew. "It was. But the reality wasn't as bad as I'd anticipated."

"I think that's often the case with life. Sometimes it's because we manage to inflate things in our head, but sometimes it's because we underestimate our ability to cope." She closed the dishwasher and straightened up. "You're a strong woman. Frankie. And you're very important to Matt."

Oh God, was this a warning?

Was she saying "Don't mess with my son"?

Was she thinking she didn't want a Cole anywhere near the family?

"I—"

"It's a relief for us. I try not to interfere, but I was worried that what happened with Caroline might have made him reluctant to get involved with a woman again. It's good to see you both looking so happy. I do hope you'll join us for Thanksgiving. I love having the whole family together." Lillian gave her a warm hug and then left the room to finish clearing the table.

Frankie watched her through the window.

She was the one with the problem, not Matt.

She saw Matt's father stand up to help his wife, in what was obviously a well-oiled routine. Partners.

Would she spend less time worrying about things going wrong, she wondered, if she'd spent more time seeing them go right?

They arrived back in Brooklyn as the sun was setting.

After the peace of Puffin Island, New York seemed frenetic. Normally Matt loved the pace and energy of the city, but right now he was wishing he was back on the island with Frankie, removed from the world in the cozy cocoon of their beachside cabin where nothing could intrude.

He'd learned more about her in the past three days than he had in twenty years.

He'd learned that she woke up early and liked her coffee strong. He'd learned that her insecurities hid depths of wild passion.

And he'd learned that she'd been carrying a secret for all of her adult life. A secret she'd shared with no one. Until now.

The significance of that wasn't lost on him.

Sharing had deepened the intimacy and connection between them, but it had also shown him that Frankie trusted him.

As they drove through the busy streets she grew quieter and quieter.

Matt glanced at her briefly. "Have you heard from Paige and Eva?"

"They have a baby shower tonight so they're going to be home late. I think Paige might be staying with Jake." She sounded distracted.

Matt was pretty sure he knew what was going on in her head, but he said nothing, instead concentrating on the traffic until finally they pulled onto their leafy street in Brooklyn.

It was a sticky summer night, airless and humid, and Frankie pushed her hair back from her face. "I miss the sea breeze."

"Me, too." He unloaded their bags and she took hers from him.

"Thanks, Matt. I had a good time."

"I had a good time, too."

Outside her apartment she paused and put her bag down, the keys in her hand.

Instead of unlocking the door, she turned to him. "My place or yours?"

He'd had no intention of letting her sleep in her place, but he'd been picking his moment carefully. The fact that she'd made the decision herself gave him a rush of exhilaration. "Are you planning on seducing me?"

"I'm not sure about seduction. I am planning to do bad things to you. Does that count?"

"That depends." He moved closer to her, trapping her between his body and the door. "How bad?"

"You'll find out." There was a naughty gleam in her eyes that he didn't recognize.

"Now you're definitely flirting."

"How am I doing?"

"You're doing fine." More than fine. He was so hot he was ready to explode. He released her and picked up her bag. "My apartment. That way we can take a drink up to the roof terrace and talk."

"You want to talk?"

"I'm trying to prove I'm not only interested in your body."

"What if I'm only interested in yours? Would that be a problem?"

Somehow they made it up the stairs. He just managed to close the door before he started to part her from her clothing. "You've turned into a sex maniac, do you know that?"

"I have a lot of years to catch up on. But I could point out that you're the one ripping at my clothes."

"I know." He groaned and shoved her jeans down her legs. "Any chance you could wear a dress with no underwear?"

"I'll think about it." She was breathless, her hand clamped behind his head as she urged his mouth down to hers.

He kissed her and lifted her at the same time, feeling her gasp against his lips as her back hit the cold of the door.

"Matt—" She was soft, tempting and unbelievably sexy and he'd never known feelings so intense.

He drove into her, his hands clamped on her hips and his mouth on hers. He heard her soft moan and felt the bite of her fingers in his shoulders as she tried to angle herself to meet each thrust. But like this, she was helpless. He controlled her and it was insanely erotic, the slick velvet heat enclosing the length of him. And then he felt the first ripples of her orgasm, each intimate movement of her body connecting with his.

Her grip on his shoulders tightened and he felt his vision darken as the intensity of her orgasm sent him crashing over the edge, too.

Recovery took a while and it was later, much later, after they'd showered together and exchanged more kisses under the cooling spray of water, that they took their drinks up to the roof terrace.

Sprawled on the soft cushions, they looked out over the night skies of Manhattan.

Matt reached for the beers he'd brought up with them. "To us." He used the word intentionally, and saw her gaze lift to his. He wondered if she was going to challenge him, but she didn't.

"To us." There was only the briefest hesitation in her voice and he pulled her against him and they lay together watching the twinkling lights of the buildings around them.

"I love New York City."

"Me, too. But I saw a different side to Puffin Island this weekend. And I forgot how lovely your parents are."

"Paige and I are lucky. When I was growing up, half of my friends used to find an excuse to loiter in my kitchen so that they could talk to my mother. She's pretty wise."

Frankie was silent. "Matt, that thing I told you—"

"You don't need to worry. Everything that happens between us, stays between us."

"I know. And I trust you." She relaxed against him. "This is the first time in my life someone has known everything there is to know about me. It's the first time I've ever been truly me with anyone."

"And how does it feel?"

"It feels good. Turns out I like the fact that you know me. It means I can relax. And I know you, too." She turned her head to look at him. "Unless you're hiding some great secret you need to share with me?"

Matt didn't answer.

He did have a secret. He had one hell of a secret, but he wasn't ready to share it. It was far, far too soon. He was afraid that if he gave her any indication of his true feelings, he'd drive her away.

And there was no way he was risking that.

"I don't have anything I need to share."

Chapter Sixteen

All you need is love. And chocolate.

—Eva

On Monday Frankie was back in the Urban Genie offices. When they'd started the business and realized that it was impossible working at home on the kitchen table, Jake had given them a corner of the impressive glass building that housed his company. So far no one saw any reason to change that.

"So tell us everything." Eva planted herself in front of Frankie's desk.

"Everything?" Frankie slid her phone into the drawer to hide the text she'd just had from Matt. "I'm not the sort of person who tells people everything."

But she'd told Matt everything, hadn't she? And she felt lighter for it, as if someone had lifted a heavy weight from her chest.

"I'm not *people*." Eva sounded affronted. "I'm your BFF. I've been there for you through thick and thin."

"She's going to burst if you don't tell her at least something." Paige didn't look up from her laptop, her fingers flying over the keys as she typed an email. "Give her a few morsels to tide her over, then we can all get on with this mountain of work."

"You make me sound like a puppy who needs a treat." Eva settled herself on the edge of Frankie's desk, sending papers flying. It was obvious she had no intention of moving until she'd had the conversation she wanted.

"You're more destructive than a puppy." Frankie leaned over to retrieve the papers.

"I need some romance in my life. I *deserve* romance. And if I can't experience it firsthand then I'm going to enjoy yours. *Please?*"

Frankie put the papers on the far end of her desk, away from Eva. "What makes you think there was romance?"

"You sent me a text."

"Careful!" Without looking up, Paige lifted a hand. "This is my brother we're talking about. I don't want details."

"I definitely want details." Eva rescued a magazine that was about to slide onto the floor. "Where did you stay?"

"Seagull's Nest."

"I know it! It's on the water, up by Camp Puffin. Idyllic spot."

"How do you know?"

"Because I'm addicted to looking at pictures of places I could never afford to stay. I saw a picture on Instagram. Someone went there on their honeymoon. Designer rustic. It looked romantic." Eva wiggled her eyebrows and Frankie sighed.

"Is that why you asked me to be here on time today? It's an inquisition?" But she was pleased to see Eva looking happier. She'd lost that pinched, tired look that came from too much crying and not enough sleep. "You told me you had something urgent to discuss."

"We do." Paige finished typing an email and looked up from her laptop. She looked tired and distracted. "New business. A rehearsal dinner."

"Another wedding?"

"Not the wedding. Just the dinner, and I know you've probably had enough of weddings to last you the whole year, but this time we need you to do the flowers."

"Who is the client? Buds and Blooms could—"

"No. We need the best, and you're the best. The client is Mariella Thorpe."

Eva slid off her desk with a gasp. *"Seriously?"*

"The editor of *Empowered*?" Frankie felt a flash of surprise, followed by a glow of satisfaction. They'd built their little business from nothing, and they'd turned into something good. People were coming to them. Important people with big budgets. "She's one of Star Events' biggest clients."

"She *was* one of their biggest clients. Not anymore. She's looking for events management and concierge services and she approached us."

"This could be huge." Eva did a pirouette and one of Jake's designers who happened to be passing in the corridor outside almost crashed into the glass window that separated their office from the rest. "As long as we don't mess it up."

"It's going to be huge," Paige said firmly. "And no one is going to mess anything up. Given that *Empowered* is one of the fastest growing women's magazines in the country, we need to impress her. She's thinking of doing a feature on us when she's back from her honeymoon. In the meantime, I need Frankie doing the flowers for that rehearsal dinner.

The team at Buds and Blooms is great, but they don't have your unique 'Frankie' signature touch."

"Flowers by Frankie," Eva said, and Paige stared at her.

"I love that." She scribbled a note to herself. "I'm going to find a way to use that. In the meantime, we need to give Mariella something no one else could give her. Can you handle it? I know Matt is keeping you busy."

"And we want to know exactly how busy." Eva sat back down on Frankie's desk and Frankie gave her a push.

"Sit on your own desk. You're messing up my files."

"I don't understand how you work with so much paper everywhere."

"I like to see things spread out in front of me. And I don't understand how you're so dreamy. We're all different."

Ignoring them both, Paige stood up and walked to the coffee machine. "We don't have long to pull this together. The rehearsal dinner is the last week of September. We're meeting with her at the end of this week. Can you be there or are you committed to Matt?"

Frankie felt her heart bump and then she realized Paige was asking about her workload, not her relationship. "I can be there. I'll talk to Matt and work around it."

"And now we've sorted out the work, tell us about the weekend." Eva refused to move from the desk. "At least tell us about the wedding. Was it very stressful for you?" The kindness in her tone melted Frankie's resolve not to tell them much.

There was no one in the world with a bigger heart than Eva.

"I thought it was going to be stressful." Frankie thought about gathering the flowers from Brittany's garden and creating bouquets on the kitchen table. "But in the end it was fun."

"Fun? Did you just say a wedding was fun?"

"People were welcoming and I didn't expect that. They treated me like an individual, not like an extension of my mother. And the wedding itself was beautiful. I liked the informality. There were dogs running around, and kids playing—" *And two people in love.* "It was about the people not the event. They managed to keep it personal and intimate and about them."

"And what about the rest of it?" Eva's expression was wistful. "You and Matt. Why didn't I see it ages ago? I guess because it was under my nose and you don't always see what's right there."

"See what?"

"The two of you. How perfect you are for each other. I mean, you need someone you can totally trust, and Matt is the ultimate strong, honorable protector—"

"That side of him drives me insane," Paige murmured, and Eva frowned at her.

"That's because he's your brother. You love that Jake is protective."

Paige thought about it and shook her head. "No, that pretty much drives me insane, too. I am not good about being swaddled in bubble wrap. It makes me want to scream. I want to be left to make my own choices, thank you."

"It isn't about having someone make your choices," Eva said quietly. "It's about having someone who cares what happens to you. You have no idea how wonderful it is to have someone who gives a damn."

"Yes, I do. And I'm sorry if I sounded as if I took it for granted." Paige closed her laptop. "You're right, I do love the fact that Jake cares about me. And I love the fact that Matt cares, too. But Eva, they care about you, too. We all give a damn. More than a damn."

"I know." Eva's smile was bright. "And then there's the fact that Matt is seriously *hot*—"

Paige returned her attention to her laptop. "No physical details, please."

Eva slid off the desk. "Romantic details would be nice. I've waited so long for this to happen." She leaned forward and hugged Frankie tightly. "I knew that one day you'd fall in love. I *knew* it."

In *love*?

Frankie stared at her friend.

"I'm not in love. That's insane." Panic uncurled inside her. "I don't even know how that feels."

Eva sighed. "It feels as if the whole of your life has been sprinkled with fairy dust."

Paige looked up and shook her head. "Get your butt back to work, Cinderella."

Frankie didn't smile.

Love?

"I have no idea what you're talking about. My apartment is covered in dust, but I don't think fairies put it there."

"I'm saying that when you're in love it adds a magical something to your life."

"How would you even know?" Frankie felt a rush of exasperation. "You've never been in love."

"That's how I know." Eva said sadly. "I haven't felt that way yet. I keep waiting and hoping. I dropped a parcel in the street yesterday to see if a handsome stranger would pick it up but everyone carried on walking. If it had been me lying in the dirt, they would have stepped over me. It's a sad world."

"It's a world that is pretty free of fairy dust, that's true," Paige said. "Unfortunately, there's plenty of the ordinary crappy type of dust that none of us ever have time to clean up since we started our own business. And talking of business, can we get back to work and focus on how we're going to impress Mariella?"

"You're on fire." Jake watched as Matt won another game of pool a few days later. "We could be in trouble, Chase."

"I was in trouble the moment I walked through that door." Chase snapped the top off another beer. "I pay more to you guys than I do in tax."

"I don't do it for the money." Matt potted another ball. "I do it to stop Jake's ego from inflating to unreasonable proportions."

Normally spending time with his friends soothed the tensions of the week, but tonight it wasn't working.

Nothing was working. Not even Jake's friendly teasing.

"Does my ego threaten your manhood?"

"My manhood is doing fine, thank you." Matt lined up the next shot and his friend gave him a speculative look.

"How was your weekend with Frankie?"

Matt lost concentration and the ball flew through the air.

Jake caught it one-handed. "You might want to put a little less spin on that," he said mildly. "I do believe that's a foul."

Matt straightened. "Are we seriously talking about fouls?"

Chase sighed. "If you want to live, Jake, I'd suggest you concentrate on the game rather than starting this conversation."

"I like to live dangerously." Grinning, Jake picked up his

cue. "I take it the weekend was good. So was it all garden design and soil samples, or did you sample anything else?"

"I'm not answering that. Maybe you should listen to Chase. He gives good advice."

"You just answered my question." Jake bent over the cue and focused.

Matt frowned. "No, I didn't."

"You are Mr. Good Guy." Jake paused and took the shot. "If there was something going on, you'd protect Frankie no matter what."

"Maybe there's nothing going on."

"Maybe, but then I'd have to find another reason for the smile on your face and your lapsed concentration, and right now I can't think of one."

"I had a great weekend visiting friends and family."

Jake straightened. "I've known you for over a decade. I know the look you get when you spend a great weekend with family. That's not it."

Chase shook his head. "Can we lose the tension? I didn't come here for tension. That's what work is for."

"This isn't tension, this is friendship." Jake stopped talking just long enough to win the game. "And I don't have tension in my work. Neither should you, given that you own your company."

"Try running a business started by your father. You don't have internal politics?"

"Only my own. You need to streamline your organization, Chase."

"Delegating works for me."

"So is it serious?" Jake looked at Matt, and this time his humorous tone had vanished.

Was it serious? On his side, yes. On Frankie's?

Maybe. Possibly. *He hoped so.*

Matt felt his heart lurch.

But he didn't know. She'd stayed at his place every night since they'd returned home, going back to hers only to pick up fresh clothes. But when he'd suggested she could pack a suitcase and move a few things upstairs, she'd resisted.

Apparently, she could spend the night, but her clothes couldn't. That added a significance, and a permanence, she clearly wasn't ready to think about.

He hadn't argued with her. He told himself that it was important to give her the time and space to adjust to the new level of intimacy between them. He told himself that if he was patient she'd realize that she didn't need somewhere to escape to, because she wasn't trapped.

He told himself all that, but there was still the one important fact he was never able to entirely forget.

Frankie had never had a romantic relationship she hadn't walked away from.

He was risking everything in the hope that her feelings for him would be stronger than her fears.

For him the risk was worth it, no question. But did Frankie feel the same way?

That was a big question.

Ignoring the ripple of unease, he glanced at Chase. "You're up. Do me a favor and win."

Chapter Seventeen

Before you hand over your heart, get a receipt.

—Frankie

The oppressive heat of August slid into the mellower heat of September. The tourist congestion eased, and locals gradually reclaimed their city.

New York Fashion Week came and went, and in between work demands Frankie and Matt explored the city that was their home.

They ate hot dogs while watching a baseball game, and sprawled on the grass in Bryant Park listening to classical music concerts. They strolled along The High Line, the elevated park built on a disused railway line, and discussed the planting and how they could apply some of the ideas to their own work. Occasionally Roxy and Mia joined them, and during those walks Frankie discovered just how smart Roxy was. She wanted to know every plant name, and not just the common name but the Latin name, too. And she never had to be told twice. She pushed Mia in the stroller, muttering about *Acer triflorum* and *Lespedeza thunbergii* under her breath.

They joined their friends for pizza at Romano's, and had movie nights up on Matt's roof, but the moments Frankie enjoyed most were the ones when they were alone. Their favorite place was Central Park and they explored hidden corners together, and soaked up the last of the summer sun on Summit Rock, the highest point in the park.

Work on the roof terrace was coming to an end and Matt had pulled his whole team onto the job to make sure it was finished before the summer weather flew south with the birds.

It was hot, sweaty work but Frankie had discovered there was nothing she liked more than getting hot and sweaty with Matt. Whether they were naked between the sheets or clothed on the roof terrace, being near him was exciting. She found herself stealing glances when she was sure no one was looking and he did, too.

Unlike her, he was never embarrassed at being caught.

Instead, he gave her a sexy smile loaded with a promise of what they'd be doing later.

Although her responsibility was the planting, she quickly understood that in a small team like Matt's, everyone had to be prepared to roll up their sleeves and she did so willingly. Everyone did the same, until the morning Roxy didn't show up.

They were all at the workshop, preparing to move the three log benches to the site, along with some of the custom-made planters, and they needed every pair of hands.

Frankie was feeling unsettled, thinking back to a conversation she'd had with Matt that morning. It was a conversation they'd had a few times. He'd suggested she move some of her things up to his apartment and she'd refused. He hadn't pushed her, but she knew that by refusing she'd hurt him, as if by holding back on moving her things she was holding back part of herself.

Why did it matter that she still kept her clothes downstairs?

Why did he need her to move everything she owned as well as herself?

Guilt mingled with exasperation, along with the uncomfortable suspicion that she was a coward.

She hated that feeling, but most of all she hated hurting Matt.

She lifted the pots into place, ready for them to be transported across to the job. Then she went to help James, who was struggling without Roxy.

"Did you call her cell?" Matt questioned James, who was hauling a bench into place.

"Four times. No answer."

"It's not like her. If we haven't heard from her by lunchtime, I'm going over there."

Frankie wiped her palm over her forehead and felt bad for Roxy. "You're going to give her a warning?"

"Warning?" Matt looked at her blankly. "I'm going to check she's okay. She's a single mother with a kid and no support. She's juggling a lot."

Frankie pushed her hair away from her face, feeling foolish. She knew Matt better than that. "I guess I'm still oversensitive about the whole job thing, having been laid off earlier this year."

"And it turns out you're a million times better off than you would have been if you'd stayed. Jake was telling me that Star Events is in trouble."

"They're losing big clients—" Frankie broke off as she saw Roxy appear in the door of the workshop. Her rush of relief lasted as long as it took for her to see that Roxy was carrying a wriggling toddler on one hip and a huge bag over her shoulder.

Matt put down his power tools and strode toward her. He caught the bag before it slid to the floor.

"What's happened?"

"Nothing. Everything is good, boss." It was obvious from Roxy's overbright voice that everything was far from good. "We just had a bit of a morning, that's all, didn't we, Mia? Fun and games all around."

"What happened to your face?" Matt lifted his hand and gently pushed her hair back from her brow, examining the livid bruise on her temple.

Roxy flinched away from him. "It's nothing."

"Mommy hurt," Mia said solemnly, and Roxy produced a smile that Frankie suspected she'd dug from somewhere deep inside.

"Mommy's fine, honey. I'm clumsy, that's all. I fell, like you do sometimes. Woops."

"Bad man," Mia said emphatically. "Bad man shouting." She covered her ears and shook her head so that her blond curls flew around her face.

Frankie saw Roxy's eyes fill, and Matt clearly saw the same thing because he immediately reached for the little girl and scooped her into his arms.

"Do you want to see something special, Mia?"

"Fairies?" Mia looked hopeful and Matt shook his head.

"Better than fairies. Butterflies."

Mia stared at Matt's mouth and tried to copy the sound. "Fies."

"Butterflies," Matt repeated. "Go with Uncle James. He'll show you."

Mia brightened at the thought of playing with James. "Play horsey?"

"Not here." James obligingly took the child from Matt. "Horsey doesn't want to put his knees on a chain saw. Horsey would never walk again. Come and see the butterflies."

"Fies." Mia grabbed a hunk of James's hair in her fist and they wandered out of earshot.

"Thanks." Roxy blew her nose hard. "I don't want her to see me upset. I know it's a lot to ask, but I was wondering if I could take the rest of the day off. There are some things I need to do. You don't have to pay me or anything."

Matt didn't answer. Instead, he took another look at her head. "Frankie, there's a first-aid kit in the drawer in my office. Were you knocked out, Roxy?"

"No! There is no way I was passing out and leaving my baby alone with—" She broke off and shook her head. "I'm fine."

Frankie hurried to the office and returned with the first-aid kit. She opened it up and found alcohol wipes and sterile dressings.

"I washed my hands while I was there, so I'll do it." She set about cleaning Roxy's head while Matt asked the probing questions.

"Headache? Nausea?" He watched as Frankie applied the sterile dressing and then closed the first-aid kit.

"You're worried about brain damage, but my mom always said I had no brain to damage." Her attempt at a joke ended in a sound somewhere between a laugh and a sob, and Matt curved his arm around her and pulled her against him in a brotherly hug.

"It's all right. You're safe now."

"I don't need help. I can handle this." A single tear spilled down Roxy's cheek and she made a furious sound and brushed it away with the heel of her hand. "It's dusty in here. We need to clean this place up."

Frankie could see that she was shaking. "Roxy—"

"Don't give me sympathy. I don't want my baby to see me cry." More tears glistened in her eyes and she blinked rapidly. "Say something annoying. Make me mad."

"No problem. Making people mad is my special gift." But Frankie moved so that she blocked the child's view. She wanted to hug Roxy, too, which surprised her because emotions usually sent her running. Maybe being with Matt had changed her in more ways than she'd thought. "What happened? What can we do?"

"I got involved with the wrong guy, that's what happened. I don't know how he found me, but he did. If he put half as much effort into finding a job maybe he wouldn't be such a loser." Roxy gave a disgusted sniff. "I'm not going back to the apartment. I grabbed what I could although I've probably left loads behind."

"Why did you have to grab your things, Rox?" Matt's voice was gentle. "Eddy did this? He hit you?"

"Sort of."

A muscle flickered in Matt's cheek. "You don't *sort of* hit someone, Rox."

"He shoved me really hard and I hit the wall."

"Did you call 911?"

"No. That would have made him mad, and he was already mad enough. I told him to get the hell out, and he got the hell out. I don't think he'll be back, but I don't want to risk it. That's why I need time off. I need to find somewhere safe for Mia and me to stay, just while I sort myself out. There's a mom at nursery I might be able to crash with for a couple of nights."

She glanced over at Mia again, checking on her constantly, but the little girl was tugging hard on James's hair as they studied the "fies," oblivious to the drama playing out close by.

"You need help, Roxy."

"Who's going to help? Eddy isn't exactly the type who lives up to his obligations. And even if he wanted to try again, I wouldn't let him. I promised myself I would never, ever stay with a man who scares me. I don't want Mia growing up thinking that's okay. I'm going to have to help myself. And that's fine. Totally fine." Despite the heat, her teeth were chattering and Matt tightened his grip on her.

"I wasn't talking about Eddy."

"Who, then?" Roxy sniffed and pulled away, her eyes widening as she saw the look on Matt's face. "You? You've already done loads, and Mia isn't even your kid. You gave me this job and your sister helped me find childcare."

"You can stay at my place."

"Hey, I've waited a year for you to make me an offer like that—" eyes glistening, Roxy gave him a playful punch on the arm "—and you do it now while my face looks like a rainbow."

"I'm serious, Roxy."

"So am I. It's kind of you Matt, but I can't stay with you in your fancy Brooklyn brownstone. I'm not that kind of gal."

"What you are is a good, kind, caring person who needs a break," Matt said. "So for Mia's sake, you're going to ignore pride and say 'Yes, Matt.'"

Roxy stared at a point on the center of his chest, her face set as she struggled not to cry. "You have a life to live. I'm not going to be a burden to anyone. And anyway, your cat would try and kill Mia."

"You can use my apartment." Until the words came out of her mouth, Frankie didn't realize she was going to say them. "It's safe and it's all one level, unlike Matt's. We won't need to do much in the way of childproofing."

She felt Matt's gaze on her and knew he was as surprised as she was by her offer.

Oh God, what had she done? She'd given up her beloved apartment. Her security. Her independence. Despite Matt's suggestions, all she'd left so far in Matt's apartment was a toothbrush. This was a huge step.

Anxiety rippled through her, and she tried to ignore it.

Of course she wasn't giving up her independence. And anyway, she already slept in Matt's bed every night. It was ridiculous to feel that keeping a few items of clothing in his apartment somehow changed things.

"That's kind," Roxy said, "but we take up a lot of space. Our things have a way of spilling over everywhere. And you told me you only have one bedroom."

Frankie felt her face heat. "I'm not using it right now."

Roxy looked puzzled and glanced at Matt. Then a smile spread across her face. "Okay, that's one piece of good news. *Finally.*"

What did she mean by *finally*?

Frankie opened her mouth to ask, but Roxy was looking anxiously at Matt.

"Before I say yes, you'd better tell me how much the rent would be."

Matt named a figure that would have covered a windowless basement in the roughest borough of New York.

Frankie felt a lump form in her throat.

Crap, she was turning into a marshmallow.

"We can go back to your apartment and pick up your things right now," Matt said. "Or you can give me your keys and a list and I'll do it myself."

"Are you my landlord or my bodyguard?"

A hint of humor lit Matt's eyes. "I'll be whatever you need me to be until you're back on your feet."

He didn't hesitate to help, Frankie thought, swallowing hard. He didn't think about his own comfort or convenience. He wasn't putting his business first, or trying to protect himself.

He was focused on helping Roxy, a vulnerable woman who had no one in the world.

He was a man in a million.

So why was she feeling so terrified because she'd given up her apartment?

What was *wrong* with her?

Something squeezed in her chest.

Roxy rubbed her palm over her cheek, undecided. "That's a really low rent. I don't want any favors."

Frankie's heart ached. If anyone needed favors, it was this girl, but as someone who had turned independence into an art form, she understood and sympathized.

"Right now that apartment is sitting empty," Matt said. "But I can't rent it to anyone else because it's Frankie's home and all her things are there. It makes sense to have it occupied, but there aren't many people I'd trust with it." With those few simple words he threw a bucket of water over the flickering flames of Frankie's anxiety.

He understood. He understood how she felt.

Frankie felt a rush of warmth and gratitude and all her worries seeped away.

It was fine. Everything was going to be fine.

"It would feel wrong," Roxy muttered, and Frankie stepped in.

"We all have moments in life when things are tough, Roxy. When that happens, it's okay to reach out and let your friends help. Look at it this way—one day you'll be able to do the same for someone else when they're in trouble."

"Pay it forward, you mean?" Roxy sniffed and chewed the edge of her nail. "I guess that makes sense. And you're right that I have to think of my baby. Her safety comes before my pride."

James walked back to them and handed over a wriggling Mia. "You're a good mom, Rox."

It was exactly the right thing to say and Frankie saw Roxy's cheeks flush.

"Don't get all soppy on me." But she straightened her shoulders and lifted her chin. "All right. If you're sure. I don't have much stuff, anyway."

"I can clear out some of my things." It made perfect sense.

Roxy needed somewhere safe to stay and it wasn't as if she was using the apartment much.

In the last three weeks she'd only been inside it to water her plants and pick up fresh clothes.

Matt held out his hand to Roxy. "Give me the keys to your apartment and a list of things you need. I'll pick them up so that you don't have to go back there."

"I'll go with you." But Roxy looked exhausted and the bruise on her head was turning an ugly shade of blue.

"I'll go with Matt," Frankie suggested. "You and Mia stay here with James."

Clearing Roxy's tiny apartment took less than an hour, and on the way home Matt stopped at the store to pick up a few things he thought she might need. Doing something practical helped to cool the anger simmering inside him.

Frankie sent the occasional questioning glance in his direction as she filled a shopping cart with food. "Are you okay?"

"Of course. Why wouldn't I be?"

"You're worried about Roxy. You want to remove Eddy's head from his shoulders."

Matt forced a smile. "Hopefully he won't come near her again, and even if he tries to he won't find her. It was generous of you to offer to let her use your apartment." The gesture had surprised him. After all the conversations they'd had on the topic, he hadn't expected it.

He pushed the cart to the checkout and started unloading it.

"Hey, it's your apartment. You're the generous one. Don't buy that—" she removed a little girl's outfit and two dolls "—you'll offend her."

"How will buying a few things for Mia offend her?"

"Because this is tough on Roxy. She needs to do it herself as much as she can."

Matt dragged his hand over the back of his neck. "I'm being overprotective again?"

"I love that side of you. And I suspect it will help Roxy to know her friends have her back. But I think we should be a little subtle, that's all. She's trying to be independent. We don't want her to misinterpret what we're doing and take it as a sign that we don't think she can cope."

"Good point." He put the outfit and one of the dolls back on the shelves. "What makes you so smart?"

"I was born that way."

"You were born sexy, too." And he couldn't keep his hands off her. Ignoring the fact that they were in a public place, he leaned across and kissed her. "I know you didn't want to move in with me. Tell me honestly—are you freaking out?"

"A little bit." She gave a half smile and he eased away, pleased that she hadn't lied to him but wishing her answer had been different.

"You've been sleeping in my apartment every night since we got back from Puffin Island."

"I know. But this feels—" she shrugged "—I can't explain."

"As if the door has closed? No escape?" He didn't need her to explain, because he understood. And the fact that she still didn't trust what they had hurt more than it should have. Telling himself it wasn't personal, he paid for the items and loaded them into bags. "You can escape anytime you like, Frankie. You can stay with Eva on a temporary basis if you'd rather."

Why the hell had he suggested that? The last thing he wanted her to do was move out.

She touched his arm gently. "I've upset you."

"No. Do I wish you'd move everything you own into my apartment? Yes. But I don't want you to feel trapped. I know this is a big deal for you, and I want you to know you're as free to leave today as you were yesterday." He kept it easy and casual, ignoring the fact that all he wanted to do was drag her back to his apartment and keep her there. "But I'm pleased we were able to help Roxy. That was a good thing you did."

"You're the one doing it." She helped him bag the items. "You've spent a lot of money, Matt."

"It's my money."

By the time they'd settled Roxy and the baby into Frankie's apartment, it was late.

James, who had taken to crawling around on all fours to be Mia's horse, announced that he was going to sleep on the couch.

"Why?" Roxy put her hands on her hips and glared at him. "You think you're going to get lucky?"

"No, but you had a bang on your head and you need someone to keep an eye on you. That's the rule with a head injury."

"I've had worse than this."

James stopped crawling. "Maybe. But I'm still sleeping on the couch. Ouch." He winced as Mia tugged at his hair and smacked her little legs against his waist.

"Horsey run."

"She's got one hell of a grip, Rox."

"Don't swear in front of my baby, you big oaf."

"Oaf," Mia said happily. "Oaf."

"Sorry." James looked sheepish and Roxy relented. "I suppose every horse needs a stable. I'll make up the couch."

"There are blankets and pillows in the basket by the bed," Frankie said and while Roxy went to fetch them, Matt took the opportunity to talk to James.

"Are you sure you want to stay? I'm upstairs if she needs anything."

"I don't think Eddy will find her here, but she's scared

and I don't like to think of her scared. I thought I'd hang around here for a while."

Matt nodded. "If he manages to track her down somehow and turns up, call me."

"Sure thing. You can come down here with that chain saw of yours and carve him into a more useful object. A doorstop, maybe."

Matt was about to respond when Roxy appeared in the doorway, her face pale.

"You don't have to talk about me as if I don't know what's going on here. I don't need a bodyguard and it seems I've got two."

"Three." Frankie took the pillows and blankets from her and put them on the couch. "I'm a black belt in karate. If Eddy shows up here he's going to wish he'd picked a different address."

"Karate? That's pretty cool." Roxy took Mia from James and cuddled her close. "I'd like to learn."

"I can take you with me next time I go." Frankie vanished into the kitchen and appeared moments later with a few plants in her hands. "These are toddler height, so I thought we'd put them upstairs. And I need to show you how the bolt on the door works because it's temperamental."

Matt handed Mia the doll he'd bought. "You didn't tell me it was temperamental."

"It's fine, but you have to bash it with your hand."

"Good, because I'm in the mood for some bashing." Roxy frowned. "You bought her a new doll?"

Matt hesitated, remembering the exchange with Frankie. "It's a gift, Rox."

"You don't need to do all this for me."

"I'm not doing it for you. I'm doing it for your daughter."

He knew that Roxy put Mia before everything, including her own pride.

Roxy chewed her lip and then gave a wobbly smile. "Thanks. That was kind."

Mia was ecstatic and insisted on smacking kisses on Matt's cheek until Roxy finally peeled her away.

By the time they returned to his apartment, it was almost dark.

Frankie arranged the plants on the windowsill in the kitchen. "Do you think he'll show up?"

"Her ex? I don't think he'd know to look for her here, but if he does James will deal with him." Matt consulted a recipe book and gathered the ingredients for a basic red sauce. He wondered how a man could father a child and then have no interest in raising it or protecting it. And in a way, Frankie's situation was even worse than Roxy's. Her father had walked out on a child he'd raised for fourteen years. What the hell made a man do that?

"Are you angry?" Frankie washed her hands and reached for a clove of garlic. "Either that onion has offended you, or you're angry."

"I'm not angry."

"You're upset about Roxy."

He stared down at his white knuckles and his fingers, clamped around the handle of the knife.

"Not just about Roxy." He put the knife down slowly. "Are you ever tempted to get in touch with your dad?"

"No." She took the knife from him and finished chopping. "I thought about it at first, but too many things happened. If we met up now it would just be awkward. I needed him back then, but I don't need him in my life now."

"I hate to think of you going through that."

"It's okay, Matt."

"It's not okay." The depth of his anger shocked him. "It's not okay, Frankie."

She shot him a puzzled look and put the knife down. "What's the matter? Normally you are Mr. Cool. I'm not used to seeing you like this."

He wasn't used to feeling like this. This dark, ugly cocktail of emotions was poisoning his usual rational approach to life. "You were left to cope with it alone. That's inexcusable." He dragged his fingers through his hair and tried to calm himself. "No parent should put a child in the position you were in."

"It was a long time ago. I've learned to live with it."

"Have you?" It was a struggle to keep his voice steady. "He's the reason you keep things to yourself and don't trust easily. He's the reason you're scared of relationships. Scared to move in here with me."

"I have moved in here with you." Her hand covered his. "And I do trust you."

He stared down at their entwined fingers. Her hand looked small and delicate against his and he felt a surge of protectiveness. "Do you?"

"Yes. I do. Calm down, Matt." She stood on tiptoe and kissed his cheek. "This will be hard for you to understand because your family is so different from mine but I don't even care anymore. I have no feelings for my father. He's a stranger to me."

"That's wrong on so many levels." Comparing it to his relationship with his own father, he pulled her against him. He didn't feel calm. He didn't feel calm at all. "I wish I'd been there for you."

"You're here now. And that's what counts." She eased

away from him and finished preparing the food. "What happened to Roxy's parents?"

"Her father was abusive. I think that's one reason why Roxy is determined not to go back to Eddy no matter what." He took the garlic from her, scraped it into the hot oil and lowered the heat. At this rate he was going to burn the food. He had to stop thinking about Eddy. And he had to stop thinking about Frankie's father. "With everything that happened today, I forgot to ask you how plans for the rehearsal dinner are going. I know it's an important event for the three of you." He tried to get a grip on his emotions, but it was disturbingly difficult.

"It's looking good. I was planning on going into the office tomorrow, but that was before most of today was wiped out."

"Go. I always build in extra time on every job. We can afford to lose a couple of days." Breathing deeply, he tipped in the chopped tomatoes and fresh chili and reached for the pasta.

They'd both widened their repertoire and it had become a seamless routine, cooking together and eating together. Sometimes they ate in the kitchen, but usually they took their plates up to the roof terrace and ate while watching the sun set over the Manhattan skyline.

Paige, Eva and Jake often joined them for their traditional movie night, but otherwise they were mostly on their own. Matt knew the others were busy, but he had a feeling they were intentionally keeping their distance.

Right now he could have used the distraction. "James and I will move the log seats tomorrow and there are a couple of guys I can call on to help if I need to."

"Most of the plants are arriving Wednesday, so I'll make sure I'm on-site for that." Giving him a searching look, she took the pasta from him and dropped it into the pan. "You're still angry."

"I'm fine."

She leaned against the counter, her gaze fixed on his face. "One of the things I love about our relationship is that we can talk about anything and everything."

That was true up to a point. They had talked about everything, from growing up on Puffin Island to their dreams for the future.

The only thing they'd never talked about were his feelings for her. Those, he kept carefully locked inside.

And it was starting to drive him crazy.

He had enough self-awareness to know that the intensity of his anger had its roots in the depth of his feelings for her.

He felt out of control and it unsettled him.

Aware that she was waiting for him to respond, he put a lid on the saucepan. "I love that we talk about everything, too."

And he loved her.

So why the hell wasn't he just telling her that?

He turned to her, saw the quizzical look in her eyes and lost his nerve.

What if telling her made her panic? What if she rejected him?

He had to wait for the right moment.

The roof garden was finished a week later, and Frankie stood back and admired their handiwork. They'd all put in extra long days and as a result they'd finished before their deadline.

Matt was hauling the last of the log seats into place and she wondered how watching him work could be so sexy.

Maybe it was the way his well-worn jeans hugged his thighs, or it could have been something to do with the way his shirt pulled against hard muscle as he hefted slabs into position.

He glanced up and his gaze met hers. His smile was intimate and personal, and she blushed slightly.

He was always looking at her, but that wasn't what unsettled her. It was the *way* he looked at her. As if they were the only two people on the planet. As if she was beautiful.

He made her feel beautiful.

Roxy strolled across the terrace. "Just makes you want to stop and gaze, doesn't it?"

For a moment Frankie thought she was talking about Matt's body, and then she realized she was talking about the roof terrace.

"Yes." Her voice was croaky. "It does. It's looking good. We've done a good job."

"Good?" Roxy stood next to her. "We're not just good, we're brilliant." In the past week she'd settled into Frankie's old apartment. There had been no sign of her ex.

James, who watched over her like a hawk, grabbed a bottle of water from the cooler. "The best there is."

But all three of them knew the real genius behind the roof garden was Matt. After working with him all summer, Frankie understood exactly how he had managed to build such a successful business at such a young age. He took jobs he knew he excelled at and he always exceeded expectations. If there was fault to be found, he found it himself and fixed it, and as a result he had happy clients and a rapidly growing business.

"Thanks, team." Matt opened his bag and took out his camera. He handed it to Roxy. "You have the best eye. Take some photos for our website."

Pleased to be asked, Roxy walked away and James followed her.

"So that's it. We're done." Frankie felt a little pang. No more roof terrace.

From next week she'd be back in the office with Paige and Eva. She loved her friends and she loved Urban Genie, but she was going to miss working with Matt nearly every day.

"We are done. And thank you." He offered her a bottle of water and she took it gratefully.

"What are you thanking me for?"

"For helping us out. We wouldn't have been able to do this without you."

"You would have found someone."

"But not the best, and I wanted the best." He tapped his bottle of water against hers. "We can pretend this is champagne."

"After hauling half a ton of soil around the place, I'd take water over champagne any day."

"I hope that's not true because I'm taking you to dinner tonight to celebrate."

"You mean like a date?"

"Not *like* a date," he drawled. "It *is* a date."

"Sounds good to me." She thought about how much things had changed in less than two months.

Then, she'd been nervous about having dinner with him, and now they were virtually living together.

With Roxy in her apartment, the option to move back downstairs had been removed.

At one time that would have panicked her, but not now.

There was a new intimacy to their relationship.

"So this dinner—am I dressing up?"

"You are. It's an excuse to wear your starfish necklace."

"I've worn it almost every day since we came back from Puffin Island."

"We should go back there soon. Make a trip to see the baby before the weather turns cold."

Emily had given birth to a little boy a few weeks earlier. They'd called him Finn after a friend of Ryan's, a photojournalist who had been killed while reporting from Afghanistan.

According to Ryan, mother and baby were doing well, and little Lizzy was so in love with baby Finn it was touching.

"That sounds good." Just how good, surprised her. Just as she was surprised by how much she loved being in a relationship with Matt. It made her giddy and dizzy with excitement.

She'd never had a long relationship before, but she was loving every minute of it.

When she was wrapped up in Urban Genie work, they talked and texted regularly and she found herself telling him all sorts of things she'd never told anyone before. Somehow Matt had become a key element of her life. She found herself wanting to share every little thing with him.

She'd been wrong to think that she wasn't capable of having a relationship, she thought happily. Wrong to think she couldn't trust.

It had been a gradual process, but little by little things had changed.

She trusted Matt totally.

She trusted their relationship.

She'd never been happier.

Chapter Eighteen

Life is like a seagull. You never know when it's going
to drop something nasty on your head.

—Frankie

Frankie was half-asleep in Matt's arms when her phone
beeped.

"It's Sunday morning. Who is texting me this early on a
Sunday morning? If it's Paige, I'm resigning." With a groan,
she reached out her hand and picked her phone up.

It was Roxy.

Warning! Your mom is on the way up.

Her mom?

"Matt, get up!" She sprang out of bed. "My mother is
here."

He eased himself onto his elbow. "It's a little early, but
that doesn't constitute an emergency, does it?"

"Yes! I'm naked in your bed and I'm living in your apartment." And she didn't want her mother to know. And the reason for that was too complicated to explore right now. She searched frantically for her clothes, some of which were strewn across the floor. In desperation, she grabbed one of Matt's T-shirts and managed to get herself jammed inside it. "This T-shirt doesn't fit. How can it not fit when it's too big for me?" She felt Matt's hands on the fabric as he carefully extracted her.

He did it the way he did everything. Thoughtful, calm and measured.

"You're trying to put your head through the armhole. You need to calm down. What's the panic?"

"The panic is my mother." Wishing some of his calm would transfer itself to her, she grabbed her hair, freeing it. "I don't want her to know I'm living here."

"Why?"

"Because she ruins everything, Matt. You have no idea. She'll embarrass me. She'll embarrass *you*—"

"Do you really think anything your mother does could change the way I feel about you?"

Something in his voice made her pause and glance at him, but his expression revealed nothing.

How could she explain that what they had was special and perfect and she didn't want it tainted?

"You don't know her."

"I've known her almost as long as I've known you."

"But you've never seen her in full flow. You don't know what she's capable of." She stumbled as she pulled on her yoga pants. "What is she even doing here? *Please* get dressed. If my mother sees your chest, I can't promise you'll be safe."

She closed the door between the bedroom and the living room and reached the door as her mother pressed the bell.

Crap, why couldn't she have a normal mother? Someone who called a few days before and arranged Sunday lunch?

Taking a deep breath, she opened the door. "Mom! This is a surprise." So was the realization that she'd forgotten her underwear. She was naked under her yoga pants and her breasts were loose and free.

Fortunately, her mother seemed distracted. "I went downstairs first. You didn't tell me you'd moved."

"It's only temporary—"

"You lent your apartment to that sweet girl with the baby. I know. I apologized for waking her, but she told me that she'd been up since five."

Frankie wondered what else Roxy had told her mother. "What are you doing here, Mom?"

"You're my daughter!" Her mother's voice rose. "Do I need an excuse to visit my daughter?"

"It's eight o'clock on a Sunday morning."

"You're always up early. You were the same when you were little. You and your father, thick as thieves, giggling away as you planned your adventure for the day." It sounded like an accusation, and Frankie tensed in anticipation of the conversation that lay ahead.

Were they going to be revisiting the past or was this about the present? More excruciating details of her mother's current relationship?

"Come in. I'll make some coffee."

"Thank you." Her mother's tone was brittle and she was paler than usual. "What are you wearing? It looks like something you bought in a man's store. It swamps you."

Given that it was Matt's T-shirt, Frankie decided not to answer that. "Are you hungry?"

"Starving, but I don't want to eat. I have this body because I watch what I eat. I look after myself. I exercise, I have a really tight butt—"

Frankie cringed and hoped Matt wasn't listening. "You're looking great, Mom."

"So why do men leave me?" Her mother's face crumpled. "Why do men always leave me? What do I do wrong?"

Frankie froze, caught unawares by the sudden eruption of emotions. "Dev left you?"

"He said he wanted to find someone his own age who could give him babies. I told him having kids is overrated but he wouldn't listen to me."

Frankie wondered why remarks like that still upset her. "I didn't know you were serious about him."

"Neither did I. But it turns out I am. We had fun together." She started to sob and the sound hammered away at the barrier Frankie had erected between herself and her mother.

"Don't cry. Please don't cry." Shaking, she put her arms around her mother and guided her to the sofa. Listening to her sobs made her chest ache. She was right back there, fourteen years old and faced with a parent who could barely drag herself out of bed every morning. "Everything's going to be okay."

"How can it be? I'm fifty-four next month. Fifty-four. My life is over."

"It's not over, Mom."

"I will never, ever find a man I can depend on." She flung her arms around Frankie, enveloping her like an octopus as she sobbed onto her shoulder. "You're the sensible one, not me. You've built a life that doesn't involve men. You have a great job, lovely friends and most of all you're independent. You never, ever give away your heart. You have more sense."

Frankie thought about Matt, getting dressed in the next room.

She thought about all the things they'd shared. The deeply personal parts of herself and her life that she'd revealed to him and she desperately tried to block out the small, traitorous voice inside her that was telling her to listen to her mother.

"Mom—"

"What? You're going to tell me this is my own fault for getting involved. And you'd be right." She blew her nose hard. "You're right to avoid relationships, Frankie. This is what they do to you." The tears flowed and Frankie held her mother while she cried, just as she'd done all those years before.

She tried to block the emotions, or at least filter them, but familiar feelings flowed back through her, an ugly mix of panic and helplessness. "Don't cry, Mom. He's not worth it."

"I know." But still she cried and still Frankie held her, her brain and her heart numb.

Matt appeared, holding coffee.

Over her mother's head, her gaze met his.

He looked rumpled and sexy and she felt dizzy with longing.

She wanted to run to him and feel those strong arms close around her, protecting her from thoughts she didn't want to have. Instead of the voice inside her, she wanted to hear *his* voice telling her in a calm, rational way that everything was going to be okay. And that in itself was terrifying.

She'd worked hard to ensure she didn't need reassurance from anyone but herself.

She protected herself. That was what she did. That was how she lived.

What did it matter whether her issues came from her father or her mother? Nothing changed the fact that they were there.

How had she let herself get this involved? Being with Matt had melted away the protective shell she'd worn for most of her life, and now instead of feeling strong she felt exposed and vulnerable.

Panic rippled through her.

What had she done?

"I should be going." Gina peeled herself away from Frankie. "I just wanted you to know that I'll be moving in with Brad so I have a new address."

Frankie was barely listening. "Who is Brad?"

"He owns the restaurant where Dev and I ate all the time. He saw how upset I was and offered me a room. Don't look at me like that, Francesca." She sniffed and took another tissue from the box. "I've finally learned my lesson. This is temporary."

Until the next person came along, Frankie thought.

Matt must have seen something in her face because he put the coffee down and walked across the room.

"I'll call you a cab, Gina."

"Oh, Matt. Always so strong and protective. I wish we could clone you." Her mother stood up and picked up her purse. "I'll be in touch, Frankie."

"Yes." Frankie's lips felt numb. All of her felt numb.

The happy, euphoric feeling had evaporated. It was as

if her mother had crawled inside her head and stamped all over her dreams.

Relationships went wrong. It was a fact of life. Even Matt couldn't argue with that.

And when it went wrong she'd lose all this. Every single thing that mattered to her.

How would she cope with it?

She'd be so much worse off than she'd been before, because she wouldn't even have Matt's friendship and she couldn't imagine how bleak her life would look without him in it.

She sat, immobilized by her own dark thoughts.

She heard the door open and close, and then came the sound of Matt's footsteps on the wooden floor.

Still, she didn't move. Said nothing until he dropped into a crouch in front of her.

"Talk to me."

What was she supposed to say? She looked at him, her brain so infected by panic she couldn't think straight. "What about?"

"I want to know what she said to you. Every word." He was steady and calm. "And I want to know what you're thinking."

"I'm thinking that you should be with Eva." The misery rolled over her like the tide enveloping a beach. A strand of hair flopped over her eyes but she didn't even bother pushing it away. "She's romantic like you. She thinks people mate for life, like ducks as she always says. You should go swim in the pond with her."

"There's only one thing wrong with that plan." Gently, he tucked the misbehaving strand of hair behind her ear. "I'm not in love with Eva."

"You should be. She's perfect for you. The pair of you could dance off into the sunset, tripping over happy-ever-afters for the rest of your life, singing like a couple of fairy-tale characters with little blue birds fluttering everywhere."

"The person who is perfect for you is the person you're in love with." Matt's thumb stroked gently over her cheek. "That's you, Frankie."

She couldn't breathe.

Was he saying—?

Did he mean—?

Now it was her heart that was fluttering. "Don't say that, Matt." Her voice cracked. If she'd felt panic before, she felt terror now. "Don't spoil everything." She felt as if she was poised on the edge of a cliff and he was about to push her off.

"How does telling you that I love you spoil everything?" His tone hadn't changed but there was a tension in the air that hadn't been there before. "I know I haven't said it until now, but I thought you'd guessed how I felt."

"I didn't—" The panic was lodged in her throat. "I can't. You're crazy."

"I happen to think I'm lucky, not crazy."

"Lucky? To be screwing a mixed-up person like me?"

"I'm not screwing you." His hand slid behind her neck, gentle but firm at the same time. "I've never screwed you, Frankie. I've made love to you. Over and over again."

Her tummy flipped. "Same thing. Just fancier words."

He pulled her to her feet and curved his arms around her. "*Not* the same thing."

"You'll change your mind once you get to know me."

"I know you, Frankie. And I'm not going to change my mind." He smoothed his hand over her hair and took a deep breath. "I hadn't planned on saying this now. I was waiting for the right moment, but I don't even know what the right moment looks like, so maybe right now is as good a time as any."

It wasn't a good time. It was the worst possible time. She tried desperately to stop him talking.

"Matt, please—I don't want to—"

"I can't tell you exactly when I woke up and realized I was in love with you, but it was a long time ago."

He'd been in love with her for a long time?

Her emotions tumbled over themselves, so many different ones she could no longer untangle them. Fear, trepidation and excitement were there and, underneath, a deep, primal thrill that came from the knowledge that this man loved her. "How long?"

"I've been in love with you for years, and I thought I knew you really well. And then I discovered I'd barely scratched the surface."

"You mean you discovered all the things I'm hiding. I'm surprised you didn't run a mile."

"You were carrying around all these feelings and secrets and finding out about those has made me care more, not less."

"Because you felt sorry for me?"

"Because you're the person I always knew you were. Sensitive, gentle, funny, generous and very, very sexy. I know you, and I know I love you. The only thing I don't know is how you feel." There was a long pause loaded with meaning and expectation and then he eased her away from him. "This would be a good moment for you to tell me."

No, it wasn't. It was a bad moment. A really bad moment.

"I—" Oh God, how *did* she feel? Excited, panicked,

sick—a horrible cocktail of stomach-churning emotions that she couldn't disentangle.

"Frankie?" He was patient, but she knew what he was waiting to hear. And she sensed something else, too. A tension, a taut pressure, that she'd never seen in him before.

He'd asked her a serious question and he deserved an honest answer.

But she had no idea what answer she could honestly give.

She tried to work out how she felt, but her head still rang with the sound of her mother's sobs.

"I don't know," she said desperately. "I need more time. I have to think."

Something shadowed his expression. Pain. Disappointment. Weary resignation. "I see."

His tone was just a little cooler than usual and she felt a flash of panic and deep regret.

She'd hurt him.

"Matt—" She tried to explain. "All my life I've seen relationships go wrong. You said you understood." She badly wanted him to reassure her, as he always did, but this time he was silent and when he finally spoke he sounded tired.

"I do understand. But I've been trying to show you the other side of that. And I'd hoped that by now you'd see that what we share is strong and real."

"It's scary, Matt."

"Scary? When we're working on the roof terrace, eating dinner alone together or with our friends, enjoying a drink, making breakfast, having sex—does any of that feel scary?" His blunt challenge made her feel like a coward.

"No, but—"

"Is that what you're thinking of when we're together? You're lying there wondering when we're going to break up?" His voice was level but there was a distance that she hadn't felt before, as if he was slipping away and she was powerless to stop it.

She'd never seen him like this. Never heard him use this tone.

"All I'm saying is that relationships end all the time. It's a fact of life."

"Yes, it is. Which makes it all the more important to pick the right person. You're the right person for me, Frankie, but only if I'm the right person for you. I don't know what your mother said to you, but I do know that as long as you listen to her, and keep focused on what happened all those years ago instead of paying attention to your own feelings and what's happening now, this is never going to work."

Never going to work? Oh *God*—

She couldn't breathe.

"Wait—stop. Are you breaking up with me?"

"No." He sounded weary. "I think you're the one breaking up with me."

Claws stalked through the apartment, swishing her tail, but for once neither of them took any notice.

"I'm not! All I'm saying is—" She broke off and his gaze locked on hers.

"All you're saying is that you don't trust me. Not enough. You don't trust us, or what we have. Maybe this was a fling to you, a way of discovering your sexuality, but it was more than that for me. Yes, the sex is off the scale but I'm not interested in a fling, Frankie. Not with you. I want the whole thing, thick and thin, richer and poorer, sickness and health, but only if you one hundred percent trust in what we have. I've seen my parents weather rough times, and they've done

it because they trusted each other and in their love, and neither one of them was ever going to give up on that."

"I don't know if you're breaking up or proposing."

"Neither. I'm asking you to think about what we have
and what you want. Because I don't want to be in a relationship where one of us doubts the other. That doesn't work
for me." He reached for his phone and his keys and she felt
an acute stab of panic.

"Where are you going?"

"I'm going for a walk, and then I'm going to the workshop."

"It's Sunday." And they'd planned on having a lazy morning followed by a long walk in Central Park. She'd been
looking forward to it.

"I know what day it is." He paused for a moment and
rubbed his fingers over his forehead, as if he was trying to
ease an enormous pressure. "We lost a couple of days because
of Roxy, so I need to catch up, and—I need some space."

"From me?"

"I'm not made of stone, Frankie. I have feelings, too. I care
about you. I care about *us*, and the fact that you don't want
the same thing—" He broke off and then shook his head.
"I'll see you later."

She'd never seen him this upset. The emotion visible in
his eyes was raw, real and almost too painful to watch. And
even more painful was the knowledge that she was the cause.

Feeling sick, Frankie opened her mouth to speak, to stop
him leaving, but Matt left the apartment without looking
back.

"Matt? Wait."

Realizing that someone was yelling at him, Matt turned

and saw Eva sprinting toward him. Her hair flew around her shoulders and she was wearing flip-flops on her feet.

The last thing he wanted right now was company, but he stopped and waited for her to catch up with him. "What's wrong?"

"Nothing's wrong. At least not with me." She was breathless and her hair was messy.

"Your T-shirt is on inside out. You look as if you just got out of bed."

"That's because I did." She tugged at it self-consciously. "Ten minutes ago I was asleep."

"What woke you?"

"Frankie, banging on my door."

He tensed. "Look, I understand you're worried about your friend, but I can't talk about this right now, Ev."

"I'm not here because I'm worried about Frankie. I'm here because I'm worried about you."

"Me?"

"Yes, you." She grabbed his hand. "Let's go to the park. It's lovely at this hour."

His chest ached, but he didn't want her to know how bad he was feeling so he forced himself to tease her. "How would you know? You hardly ever see this hour?"

"True. So let's go and see if the rumors are true. I'll buy you coffee and we can talk."

He didn't want to talk, but he couldn't think of a way of telling her that wouldn't offend her so he gave in and walked with her along the street toward the park.

It was a slow Sunday morning and the neighborhood was just waking up. They strolled past family-owned stores brimming with fresh produce, and Eva dragged him into

Petit Pain, the artisan bakery that also sold the best coffee in the area.

"Here." She handed him a tall coffee and a bag containing a still-warm pastry. "Let's go and find a comfortable bench to sit on."

"You don't have to—"

"Never argue with a woman who's just woken up."

He gave up arguing and they walked in silence until they reached the park.

It was still relatively quiet, with only a few families with young children already in evidence. Matt pushed open the gate and then paused, his fingers digging into the smooth wood. "Was she upset?"

Eva nudged him through the gate toward the nearest seat. She didn't ask who he was talking about. "Yes, but so are you."

Upset? His gut twisted. His feelings were more complicated than that. He felt sad and sore, as if his emotions had been dragged across a rough surface. "What did she tell you?"

"Nothing. She asked if she could stay in Paige's room for a while. Then shut the door on me, which is what she does when her mother gets in touch." She sipped her coffee and watched the squirrels playing on the grass. "Roxy texted me and told me her mom showed up in person, so I don't need to know much more than that. Her mom messes with her head."

"I know, but I was hoping we'd moved past that." And that was the other emotion he was feeling. Bone-deep disappointment. He'd truly believed her feelings for him were strong enough to overcome her reservations about relationships.

"I was hoping so, too. If she messes this up I will kill her."

"Messes what up?"

"Your relationship. In fact, I'm so stressed I need to eat half your pastry." She reached across and took the bag from his hand.

"You should have bought one for yourself."

"I'm on a diet. If I steal yours it doesn't count." She broke off a piece and ate it, sugar dusting her lips. "That's *so* good. You're right. I should have bought myself one. Or five."

"So what are we doing here, Ev? Did you want to give me wise advice?"

She licked the tips of her fingers. "You're talking to a woman who hasn't had sex in—oh—" she counted on her fingers and then shrugged "—more time than I'm prepared to admit, so I'm not in a position to dish out advice. I'm here because you're sad, and sometimes when I'm sad it helps to have company." Something in her voice made him glance at her.

"Are you sad, honey?"

She stared intently at the bag in her hand. "We were talking about you."

"Well, now we're talking about you."

She reached into the bag and broke off another piece of pastry. "Sometimes. There are days when I'm okay, and other days when I'm so lonely it feels as if I'm the only person on the planet. What is wrong with me, Matt? Why can't I meet someone special?"

"There's nothing wrong with you." He looped his arm around her shoulders, trying to push his own pain to one side so that he could focus on hers. "You're one of the best people I know."

"I live in this amazing city, surrounded by all these people and I'm on my own. That's sad, but what makes me even sadder is that you've met the right person and it still isn't working out."

"Some things aren't meant to work out."

"This shouldn't be one of those things."

"If you have any words of wisdom, I'm listening."

She handed the bag back to him. "I don't have words of wisdom. Just a shoulder for you to lean on. And coffee and calories."

He smiled, touched. "You're a generous person, Ev. And a good friend. Somewhere out there in Manhattan there is a hot guy waiting for you."

"I'm glad you mentioned the *hot* part." She peeled the top off her coffee and blew on it. "I definitely deserve someone superhot."

"You do."

"With great abs."

"Great abs are important."

She sipped her coffee. "Good shoulders would be nice, too."

"Shoulders." He nodded. "Anything else?"

"Stamina, because I haven't had sex in a *long* time."

Matt hadn't thought he was capable of smiling right now, but he found himself smiling. "Stamina. Is that it?"

"He has to not mind that I still have the stuffed kangaroo Grams gave me when I was five."

"So he needs to be either visually impaired, CEO of a soft toy company or tolerant."

"And he needs to be kind," Eva said softly. "I don't want a player who is going to break my heart. I've cried a lot this year since—well, you know. My New Year's resolution is not to cry once."

"It's only September."

"Which means I have a little over three months to get my crying done. Then that's it. Oh, and I bought a new condom to replace the one that expired, so I need to use that before it goes out of date like the last one. Because I'm a person who hates waste."

"Naturally. It's the eco-friendly thing to do." He stirred. "Just the one condom?"

"That's all I carry. And I probably won't even need that one. I have so much love to give," she said gloomily, "and no one wants it."

"Some lucky guy is going to want it."

She roused herself and nudged him in the ribs. "He'll probably use my condom and then leave me with a broken heart."

"If anyone breaks your heart, Jake and I will take him down." He lifted his arm away from her shoulder and finished his coffee. "You deserve someone special."

"Trouble is we don't always get what we deserve." She leaned her head on his shoulder. "I love you, Matt. You're the brother I never had." She said it easily, wearing her emotions as comfortably and effortlessly as she wore her clothes. There was no embarrassment. No awkwardness. No qualification. Just Eva, whose heart was big enough to fill the whole of Manhattan.

"I love you, too, honey."

"When you hurt, I hurt."

"I'll survive. I'm big and strong."

"I know you're big and strong, and I know you'll survive, but I want more than that for you. I want you to live happily ever after with Frankie."

Thinking about it tore at him and the pain was made

worse by the fact that for a while he'd actually believed it was possible.

"You have a way of making things sound so simple."

"When two people love each other, it should be simple." She stared into her empty coffee cup. "It really should be simple."

They watched the squirrels for a moment and Matt tried to pull himself together. He needed to talk about something other than Frankie. Think about something other than Frankie. He needed to stand up, put one foot in front of the other and go home. Or go to work. He couldn't spend the rest of his life hiding out in the park. "It's Christmas in three months. Have you started counting days and hours yet? Normally by now you're telling me how many days it is."

"I haven't started counting this year."

He glanced at her. "You love Christmas. You start planning Christmas in January."

"I know. But it's—" She broke off. "Last year, my first Christmas without Grams—it was awful. I'm dreading it, to be honest. Christmas is for families, and I don't have family. I'm alone. Alone, alone, alone. I hate that word."

"You're not alone. You have us. We're your family. Mom would love to see you for Thanksgiving if you're free, and my parents are thinking of coming to New York for Christmas. We'll probably spend the day with Maria, Jake and Paige."

"That sounds good." She was silent for a moment. "I'll come if I'm not busy."

"You have plans?"

"Yes. I plan not to spend another Christmas missing Gram and feeling sorry for myself. She'd be so ashamed of me." She straightened her shoulders. "If Frankie can face everyone on Puffin Island, I can face Christmas. I'm staying in New York City and I'm going to party."

"Are you planning on partying with anyone in particular?"

"Yes. I will be partying with the hot guy that Santa is delivering for Christmas."

"Will he be coming down the chimney? Because that might be a challenge."

"I don't care how he comes, or where he comes, as long as he comes."

Matt grinned. "You're a bad girl, Ev."

"Not in a while, but I'm going to be."

"You'd better not tell Santa that until after he has delivered your hot man. Bad girls don't get gifts from Santa."

"I'll keep wearing my good girl disguise until the moment I get my man naked."

"You'd better write to Santa pretty soon, then."

"Already done. I thought it might take him a while to find the perfect guy."

"With abs."

"And shoulders." She stretched out her legs and tilted her face to the sun. "He is going to sweep me off my feet and that will be that."

"That will be what?"

"My happy ending. Right there."

"Tied with a big red bow?"

"I prefer pink, but red would do."

Frankie watched from the gate in the park feeling as if she was alone on a desert island, watching a ship sail away into the distance.

Matt and Eva sat close together talking. She saw the moment Matt put his arm around Eva, and saw her lean her head on his shoulder.

Her throat felt thick and her eyes stung. Inside she felt raw and vulnerable.

She should be the one sitting with her head on Matt's shoulder. And she would have been, if she wasn't so stupid.

"Walk with me." Paige's voice came from behind her and Frankie turned to see her friend dressed in workout gear, her hair pulled into a ponytail.

"What are you doing here? I thought you were at Jake's." She'd been relying on the fact she could stay in Paige's room. Roxy was in her apartment. Staying at Matt's wasn't an option after what had just happened. Where would she go?

"I was there last night but he has to work today so I came back for my spin class."

Frankie noticed the bottle of water in her hand. "So you'd better go. You don't want to be late."

"I'm not in the mood for a spin class. I'd rather talk to you." Paige glanced across the park to where Eva and Matt were sitting.

Frankie rubbed her fingers over her forehead, scared by how close she was to crying. "I'm not good at talking." Maybe if she was better at talking and sharing her feelings, she wouldn't be in this mess.

"So I'll do some of the talking." Paige slipped her arm through Frankie's and started to walk, giving Frankie no choice but to walk with her. "You know there's nothing going on there, don't you?"

"What? Oh, yes. She's giving him a shoulder to cry on. Being a good friend, because he's upset." And that was her fault. Her fault. She wanted to talk to Paige, but as usual the words wouldn't come. The only person she'd found it easy to talk to was Matt. What did you do when the problem you wanted to talk about was with the only person you could talk to? "I hurt your brother. I'm sorry." *Sorry* was a pathetically pale apology for the guilt and regret she was feeling right now.

"He's tough. He'll survive. Right now I'm more worried about you." It was typical of Paige. Her loyalty to her friends was unshakeable.

Frankie stopped. "Mom came to the apartment this morning."

Paige nodded. "Ev texted me."

"Is that why you're here?"

"I was coming, anyway," Paige hedged. "What did she say? Another boyfriend? She's moved on from that guy we met in the flower market?"

"He dumped her. But this time she cared. She really cared. She was crying." Frankie wiped her hand over her forehead, feeling her tension levels rise. "It reminded me of before."

"Those were bad times." Paige's gaze was sympathetic. "I'm starting to understand why you freaked out."

"She told me that finally she agreed with me that avoiding relationships was a good thing."

Paige twisted the top off her water. "And since when did you ever find yourself in agreement with your mother?"

Frankie felt even more foolish. But she knew that it wasn't enough to know intellectually that she was being stupid. She needed to feel it. She needed to *believe* it.

"How do I stop feeling this way? I don't want to feel this way." She was desperate and Paige gave her a searching look.

"I presume I'm right in thinking that you're in love with Matt?"

It was the same question Matt himself had asked, and she hadn't been able to answer him.

It was as if the words and feelings were jammed up behind everything in her past.

"I don't know." But she did know, didn't she? That was the problem. She knew, and that was why she was so scared. Of all the situations she'd faced in her life, she'd never faced this one. She sent her friend an agonized glance. "All right, yes! I'm in love with Matt. I'm crazy about Matt. And it's the most terrifying thing that's ever happened to me."

Paige's gaze softened. "Have you told him?"

"No. And he hadn't said anything to me, either, until this morning. It came out as part of this weird conversation about my mother."

Paige's eyebrows rose. "Matt told you he loved you in front of your mother?"

"It was after she left."

"Bad timing." Paige took a sip of water. "Now I understand why you're terrified. But you're not your mother, Frankie. You've never lived your life the way she lives hers. You make your own choices, and you always have. If she told you to give up your work, would you do it?"

"Of course not."

"If she told you to move out of your apartment, would you do that?"

"No!" Frankie frowned. "What are you—"

"So why are you letting her dictate your love life? Why are you letting anything she says influence the decisions you make about your life?"

Frankie moved to one side so a couple with a stroller

could walk past. "Because she pushed all my buttons. It was like being transported in a time machine. I was right back there, to the time my dad moved out."

"Answer me one more question." Paige looked thoughtful. "Before your mother showed up, were you and Matt happy?"

"We were half-asleep. And yes, we were happy. We were going to spend the day together. We had it all planned. I was going to cook breakfast, play with my plants for a while and then we were both going to take a long walk in Central Park." Her eyes filled. "I hurt him. I hurt Matt. How can I hurt someone I love so much?"

"Because you were scared and panicking. But now you need to fix it, Frankie."

"How?"

Paige rubbed her shoulder. "You're the one who knows my brother. You'll find the right way."

Chapter Nineteen

Love isn't something you see, it's something you feel.

—Eva

"Someone's dogwood has mildew. I presume that's a plant, not an animal." Paige scanned the requests they'd received overnight. "What is a dogwood?"

Frankie stirred. "Email me the details. I'll deal with it."

She felt listless and unmotivated, as if someone had drained all the life out of her.

She missed Matt horribly. She missed being snuggled next to his warm strength; she missed sharing those intimate thoughts and details she never shared with anyone else and she missed the sex.

She wanted to talk to him, but she didn't know what to say. She didn't know how to prove to him that she trusted what they had.

And in the meantime, she was sharing an apartment with Eva.

"I used the last of your shampoo this morning."

Eva glanced up. "The expensive one that is supposed to make me look like a Greek goddess?"

"Is that what they promised you?" Her friend had said nothing about her exchange with Matt, but Frankie knew she hated any kind of tension. "Are you mad at me?"

"Of course I'm not mad at you."

"You hate having me live with you."

Eva sighed. "I love having you live with me. The only thing I hate is the reason for it. You should be upstairs with Matt. I hate seeing two people I love upset. I want you both to be together."

"I want that, too," she admitted. "And don't tell me to fix it, because if I knew how to do it, I would. I'm not like you. I don't know how to be in a relationship."

And yet being with Matt was the easiest thing she'd ever done. It hadn't felt hard, or stressful or even complicated. It had felt fun, safe, exhilarating and— perfect. It had felt perfect.

"You don't have to flirt. Matt loves you," Eva said gently. "All you have to do is show him you love him back. That's it, Frankie. You have to trust him with your feelings. Is that really so hard? Can't you do that?"

She'd already trusted him with things she'd never shared with anyone else. Her body, her secrets, those inner parts of herself she'd kept hidden for almost all her life.

Could she trust him with her heart, too?

Yes. Yes, she could.

But how did she tell him that? How did she show him in a way that he'd believe?

Without saying a word she stood up suddenly, knocking a pile of papers to the floor. She reached for the can of diet cola that was sitting on her desk, slid the tip of her finger into the pull tab and opened the can.

She stared at it for a moment.

"Are you having second thoughts about drinking that stuff?" Eva gave her a reproving look. "Because you should. If you're going to be living with me, you're going to have to accept that I pay as much attention to what I put into my body as I do to what I pour over my hair. I won't have that stuff in my fridge."

Frankie ignored her and stared at the can, her mind working. "Where's Matt today?"

"I think he's working at home," Paige said. "We had a conversation about Thanksgiving plans earlier. Why?"

She had to talk to him. She had to talk to him right now.

Frankie grabbed her purse. She'd never felt such a sense of desperate urgency. "I need to take the rest of the day off. Is that okay?"

"This is your company, too. You do what you need to do." Paige gave her a quizzical look. "Are you going to see Matt?"

"Yes." She fumbled with the strap of her bag. "But first I need to talk to my mother."

She knew she had to do that before she could take the step she needed to take and say the things she needed to say.

Eva looked alarmed. "Are you sure? You and Matt were doing great until your mother showed up."

"Exactly. Before I talk to Matt, I need to talk to her. I have to fix this. It's time I was honest with her. It's time I told her how I really feel." She strode to the door. "And while we're on that topic, there's something I want to say to you, too."

"You're resigning from Urban Genie so that you can work with Matt?"

"Are you kidding? Resign from a job where I get to work with my two closest friends every day? No way." She shook her head and forced the words through the barrier that always prevented her from expressing her feelings. "I just wanted to say that I'm lucky to have you."

Eva's gaze softened. "Oh, *Frankie*—"

"I'm not done yet. I—" She could feel the barrier weakening. "I love you both. Very much."

There was silence.

Paige was the first to speak. "Well—" Her voice cracked. "Was that a practice run for the real thing?"

"No. This was the real thing, too. I meant every word. You're the best friends any woman could have, or want in her life."

Eva's eyes filled. "Group hug?"

Frankie gave a wobbly smile and pulled open the door. "Don't push your luck."

Her mother was already at the coffee shop. "I came as soon as I got your text. What's wrong? You normally refuse to meet me in the middle of your working day."

"I need to talk to you, Mom."

"Of course. That's why I'm here. I came right away. I ordered you a diet cola. That's what you like, isn't it?"

"I mean *really* talk." Frankie slid into the booth opposite her mother. "About stuff we probably should have talked about a long time ago."

"You mean about what happened with your father? I know it affected you. How could it not? Him walking out like that with no warning—"

"I knew, Mom."

The silence that followed stretched on for so long she wondered if her mother had heard her.

"Knew?" Her mother looked shocked. "You mean about the affairs?"

"Affairs?" It was Frankie's turn to be shocked. "He had more than one?"

"Oh—I—" Her mother looked thrown. Then she lifted her chin. "Yes. Yes, he did."

"Why didn't you tell me?"

"Because you worshipped the ground your father walked on, and I didn't want to be the one to kill your feelings. But it seems that happened, anyway." Her mother looked tired. "But if you knew about the last one, why didn't you tell me?"

"Because he made me promise not to. He told me it was the first time he'd done it, and that he was never going to do it again. I didn't know he was still seeing her until the day he walked out. And I didn't know how to handle it. I knew you loved him and I didn't want to hurt you. I lived with it, stored it inside me like some toxic virus that isn't allowed to meet with the air in case it combusts. And I always wondered whether if I'd told you the moment I'd found out, if I hadn't kept my silence, you might have been able to fix it."

There was a long, pulsing silence.

"Oh, Frankie. Oh, sweetheart." Her mother reached across the table and took her hand. "Nothing you did or didn't do would have made a difference. He was playing you, just as he played me. His first affair was when I was expecting you. I found out because I went into labor early and no one could find him. It turned out the reason they couldn't find him was because he was having a very intimate meeting with a coworker. After that things went quiet for a couple of years, but then it started again."

Her mother talked, outlining a catalog of infidelity that Frankie struggled to comprehend. She'd thought she was the one with secrets, but it turned out that her mother had plenty of her own. Deep, painful secrets that she'd never shared.

"Why did you stay?"

"Because I loved him. And because of you." Her mother poked at the foam on her coffee. "I thought that staying together was best for you. I didn't realize that what I was doing was damaging you."

Frankie's chest ached. "Because of what I saw as a child, I grew up believing there was no relationship that couldn't be destroyed. And I saw what Dad's leaving did to you. I've lived my life trying to avoid that sort of pain happening to me."

"I know. And you've been so much more sensible than I ever was. You've made your own life and made great choices. Look at you, Frankie—" her mother waved her hand "—you're so independent. You have a great apartment, a fabulous job, friends who love you and no romantic attachments."

"I'm in love with Matt."

"I—" Her mother gaped at her. "What did you just say?"

"I'm in love with Matt." Saying it felt so easy. So real. So *right*.

There was nothing holding her back now. Nothing.

Her mother's eyes widened. "*The* Matt? Sexy Matt?"

"Yes, sexy Matt, but I'd appreciate it from now on if you'd just call him Matt. No innuendos. No squeezing his butt. No behaving in an inappropriate fashion. I want to see you, Mom. I want to start fresh, but I don't want to dread every visit in case you embarrass me."

Her mother was still gaping. "But—I thought you were living in his apartment because that girl—"

"Roxy."

"Because Roxy needed a place to stay and had moved into your home."

"I'm living there because I want to be with Matt. My home is wherever he is."

"It's that serious?"

"Couldn't be more serious." Except that she felt like smiling. Never before had something so serious made her want to smile so much.

"Has he proposed to you?"

"The details are my business."

"That means he hasn't." Her mother's eyes lit with anxiety. "It might just be sex, Frankie. He might hurt you. He might not want—"

"It isn't just sex, Mom, and I know what he wants because I want the same thing. And Matt would never intentionally hurt me." But she'd hurt him. Badly. She felt a flicker of trepidation. What if she'd hurt him so badly he wouldn't want to take a risk on her? No. That wouldn't happen. She trusted what they had and no one, especially not her mother, was going to put doubt in her mind. "I don't need your help with my relationships. I don't want it. It's time to take my own risks and make my own mistakes. But this isn't one of them. Nothing I do with Matt could ever be a mistake. I'm going to find him to tell him, but first I wanted to talk to you."

"Well—" Her mother was silent for a moment and then breathed deeply. "I guess we should talk about something else, then. I got a job. Not a fancy job like yours, but it's still a job. I'll be working in a deli."

"That's great, Mom."

"And Brad is taking me to dinner tonight."

"Right." Frankie wondered how long Brad would last,

and then decided it wasn't her business. Her mother was an adult and it was up to her how she lived her life.

And Frankie was going to live hers. Really live it, not do what felt safe.

"You should be going. We can have a longer chat another time, but right now you have more important things to do." Her mother reached for her purse. "I've got this."

Frankie hid her surprise. "Thanks, Mom."

Gina Cole stood up. "If you feel like texting me later to let me know how things went, then do that. And if you want to talk—or anything—" she breathed "—I'm not giving you any advice. Just carry on doing what you're doing. You do it so much better than I do, anyway."

Frankie hesitated and then leaned forward and gave her mother a hug. It felt tense and a little awkward, but it was still a hug. "I love you, Mom."

Her mother held her so tightly she couldn't breathe. "I love you, too. Now go."

Before going home Frankie paid a visit to one of Eva's favorite stores and bought herself a dress in a beautiful shade of green. She paid, ignoring the cost, and wore it right away. It showed more leg than she'd ever shown in her life before and it felt strange, wearing a dress, but it also made her feel oddly confident.

With the rest of her clothes stuffed into a bag, she rode the subway home, her palms clammy.

The closer she got to Brooklyn, the more nervous she became.

What if Matt had lost patience with her insecurities?

No. No, that wasn't going to happen.

All the same, she was desperate to put things right and she virtually ran the distance from the subway to their brownstone. She was about to head straight up to Matt's apartment when she saw that the door to her own apartment was open.

Wondering if Roxy had left it open by accident, she went to investigate.

Maybe they needed to fit some sort of child lock. If Mia wandered out onto the street it could be dangerous. She'd talk to Matt about it.

"Roxy?" She walked through the open door and sensed immediately that something wasn't right.

The apartment was empty.

Where was Roxy and why had she left the door open?

She wandered through to the kitchen and heard glass crunch under her feet.

"Crap." The small window that opened from the kitchen into the garden was broken, and glass glittered over the tiled floor.

She stepped back gingerly, trying to avoid the worst of it. Was it burglars? That seemed the most obvious explanation, but there was no sign that anything had been taken. And why break the window and then come in through the front door? Or had they gone out through the front door?

She tried to make sense of it, and while her mind was working she heard a sound behind her and realized the apartment wasn't empty.

She'd been wrong about that.

Her stomach dropped with fear and she turned quickly but she was too late.

A hand came over her mouth and she was slammed up against the wall.

"Where's Roxy?"

She felt a hand tighten around her throat and then a man's face pressed up close to hers, his expression ugly.

Frankie forced herself to stay still and think. She had no idea where Roxy and Mia were, but their new favorite place was the park and she was guessing they'd gone for a walk. Which meant they could be back at any moment.

Using a move she'd practiced hundreds of times, she knocked the man's hands away from her throat and brought her knee up hard.

He gave a grunt of pain and made a grab for her, but she hooked her leg under his and brought him crashing to the floor.

"You crazy bitch." He howled in agony as his head smacked into the floor and his shoulders landed on the broken glass.

Frankie hit the floor with him and felt pain shoot through her knee.

"Yeah, that's me. Pleased to meet you." She yanked his arm behind his back and twisted it hard, thinking they could probably hear his yells up in Harlem.

She *hoped* someone would hear.

And then she heard a sound at the window and saw Claws, standing in her usual place.

"No!" Frankie glanced at the glass scattered across the floor. "No! Claws! Don't jump."

But Claws ignored her and jumped.

Matt finished the proposal he'd been working on, removed his earphones and stood up. Mozart helped him concentrate and blocked out the noise from the street.

Claws appeared and rubbed herself against his leg.

He looked down and saw spots of blood on the floor.

"What the—" He dropped into a crouch and caught her gently. "What have you done?" Lifting her carefully, he examined her paws and winced.

"You trod on glass?" He stood up, intending to investigate on the way to the vet, when he heard Roxy scream his name.

Cursing fluently, he locked the cat in the safety of his apartment and sprinted to the ground floor.

Frankie's door was open and the lock was hanging off.

Matt strode into the apartment and saw Frankie kneeling on the floor next to the twisted body of a man who was letting out a stream of curses interspersed with grunts of pain.

There was blood on the floor, but whether it was from the cat, the man or Frankie, he wasn't sure.

His stomach lurched.

"Oh, Matt—" Roxy was clutching Mia, pressing her daughter's head into her shoulder. "I went to the park and when I came back the door was open and—

"Take Mia up to my apartment, Rox."

"But—"

"Just do it." He handed her his keys. "I've got this."

Frankie looked at him. "*You've* got this? I hate to bust your knight-in-shining-armor aspirations, but from where I'm sitting it feels as if I'm the one who's got this." She adjusted her hold on the man and he gave another howl of pain.

Matt felt a rush of relief that she seemed to be alright, closely followed by admiration. "So you don't need any help there?"

"Thanks, but I'm good."

"I'll call 911."

"Way ahead of you."

He scanned the broken glass, the trail of blood and the bruise on her head. He wondered how he had missed hearing the commotion, and then remembered he'd been listening to music. "You already phoned this in? How?"

"This guy isn't much of a challenge. Brought him down with my right leg and my right hand, so my left hand was free. It's called multitasking."

Matt leaned against the door. "So you don't need me for anything at all? How about compliments?"

"Compliments are good. I've discovered I like them."

He scanned her slowly. "Nice dress, honey."

"Thank you. I'm glad you noticed."

"I'm noticing the legs, as much as the dress. They're incredible. Anything else you need me for?"

"I need you for a lot of things. That's why I came home. To tell you all the ways I need you. And I came to give you something. Keep still—" She growled at the man who was trying to extract himself from her hold. "I'm talking. Don't interrupt me when I'm talking. I love you, Matt. That's what I came to say."

His heart kicked against his chest and his gaze locked on hers. The look in her eyes was something he'd given up hope of ever seeing. "You love me?"

The man on the floor squirmed. "For fuck's sake—"

Neither Frankie nor Matt spared him a glance.

"I love you." Her smile was wobbly but her voice was full of conviction. "I've been in love with you for years."

"So you're saying you want to have a fling?"

"I'm not interested in a fling. Not with you. I want the whole thing, thick and thin, richer and poorer, sickness and health, but only if you one hundred percent trust in what we have."

For the first time in his adult life Matt found it difficult to speak. "That's what you came here to say?"

"Yes. And I came home to give you something, too, but then I found this scumbag in my apartment." She dug her elbow into the man's back. "You hurt the cat and got glass in my *Ocimum basilicum*."

"Your what? Lady, I wouldn't touch a single part of you, let alone your—whatever that thing is."

Matt didn't shift his gaze from Frankie's face. "What did you want to give me?"

"A token of my feelings. And they're strong feelings, Matt. I hope you're up to handling them."

"He'd have to be a sadist to want to go anywhere near you," the man on the ground screeched and Frankie frowned.

"I think the word you're looking for is *masochist. Sadism* would describe what I might do to you if you don't stop interrupting what might be the most important conversation of my life. Matt, I love you."

"You already said that." The man on the ground squirmed. "And I don't want to hear this shit."

"Well, tough. You're hearing this shit. And if you're sensible you'll take something away from it, like the fact that when a woman says she doesn't want you in her life, she means it. Love isn't something that can be extracted through pain, fear or extortion, Eddy. It's something that is given. Watch and learn." Her eyes locked on Matt's. "I'm giving my love to you, Matt. All of it. All of me."

The air left his lungs in a rush. "Frankie—"

"Shut up!" Eddy squirmed like a fish on a hook. "It wasn't my fault! I never wanted the baby. She was the one who insisted on keeping it."

"That's because Roxy is a wonderful human being. You can think about that when they lock you up. And if you ever come near Roxy or Mia again, I will personally make sure you are never again able to make a baby you don't want."

"I'm going to fucking kill you. One dark night when you've forgotten all about me, I'm going to be waiting for you in the shadows. And what are you going to do then?"

Matt felt anger rip through him and took a step forward but Frankie shoved Eddy's arm higher and gave him a thoughtful look.

"I guess I'll do the same thing I'm doing right now. Pin you to the ground and give you a piece of my mind. You're a wimp, Eddy. A bully and a wimp. And it's time you took your bullying wimpy ways and left Roxy the hell alone. How can I put this so that I'm sure we understand each other?" She paused, thinking. "If you *ever* lurk in the shadows and try to scare me or anyone I love again, I will personally kick the shit out of you."

"You won't have to, because I will already have done it." Roxy stood there, her face set and angry. "You stay away from me, Eddy. And you stay away from Mia."

Eddy's expression was ugly. "You're all big and tough when you have your friends here, Roxy, but we both know you don't have the guts."

"Try me." Roxy braced her shoulders. "You come within a hundred feet of my baby again and you'll find out how much I've changed since I had the sense to walk away from you." She turned to Matt. "The police are here. Can I leave you to handle it for a minute? I left Mia with James."

"James is here?" Matt wondered how it was that his whole team suddenly seemed to be camping out in his house.

"I called him and he came right away. That's what friends do." Roxy glared at Eddy. "I'm making a statement. I'm telling them everything. You don't scare me anymore."

Matt hoped Eddy couldn't see what he could see. That Roxy was shaking.

Eddy squirmed. "I have rights!"

"And I have a black belt in karate," Frankie said pleasantly. "Want me to show you a few more of my moves? I'm having fun trying them out in a real-life scenario."

Two uniformed officers entered the apartment and Eddy started to howl.

"Get her off me! This is assault."

Matt felt a ridiculous urge to smile, an urge that faded as soon as Frankie stood up and he saw the blood pouring from her leg.

"You're hurt—"

"I knelt on glass. If I hadn't been wearing this stupid dress I would have been okay. I should have stuck to yoga pants." Wincing, she pulled out a large shard and frowned at the kitchen floor. "This place is a mess. Roxy can't bring Mia back in here until we've properly cleaned it up."

"She can use our apartment for the moment." He was by her side, grabbing a towel to stem the bleeding. "I'm taking you to the hospital."

"I'm fine. But I don't want to get blood on my new dress. It's the only one I own. Did you say *our* apartment?"

"Frankie, you're not fine. And yes, I said *our* apartment. That's what it is, providing you meant all the things you said back there."

"I meant every single word. And I still have to give you something. I had it all planned, and then this happened. He messed it all up!"

Matt looked into her eyes, but decided that this wasn't the right time to tell her everything he wanted to say. "Let's deal with Eddy, speak to the police, get your knee seen and then we can talk."

"We need to get Claws to the vet, too. She stepped on the glass."

"I'll do that." Eva stepped into the room and Matt felt a rush of affection for her.

"You hate my cat."

"I wouldn't say I hate her, exactly. It's more that she scares me. But she's injured and she needs attention, and so does Frankie. You can't do both, so I'll deal with the cat." Eva glanced at Roxy and smiled. "Sometimes it's good to face the things that scare you."

James walked into the room holding a tearful Mia. "If you all take yourselves off and stop tramping glass around, I can clear this place up."

"Bad man," Mia sobbed. "Bad man shouty."

"He's gone, honey. You're safe." James stroked her back and Mia hugged him tightly and covered him in kisses.

"James horsey."

"Later." He unpeeled her arms from his neck and handed her to Roxy. "Take her for a walk in the park. Give me a couple of hours. I want to make sure there's not a speck of glass left in this place. Don't want her to hurt herself. Or you."

Roxy stood on tiptoe and kissed him.

Color spread across his cheeks. "What was that for?"

"For coming when I called you. And for caring about my daughter."

Matt suspected that James cared about more than just Roxy's daughter, but he didn't say anything.

He had his own relationship to think about.

And finally, finally, it was almost time to focus on that.

Chapter Twenty

Never guess the ending before you've read the whole book.

—Matt

They talked to the police and then Matt insisted on taking her to the hospital.

By the time they left, it was late afternoon and she still hadn't said what she wanted to say.

Now that it was over, she felt shaken and sick.

Matt had refused to leave the room when she was being treated, as if he was afraid to let her out of his sight.

"You gave me heart failure, Frankie. When I walked into that apartment and saw you in the middle of the broken glass with Eddy—" He ran his hand over his face and she gave a rueful shrug.

"He had his hands around my throat. I had no choice but to throw him."

"I wanted to put my hands around his throat for touching you."

"You have hidden caveman tendencies. I've suspected it for a while."

"He could have had a gun. Or a knife." Matt's tone was raw and she knew he was feeling the same aftereffects she was.

"A knife I could probably have dealt with. A gun—" she frowned "—I prefer not to think about that."

"I prefer not to, either, but I can't get the image out of my head. The broken lock. The look on his face."

"How about the image where I sat on him and almost dislocated his shoulder? Can't you replace it with that one?"

"I'll try. So you were, what, seventeen when you took up karate?"

"Yes, but I'm a quick learner. Turned out I had a talent for it."

"And we're all relieved about that."

"Eddy didn't seem too pleased."

Matt gave a reluctant smile and then his phone beeped and he dug it out of his pocket. "It's James. He says that the apartment is clean, the window is fixed and he's spending another night on the couch so that Roxy and Mia feel safe."

"Do you think he's in love with her?" Frankie gave a half laugh. "Listen to me—I sound like Eva."

"Yes, I think he's in love with her. I think he's probably been in love with her for a while, but nothing is going to happen."

"How do you know?"

Matt typed a reply and slid his phone back into his pocket. "Because Roxy thinks James is too good for her. She didn't finish high school and before James threw it all in to work in landscaping, he worked as a lawyer."

"I didn't know that, but I can't imagine James caring about that."

"I agree, but Roxy won't. And she's pretty stubborn."

"She's also brave. And very smart. Poor Roxy. How did she cope when she was pregnant and living with that monster? She must have felt so alone."

"She told me once that if it hadn't been for Mia, she'd probably still be living with him. Mia spurred her into leaving. But she never had the courage to give a statement to the police before now."

"She's a great mother." Frankie looked out the window of the cab. "We're going the wrong way. This isn't home."

"I'm not ready to go home yet. There are things I need to say to you and things I want to hear you say to me. And I don't want to do it in the chaos of the house. I love our friends, but today I want you to myself."

"What about Claws?"

"Eva texted when you were in the emergency room. The vet has given her some antibiotics and we're to watch for infection, but they didn't seem too worried. Eva has agreed to keep her in her apartment until we're home."

"Claws and I can heal together." Frankie glanced out the window again, nerves fluttering in her belly. She'd had a plan, but that had all gone awry thanks to Eddy. Now she didn't know what to do. When was the best time to say what she wanted to say? "So where are we going?"

"Central Park?" Matt looked at her leg, the bandage exposed by the dress. "Will you be able to walk?"

"Of course." She settled back in her seat and watched New York slide past her, store windows, jostling crowds, people jabbering into cell phones. A million lives blended into a small island. Small, and yet big in so many ways.

The cab dropped them off near Columbus Circle and

they walked toward Bow Bridge along winding paths, past small children playing baseball and families with strollers.

It was a perfect late-September day.

"Another month and the ice rink will be back." She slid her arm through Matt's. "We should go. All of us."

"You hate ice-skating."

"I know, but it's Eva's favorite thing. Last Christmas was so hard for her. I want this one to be better. Shall we suggest it?"

"That depends. Will you still love me if I land on my butt?" They'd reached the bridge and they both stopped, as if subconsciously they'd both been aiming for the same destination.

Matt leaned on the graceful arch and looked over the lake.

Frankie glanced at him and then at the water, watching the reflections play across the surface.

"Nothing will stop me loving you." The words came naturally and when he turned to her she continued in a rush. "Before you say anything, there are some things I need to tell you. I spoke to my mother this morning."

"She called you again?"

"No. I called her. I asked her to meet me. We talked. Properly. In fact, I think it's probably the first honest conversation we've ever had."

"How honest?"

"I told her about my dad."

"All of it?"

"All of it. Turned out that wasn't his first affair. He'd had others. He even had one when she was expecting me." It still hadn't really sunk in. "She forgave him. But she had no idea that I knew about the last affair."

"Do you feel better now that she knows?"

"Yes, but what really helped was telling you." She paused, wondering how she could make him understand. "I'm not like Eva. I don't find it easy talking to people about emotional things. I guess it makes me feel too vulnerable. Naked."

"I like you naked."

"When my mother arrived, and she was so upset, it was like being catapulted back in time. I felt as if everything was unraveling. As if suddenly I was unlearning everything I'd learned." She leaned her head against Matt's shoulder. "I know I hurt you, and I'm sorry."

"Don't apologize." He curved his arm around her and pulled her close. "Your mother spent her whole visit giving you a bunch of reasons not to fall in love, reminding you of all the reasons you've spent your life avoiding it, so it was hardly surprising you started backing off. I should have given you space instead of pressing you. My timing couldn't have been worse."

"I shouldn't have let her words affect me the way they did. I *do* trust what we have. It's special, and real and the most powerful thing I've ever known." Her throat felt thick. "Back there in the apartment you said that I didn't need you for anything, but that isn't true. I need you for so many things, Matt. You're the only person I've ever been truly myself with. I love every single moment we spend together, whether we're up on a roof terrace hauling paving stones, or naked in bed. With you, I'm allowed to be me."

"And I love who you are." He slid his fingers into her hair. "I thought I knew you so well, and then that day in the apartment when you forgot to wear your glasses, I realized I didn't know you at all. And the more I learned about you, the harder and deeper I fell. I thought I was in control of everything, and before I knew what was happening I was out of my depth. There was so much I wanted to say to you, but I was afraid I'd send you running. I knew you had feelings for me, I just didn't know if they were as strong as mine. I could see that your mother had put questions in your mind, and instead of leaving you to work it out, I waded in clumsily. I really thought I'd lost you. I thought you didn't trust me."

"Why do you think I told you all those things about myself? Because I trust you. I love you. I think I've loved you for a long time. And the reason I freaked out was not because I didn't want what you were offering, but because I wanted it so, so much." She could barely see him through the sheen of her tears. "None of my relationships have ever mattered before. I didn't want them to matter. I saw what happened when they mattered. And then there was you—"

"Frankie—"

"You broke down every barrier I've ever put up. Being with you was exciting, it was fun. And it was relaxing because for the first time in my life I wasn't carrying secrets. I've spent my life being scared of intimacy but I see now that intimacy can be good. There's nothing better than being with someone who really knows you, and you know me. I'm terrified of loving you." She swallowed. "But I'm even more terrified of losing you. I want to hold on to what we have and never let it go and I don't know how to do that. I—I'm new to this. I'm going to need a manual or something."

"I'll be your manual. We'll work it out together." He stroked his fingers through her hair. "Earlier you said you had something you wanted to give me?"

"Yes." She dug her hand into her pocket and pulled out the object she'd been carrying around. "Here." She pushed it into his hand and he studied it with raised eyebrows.

"You rushed home to give me the ring pull from your soda can?"

"I was improvising. You need to use your imagination." Nerves fluttered in her stomach. "It's a ring. Maybe not the prettiest ring, or the most valuable ring, but that isn't what counts, is it? It's symbolic."

His expression changed. "Is it?"

"Yes. It signifies how much I love you."

There was a gleam in his eyes. "You love me as much as a can of cola?"

"In case you hadn't noticed I love diet cola, so in fact, that would be a lot." She knew he was teasing her, but suddenly her courage faltered. "Of course, if you've changed your mind—"

"I am never going to change my mind, and it so happens I've been carrying something around, too." He dug his hand into his pocket and pulled out a box. "This is for you."

She stared at the box, recognizing the delicate logo of Tempest Designs, Skylar's company. "This is from Emily's store on Puffin Island. You already bought me a starfish necklace—"

"This isn't a starfish necklace. Open it."

She took it from him and discovered that her fingers were shaking. Flipping open the lid, she saw a large diamond in an unusual and beautiful setting. "Oh. Oh, Matt. You bought this when we were on the island?"

"Yes." He took the ring and slid it onto her finger. "Francesca Cole, will you marry me?"

She could hardly breathe. "That depends—"

His gaze grew wary. "On—?"

"On whether you can keep up with my sex drive. I've wasted a lot of time."

The corners of his mouth flickered. "Are you flirting with me?"

"I don't know how to flirt. I'm telling the truth." She slid her arms around his neck and pressed her mouth to his. "Have I scared you?"

He gave a slow smile. "Nowhere near as much as you scared Eddy."

"I was thinking that we could let Roxy stay in my apartment as long as she needs to."

"You're going to move more than your toothbrush?"

"I think it's time. Does this mean I get to adopt your cat, too?"

"I'm afraid so. Does that affect your answer?"

"No. I want to marry you, Matt." She eased her mouth away from his, happiness engulfing her like a burst of sunshine. She was marrying him. She was marrying Matt. Her best friend. *Her lover.* "So is that it? Have we finished here?"

"Finished? I haven't even started." And then he was kissing her, a hot, hard kiss that made her brain melt and her limbs shaky.

When he finally lifted his head, Frankie realized they'd attracted a small crowd of people, some with cameras, all of them watching with rapt attention.

"Oops." She buried her face in Matt's chest. "This is embarrassing."

He grinned. "Honey, this is New York City. The most romantic destination on the planet. The department of tourism will thank us."

And he kissed her again, until happiness rippled through her and the last rays of the sun set over Central Park.

* * * * *

Acknowledgments

I'm grateful to all my wonderful readers. So many of you take time to email and chat to me on Facebook, and your kind comments and supportive messages always make my day. To those of you who take the time to leave reviews and post about my books on social media—thank you a million times. It really helps! To all the wonderful bloggers who are always so kind, enthusiastic and vocal about my books, I'm so grateful for your time, energy and support.

Seeing my books on sale around the world is a dream come true for me, made real by the team at Harlequin, who has always encouraged me to write whatever story excited me. I'm fortunate to have such fantastic support from my publisher.

I definitely struck lucky the day I was given Flo Nicoll as my editor. Working with her is such fun, and I'm thankful for the vision, patience and enthusiasm she displays as we work together on each book.

I'm grateful to my agent, Susan Ginsburg, and the team at Writers House for everything they do.

I have the best family in the world and I'm continually grateful for their unwavering support. You're the best!

Hopeless romantic Eva Jordan loves everything about Christmas. She might be spending the holidays alone this year, but when she's given an opportunity to house-sit a spectacular penthouse on Fifth Avenue she leaps at the chance. What better place to celebrate than in snow-kissed Manhattan? What she doesn't expect is to find the penthouse still occupied by its gorgeous—and mysterious—owner...

Read on for a sneak peek of MIRACLE ON 5TH AVENUE, the third book in Sarah Morgan's fabulous new trilogy!

Eva held her breath and then heard another noise—this one definitely inside the apartment. It sounded like a footstep. A stealthy footstep…as if the owner didn't want to reveal himself.

She glanced up and saw something move in the shadows up above her.

Fear was sharp and paralyzing.

She'd interrupted a break-in. The hows and whys didn't matter. All that mattered was getting out of here.

The door seemed a long way in the distance.

Could she make it?

Her heart was racing and her palms had turned sweaty.

She wished now that she hadn't removed her shoes.

She made for the door and at the same time grabbed her phone from her pocket. Her hand was shaking so much she almost dropped it.

She hit the emergency button, heard a woman say, "911 Emergency," and tried to whisper into the phone.

"Help. There's someone in the apartment."

"You'll have to speak up, ma'am."

The door was there. *Right there.*

'There's someone in the apartment.' She needed to get downstairs to the doorman—Albert. He'd—

A hand clamped over her mouth and before Eva could utter a squeak she'd landed on her back on the floor, crushed by the hard weight of a powerful male body.

The man pinned her. One of his hands was still across her mouth and the other gripped her wrists with brutal strength.

Holy crap.

If she could have screamed she would have done, but she couldn't open her mouth.

She couldn't move. She couldn't breathe—although, bizarrely, her senses were still sufficiently alert for her to realize that her attacker smelled *really* good.

It was an irony that finally, after almost two years of dreaming and hoping, she was finally horizontal with a man. It was a shame he was trying to kill her.

A shame and a tragic waste.

Here lies Eva, whose Christmas wish was to find herself up close and personal with a man, but who didn't specify the circumstances.

Was that really going to be her last thought? Clearly the mind was capable of strange things in the last moment before it was robbed of oxygen. And, having written her eulogy, she was going to die—right here in the dark, in this empty apartment, three weeks before Christmas, flattened by this gloriously smelling hunk of solid muscle. If Lucas Blade, the owner of the apartment, decided to postpone his return her body might not be found for weeks. They were in the middle of a snowstorm—or a "winter weather emergency" as it was officially called.

The thought rallied her.

No! She didn't want to die without saying goodbye to her friends. She'd found Paige and Frankie perfect Christmas gifts and she hadn't told anyone where they were hidden. And her apartment was a total mess. She'd been meaning to tidy up for ages, but hadn't quite found the time. What if the police wanted to look through her things for clues? Most of her possessions were strewn across the floor. It would be horribly embarrassing. But most of all she didn't want to miss enjoying New York City at Christmas, and she didn't want to die without having amazing, mind-blowing sex at least once in her life.

She didn't want this to be her last experience of having a man on top of her.

She wanted to *live*.

With a huge effort she tried to head-butt the man, but he took evasive action. She heard the rasp of his breath, caught a glimpse of jet-black hair and fierce, smoldering eyes—and then there was a hammering on the door and shouts from the police.

Relief weakened her limbs.

They must have traced the call.

She sent silent thanks and heard her attacker curse softly moments before the police burst into the apartment—followed by Albert.

There were no words for how much Eva loved Albert at that moment.

"NYPD—freeze!"

The apartment was flooded with light and the man crushing her finally relieved her of his weight.

Sucking air into her starving lungs, Eva screwed up her eyes against the lights and felt the man wrench the hat off her head. Her hair, released from the confines of wool and warmth, unraveled itself and tumbled over her shoulders.

For a brief moment her gaze collided with his and she saw shock and disbelief.

"You're a woman."

He had a deep, sexy voice. Sexy voice, sexy body—shame about his criminal lifestyle.

"I am. Or at least I was. Right now I'm not sure I'm alive." Eva lay there, stunned, gingerly testing various parts of her body to check they were still attached.

The man sprang to his feet in a lithe, fluid movement and she saw the expression on the police officer's face change.

"Lucas?" There was shock on his face. "We had no idea you were here. We had a call from an unknown female, reporting an intruder."

Lucas? Her attacker was Lucas Blade? He wasn't a criminal. He was the owner of the apartment.

She took her first good look at him and realized that he did look familiar. She'd seen his face on book covers. And it was a memorable face. She studied the slash of his cheekbones and the bold sweep of his nose. His hair and his eyes were dark. He looked as good as he smelled, and as for his body… She didn't need to study the width of his shoulders or the power of those muscles to know how strong he was. She'd been pinned to the ground under the solid weight of him, so she already knew all there was to know about *that*.

Remembering triggered a fluttery feeling in her tummy. What was *wrong* with her?

This man had half killed her and she was having sexy thoughts.

Which was yet more evidence that she'd gone far too long without sex. She was *definitely* going to fix that this Christmas.

In the meantime, she dragged her gaze away from the magnetic pull of his and tried to be practical.

What was he doing in the apartment? He wasn't supposed to be home.

"*She's* the intruder."

His expression was grim, and Eva realized that everyone was glaring at her. Everyone except Albert, who looked as confused as she felt.

"I'm not an intruder. I was told the apartment was empty." The injustice of it stung. "You're not supposed to be here."

"And how would you know that? Do you research which apartments are empty at Christmas?" He might be sexy, but he didn't give away smiles lightly.

Eva wondered how she'd suddenly turned into the bad guy. "Of course not. I was asked to do this."

"You had an accomplice?"

"If I were an intruder, would I have dialed 911?"

"Why not? Once you realized there was someone home it would have been the perfect way of appearing innocent."

"I *am* innocent." Eva looked at him in disbelief. "Your mind is a strange, twisted thing."

She glanced at the police officer for support, but found none.

"On your feet."

His tone was cold and brusque and Eva eased her bruised, crushed body into a sitting position.

"That's easier said than done. I have at least four hundred broken bones."

Lucas reached down and hauled her upright. "The human body does not *have* four hundred bones."

"It does when most of them have been snapped in half."

His strength shouldn't have surprised her, given that he'd already crushed her to the ground under his body.

"Why is everyone glaring at *me*? Instead of interrogating me about breaking and entering, they should be arresting *you* for assault. What are you doing here, anyway? You're supposed to be in Vermont—not skulking here."

"I own the apartment. A person can't 'skulk' in their own apartment." His brows came together in a fierce frown. "How did you know I was supposed to be in Vermont?"

"Your grandmother told me." Eva tested her ankle gingerly. "And you were definitely skulking. Creeping around in the dark."

"*You* were the one creeping around in the dark."

"I was admiring the snow. I'm a romantic. As far as I know that isn't a crime."

"We'll be the judge of that." The officer stepped forward. "We'll take her down to the precinct, Lucas."

"Wait—" Lucas barely moved his hand, but it was enough to stop the man in his tracks. "Did you say my *grandmother* told you I was in Vermont?"

"That's right, Mr. Blade." Albert intervened. "This is Eva, and she's here at the request of your grandmother. I verified it myself. None of us knew you were in residence."

There was a faint hint of reproach in his voice. Lucas ignored it.

"You *know* my grandmother?"

"I do. She employed me."

"To do what, exactly?"

His eyes had darkened. It was like looking at a threatening sky before a very, *very* bad storm.

His grandmother had told her many things about her grandson Lucas. She'd mentioned that he was an expert skier, that he had once spent a year living in a cabin in the Arctic, that he was fluent in French, Italian and Russian, was skilled in at least four different forms of martial arts and that he never showed anyone his books until they were finished.

She'd failed to mention that he could be intimidating.

"She employed me to prepare your apartment for Christmas."

"And...?"

"And what? That's it. What other reason could there have been?" She saw the sardonic gleam in his eyes. "Are you suggesting I broke in here so that I could meet *you*?"

"It wouldn't be the first time."

"Women *do* that?" Outrage mingled with fascination. Even she couldn't imagine ever going to those lengths to find a man. "How exactly does that work? Once they get inside they leap on you and pin you down?"

"You tell me." He folded his arms and looked at her expectantly. "What plan did you cook up with my grandmother?"

She laughed—and then realized he wasn't joking.

"I'm good in the kitchen, but even *I* have never managed to 'cook up' a romance. I wonder what the recipe would be? One cup of hope mixed with a pinch of delusion?" She tilted her head to one side. "Not that I'm not one of those women who thinks a guy has to make the first move, or anything, but I've never gone as far as breaking into a man's apartment to get their attention. Do I *look* desperate, Mr. Blade?"

In fact she *was* pretty desperate, but he had no way of knowing that unless he searched her purse and found her single lonely condom. She had hoped to give it a spectacular end to its so far uneventful life, but that was looking increasingly unlikely.

"Desperation wears many faces."

"If I *were* to break into a man's apartment with the intention of seducing him, do you really think I'd do it while wearing snow boots and a chunky sweater? I'm starting to understand why you need such a large apartment, even though there's only one of you. Your ego must take up a lot of space—*and* need its own bathroom—but I forgive you for your arrogance because you're rich and good-looking, so you're probably telling the truth about your past experience. However, the flaw in your reasoning is that you are supposed to be in Vermont."

His gaze held hers. "I'm not in Vermont."

"I know that *now*. I have bruises to prove it."

The police officer didn't smile. "Do you believe that story, Lucas?"

"Unfortunately, yes."

Loved this book?

Visit Sarah Morgan's fantastic website
at **www.sarahmorgan.com** for
information about Sarah, her latest books,
news, interviews, offers, competitions,
reading group extras and much more...

...and connect with her online, at:

 @SarahMorgan_

 facebook.com/AuthorSarahMorgan

 goodreads.com/SarahMorgan_

instagram.com/sarahmorganwrites

pinterest.com/SarahMorgan_

What if the person who broke your heart, is the only one who can help you find your future?

Great friends. Amazing Apartment. An incredible job. Paige has ticked off every box on perfect New York life checklist… until disaster strikes. Her brother's best friend Jake might be the only person who can help her put her life back together. He also happens to be the boy she spent her teen years pining after, and Paige is determined not repeat her past mistakes. But the more time she spends with Jake, the more Paige realises the one thing that was missing from her world all along…